Praise for Jennifer

D1321719

'The Greek gods engage in modern-day power struggles in the solid inaugural installment of the Titan series. Armentrout dives deep into the psyches of both hero and heroine, deftly switching from one point of view to another, while creating a drum-tight sense of suspense and sexual tension from the first page to the last. This is a very promising start to the series'   *Publishers Weekly*

'Sizzling, forbidden romance and non-stop action make *The Return* an addictive read. Sign me up for the sequel – I am now officially a Seth-aholic'   Jeaniene Frost, *New York Times* bestselling author

'Oh my Gods! Wow! Jennifer L. Armentrout is such an amazing writer; my heart is still beating hard against my rib cage'
Book Gossips

'I am completely hooked on Jennifer L. Armentrout's Covenant series'   *Love is Not a Triangle*

'Holy Daimon babies! The stress of the last book. The finale. The close. The goodbye . . . It was perfect. It had all the action, all the romance, all the snark, and all the wit I desperately desired with unexpected surprises that left me holding my breath and in tears by the last page'   *Vilma's Book Blog*

'When I first read *Half-Blood*, I devoured it on one sitting. I absolutely adored it and I couldn't believe the magic of Jennifer's writing style. I was completely under the spell Jennifer had woven and I have never looked back'   *K-Books*

'A great blend of action, drama, and romance . . . simply amazing from beginning to end'   *The Reading Geek*

'Ramps up the action, suspense, and romance without ever losing a step'   *Dreams in Tandem*

'Oh. My. God. Oh my God. Oh my God! Jennifer L. Armentrout just keeps getting better and better . . . I am BLOWN AWAY!'
iSoul Reviews

Also by Jennifer L. Armentrout and available from Hodder:

The Covenant Series
Daimon (novella)
Half-Blood
Pure
Deity
Elixir (novella)
Apollyon
Sentinel

The Lux Series
Shadows (novella)
Obsidian
Onyx
Opal
Origin
Opposition

Standalone Titles
Cursed
Don't Look Back
Unchained (Nephilim Rising)

Writing as J. Lynn:

The Gamble Brothers Series
Tempting the Best Man
Tempting the Player
Tempting the Bodyguard

JENNIFER L. ARMENTROUT

The Return

A Titan Novel

HODDER

First published in the United States of America in 2015
by Spencer Hill Press

First published in Great Britain in 2015
by Hodder & Stoughton
An Hachette UK company

1

Copyright © Jennifer L. Armentrout 2015

The right of Jennifer L. Armentrout to be identified as the Author of the
Work has been asserted by her in accordance with the Copyright, Designs
and Patents Act 1988.

All rights reserved. No part of this publication may be reproduced, stored in a
retrieval system, or transmitted, in any form or by any means without the prior
written permission of the publisher, nor be otherwise circulated in any form of
binding or cover other than that in which it is published and without a similar
condition being imposed on the subsequent purchaser.

All characters in this publication are fictitious and any resemblance to real
persons, living or dead is purely coincidental.

A CIP catalogue record for this title is available from the British Library

Paperback ISBN 978 1 473 61157 3
eBook ISBN 978 1 473 61158 0

Printed and bound by Clays Ltd, st Ives plc

Hodder & Stoughton policy is to use papers that are natural, renewable
and recyclable products and made from wood grown in sustainable forests.
The logging and manufacturing processes are expected to conform to the
environmental regulations of the country of origin.

Hodder & Stoughton Ltd
338 Euston Road
London NW1 3BH

www.hodder.co.uk

FOR ALL YOU SETH FANS... ENJOY.

Dorset County Library

Askews & Holts	2015
	£7.99

"But these sons whom he begot himself great Heaven used to call Titans in reproach, for he said that they strained and did presumptuously a fearful deed, and that vengeance for it would come afterwards." (ll. 207-210)

The Theogony of Hesiod
(translation by Hugh G. Evelyn-White)

CHAPTER

1

THE MANSION was as silent as I wished the inside of my head could be. No noise—not even a ragged inhale of breath or a whispered word. Truly blissful.

Peaceful.

The scenery was a whole different story.

From my vantage point at the top of the grand staircase, the opulent, open-floor design of the first level looked like a truck had backed up to the bronze double doors and dumped a load of SpaghettiOs all over the floor. Everything was splattered with red and gunk, like a fleet of cannons had shot an endless stream of beef ravioli against the walls and ceilings—lots of chunks of lots of different types of matter that usually belonged *inside* a body.

I'd never look at a can of Chef Boyardee the same way again.

However, there wasn't a drop of blood on me. My black boots were shiny; the black tactical pants and Under Armour shirt, the standard uniform of a Sentinel, were free of the gore. I had skillz—major skillz.

My gaze flickered over the room below. This had to be, by far, one of my best *Remediations*—as in, search out hideouts and destroy the traitors who over a year ago had supported Ares when he'd attempted to take over the mortal world.

1

Their sorry asses didn't have a chance in Hades.

Good old, average mortals who'd gotten mixed up in the wrong thing lay dead among the offspring of the Olympians. But most of those who littered the floor below were pure-bloods. Their official name was *Hematoi*. I rolled my eyes. They were as pompous as their name suggested. They were the products of two demigods getting it on. Their blood was considered *pure* compared to their counterparts, the half-bloods, which was what happened when a pure and a mortal got together. By simple genetics, halfs were weaker than the pures. They had less *aether* in them, the substance that surrounded Olympus and was also the very life force that flowed in the blood of the gods and all their creations. The *aether* was what enabled us to sense each other. The pures had more *aether* in them than halfs, which was why pures could wield control over the elements, just like the gods, but the halfs couldn't. Our society had been stratified for thousands of years, because the pures always held themselves higher than the halfs, virtually enslaving them up until a year ago, all because they genetically carried more *aether*.

But in death, they were all the same, which was stinky, messy, and dead.

My gaze shifted back to the gaping double doors. Sentinels were here. I could feel their wariness to enter the building, taste their anxiety on the tip of my tongue. A slight smile lifted the corners of my lips. They knew *I* was here. They could feel me, too, but I was something far different than them.

I was a half-blood, but I was also the Apollyon, a child of a pure and a half, a union that had been forbidden for thousands of years because an Apollyon was more powerful than any pure or half could ever hope to be.

And I always got to the traitors' hideouts before they did, so the Sentinels were usually left with the cleanup, which I was sure absolutely thrilled them.

The first to enter was a female half-blood dressed just as I was. Her black hair was pulled back in a neat little knot at the top of her head. She was older, probably in her mid-thirties. It was pretty rare for a Sentinel to live that long. Her dark skin paled as she stopped just inside the entrance. She clenched titanium daggers in her hands like she expected something vicious to pop out from under the bloody mess.

The female Sentinel tipped her chin up, and the overhead light sliced across her broad cheekbones. She bore a jagged scar under her right eye, the skin lighter in tone. She saw me and froze.

My smile widened.

Behind her, another Sentinel rushed in, almost mowing her over. He saw me and whispered, "Seth."

He'd said my name like I was the monster under his bed, and I sort of liked that. Then another Sentinel and another rolled in. The fifth took one look at my interior design work and keeled over. Slamming his hands on his knees, he hurled up his dinner.

Nice.

Our society existed completely unknown to the average mortal and had operated under what was known as the Breed Order for thousands of years. The Order had been dismantled, which meant halfs were no longer forced to choose between becoming Sentinels—hunting down violent creatures, protecting pures, enforcing laws, and otherwise usually dying pretty damn quickly on the job—or servants, which was a job that really wasn't a job, but more like slavery. Since then, many pampered pures had signed on to be Sentinels, making up for the loss of the halfs who'd pretty much said *"screw this shit, I'm out."*

This wasn't necessarily a good thing.

For example, the dumbass puking all over my blood-covered floor was a pure. When he straightened, his face a greenish hue, he backed away, shaking his head. "I can't," he gasped out. "I can't do this."

Then he turned and hauled ass out the doors.

I sighed. This was why we couldn't have nice things.

The female Sentinel had more balls than any of the males with her. She moved closer, stepping over a leg that used to belong to

3

the guy by the—no, *his* leg was by the stairs. I didn't know where that first one had come from. Her mouth opened as if she was going to speak, and I couldn't wait to hear what she had to say, but then the air in the room shifted, filling with electricity and a ripple of power. Ancient glyphs bled out on my skin, swirling and forming wards of protection all along my flesh.

A column of shimmery blue light pierced the cathedral ceiling, shooting down to the floor a few feet from the female Sentinel. As the light faded, a god was revealed.

The Sentinels hastily backed off. A few even dropped to their knees, unmindful of the mess on the floor. I, on the other hand, raised my right hand and scratched my brow with my middle finger.

My least favorite person in the whole mortal realm, Olympus, and Tartarus smirked as he crossed his arms over his chest. He tilted his self-important, pretentious, woefully and generally unhelpful head back and eyed me with eyes that were pure white— no pupils, no irises. Freaky shit right there.

"I sensed a disturbance in the force," he said.

I narrowed my eyes as I blew out an aggravated breath. "Did you seriously just quote *Star Wars*?"

Apollo, the god of the sun and other annoyingly important things that made killing him virtually impossible unless one wanted to end the world, shrugged a shoulder. "Maybe I did."

I'd been having a good night. Ate filet and lobster for dinner. Killed some people. Scared some pures and halfs. Planned on making another visit to the all-girls' college I'd discovered about three months ago. Those girls could cheer up any dude. But now *he* was here. Everything was going to go down the shitty pipe from this point.

Irritation pricked at my skin, causing the glyphs to agitate restlessly across it. Apollo and I had a history—a very bad history. He couldn't kill me. I wasn't sure how any of the Olympian gods could kill me, but I knew they would, eventually. Just not yet— they still needed me. "What do you want?"

He tilted his head to the side. "One of these days you will speak to me with respect, Apollyon."

"One of these days you will realize I don't respect you."

The Sentinels in the room stared at me like I'd just pulled down my pants and shaken my junk in their faces.

A tight smile appeared on the god's lips, a hide-your-kids-and-loved-ones kind of smile, but since I had neither of those things, I wasn't intimidated. "We need to chat."

Before I could respond, he snapped his fingers, and I was suddenly standing outside the mansion, my booted feet in the sand, the smell of salt overwhelming my senses, and the rolling ocean at my back.

A growl of anger rose in my throat. "I hate it when you do that."

The smile on his face increased. "I know."

I absolutely loathed it, and the bastard did it every chance he got—usually about every five minutes whenever I was in his presence and mostly without any purpose. Sometimes he would just pop me from room to room for the hell of it. The last year or so of my life had been a real test of my short patience.

"What do we need to talk about?" I ground out, folding my arms to keep myself from hitting him with a blast of *akasha*, the fifth and most powerful element only the gods and the Apollyon could wield. It wouldn't kill him, but sure as hell would sting like a bitch.

Apollo shifted his gaze to the dark ocean. "Do you have to always be so messy?"

My brows rose. "Huh?"

"Back there," he said, jerking his chin to where the lights from the mansion twinkled in the distance. "Do you always have to be so messy when you dispatch those who betrayed us?"

"Do I *have* to? No."

"Then why?" He looked at me.

Killing them the way I did was unnecessary. I could just blast them into nothing, make it quick, neat, and painless, but that's not how I rolled. Maybe in the beginning I'd been less...violent, but not anymore. Not when my sole purpose of existence was carrying out the gods' dirty work. Because every time I saw one of their faces, I thought of my own major screw-ups, and they were plentiful, and that made me think of— I cut that thought off. I was *so* not going down that road tonight without a bottle of whiskey.

"You all turned me into the Terminator. What did you expect?" I shrugged. "Is this what you wanted to talk to me about? My method of carrying out your orders? I'd think you'd have better things to do than pop up just to bitch at me because I made a mess."

"It's not just making a mess, Seth, and you know that. It's *you*."

A muscle began to thump along my jaw. I got what he was saying. "It's what I am now. So deal with it." I started to turn away. "If that's it, I'm out. There are these girls I want—"

"That's not why I'm here."

Closing my eyes, I swallowed a stream of curses. Of course not. I pivoted back to him. "What?"

Apollo didn't answer immediately. "Remember Perses?"

"Uh. No. I've forgotten all about the seven-foot Titan I helped free from Tartarus. Totally slipped my mind." My voice dripped sarcasm, and the flare of static crackling out from his all-white eyes showed that he noted it. That made me ridiculously happy. "Did you guys catch him?"

"Not quite."

I rolled my eyes. "Big surprise there."

Freeing Perses had been a last-ditch effort in the fight against Ares. The Titan was probably the only thing the God of War had feared, and the decision to roll out the red carpet to the mortal realm had been risky. Perses had been promised an eternity in the Elysian Fields for his help—if he behaved. Obviously, he had *not* behaved, and the moment Ares had been taken out, the Titan had disappeared—off to do whatever ancient gods did after they'd been asleep for a few millennia.

I bet it involved getting laid. A lot.

"Your sarcasm and general assholeness are not necessary," Apollo remarked casually.

I grinned at him. "I don't think 'assholeness' is a word."

"It is if I say it is." Apollo drew in a deep breath, a sure sign his temper was reaching its knock-Seth-into-the-nearby-ocean point. "Perses has managed to do the unthinkable."

There were a lot of things I'd consider unthinkable, like say half of what the gods did every day. "You're going to have to narrow that down."

He blinked and when his eyes reopened, they were more normal. Not completely normal, but he now had pupils and irises. His eyes were an intense, denim blue when they met my amber-colored ones. "He's freed more Titans."

"That's not—*wait*. What?"

"He's freed more Titans, Seth."

Now he had my full attention. "*All* of them?"

"Seven of them," Apollo confirmed. "Including Cronus."

Holy shitstorm in Hades—that was *not* something I'd expected. I took a step back, dropping my hands to my hips as I mulled that development over. "How in the fuck is that even possible? Was Hades sleeping on the job or something?"

"Yes, Seth, he took a nap and Perses snuck in the back door and let them out. Then they skipped through the Vale of Mourning, stopped to have a pic-a-nic and then decided to leave the Underworld all slow-like, and all the while Hades was chillin' and doing nothing."

That sounded probable.

"No," he snapped, blue eyes flaring brightly. "Hades wasn't sleeping on the job. None of us were, you little punk ass."

I arched a brow. "Well, *that* was unnecessary."

Apollo ignored that. "Use your brain for once, Seth. You're a smart guy. I know you are. And you knew damn well that when Ares was taken out there would be ripple effects."

"Yeah. I *might* remember that."

7

He stepped a good foot back from me, and I knew it was to stop himself from attempting to pummel me into next week. "We knew there'd be side effects. It was a risk we had to take—just like freeing Perses. But when Ares died, all of us were weakened in one way or another. We did not realize that one of the biggest chinks in our armor would be the wards entombing the Titans. How Perses realized that and made it into Tartarus to free them is unknown and really doesn't matter at this point. Some of them are free. So are some souls—shades. And not just any ordinary souls, but ancient souls who supported the Titans when they ruled."

Dumbfounded, I stared at the god. "So, you're telling me that not one of you considered that this might happen?"

He returned my stare with a glare.

I coughed out a dry, humorless laugh. "This is great, Apollo. We have Titans roaming around?"

"They are somewhere. Where? We have no idea. They are blocked from our viewing." Apollo reached up, scrubbing a hand through his blond hair. "They are plotting to overthrow us."

"You think? I mean, I'm sure they're still pissed about being overthrown by Zeus and the douche-canoe crew in the first place." I wanted to laugh again, but none of this shit was funny. If I cared about much of anything, I'd probably be more concerned than I was annoyed. "So you guys want me to hunt them down or something?"

That had to be the reason why he was here. As twisted as it was, I was pleased by this request. Dealing out *Remediations* was getting boring, and locating the Titans would most likely end in me ceasing to exist on this level. As powerful and awesome as I was, I couldn't take down a bunch of Titans without ending up dead. All that meant was that I'd be dying sooner than I expected.

Oh, well.

Due to the deal I'd made over a year ago that put my ass on the eternal chopping block in place of my second-least-favorite person's ass, there was a giant ticking clock counting down above my head. When the gods no longer thought I was useful to them, they'd find a way to end me. Then my eternity as a servant to Hades began. But the deal...yeah, it had been worth it. Not for *him*, but I'd owed it to *her*.

Apollo watched me closely, intently. "No."

My eyes narrowed. "No to what?"

"I'm not sending you after them. Not yet," he said, surprising me into silence—a rarity. "I have another task for you. You need to leave for southern Virginia immediately. I'd snap your sunshine-and-rainbows ass there, but now that you've annoyed me, you'll drive the twenty or so hours to get there."

Okay. That was irritating, but I kind of liked road trips, so whatever. "What's in southern Virginia?"

"Radford University."

I waited.

I waited some more, and then sighed. "Okay. You want me to enroll in college?" I asked, and Apollo tipped back his head and laughed so loudly, he actually whooped. I frowned. "What the hell is so funny about that idea?"

"You. College. Using your head. That's what's funny."

I was seconds away from blasting him with *akasha*.

The smile slipped off Apollo's face. "There is someone important there you must protect at all costs, Seth."

My lips curled into a smirk. Sending me to be a guard—how cliché. "Well, that's very little detail."

Apollo's grin turned cheeky. "You will know who it is when you see them." A puff of smoke appeared as he waved his hand, and as it faded into the night, I saw that he had a slip of paper. Neat ability. "This is their schedule. You shouldn't have any trouble finding them."

Frowning, I took the paper and quickly scanned it. It was a class schedule—a boring class schedule full of psychology and sociology classes. "Okay. And what exactly am I supposed to do with this person?"

"Keep them alive."

I exhaled noisily. "No shit, Apollo."

"You will both need to go to the Covenant in South Dakota— to the University there."

My spine straightened as if someone jacked me up. That was the last place I wanted to go. There were people there I didn't want to see. "Why? Who is this person?"

Apollo's smile returned, he winked, and then he was gone. Just like that. Poof. There one second and gone the next. Son of a bitch, I also hated that. More than just a little annoyed, my gaze dropped to the slip of paper. There were initials on the schedule.

J.B.

Sounded like a dickhead name.

Turning to the ocean, I let out a string of curses directed toward Apollo, and as the wind lifted the shorter hairs that had escaped the leather thong holding the hair back from my face, I swore I heard that bastard laugh.

I couldn't say I was surprised that Apollo hadn't given me a lot to work on. The jerk was known for delivering little to no information, or handing out what he did know in doses at the most inopportune moments, usually *after* the information would've been helpful.

One thing for sure; whoever I was supposed to keep safe really got the shittier end of the deal, considering the last person I'd been tasked with protecting had ended up with a titanium bullet in his forehead.

2

MOM HEAVED a huge sigh, causing the connection between us to crackle in my ear. "Baby, I wish you weren't so far away, where I can't help you or be near to you when you need me."

My mom was mentally unstable.

Not in the "ha ha, your mom is so cray cray" kind of way, but in the way she was one hundred percent convinced that, twenty years ago, an honest-to-God angel had visited her in the middle of the night and gotten her pregnant with me.

Yep.

A diagnosed schizophrenic, she'd been doing okay the last couple of years because she'd stuck to her medical regimen, but all those years before then had been rough, sometimes scary, and always exhausting.

It didn't help that Mom had been young when she'd gotten pregnant, barely seventeen, and in the small town I'd grown up in, people hadn't been kind to young, unwed mothers. And the community sure as hell hadn't been understanding of her mental illness, either.

"Mom, I really need to go," I said into my phone, glancing over as the door to the dorm room sprung opened. Erin Fore sashayed in, practically glowing from her morning run along the New River Valley of the Blue Ridge Mountains. She preferred to do her runs outside even though we had a fitness center in our residence hall. I preferred to lollygag on an elliptical machine. Screw the hard, running-outside crap–that required effort.

"I really wish you'd come back home. You're all the way across the world," she said.

I fought the urge to sigh. This was hard for Mom. I kept telling myself that. "It's not 'all the way across the world.' You're in Missouri. I'm in Virginia. It's not that far, Mom."

Erin's dark brown eyes caught mine and sympathy filled her gaze. We'd been roomies for the last three semesters, almost two years. She knew all about my mom troubles, and she totally understood why I was majoring in psychology. Because of my mom's illness, I was fascinated with how the human brain worked–and all the things that could go wrong with it. Growing up dealing with mental illness had given me a unique perspective on the ripple effects on other family members. I wanted to help those with the illness, and I also wanted to help those who were caregivers.

But it was more than that. Maybe if I understood how the mind worked, I'd be able to avoid the same fate as my mother.

"I'd feel better if you just came home," she continued as if I hadn't even spoken. "There are good colleges here. When you left after this summer, it was hard, Josephine. I want you home. Things aren't right."

I froze as I was sliding my flats on my feet, halfway bent over with long strands of light brown hair hanging in my face. I stared at my hair, seeing the almost-white streaks mingling with the more normal color. I hadn't put those blonde streaks there. They'd formed when I was in middle school.

Mom had said they were my angel father's grace showing up. That sounded cool, but they more than likely had formed from spending my summers outside by the lake. For some reason, they'd never faded, and since I kind of liked them, I never dyed my hair.

Guilt roiled in my stomach, and I thought the same thing I'd thought every day since I'd left for college. *I shouldn't have left her.* But the town had been slowly killing me. I'd had to get away, I had to *live*, and my grandparents had supported that need. They wanted me to have a normal life, so much so that they had saved every red penny to send me to school, to get me away from the bigotry and the soul-consuming responsibility of being my mom's daughter.

"Josephine," she whispered.

No one called me Josephine except for my mom, but that wasn't what made my heart skip a beat. I straightened, turning away from Erin as I headed to the tiny dresser and plucked up a faux-gold bangle. I lowered my voice, even though it was pointless to do so in our cramped dorm room. "What's not right?"

"The world is in its last stages." While her hushed words were dire, the tension seeped out of my shoulders. This was nothing new. "You can't have forgotten what happened last year."

No one in their right mind could have forgotten all the cataclysmic destruction that seemed to have rippled across the world. A water cyclone had wiped large chunks of the North Carolina coast off the map. Volcanoes, large-scale earthquakes, tsunamis—entire cities had been destroyed. Countries had been on the verge of World War III. It really had seemed like the end of the world, and there had been a teeny moment when I'd been afraid that maybe my mom had been right all along, but then it all had stopped, simply just stopped, and since then, everyone— the whole world—was all let's-hold-hands-and-love-one-another. Even countries that'd been fighting with one another since forever had stopped their bloodshed, and peace now prevailed and all that good stuff.

It took millions of people to die to wake everyone up, but it hadn't been the movie *2012* coming to life. The world hadn't ended. It had just been Mother Nature bitch-slapping humanity into its place.

"Mom, the world's not ending." I grabbed another bangle, this one a more dirty-gold color, and slipped it onto my left wrist. "Everything is fine. I'm okay. And you're okay, right?"

"Yes, baby, but I just...I have a bad feeling," she whispered into the phone, and that poured the tension back into my shoulders. "You know, a *real* bad feeling."

It was hard to drag in the next breath as I closed my eyes. A "bad feeling" was our code word for relapse—for auditory and visual hallucinations, for her slipping away from my grandparents and inadvertently putting her life in danger. My heart started pounding fast. When I turned, Erin was sitting on her narrow bed, kicking off her shoes. Concern pinched her downright gorgeous face. "What kind of 'bad feeling' do you have?"

Mom started talking about how she was having dreams about my father. "A great change is coming. Everyone is going to..."

As she spoke, Erin mouthed *is she okay?*

I shook my head, feeling heartsick. By the time I got off the phone, I knew I was going to be late for Abnormal Psychology if I didn't book it, but all I wanted to do was climb into my bed and pull the patchwork quilt my granny had made me over my head.

"Is she relapsing?" Erin asked as she tugged her hair free. Black, loose curls fell around her shoulders. There wasn't even a crimp in her hair from the ponytail.

Erin was perfect.

She was also a sweetie.

"Yeah." I flipped my hair—my heavy hair that never held a curl, but sure as hell showed a crimp if it were up in any ponytail for a second—as I grabbed my backpack off the floor. "I'm going to call Granny after class. They probably already know, but didn't want to worry me."

She rose to her feet gracefully, showing off incredibly long, incredibly smooth, dark legs. I was convinced that hair didn't grow on her legs. Seriously. "Is there anything I can do?"

"Sneak me some tequila tonight?" I slugged the bag over my shoulder.

Her full lips curved in a grin. "I always know where to get the good shit."

That she did. It was kind of odd, since she was only twenty, like me. I had no idea where she got the endless supply of alcohol. I swear she could just walk into a liquor store, flash those killer legs and beautiful smile, and they just handed over anything she wanted.

I, on the other hand, would get laughed right out of the store.

"I'll also get us some junk food—like rocky road ice cream, dill-flavored potato chips, and—oh—those chocolate-covered pretzels." She opened the door for me. "How does that sound?"

"You're amazing." Springing forward, I hugged her quickly and then pulled back, flushing as I backed away. I was such a dork, it was embarrassing.

Erin simply allowed me to be on the receiving end of a stellar smile. She didn't get it, though. She grew up outside of DC, in a big city, in a big family, surrounded by friends she'd made on the track team. Me? Growing up virtually friendless in a town that saw the kid of an unwed mother as the devil's spawn made me truly value the friendship I had with her.

Before I made things even more awkward by throwing myself at her feet and thanking her for being my friend, I wiggled my fingers in a wave and hurried out of the room. As I all but raced down the hall, I had to compartmentalize, placing what was happening with Mom in the corner of my mind to revisit after class. I needed to pay attention today. This was our last lecture before the exam on Friday.

I stepped outside Muse Hall, tugging the loose cardigan close as my feet hit the paved walkway. Spring was in the air and tiny leaves were sprouting from the branches, but the chill of winter hadn't left the campus yet. The dorm was great—co-ed, fun, had its own dining hall—but it was a heck of a walk to Russell Hall, where the Ab Psych class was held, and I had a feeling I'd be blown into the trees before I reached the building.

The wind was whipping down through the valley, tossing my hair back from my face. I hunched my shoulders, keeping my chin down as I stepped out from under the stone awning, not paying attention to the array of students hanging out at the entrance or lounging on the benches. On a good day, I was easily distracted, but when I became nervous or stressed, *everything* was a bright, shiny object and I had the attention span of a goldfish. I couldn't afford getting lured into a conversation and inevitably missing class.

I followed the path around the neatly landscaped park. On nicer, warmer days, I'd spent time studying under the large, black oak trees. The campus was truly beautiful. It was one of the reasons why I'd enrolled.

That, and no one knew who I was here, or who my mother was.

Folding my arms more tightly across my chest, I'd just reached the halfway point when I felt something...something *weird* and *familiar* and definitely *unwanted*. It started off as a shiver exploding at the base of my spine and then shimmying up. The odd tremor spread over the nape of my neck, dancing along my shoulders. Tiny hairs rose all over my body, and my feet somehow got tangled with the flat ground. I tripped as unease bloomed in the pit of my belly like a noxious weed determined to take over.

I glanced over my shoulder, my gaze darting across the swaying branches and the benches, but I didn't see anything abnormal. Students were everywhere, talking in groups, doing their own thing, but I couldn't shake the distinct feeling of eyes on me, drilling into my skin, muscle, and bone.

But no one was paying a damn bit of attention to me. They never were, when I had these feelings. It was all in my head.

Picking up my pace, I couldn't outrun the unease that was steadily growing into a pungent, bitter ball of panic in the back of my throat. My heart picked up, pushing my pulse into cardiac workout territory, and I could feel the sweat dotting my palms.

"Crap," I muttered.

I stopped, forcing myself to draw in several deep, slow breaths, but pressure clamped down on my chest. The shivers extended up the back of my skull. Was this it? A warning symptom? Was this how it'd started for Mom? A bunch of studies linked genes to mental illness. There was roughly a twenty-five percent chance I would develop schizophrenia. And I was in the right age group for the onset of the disease.

I'm not getting sick. I'm not getting sick.

Closing my eyes, I wrapped a trembling hand around the strap of my book bag. This was not a symptom of a mental disorder. I was just tired. Stressed. I was totally okay. Everything would be fine.

It had to be.

Turned out, I made it to class on time and was able to focus during the lecture, so I figured I was prepared for the exam on Friday. When Jesse Colbert, another psych major who took a bunch of classes with me, lingered in the seat beside me while I gathered up my stuff, I tried not to act like a total goober.

He was a tall guy, around my age, with hair as dark as polished obsidian. Good looking. Nice. Great cheekbones. Really cute and always had an easy smile on his face. Awesome hands. I had a thing for male hands for some reason and his hands—rough, masculine, long-fingered. I liked them.

Pulling my thoughts away from my weird semi-fetish, I forced what I hoped wasn't a creepy smile. "Hey."

Grabbing his books, he sent a slight grin in my direction. "We still on for tomorrow night?"

Standing, I shoved the massive text into my bag. "Yep. It's a date..." My brain winced, backpedaling away from that comment. "I mean, not a *date* date. Like going out and stuff. Dinner.

17

Whatever." Feeling my cheeks burn, I focused on the corner of his shoulder. "Study date, but without any real dating stuff."

Oh my God, I needed to shut up, because this was why I never got a *date* date. Oh Lord, now my face was really burning, because I was standing in front of Jesse thinking about why I was still a virgin. I wish my brain had an off switch.

He watched me through the whole ridiculous ramble, and when I finally clamped my mouth shut, he chuckled. "Yeah, I know, Josie. See you tomorrow at six?"

"Yeah. Six. In the evening, right?" Shoot me in the head. Please? "Of course. Perfect."

He hesitated, and then with his grin lifting up the corners of his lips, he wheeled around. Sighing, I mentally listed the ways I was the Queen of All Dorks as I headed out the door. I made a pit stop in the restroom, mostly so I could put off calling my grandparents for a few more minutes. I wasn't ready to hear what I already knew, and I hated that, because it made me a coward. But I washed my hands twice, worked a tiny brush through my wind-tousled hair, reapplied my lip-gloss, and then moseyed out into the hall. Classes had already started up and I headed to the closest stairwell, letting the door swing shut behind me. Thoughts once again focused on my mom and calling Granny. I needed to get this over with. I tugged my bag around and reached in for my phone.

I have no idea how what happened next went down.

Only a few steps from the second-floor landing, a cold blast of air whipped up from the floor below, shooting right through me, strong enough to startle me. I reached out to grip the railing as my bag slipped off my shoulder, hit the step by my foot, and then bounced its way down to the landing.

What in the world?

For several seconds, I stared at my bag and then I looked over my shoulder. I had no clue what I expected to see standing there—maybe Casper the pervy ghost or something? A little wigged out, I turned around and almost fell backward out of shock.

A guy stood in front of me. Well, he wasn't standing. He was bending down to pick up my bag. But how in the world did he get there? I hadn't heard anyone walk up the stairs, and there was no way anyone could get up them that fast in the first place...unless he'd sprouted wings and flown up the stairs, but I didn't think that was likely.

I could only see half of him, and even from that, I could tell he was tall. I wasn't a small girl, coming in close to five foot nine, but this guy would make me feel...*dainty* standing next to him.

A deep-brown henley stretched taut over broad shoulders and extremely well-defined upper arms. Blond hair was pulled back at the nape of his neck by a brown leather band. Shorter strands had slipped free, obscuring his face as long fingers wrapped around the strap of my bag.

Oh my, my—he had beautiful hands.

His skin was golden, all the way up to where the sleeves were pushed up his forearms. I'd never seen a complexion like that. It wasn't tanned, but something...something *else*. My breath floated up my throat, and then stopped as he straightened.

Holy Hottie-McHotters!

A curved, almost-stubborn chin was paired with a cut, strong jaw. The upper lip was only slightly thinner than his bottom one and those loose strands of hair now caressed broad, high, golden cheekbones.

Then I saw his eyes.

I jerked back, lost my balance, and my ass plopped down on the step behind me. Maybe later I'd be embarrassed, but at that moment, all I could do was stare at him.

He had to be the most beautiful guy I'd ever seen, and that was no joke. I couldn't even think of anyone on TV, in the magazines, or in movies who looked like him. His male beauty was delicate and yet hard at the same time, rough and smooth, a total conundrum of splendor, but his eyes...

They were the strangest color—a tawny amber. There was no way they could be natural. But damn, he worked those contacts, paired with surprisingly dark lashes and brows a shade or two darker than his hair.

I suddenly wondered if it was possible to have a visual orgasm, because I think I might have just experienced that, except he... this unreal, beautiful man was staring at me with honey-colored eyes that kept getting wider.

And the way he was staring at me was not good—almost like he couldn't believe what he was looking at—as if I had grown an extra head. While I knew I wasn't going to be winning Miss USA anytime soon with the hip span I had going on, I had no idea why he was looking at me like he suddenly wanted to vomit.

Or hit something.

"Son of a bitch," he said, and my bag slipped out of his fingers and landed once more with a heavy thud.

If I hadn't already been sitting on my ass, I would've fallen on it again. His voice... I slowly shook my head, wanting him to speak again, because it was the deepest, smoothest voice I'd ever heard, with a slight accent I couldn't place.

I needed to say something, but all I could do was sit there and stare at him in open wonder. And think about the fact that the only makeup I was wearing was lip-gloss, and I was the kind of girl who needed at least some blush, mascara...and an entire painted face.

"What's your name?" he asked.

My mouth dried as I continued to stare at him like my brain had shorted out, which was possible. It felt like I'd lost some brain cells, maybe a few synapses, and maybe a few other important things...stuff.

He shot forward, moving as quickly as the striking rattlesnake I'd seen once by the lake back home—so fast that I had no way to move. One hand landed on the railing by my head, and the other two steps above me, and he was right there, in my face, breathing the same oxygen as I was. The wide stairwell with its red-washed walls constricted and the space seemed much smaller than before.

Our gazes locked, and…and as crazy as it sounded, his eyes… They looked as if there were some kind of light behind the pupils. "Are your initials J.B.?"

Way in the back of my head, I realized that was a weirdly on-point question. "How do you know that? We haven't met. I'm sure of that, because I would've remembered that." There I went again, rambling like an idiot. "I mean, I'm good with faces."

Especially extraordinarily gorgeous faces—yeah, I remembered those.

Thick lashes lowered, covering those eyes briefly as he muttered, "Shit."

I blinked. "Excuse me?"

"Your name?"

Part of me wanted to ask him what the hell his name was, but I was caught off-guard and I answered. "Josie. Josie Bethel."

His gaze flew back to mine and for a long moment he didn't speak. A sense of hyperawareness rushed over my skin, forming tiny little bumps. Tension poured into the air like kegs of it had been tapped open above us. My pulse picked up as I drew in a shallow breath. A muscle spasmed along his jaw and his lips parted as he said, "What in the *fuck* are you?"

MY EYES had to be deceiving me, like some kind of twisted-off-its-ass wish fulfillment or something. The hair was the wrong color. Hell, I wasn't even sure what color hair this girl had. Light brown? Blonde? Pale blonde? All the shades rolled into one? And her nose was too small, but this girl, she looked...

I couldn't even bring myself to finish that train-wreck of a thought.

Her eyes, a shade of deep denim that was familiar in a nagging sort of way, were fixed on mine. When she didn't answer my question, I decided to take a more touchy-feely kind of approach. My hand shot out, wrapping around her wrist.

I waited for something—a zap, a fissure of power signaling what she was.

Nothing.

Her eyes widened, almost consuming her face, and there was a quality of innocence to her suddenly wary gaze that I hadn't seen in a long time.

"W-what are you doing?" She pulled on her arm, but she didn't get very far.

Her question fell to the side. I was focused on trying to puzzle out what the hell she was and why in the hell I was here.

There'd been no awareness of her when I'd entered the stairwell—late, according to the schedule I had. I hadn't even expected to find the mysterious J.B. after this class. Shit, I hadn't even felt her until I'd zipped up the stairs, too fast for any human to track, and startled her. She was definitely not a pure or a half, because I would've sensed that. So she wasn't hiding out in the mortal world, like some of them had managed to do in the past. But when I'd straightened and had seen her face, I knew—I just *knew* this had to be the person Apollo had sent me to find, and her initials had confirmed it.

There was nothing special that jumped from her skin to mine—no awareness of anything that would make her unique. She felt *mortal*, but she couldn't be, because there'd be no reason Apollo would want me to guard a mortal college chick. Unless this was another warped form of punishment, and hell, that actually wouldn't surprise me.

"You're hurting me," she whispered.

Her voice broke through my thoughts. My gaze dropped to where my fingers curled around her slender wrist. The skin around my hand was turning white. Shit—I *was* hurting her. I dropped my hold as if her skin had scalded mine. Surprise flitted through me, but I had no idea if it was real or just wishful thinking that I hadn't truly intended to harm her.

Sometimes I wasn't quite sure what my intentions were anymore.

"What are *you*?" she asked, her nose scrunching as she spoke. "Other than a heart-stopping hot guy with obvious boundary issues and problems with anger management?"

I blinked at her. She thought I was a heart-stopping hot guy? Well, of course she did.

"God. Just my luck," she went on, rubbing the skin around her wrist and eyeing me with more than just a hint of distrust. "Why do all the hot ones have to be such freaking D-bags?" She pushed up to her feet. Her eyes met mine as she stepped to the side, pressing against the wall. "What do you want?"

23

Seth, what do you want? Those words from the past were accompanied by angry, whiskey-colored brown eyes. I drew back so fast I was surprised I hadn't given myself whiplash.

"You know what? I don't want to know. It's probably a good thing that I don't. I'm just going to get my bag and keep on going. Okay? All right, sounds good to me." She edged down the wall. "This is me leaving."

An odd sense of déjà vu washed over me as she pushed past me—literally knocked her shoulder into mine—and snatched up her bag.

"Crazy asses," she muttered under her breath. "I am a weirdo magnet."

I turned as she hurried down the steps, away from me like I was the maniac people didn't want to meet in a dark alley. And well, that wouldn't be too far from the truth. Some would probably prefer to come face to face with a harpy instead of me.

At a set of doors, she stopped to look over her shoulder, and again, I was struck by the familiarity of those deep, dark-blue eyes, of the curve of a stubborn jaw and chin, and bow-shaped, pouty lips. From my vantage point, I could really see her now. If that oversized sweater weren't hiding her ass, I bet it would match her heart-shaped face.

It was like taking two people I knew and mixing them together to form a brand-new person, and that was entirely unnerving.

Then she was gone, slipping out the doors, and I was left standing on the landing like a dickhead.

Seth, what do you want?

Everything and anything and nothing at all?

Yeah, that sounded about right. My hands tightened into fists. Closing my eyes, I tried to center myself, but I couldn't shake the feeling I'd been here before, but with someone else.

A crack of loud thunder from outside reverberated through the stairwell and echoed inside my skull. A storm was brewing, matching the warring emotions inside me.

What do you want?

My eyes flew open and the stairwell was tinted in amber. No, *fuck* no. I staggered back against the wall. It didn't make sense, but godsdammit I *had* been here before.

Dammit.

I was going to commit god-slaughter on Apollo.

Too freaked out from the run-in with the kind of scary, yet extraordinarily hot, guy in the stairwell, I didn't end up calling my granny before the start of Statistics. I shouldn't have even bothered going to class, because when the fifty minutes had passed, it felt like I'd only just sat down and cracked open my notebook.

I'd taken about two sentences worth of notes and somehow ended up with a doodle of something that looked like a zombie in the margin of my page. Real effective note-taking skills right there.

Once outside the class, feeling like I'd somehow just gotten dumber rather than smarter, I checked in with my grandparents. Like I'd expected, they were totally aware of Mom's feelings and were watching her closely. Granny told me not to worry, and while that was easier said than done, it did ease some of the stress. Mom had support. She wasn't alone.

As I walked to my dorm, my thoughts coasted back to the stairwell in Russell Hall. Who was that guy, and why in the world had he asked *what* I was? Like there was some other option besides human? That had be the oddest question I'd ever been asked, and I'd been asked some peculiar crap.

God, I really knew how to attract some weirdos.

I had an elaborate history of them, starting with Bob. I'd never known his last name, which was probably a good thing, considering the whole weirdo magnet thing. But when I was a little girl, he'd been my world for one summer.

I'd spent most of my days at the lake that was hidden by the sad willows and the bright-yellow oak trees that butted up to my grandparents' property. At that age, the lake had appeared the size of an ocean. And it was there that I'd met Bob.

He'd shown up while I'd been playing by the dirt-and-pebble shore one afternoon—an important afternoon to me. One of the girls at school had had a huge slumber party that night in celebration of school ending and the beginning of summer. I hadn't been invited—I'd never been invited to any of those things— and I'd been sad and confused, because all I'd ever wanted was for the other kids to like me. And the boys didn't like me until high school, but then they'd done so for all the wrong reasons.

When I'd first seen Bob, I'd been scared out of my mind, frozen in place when he stepped out from among the trees. Dark-haired and with eyes the color of the sky, he'd been as big as the superheroes in the stash of comics that my grandfather had in his office that I'd been warned away from ever touching.

I'd touched them a lot.

Bob had claimed to live further down the lake, and I hadn't thought to question him, because the world was too big then for me to know that there were no cabins or houses there, other than my grandparents'. The first time we'd met, he'd talked about the catfish in the lake and the bigger fish he'd seen in the oceans, telling me stories that had fascinated me. I'd liked him and had been happy when he'd returned the following week, on the same day at the same time, bearing candies. A once-a-week ritual had started, and being relatively friendless with the exception of the random new kid in town who'd either never stayed around long or stayed nice, Bob had become my best friend over the course of a summer.

And the baby dolls that he'd brought me had helped.

Even to my young eyes, they had appeared rare and expensive—as if he'd gathered them around the world—because the pretty, painted faces had come from many cultures I'd never heard of.

Looking back, I totally saw how creepy all of that was, but then, I'd been so starved for friendship, I probably would've warmed up to the Grim Reaper if he'd wiggled his bony fingers at me.

Truth.

The friendship had ended when my grandfather had stumbled upon us one afternoon. Bob had been sitting cross-legged by me, showing me how to fold grass between my fingers and turn it into a whistle. Needless to say, Pappy freaked and I'd been carted away from the lake. They'd found the dolls, and all of them had gone into the trash. Mom had cried for some reason, and then I was sat down and taught all about the whole stranger-danger thing.

I'd never seen Bob again.

I'd collected more weirdos over the years, like the old lady who was always at the convenience store when I was stocking up on junk food because my grandparents were health-food nuts. Somehow we'd struck up an oddball friendship—me, her, and her nine cats. Then, there had been the high-school librarian. She'd been the closest thing to a BFF I'd ever had.

There had been more, and as ridiculous as it sounded, sometimes I wondered if there was some innate crazy that other crazy folks could sense in one another, like a homing beacon. So I guessed I shouldn't have been so surprised by a random, crazy—albeit hot—guy running into me on a campus with thousands of people.

I entered my dorm and took the elevator the ten floors up. Adjusting my bracelets, I shifted from foot to foot, impatient. When the elevator stopped, I barreled out the doors and almost knocked down a smaller girl. She stumbled back, catching herself on the opposite wall.

"Sorry. So sorry," I said, wincing as she righted herself. "Really sorry."

"No biggie." She smiled as stepped in the elevator.

Shaking my head, I pivoted around and walked down the long hall to my dorm room. As I reached the door, the shiver was at the base of my spine again, dancing its way up until it traveled across my shoulders. My heart turned over heavily and I closed my eyes.

Twice in one day.

Oh God.

I'd never felt this more than once in any span of several days. Swallowing hard, I wrapped my fingers around the doorknob, battling the urge to turn and scan the hall, because I knew no one would be there.

Dragging in a deep breath, I opened the door and stepped inside the room. My brows flew up, and I forgot about the feeling as I closed the door behind me.

Erin was sprawled on the floor, palms pressed down on a mat, her spandex-covered behind jutting up toward the sky. She turned her head, peering at me from under her armpit.

Her *armpit*.

"How in the world do you get your neck to bend like that without killing yourself?" I asked.

"Skills, yo."

Erin did yoga and meditation religiously, saying it helped merge her yin and yang together or something. She'd once told me she had a hell of a mean streak, and contorting herself into painful-looking positions helped keep "good vibrations" around her. Which was strange, because I'd never seen Erin lose her temper in the two years I'd known her.

Erin unfolded herself from some kind of downward dog or upward pony and grinned at me. "Check under the bed."

Curious, I dropped my bag and stepped over her legs. Bending down, I lifted the bedspread and my eyes grew to the size of saucers when I spotted the bottle. I snatched it up and clutched it to my chest as I whipped toward her. "José!"

Her grin spread into a smile. "The best boyfriend ever."

Standing in the middle of the penthouse suite in the hotel not too far from Radford, I yelled for Apollo for the fourth time since I'd walked through the door.

Finally, there was an answer in the form of a fissure of energy permeating the room. Warm air blew over the back of my neck. I spun around, cursing when I saw Apollo standing *right* there. As in, he'd zapped himself into the room practically on top of me.

"Gods," I barked. "There's at least eight hundred square feet in here, buddy, you didn't need to land on my ass."

Apollo snickered as he folded his arms. "You called?"

I squared off with the god. We were nearly the same height, putting him at maybe an inch or two over my six-foot-four. "Who is she?"

There was a pause. "Josephine Bethel."

I stared at him as irritation spun up like a high-speed cyclone. "I've figured that out. Thanks."

"Is that so? By the way, you're off to a good start with this whole 'protecting her' thing. Are you doing it remotely? Is that a new ability of yours I'm unaware of?" He turned, tilting his head to the side. He seemed to be staring at the chain hanging from the ceiling fan. Seconds later, he confirmed this by reaching out and tugging the chain.

Light clicked on.

He tugged the chain again.

Light went off.

Oh for gods' sake, he had a mean case of ADD sometimes. "Apollo," I snapped.

Seeming to have forgotten he was even in the room with me, he lowered his hand slowly. "You haven't asked the correct question, Apollyon."

I forced myself to take a step back before I tapped into the air element, wrapped the shiny gold chain around his thick neck, and turned him into a sun god piñata. "She's not a half or a pure. She feels like a mortal, but she…" I shook my head, turning away. Moving to the large window, I pulled back the curtain. Dusk had fallen, bringing a haze of fog to the tops of the tree-covered mountains.

"What, Seth?" Apollo asked softly.

I couldn't believe I was going to say this, but Apollo wasn't going to feed me information. That wasn't how he rolled. Slipping my fingers off the curtain, I closed my eyes. "She looked...she reminded me of Alex."

Alex.

Alexandria Andros.

The girl I once had thought was just an ordinary half-blood, but had turned out to be another Apollyon—the *real* Apollyon. I was the one who was never supposed to have happened, even though I'd been born first. I'd come into existence because Ares had sought to control Olympus through controlling me. And worse than being a descendant of that asshole, he'd almost succeeded in turning me into the God Killer, the supreme being that was the result of one Apollyon absorbing the abilities of another. It was why having two Apollyons in one generation was forbidden.

And I'd played right into Ares's games. I'd fucked up—fucked up in a way that had ended with Alex spending a good part of the year—and of every year for eternity—in the underworld. That was something I could never forgive myself for. No matter what amends I'd made or deals I'd offered.

I cleared my throat and continued. "Not completely. Different hair. Different nose and eyes, but she even sounded like her for a second." I laughed, and it sounded harsh. "If I didn't know better, I'd think they were somehow related, but that's not possible. Right?"

There was no answer as Apollo stared at me.

And then I lost my shit.

Glyphs snapped over my flesh. The lamp on the executive-style desk exploded in a shower of sparks and tinkling glass. The smell of burnt ozone filled the air. Wind picked up, blowing the little courtesy notepads off the nightstands. "It's not possible, Apollo."

He arched a blond brow. "I'm not surprised that she reminds you of Alexandria."

For a moment, I couldn't move or say anything. My lips pulled back into a sneer as I stumbled a step back. I waited for him to say something else, anything else. Apprehension ran its bony fingers over my neck.

"What is she?" I rasped, tensing up. The need to destroy something rippled over me like a shockwave.

Apollo dipped his chin and the seconds ticked away before he spoke. "She is a demigod."

THAT HAD to be the last thing I was expecting Apollo to say.

"A *demigod*?" I repeated like I'd just learned to speak a few seconds ago. "A real, live demigod?"

"Opposed to a fake, dead one?" He chuckled, proud of himself, and then sighed when my eyes narrowed on him. "You used to have a sense of humor, Seth."

"I used to have a lot of things," I retorted. His features sharpened and his mouth opened like he wished to expand on that, but that wasn't what was important here. "There hasn't been a true demigod in thousands of years—not since mortals worshipped the gods."

"That's true. We agreed not to create anymore when we retreated to Olympus, but what is also true is that she's not the only one."

I stared at him, and then I barked out a short laugh. "There are demigods roaming the Earth? You know, this might have been good to know a year or so ago, when we all were getting our asses kicked." Demigods were like the Apollyon, their powers second only to the gods'. They were major ass-kickers. And they were also like Pegasus. Supposedly it existed, but since it did so in Olympus, I'd never seen it. "Wait. This doesn't make sense.

I felt nothing around that girl. She sure as hell didn't act like a demigod, and that doesn't explain why she reminds me of...her."

"Is it so hard to say her name?" Apollo asked. "I think a few minutes ago was the first time you've said her name since after you two fought Ares."

My jaw ached from how hard I was grinding my molars.

"Whatever," Apollo said, his attention returning to the godsforsaken ceiling fan chain. "Don't talk about it. Be the best issues-boy you can be."

I took a deep breath. It didn't help. "I *don't* have issues."

He tipped his head back and roared with laughter. Paintings of the nearby Blue Ridge Mountains rattled. "You have more baggage than United Airlines. Cross that out. You have more issues than Medusa, and that woman makes the inside of a cat lady's thoughts seem like a calming place."

"I hate you."

"You wound me straight to the heart, bud."

My patience was just about the same as that of Cerberus after someone tried to take a squeaky toy away from him. "What about the girl, Apollo?"

He dropped down into the leather chair, his large form nearly swallowing it. "It's a long story."

"Go figure."

That comment went largely ignored. "It all started with your birth, so there's something else you can add to your mountain of suck."

I wondered if there was an anti-god repellent and where I could find it.

"We knew the moment you were born that there would be the possibility of a God Killer, since Alexandria was on schedule to make an appearance a few years later. We didn't know who among us was responsible for your birth, but we knew they'd want to use you for their own gain."

"This walk down history lane is boring me." I crossed my arms.

Unaffected, he eased himself closer to the bed, kicked his booted feet up on it, and stretched out leather-clad legs. "The risk of you two joining forced us to come up with a contingency plan in case the proverbial poo hit the fan."

My brows knitted. There was something wrong with hearing Apollo use the word "poo" in a sentence.

"The Twelve agreed we had to do something," he continued. The Twelve were the core of the Olympians, the most powerful. There were more gods, so many that no one could keep track of them, since they populated like rabbits, but the Twelve called the shots. "So we decided to do something none of us had done in thousands of years. We created twelve demigods."

Twelve? Holy roasted Hades's balls. "So, let me guess. You and Zeus, Hephaestus, Dionysus, Poseidon, Hermes, and Ares," I spat that bastard's name out, and then moved on, "got human women knocked up, and then Hera, Artemis, Athena, Aphrodite, and Demeter got pregnant?"

"That's usually how making babies works," he replied dryly. "Once our lovely ladies conceived, they transferred their offspring into mortal women. And before the twelve demigods were born, their abilities were bound so that they, until needed, would be nothing more than mortal. We couldn't have demigods running amuck in the mortal world."

I rolled my eyes.

"Demigods are more powerful than pures. You know that, Seth. The *aether* we pass onto them has not been diluted. They can control all the elements, including *akasha*. We could not allow them free reign."

"Of course," I muttered.

"Two of them were killed off immediately. Zeus got jealous and took out Hera's child, and in retaliation, she snuffed out his. You know how those two can be."

Gods.

"That left ten. Of course, as we know, Ares had a stick up his ass and was planning to turn the mortal world into his personal playground of carnage. He knew of our plan. He went right along with it. He knocked off four more during his little reign of terror, leaving six remaining. Of course, his own kid wasn't one of the ones he killed."

A muscle began to thrum along my jaw. During my time with Ares, he'd mentioned none of this. Not that I was surprised. There was a lot he hadn't told me, and even more I simply hadn't questioned, because I hadn't cared. Not at first, at least. Tension crept into my shoulders. "If you had at least six demigods, why weren't they used to help defeat Ares?"

He wiggled his booted feet. "Everything we do has a cosmic checks and balances system. The demigods' powers can only be unbound two ways. At least six of them have to be in the same location at one time, and then it's like a universal remote. All of their abilities are released naturally, like a system hitting critical mass. The second way is for us to release their powers, but that's... that is messy, and we can only unbind the demigod who belongs to us. If we make that decision, it weakens us considerably and it would take time for us to recover. Another cosmic check and balance."

Rolling my shoulders, I worked out the creeping tautness. "I still don't get why you guys didn't pull the demigods into the fight against Ares. They could've changed the—"

"The outcome wouldn't have changed. Alex would still be where she is now. Moving on," he said. "What matters now is that we need them to entomb the Titans. Besides the fact there are no longer twelve of us, we don't have the cosmic mojo to do so. Now that they've escaped, we can't put them back. The chore would fall to those who carry our blood. It won't be easy for them. There are things they must accomplish first. You know, checks and balances, Seth."

I didn't care about the checks and balances. "Then get them together, power them up like it's a game of Super Mario, and get this shit over with."

35

"It's not that simple. We don't know where all of them are. We have our guesses."

"How in the hell do you not know where they are?"

"When we bound their abilities, it also blocked us from sensing them. Over the years, we've been able to keep track of a few of them. It really depended on the god who fathered or mothered them and how interested they were in keeping tabs. Many weren't."

"Yeah, because you guys are paradigms of good parenting."

He smirked as he crossed one ankle over the other. "Can't argue that. But, we're actively searching for them. Two that *we did* keep track of went missing about three weeks ago. They disappeared. Poof. Gone."

This crap was causing my temples to pound. "Then how do you know there aren't just four left now?"

"Because Athena and Hermes would've felt their loss. They haven't. But we suspect that the Titans have something to do with their disappearance. Just because *you* can't sense their blocked powers doesn't mean the Titans can't."

"Why would the Titans take two demigods—the only things that can put them back in Tartarus—and not kill them?"

"Your favorite thing. Cosmic checks and balances." He sighed as he smoothed a hand over the white shirt he wore, inspecting a gold button with an interest that bordered on weird as he spoke. "There was a reason why we couldn't just kill the Titans when we overthrew them. We derived our power from them. They are our fathers and mothers, after all, and that works both ways. They've been entombed for thousands of years, Seth. They are weak now and they need to be charged up to enter Olympus, but they need a god or something of similar power to do so."

"Something that carries undiluted power in them?"

Apollo nodded. "They can feed off the demigods, drain them of their *aether* like a daimon would, but not as messy and bitey. But you know there are different ways to drain *aether*, don't you?"

I sucked in a sharp breath as I drew back. Yeah, I did, and that was a nice homerun slam against me. Asshole.

"So they just won't kill them. They will capture them and feed off them until they are at full strength and the demigods... Well, they will be nothing but dried-out husks of what they used to be." He kicked his feet off the bed and stood. "They already have two of them, and Josephine needs to be safely stowed away at the Covenant."

"Because she's a demigod?" I still couldn't believe it—a freaking demigod. "An untrained, weak, virtually mortal demigod?"

"Mortals are not always weak, Seth. You will be wise to realize that. And there are other reasons why it's imperative that Josephine remains safe."

"Whatever." I turned, snatching my bag off the chair and tossing it on the bed. I pulled out the Glock that was loaded with titanium-encased bullets and shoved it in the back of my jeans.

Just as I tugged my shirt down over the butt of the gun, it hit me. I turned slowly to Apollo, and he must've read something in my gaze, because he arched a brow.

Son of a *bitch*.

"The eyes," I said, taking a step toward him. "Her eyes were familiar."

A slow smile formed on his mouth, and then he blinked. When he reopened them, I let out a harsh curse. They were the dark, denim blue—almost-normal mortal eyes. The same eyes that had been behind thick, long lashes, and the same eyes Josephine Bethel had stared up at me with.

"She's yours, isn't she? That girl back there?" I swung my arm, jabbing a finger in the direction of the campus. An odd feeling opened up in my chest. It was unfamiliar, but I knew what it was. Dread. "She's your kid."

Apollo's smile spread until he was flashing even, white teeth. "She is. And when her abilities are unlocked fully, she'll have every power that I do, not like Hercules or Perseus or any of the

37

original ones who only had *some* of our abilities—we've figured out a few things since then. And that means she could turn you into a bush that smells like cat piss, so remember that when you're around her."

Hmm, how would he react if he knew I'd been checking out his *daughter's* ass? But I really didn't care if she could turn me into the damn Kraken. What I cared about was the fact that she was related to *her*—to Alex. That was why they seemed similar. After all, Apollo was Alex's great-great a thousand times great-grandfather, and they all shared the same basic flavor of *aether*. So even though the girl's powers were bound, I was still picking up on something.

My eyes met his. "This is messed up, Apollo. You know that, right?"

He inclined his head. "I could see where it could be... uncomfortable for you."

Uncomfortable? I almost laughed, but I didn't, because I wanted to punch him in the face. The last thing I wanted was anything that reminded me of how badly I'd messed up, of all the poor choices I'd made, and this girl would be a constant reminder. I could feel my chest constricting with anger and unease, because there was nothing I could do. The gods, namely Apollo, owned my ass. I could fight it, but ultimately I'd be forced to play along, and the forcing part would not be pretty. It was the deal I'd made.

Apollo turned so that his profile was visible, and a look that said he was thinking of something or someone far removed from this room flickered across his face. "To the best of my ability, I've kept her safe over the years, but with the Titans, I...I fear that it won't be enough." His large body shuddered with his next breath. "You think *we* are bad. You think *we* are uncaring, but the Titans are truly monsters, unnaturally cruel, and all they've had to survive on these thousands of years is thoughts of vengeance. And I fear that some of them don't even care about taking back Olympus, that some of them would be more concerned with payback."

Was this...actual apprehension I was sensing from Apollo? Holy shit, I hadn't suspected he was capable of such a thing.

"I fought Hyperion and was the one to seal him into his tomb. It was a bloody battle and...well, let's just say that Hyperion has every reason to strike back at me. The moment he realizes that we have demigods on Earth, he'll be looking for my child." Apollo turned to me. "He wouldn't just feed from her. He would *destroy* her to get back at me. She is my daughter, Seth. Take care of her, and I won't forget that."

Whoa. All I could do was stare at him. That had to be one of the most compassionate things I'd ever heard come out of Apollo's mouth—or from any god, for that matter.

And then he vanished in the way all gods did when they were done with a conversation.

Tipping my head back, I closed my eyes and exhaled slowly. "This is so messed up."

39

DUSK WAS already chasing the sun out of the sky, and I couldn't even stifle my yawn as I hurried across the lawn, running late for my Thursday study-date-that-wasn't-a-real-date with Jesse. I'd stayed up way too late last night with Erin and my bottle of José, and I'd been paying for it with a mushy brain all day. I had no idea how this study-session was going to have any bennies. Well, I'd probably spend the whole session staring at Jesse's face, and well, that was a benefit, and it was better than thinking about the Crazy Hot Guy from yesterday.

Cutting around a cluster of funky-smelling bushes, I hopped up on the veranda along the side of the library. Out of the corner of my eyes, I saw that someone was leaning against the exterior wall, someone tall, and as both my feet hit the stone walkway, the person pushed off the wall.

"Josephine."

My breath caught at the sound of the voice I couldn't easily forget and I spun around.

It was *him*—the Crazy Hot Guy who lurked in stairwells. Even in the dim overhead lighting and the rapidly increasing darkness, there was no way I wouldn't recognize him. Dumbly, all I could think was he knew how to make a pair of distressed denim jeans look like a work of art on long legs, because you know, that was an important observation. He also was wearing a henley again, the sleeves pushed up to the elbows, but it was black this time. Yet another helpful, essential observation.

My gaze trekked up his body, and I felt a little dizzy. My memory had not done that face justice. Every angle and plane, every square inch of his face, was something an artist would crave to sketch or paint. His beauty...the longer I stared at him, the only word that came to mind was "unearthly."

"We didn't get off to a good start yesterday." Crazy Hot Guy shoved his hand out, extending long fingers. "My name is Seth."

I stared at his hand, and then I stared at his face some more.

One golden eyebrow arched. "This is the part where you shake my hand and say, 'Hi, Seth, it's so nice to meet you outside of a stairwell.'" There was a teasing, cajoling tone to his voice that left me unsettled as he lowered his hand to his side. "Or not."

My heart jumped a little as I started backing away. "I'm sorry, but I'm running late and I...I really don't know you."

"We've actually met. In the stairwell. Yesterday."

"That doesn't count." I took another step back.

"It does to me." He tilted his head to the side. A strand of blond hair slipped free, kissing the curve of his high cheekbone. "We need to talk."

"I don't even know who you are, other than being the crazy hot guy from the stairwell. There's nothing to talk about."

Seth's one-sided grin went up another notch. "You think I'm hot."

My cheeks heated. I *had* said that, because I was an idiot and tended to babble when I was nervous. "I also said you were crazy."

"I have subjective hearing, but you and I *do* need to talk, Josephine."

"Josie," I corrected absently.

"How about I call you Joe?"

My brows knitted. "What? Don't call me Joe." I shook my head. "Why am I even standing here, talking to you? I have to—"

41

"Hey, Josie, I've been looking for you. What are you...?"

I turned toward the sound of Jesse's voice. He was standing behind me, his textbook dangling from his fingertips. He wasn't looking at me. He wasn't talking.

Confused, I glanced over at Seth. His profile was to me and he was staring at Jesse. My gaze darted back to him, and he was just standing there, arms hanging limply at his sides.

"Go away," Seth said, his voice low.

Jesse blinked slowly, his lips forming a word that never came out, and then he pivoted around, stiffly walking off.

What in the holy hell?

My mouth dropped open as my heart kicked in my chest. Jesse seriously had just turned and walked away, leaving me with Crazy Hot Guy! I spun back to Seth, and he was closer now, maybe a foot away.

He winked at me.

Whoa. Most guys looked like total douche-wads when they winked, or a caricature of a guy who belonged on a cheesy sitcom. Basically, guys winking was just something awkward that shouldn't be done, like ever. He, however, looked damn sexy and confident. But, more importantly, hot winking aside, something wasn't right. Tiny goosebumps formed on my skin.

"I hate interruptions." He dipped his chin in a way that made him come off ridiculously angelic. "So, *Josie*..." His gaze slowly traveled over my face, his stare so intense it felt like a caress. He reached out, lifting a strand of my hair.

I locked up. Every muscle. Every cell. I didn't even breathe. This was weird, really freaking weird.

He twisted the strand around three of his fingers. "You have interesting hair. Blonde. Brown. A gold color. Some strands so pale, they could be white. All mixed together. Never seen anything like that, and I've seen a lot of things."

My eyes widened. Was he...*feeling up* my hair? Was that what he wanted to talk about? My gaze darted from where he held my hair to his face. Our eyes locked, and my heart dropped

42

somewhere into my belly. His eyes...that tawny color was unreal, but I suddenly doubted my assumption from yesterday that they were contacts.

Instinct roared through me, demanding that I remove myself from this situation, pronto. The feeling I got sometimes for no reason, the sensation of being watched, had nothing on what I was feeling now. Pressure clamped down on my chest. A series of shivers slithered down my spine like icy eels. I snatched my hair free and turned, not even bothering to say anything to— *Holy Christ*, he was in front of me.

I stumbled back, gaping at him. How did he get in front of me when he was on the other side of me?

"I believe you are making a habit of running away from me." He was grinning, but the action didn't reach his eyes. Not only were they an extraordinarily weird color, they were now as cold as the first snowfall.

Fear trickled over my skin, which caused a different kind of emotion to punch loose—anger. I latched onto it as my hand tightened around my bag. "Are you a stalker or something?"

"I've been called that a time or two, oddly enough."

My jaw unhinged.

"And it's funny, considering who the last person was to ask me that." His arresting features tensed. "A relative of yours. A cousin, I guess." His lips pursed thoughtfully. "Or maybe a sister? Honestly, I have no idea how that works out, but it's about a thousand different kinds of disturbing."

"I don't have a sister. I don't even have any cousins." Mom was an only child. "You don't—" My words ended as a sharp squeak. One moment he was standing several feet away from me, and then he was right in front of me. I hadn't even seen him move. I jerked, pressing my back against the wall of the library. My bag slid off my shoulder, landing next to my feet. "Holy crap, you can move."

"I can do a lot of things." Angling his body, he pressed one palm against the wall beside my head. Good God, he was tall. "Some of them fast. Some of them *real* slow."

My mouth opened. "Was that a s-sexual innuendo?"

His lips twitched. "Something along those lines."

The heat was back in my face and throat, despite the chill bleeding from the wall through my lightweight sweater. "Well, it was a crappy one."

"I can do better," he offered, and those golden eyes finally lightened.

I inhaled sharply, which was a mistake, because his scent invaded my senses. It was wild—a mix of the outdoors and something heavy, sultry. "That won't be necessary. Thanks."

He chuckled and the sound was deep, masculine, and would've been nice if he hadn't been a stalker. "Okay. We are getting off to another bad start. I have that effect on people."

"I can imagine." I twisted to slide out through the opening, but as soon as my body twisted, his other hand landed on the wall, caging me in. My gaze swung back to him. "This isn't cool," I said, my voice scratchy, barely above a whisper.

"I know." His tawny gaze latched onto mine. "I also have a problem with personal space. I don't really believe in it."

"Knowing is half the battle, I guess." My heart rate had picked up. "Step back."

He shook his head slowly.

I drew in a deep breath as I raised my hand to push him back, but his shot out and his fingers curled around my forearm again. I gasped at how quick his reflexes were and how *warm* his hand was.

"Please, gods, tell me you don't have a hitting problem, too," he said. I snapped my mouth shut. Gods? As in plural? His gaze dropped to the arm he held between us. His lips parted. "You're bruised."

What? My gaze followed his and I really couldn't see anything, but I realized he was holding onto the same arm he'd gripped yesterday. There were marks there, his fingerprints, but I could barely see them in the dim light. "How do you see them?"

"I did that." Emotion churned in his eyes as his gaze flicked back to mine. "I'm sorry."

Before I could respond, he lifted my arm and pressed his lips against the skin of my inner wrist. A soft exhale crashed out of me. My entire arm tingled, buzzed even after he lifted his mouth from my skin. He slid his hand up my arm, stopping just shy of closing around my wrist. He smoothed his thumb over the area where his lips had just been.

The breath in my chest quickened. "What...what are you doing?"

An eyebrow rose as he spoke. "I'm going to handle this like a Band-Aid being pulled off, try to make it as quick and painless as possible."

I tensed. That didn't sound good.

"Do you know anything about the Greek gods?"

Okay. That wasn't a question I was planning to have to answer today. And I really shouldn't have needed to answer it. I needed to be plotting ways to get myself out of this situation, but he was still gliding his thumb in a slow circle.

"Josie?"

"Yes. I know what the Greek gods are." I wet my lips, and the hue of his eyes seemed to have brightened when his gaze dropped to my mouth. Oh holy smokes, everything about this guy was potent and dangerous and absolutely crazy. "Can you let me go and back off now?"

"Not yet," he said. "I'm sure you know some of the more famous legends then? About the gods? But what you probably don't know is that, a long time ago, the gods got it on with mortals."

"Uh..."

"And when they produced happy, bouncing babies, those kids were called demigods. When they got together with each other, their kids were called pure-bloods. Then some of those pure-bloods got a little frisky with mortals, and they created half-bloods," he went on. "And sometimes, not always, and who knows how or why, when a pure and a half got together, they created an Apollyon."

"Okaaaay." I drew the word out.

That playful but edgy half-grin appeared on his lips again. "I'm an Apollyon."

I opened my mouth, closed it, and then reopened it again. "You're...a polly-yon?"

"Apollyon." Seth, or whatever he was calling himself, corrected. "And you, Josie, are something that hasn't been seen for a long time."

"I am?" I squeaked.

"Yep." He leaned in and there was only a hairsbreadth between us. The entire front of my body warmed with acute awareness. "You're a demigod."

I stared at him, thinking I surely heard him wrong, but as he continued to stare right back at me, waiting for a response, I realized I'd heard him clearly enough. "I'm a demigod?"

He nodded.

The laugh burst out of me, and he drew back maybe an inch, cocking his head to the side as he dropped my arm. A tautness crept across his face. "Okay. Did someone put you up to this? I mean, someone had to have—"

"Someone *did* put me up to this, but not the way you think," he cut in, his expression relaxing. "It was your father."

"My father?" I laughed again, but the sound was rough. Absentee Dad? Oh, this was fabulous.

"Yeah, your daddy. And your daddy is one of the biggest pains in my ass—in probably a lot of people's asses. He's Apollo, also known as the sun god, and he's a major dick."

"Apollo?" Another wheezing laugh escaped me.

His eyes narrowed. "The gods are real, Josie. And there's a whole world living right among the mortals, moving in and out of what you think is 'normal' every day."

All the humor dried up inside me. "You're saying I'm a demigod? You're a Pollyanna or something, and my dad is Apollo?"

"Apollyon," he corrected drolly. "And now you and I have a six-and-a-half-foot-and then some tall, asshole god in common."

I continued to stare at him until I finally found words. "You're being serious."

"As serious as the Titans busting loose from Tartarus—which is also a real place—and gunning for your sweet ass."

My mind got hung up somewhere between Titans and my sweet ass. I couldn't believe this conversation was actually happening. "You're...you're mentally unstable."

He leaned in again, so close I could feel his breath on my cheek, and boy, did that do a variety of things to me. "I wish I were. It would make things so much more fun. Sadly, I'm not. At least, not yet. And I know this is a lot to swallow, and it would be great to give you time for a learning curve, but I have a feeling we aren't going to have that luxury."

This was *so* not normal. I squeezed my eyes shut, and when I reopened them, Seth was still there. My palms were getting clammy, and in the back of my head, a horrible little voice had picked up in the background. *You've gone off the deep end. This is it. You're totally crazy.* "Is this real?"

His brows knitted. "This is real."

It couldn't be. There was no way any of this was real. I dragged in a breath, but it got stuck, and I looked around wildly as a flutter of panic began in my chest. We were outside, but there were invisible walls closing in. Schizophrenia—one of the main symptoms was hallucinations—seeing things that weren't there. I could've totally conjured up a hot guy who thought he was a polly-poo. "I need air."

He was frowning. "You have air. You're—"

"No!" My voice exploded harshly. "I need air. Space. I need *space!*"

For a moment, he didn't move, and the flutter of panic in my chest turned into a freaking bird of prey, clawing at me from the inside. He must've read something in my expression, because he actually backed off.

Flying off the wall, I took a step to my left and tripped over my forgotten bag. I wheeled around, my foot getting tangled up in the strap. Seth shot forward, catching my arm before I turned into a flailing Muppet.

"Hold on," he said gruffly, bending over. Within a second, he had my bag detached from my foot. "There you go."

The moment I was free, I yanked on my arm and he let go. I started backing up, trying to get my throat and chest to unconstrict. "This isn't real."

This whole thing was a hallucination. My head had drummed up this Seth. Maybe Jesse hadn't even been meeting me in the library. Maybe *none* of this was real. I knew—I *knew*—it was possible. I'd witnessed week-long episodes where Mom thought we were in NYC or in China, even though we hadn't left the house. Or when she would talk to people who weren't there, hold entire conversations with them.

Holding my bag in his hand, he straightened. "Josie—"

I spun around and ran. I ran faster than I ever had before, maybe even faster than Erin could run, and I didn't look back to see if the apolloanna gave chase. Muscles strained and my arms pumped. People I passed were blurs. I thought I heard someone shout my name. I didn't stop running when I hit the steps leading to my dorm or when I barreled past the occupied couches in the lobby. I only skidded to a stop once I'd slammed my hand on the elevator button.

I was going crazy. My brain had just shit the bed on me.

CHAPTER
6

YOU HAVE *interesting hair?*

Had I seriously said that? Yeah, I had, and if I had time, I'd punch myself in the nuts, but alas, my show-and-tell with the girl had gone about as well as walking into Hades's palace with slabs of meat hanging around my neck while calling for his "puppies" to come out and play.

Perhaps I could've handled it better. Then again, how did one gently break that kind of news? Over tea and crumpets? My stomach grumbled. Gods, I was hungry.

With Josie's book bag in my hand, I stepped off the porch circling the library and cut across the lawn. I knew where her dorm was, which floor she was on and what room was hers. I could give her some time to digest the information, but I'd seen the panic in her blue eyes—so strong and raw I could taste it. Giving her time would backfire. She'd use those hours to further convince herself that none of this was real.

My hand tightened around the strap. Too bad I couldn't bop her on the head or something, transferring the truth and the knowledge of our world to her. A nifty-ass trick like that would come in handy right about now.

Even more fucked up was the fact that, when I bit down on my lower lip, I could taste her skin, and that sent a bolt of oh-yeah straight through all my happy places. Not that it took much. A breeze could get that same kind of effect, and Josie...she wasn't the kind of girl I'd go for. I tended to go for more of the in-your-face kind of hotness. Not *pretty* girls who existed somewhere between plain and sweet.

Her hair wasn't plain, though.

Neither were her lips. Pouty. Bow-shaped. Soft-looking.

Or her eyes. Even though she clearly got them from her father's side, there was always something...sexy about a pair of deep-blue peepers.

And she looked like she had a body under the chunky sweaters.

Fuck. Now my happy places were *really* happy.

I'd just crossed the midway point in the long stretch of lawn when I felt a sudden, oily heaviness slinking over my skin. I stopped, my narrowed gaze swinging over the trees and the students hurrying back and forth in the chilly night air. My attention landed on a middle-aged guy holding a briefcase. Glyphs raced across my skin in warning, but even without them, I would've known something wasn't right about the dude.

He was standing in the middle of the lawn, staring right back at me. In the pale moonlight, his lips pulled back in a sneer.

Interesting. Looked mortal, but I'd bet my punching arm that he wasn't—at least, not anymore.

The man pivoted, walking off quickly in the opposite direction. I glanced quickly to where Josie's dorm rose in the distance, but then wheeled around. It took no time to catch up to the guy as we passed under a cluster of oaks. Dropping her bag on the ground, I reached out and clamped my hand down on the man's shoulder. A jolt traveled up my arm, and the murky and thick feeling increased.

Yeah, something was *not* right about this dude.

I spun him around and stared into watery eyes, a washed-out color devoid of life. Inhaling, I caught a stale, musky scent that reminded me of when I'd been in the Underworld. Not a very pleasant smell.

Slamming my hand into the center of his chest, I pushed him back against the trunk of a thick oak, moving us out of the path of unsuspecting bystanders. My lip curled. "You smell of death."

The thing inside the man cocked its head to the side and laughed a high-pitched wailing sound that most likely caught a bit of attention. "Funny that you know the smell," it said, its voice distorted as if standing at the end of a long tunnel. "Since you reek of death yourself."

I rolled my eyes. "Wow. That was a clever comeback."

"Fuck you," it snarled.

"Even more ingenious. I bet you can carry on a real deep conversation. Let's talk about the shitty economy next."

The thing wearing the man smiled. "And I bet Hades is going to enjoy shoving every imaginable item up your ass when you finally get down there and become his personal chew toy." It laughed as my hand tightened around the collar of its shirt. "What? Everyone knows about the deal you made, Apollyon."

My eyes narrowed as my gaze drifted over it. There had to be a reason why it smelled like it'd rolled around in the Underworld and spritzed himself with cologne of death with an extra side of River Styx. My gaze shot back to his face as I remembered what Apollo had said about when the Titans had escaped. "You're a fucking *shade*."

It arched a brow, and those washed-out eyes turned all-black. "And you're too late."

The thing threw its head back against the tree with such force that the man's skull cracked like a clap of thunder. It opened its mouth and pulled a *Supernatural*—the TV show Deacon always seemed to be watching whenever I was within a ten-mile radius of him. Black smoke poured out of it, whirling up into the trees, blacking out the branches before it disappeared into the night. I dropped my hand, and the guy hit the ground, dead on arrival.

I glanced down at the body. Next to him was the fallen briefcase. There was a name engraved—something ending in Ph.D. "Well, shit."

Spinning around, I snatched the bag off the ground and picked up my pace. Shades were on campus, and there was no doubt in my mind that they were the ones that had escaped with the Titans. Which meant there was a damn good chance that the Titans were aware of Josie's location.

I kept to the thicker shadows, moving faster than the mortals could track, becoming nothing more than a burst of wind until I hit the paved walkway leading up to Muse Hall.

Slowing, I jogged up the steps and threw open the door while I hoped Josie had calmed the hell down. The last thing I needed her to do was freak out and run screaming into the hills while I had damn shades roaming the campus, and worse yet, a possible Titan or two or five.

As I headed toward the elevators, a dark-haired brunette swung around from where she sat perched on the arm of the couch. Her glossy lips turned up at the corners as her gaze tracked my progress across the lobby. I got an eyeful of her chest as she bent over, folding her arms under her breasts. The low-cut sweater showed more than enough to get my notice.

Damn.

By the time I stepped into the elevator, I felt sort of molested. A grin tugged at my lips as I turned, facing the closing door. The girl was still staring. I wiggled my fingers at her, and then I got down to focusing on less interesting—but sadly, more important—topics. Like how to convince Josie this was real and neither of us was clinically insane before another shade—or something worse—popped up.

From what I knew about shades, they could possess mortal bodies and will them to do just about anything. And they were dangerous in their shadowy, spirit form, too. They could kill mortals easily, so that begged the question—why was Josie still up and walking around if shades were already here? Why hadn't they taken her out? Unless that meant their orders weren't to kill the demigods.

Or, unless the shade's taunt that I was already too late meant Josie was lying somewhere in a bloody heap.

"Shit," I hissed, tempted to wing the bag through the elevator walls. I doubted Apollo would be thrilled if I were already too late. Unease stirred in the pit of my stomach, and admittedly, I'd be less than thrilled myself. Hysterics and calling me Pollyanna aside, she seemed like she could be a cool girl.

But she was a pretty, cool girl with a short life expectancy, since she had Titans after her.

When the doors opened, I moved into the hall, heading for her room at the end. I might've been a handful of steps away when I felt the coiled awareness of something packing a whole bunch of *aether*–more than a pure would carry in their blood, even more than what I had.

That meant somewhere on this floor there was something very godlike. Not a pure or a half, and definitely not another Apollyon, since I was the only one currently topside. And it wasn't the same feeling I got when I'd sensed the shade. The sensation increased as I reached Josie's door, and as I gripped the handle, I swore under my breath. Yep, something packing a whole lot of *aether* was in her room. And dammit if I didn't feel that hollowing in my stomach, that emptiness that begged to be filled with the power only draining *aether* could fill. I usually could ignore the urge whenever Apollo was around, because his general dickheadedness overshadowed everything else.

But fuck. I was like a damn daimon jonesing for a fix.

And that pissed me off.

Twisting the doorknob, I tapped into the element of fire and melted the internal gears. Open Sesame. There was a shriek from inside the room as I stepped in, kicking the door shut behind me. Took no time to find Josie, since the room was the size of a shoebox. She was sitting on a bed to my right, her back pressed against the wall, eyes wide and the odd, multicolored hair hanging down over her shoulders, past her breasts. Her face was as pale as a daimon's.

"I brought you your bag," I announced, tossing it to land on a skewed blue mat on the floor.

"Holy crap," she whispered, blinking several times. "You're not real. You're not real."

I sighed, widening my stance. "Not this again."

She opened her mouth, but then the narrow door near the foot of her bed opened. I would've thought it was a closet door, but it couldn't have been, unless a half-naked chick had been hiding in there.

If so, this was my kind of dorm.

But the moment I got a really good look at the tall girl wearing shorts that barely covered what she had going on and a sports bra, I knew I'd found the source of all that *aether* goodness.

The girl looked to be Josie's age, which based on what Apollo had said had to be around twenty. Her head whipped toward me, the movement very snakelike.

My muscles tightened. Our eyes locked like two bulls ready to knock horns.

"Do you see him?" Josie asked, clutching fists full of the blanket. "Do you see him, Erin?"

"Yeah, I see him." Squaring off with me, a wall of red-hot fury radiated from her, practically coating the room.

"Do I know you?" I asked.

Her features sharpened as she pulled back her lips, baring shark-like teeth. "You killed one of my sisters."

"What?" squeaked Josie.

I squinted at the girl. During the time I was with Ares, I...I'd killed a lot of people. Some were pures. Some were halfs. Some were even mortals. Basically, anyone who'd gotten in his way. Not too different from what I did now for the remaining gods. "You're going to have to narrow that down for me."

She drew back as if she'd been slapped, and yeah, maybe I could've been a little more sensitive about my request for additional info, but I was a jackass—and apparently everyone else knew it too.

The smile that appeared on her face was almost nice, except for the jagged teeth and barbed-edged quality to it. Then the girl who called herself Erin stepped forward, shedding her mortal façade.

Her flesh turned a murky gray, washing away the deep hue of her skin. Gray wings sprouted out of her back, reaching at least six feet—a huge-ass wingspan that was sort of impressive. Her fingers elongated, forming claws that could disembowel someone with a flick of the wrist. Her black hair thinned all around her head, forming a thousand tiny black snakes that snapped at the air around her. The dark eyes disappeared, and all-white ones appeared.

"Oh my God," Josie whispered, looking like she was trying to become one with the wall behind her. "Oh my God. Oh my God."

"Furie," I groaned. "Seriously?"

Erin—the name was so funny now, considering the actual Greek word for furie was *Erinyes*—rose up off the ground. "Yeah," she spat. "Seriously."

Whatever guilt I'd felt inside me for killing her sister had washed right away. Godsdamn furies. Yeah, I'd taken one of them out when I'd been all juiced up on the *aether*, but gods, those bitches had been gunning for my ass long before I'd done that. Furies were used by the gods to search down those who'd escaped justice, and they were a sign of a very unhappy pantheon. There could only be one reason why she was here—to protect Josie—and I had to remind myself of that.

"Okay. So I did kill your sister. But how many more do you have? Hundreds?"

She let out a low rumble of warning. "I should rip out your intestines and string them around the ceiling."

My brows rose. "That paints a pretty picture."

"This isn't real," Josie said, scooting along the wall. One leg made it over the edge of the bed. "This cannot be real."

"Oh, it's real. Your roomie here is a furie." The creature drifted to the side, blocking Josie as she came to her feet, forcing her back, away from me. Suspicions confirmed. "And Apollo sent you."

The furie snapped at the air, baring those attractive teeth. "Boy, you're a smart Apollyon."

Akasha zapped over my skin, appearing as a shimmer of golden light along my right forearm. "Do you want to join your sister?"

She hissed. "I'd like to see you try."

"What's happening?" Josie whispered.

A pulse of energy rolled out from me. The overhead light flickered. Loose pieces of paper rattled. The furie flew forward, swiping out at me with razor-sharp claws. I spun out to the side and dipped under a wing, coming up with my back to Josie and the furie in front of the door.

"Oh, you are really starting to irritate me," I warned, dodging her leg as she kicked out. I snapped forward, catching hold of her ankle. I let go with *akasha*, enough to send a friendly little buzz through her. She growled as she swung her arm toward me. Releasing her ankle, I caught her hand before it connected with my face. "Knock it off."

Rage poured off her as she aimed her other arm at me. Catching that one, too, I yanked her down so her feet were on the floor.

"What is happening?" Josie shrieked.

I dipped and kicked out, sweeping the furie's legs out from under her. Wings folded in as she hit the floor on her back. I sprang forward, dropping down so my knees held her legs immobile. Grabbing hold of her wrists, I pinned her down, keeping those damn claws away from my face. "You must be young, if that move took you down."

"I *am* the youngest of my sisters, you dickhead," she spat back. "But that won't stop—"

"Dammit." I kicked my head back as Josie darted around us, stumbling over as the door flung open. She skidded to a halt.

Underneath me, the furie used the distraction to her advantage. Rolling her powerful hips, she flipped me off her just as the heavy scent of death and decay entered the room. A shade.

I landed on my side and rolled as Erin's claws came down, digging and ripping through the carpet. Gods—she *really* didn't like me. Flipping to my feet, I jumped back as her razor-sharp nails caught the front of my shirt, slicing it open over my abs. Hot pain flared across my stomach.

I was *so* done with this shit.

Throwing my arm out, I let go with of a bolt of *akasha*. The shimmery blue light crackled like lightning as it smacked into her leg, spinning her up and back. She hit the wall beside the bed. Plaster cracked as she recovered, pushing off. On a hunch, I ducked as I pivoted, and the furie flew over my head.

"Josie!" I yelled, seeing her going toward the thing that had walked through the door like it was her own personal savior. "No!"

She whirled toward me as the guy, who looked like an average student, grabbed for her.

"Come with me," it said, wrapping his hand around her wrist. He twisted her arm hard, his eyes going completely black, and she cried out as she yanked back against him.

I launched forward as Erin *finally* realized the change in the situation. She spun, reaching for the shade as her wings roared through the air at the same moment Josie pulled herself free. A wing hit her in the chest, lifting her up off her feet. I lurched toward her, but it was too late. She smacked into the blinds covering the narrow window. Glass cracked, and then she was falling forward. Cursing, I slid across the floor, catching her around the waist before she ate the carpet. I turned her, pulling her to my chest. Lowering her to the floor, I slipped a hand under her neck as I straightened her body out.

Thick eyelashes, a dusty brown, fanned the tops of her cheeks. Her skin was pale as I pressed a hand above her breasts. Her heartbeat was steady under my palm. I quickly skimmed my fingers over her chest, ignoring the soft swells as I checked out her ribcage. Maybe the keyword was "trying" to ignore the curve of her breasts, which appeared fuller than I'd expected.

I was a total fucking creep sometimes.

Grinding my teeth together, I reached up and brushed the thick mass of hair back from her forehead. Nothing appeared broken. Out cold, but still alive—for now.

I looked up just as the furie caught the shade in the stomach. Blood squirted, and gore erupted. The shade threw its head back, releasing itself into black smoke that slammed into the ceiling, rattling the walls.

"Oh, I don't think so." The furie shot up, opening her mouth. Her chest rose as she inhaled. The black smoke stilled, its center bubbling and wiggling as tiny, finger-like tendrils whipped out.

The furie inhaled again, and the shade was pulled back, sucked down through her wide mouth. Her throat bulged as the last wisp of smoke snaked out, flailing before it too disappeared into the furie's belly.

"Yeah," I murmured, my fingers stilling in Josie's hair. "That was...gross."

She whirled toward me, but her gaze landed on Josie's prone body. Immediately, she shifted back into her mortal form as she dropped down on the other side of her. She reached for Josie, but for some reason that was beyond me, I moved one hand to the back of Josie's head and the other to her hip, guiding her into my lap. The look I sent the furie must've been read loud and clear, because she withdrew her hands.

Our stares held once more, and then she sighed, her shoulders shuddering, and dipped her chin to her chest. "They've found her."

I KNEW I was dreaming, because I was back home, sitting at the golden oak table in the old, country-style kitchen in my grandparents' house, and I was wearing a grown-up version of the red cowgirl outfit that I'd loved dearly and had worn almost every day for several months before my granny took it away from me. The skirt was red with white ruffles, and the shirt had a red vest attached to it, also full of white ruffles that formed a "V" on each side. When I'd been four, this outfit had been cute—adorable even—but as a twenty-year-old, not so much.

Mom was sitting across from me, looking so very young and so very vulnerable as she stared into her teacup. My breath caught as she tilted her cup to the side.

Oh God, I remembered this morning. I would never forget this morning.

Closing my eyes tightly, I reopened them to find my mom staring at me. Her lips parted, and every muscle in my body strained to give flight, but I was rooted to my seat in that damn cowgirl dress, reliving the morning from sixteen years ago.

"You're destined for something great, baby." Her deep-brown eyes roamed over my face, unfocused. "You have to be. I keep telling myself that's the reason why you're here. There has to be a reason why my life ended when yours began. There has to be a point to all this."

Like before, when I first heard those words, a very real pain sliced through my chest, cutting deep through tissues and organs. At four years old, I didn't understand that those words meant I was unplanned and a mistake, but I had *felt* their meaning, and I had known in that moment that my mom hadn't wanted me. I knew she loved me, but she hadn't *wanted* me.

The kitchen blurred as the dream faded away before Granny entered. Even as I was pulled out of the dream, existing somewhere between asleep and awake, I remembered that Granny had overheard Mom, and it hadn't been pretty. Mom had spent the rest of the day in her bedroom, and my grandparents had taken me out for ice cream.

Consciousness pressed against me as I dragged in a deep breath. It got hung up around the messy ball in the back of my throat, but there was a nagging suspicion that there was something more important that I needed to pay attention to, something other than what my mom had said so many years ago.

Nearby footsteps tickled my ears, and I forced my eyes open, blinking my surroundings into focus. The ceiling was unfamiliar. Satiny-white, with polished, exposed beams, it was a hell of a lot more fancy than the drop ceiling in my dorm. My gaze crawled past a huge ceiling fan to a flat screen the size of a small car mounted to the wall, and then to the large desk under it.

This was *so* not my dorm, and come to think of it, the bed in my dorm wasn't this fluffy-cloud comfortable, and neither were the sheets or the blanket practically tucked up to my chin.

Holy crap.

My gaze darted to the left, to a door that was ajar. I caught sight of a massive bathroom. Heart thumping, I checked out the scenery to my right and my mouth dropped open.

Seth stood by a large window. The blinds were up and the curtains were pulled back. It was night out, but who cared about that? He was missing a shirt. Looking out the window, he had his back to me and all that golden skin was on display.

Muscles along his back and his shoulders rolled, flexed, and did a myriad of fascinating things as he dragged a white towel through his wet hair. When he lowered his arms, the ends of his blond hair brushed his shoulders. He turned around, and goodness, the nylon sweats he wore hung so low on his hips it was almost indecent.

That boy worked out—and then some.

On either side of his hips, there were these indentations that begged to be touched, but then there were his abs. Six-pack? Was it possible to have an eight-pack? I think he had one. Smooth skin stretched over tightly rolled muscles. I bet I could've done a week's worth of laundry on his stomach. Probably would be a heck of a lot more fun way to wash clothes. The near-perfect, if not completely perfect, body came complete with actual pecs, and I'd never really seen a guy in real life with actual pecs. They were unreal, but totally—

"Do you want to touch?"

Eyes darting up to his face in surprise, I felt my body burn red-hot. "E-excuse me?"

His lips curved up and his bicep tensed as he tossed the towel across the room. He stood at the side of the bed, arms at his sides, completely comfortable with how much flesh he was showing off. Then again, I'd walk around naked if I were a dude and had a body like that, so...

"You were staring at me for so long, I was asking if you wanted to touch," he repeated, and my face started flaming.

"I don't want to touch. And I wasn't staring."

The half-grin spread. "You weren't?"

I shook my head. "No, I wasn't. I was just...lost in thought." Blowing a strand of hair out of my face, I pushed myself up into a sitting position. "And it's rude to point out if someone is staring at you."

He arched a brow as he folded his arms across his chest. Yikes! More interesting muscle movement. "Isn't it more rude to *be* staring at someone?"

I could see a nipple peeking out from where his arms were folded. Who knew a nipple on a guy could be so...attractive? The skin was flat, dusky, and the nip—

"I think you're wrong," he replied dryly. "And you're staring. Again."

Crap! I was. I forced my gaze to the forest-green comforter. "I was not staring. I dazed off again. I have a habit of dazing off. So don't flatter yourself."

"I'm totally flattered."

I huffed.

"So, let me guess. You like shiny things?"

"What?" I looked at him again, but this time I kept my gaze on his face. "Shiny things?"

He was fully grinning now. "Yeah, shiny things. Like ADD. Your dad has a mad case of it."

"My dad..." I trailed off as the last couple of hours rushed to the surface. "Oh my God!" Here I was, sitting here and staring at this guy, arguing about shiny things when my entire world had imploded with crazy.

Seth moved closer to the bed. "Are you going to freak out and run again? If so, I'd like to put some shoes on."

Ignoring him, I pressed the heel of my palm against my forehead as I stared at the comforter again. My head spun like I'd drunk half a bottle of tequila in less than an hour. My stomach roiled and I swallowed down the sudden rise of nausea. I remembered being outside the library and the odd way Jesse had looked as Seth had sent him off. I remembered every insane thing Seth had said, and I remembered running to my dorm, to Erin... and holy crap, what had she turned into? A giant bat?

Start small. That's what I told myself as my heart rate picked up. I needed to start with the small stuff. "Where am I?"

"You're in my hotel room. We're about a mile off campus." He paused. "You're safe here."

Safe from what? Oh yes, flying creatures, Titans, and guys with creepy, all-black eyes. "Did I...pass out?" That was kind of embarrassing.

He nodded. "You hit your head. Kind of got in the way of a wing. I know it's a lot to deal with," he continued, his voice low, as if any loud noise would send me scurrying into a panic. "Everything you thought you knew about the world is wrong and blah, blah, but we really don't have time for another freak out. Like I said, you're safe, but just for now. That thing back there—it was a shade, a soul that escaped Tartarus along with the Titans. They're dangerous in spirit form and they can also ride mortal bodies. It wasn't the only one here, but that's beside the point. It knows you're here, so that means *they* know you're here."

Lowering my hand, I looked at him sharply. "Wow."

One shoulder rose. "It's the truth."

My gaze dipped, and I pursed my lips. "Can you put on a shirt?"

A small grin formed. "No."

Frustration rose, mixing with confusion, as my head sought to catch up with everything. Denials formed on the tip of my tongue, but as I looked away, I shook my head slowly.

"Do you think none of this is real?" he asked, and the bed dipped as he sat beside me. I hadn't even heard him move. "You're awake. And you're holding a conversation with me again." He reached out, trailing his fingers over my forearm. "And you feel that, right? It's real."

I sucked in an unsteady breath. Yeah, I felt the wave of tingles that traveled to the tips of my fingers. "My mom is sick," I blurted out, and he pulled his hand away as he tilted his head to the side. Damp strands clung to his cheek. My fingers tightened on the edge of the green comforter. "She has a mental illness— schizophrenia. And there were times when she'd have episodes that lasted days and she would hallucinate people and locations. And schizophrenia—it can be hereditary."

His golden gaze swept over my face, intense and strange. "And you think that is what this is? That you have this sickness?"

A moment passed as embarrassment scaled my cheeks. Developing the illness was one of my greatest fears, because I knew firsthand how hard it was to deal with. "I don't know what to believe." My head felt woolly, my throat dry. I remembered hitting a wall. "Maybe it's a concussion and—"

"You don't have a concussion. We checked you over."

We. A cold air swept through my chest as the events in my room replayed in my mind. "Erin. Oh my God. What...what is she?"

Seth placed one hand on the bed next to my legs as he raised the other, shoving his fingers through his damp hair. "She's a furie. They usually go after those who've escaped judgment, and the gods use them as a warning system. Your friend can get pretty vicious, as you saw. Furies are no joke. They aren't a big fan of me."

A furie. My friend and roommate was a furie. A laugh escaped me and it quickly faded as an empty feeling opened up in my chest. "Is she really my friend?"

His brows rose. "I'd say so. She's rather protective of you. You should've seen her when I took you. Not fun."

I didn't say anything, because I doubted he'd understand, but everything Erin had told me had to have been a lie if she was some kind of furie. I didn't know if I should laugh or cry. "Where is she?"

"There was a bit of a mess to clean up, and she's gathering up your stuff, but that's not really important right now." He shifted closer and our gazes met. "I'm going to try this again, okay?"

Pressing my lips together, I nodded. My knuckles started to ache from how tightly I was clenching the blanket.

"Your father is Apollo, and that *does* make you a demigod."

"But...I'm not special," I said, and then realized how lame that sounded when he grinned. "I mean, demigods have powers, right? I remember reading about Hercules and some others. They were super-strong, and I can't even jog a mile without getting out of breath or having a leg cramp."

"Well, that's good to know, in case I need you to run fast." He cast a bland look in my direction. "Your abilities were bound at birth, along with those of the others."

"Others?"

He nodded. "I don't know how much you know about Greek mythology, but only half of what they teach in the mortal schools is true. The one thing you do need to know is that the gods are very powerful, but they suck at cognitive thinking skills."

"Um." An ache started at my temples. "Alrighty, then."

"They do things without really thinking them through, which is how we're in this situation now," he continued as he turned his gaze to the open window.

I wasn't sure I was ready to hear about this situation. "And, you're not a demigod. You're the pollen-ann?"

"Apollyon," he said, sighing. "Like I told you before, my mom was a pure and my father was a half. I didn't know him."

"I didn't know my dad, either." When he glanced back at me, I felt my cheeks heat. "Well, duh. You know that."

"Well, I guess we also have that in common, don't we?" His eyes flashed a bright amber, startling me with their intensity. "You and I might have some things in common, but we're nothing alike and there's nothing to bond over."

Drawing back against the headboard, I was stung, and I wasn't quite sure why, but the tone of his words had been harsh. "I wasn't trying to bond with you."

He turned his gaze back to the window and didn't say anything for a long moment. "Not every pure and half who get together create an Apollyon. Usually there's some kind of divine intervention, but relationships between pures and halfs were forbidden because of the threat of an Apollyon being born."

65

Pushing away the sting of his earlier words, I focused on what was important. "Why?"

"There's only supposed to be one Apollyon in a generation. We're as powerful as a demigod, able to control the four elements—air, water, fire, and earth—and we control the fifth—*akasha*. But when there are two Apollyons, we can...we're connected in a way that's hard to explain. We can pull energy from each other, and one of us, if we do a certain ritual on the other, can become a God Killer, something a demigod cannot do. And being a God Killer basically means what you'd think it does. Needless to say, the gods aren't thrilled whenever there are two Apollyons, because of that potential."

All of this was Greek to me. Literally. But it was fascinating.

Twisting at the waist, he faced me again. "I'm going to give you the CliffsNotes version of what went down."

I was surprised he hadn't said he was going to give me the version for dummies, but I kept my mouth shut.

"I shouldn't have been born," he stated pointedly.

"Whoa." My eyes widened. "That's a bit harsh." And also a bit too close to home for my liking.

He shrugged, but there was a hardness to his jaw that said it affected him more than he led on. "There was already another Apollyon lined up to be born. All of them are descendants of Apollo, one way or another. But I was born before...before her, and I was raised to be the Apollyon—schooled, trained to fight from the moment I could walk. My duty was to step in and handle situations the Sentinels couldn't handle."

"Sentinels? Isn't that a Transformer?"

He chuckled, smiling slightly. "Sentinels are halfs and pures who train to keep things in order—to make sure no one gets out of hand and that the mortal world remains oblivious to what coexists among them. There's a whole society—schools, universities, communities, clubs—you name it. It's out there and mortals have no idea about any of it, Joe."

I frowned. "Don't call me Joe. I'm not a dude."

Seth ignored that. "Anyway, I was raised believing I was the only Apollyon. Until I was brought to Deity Island—a small island off the coast of North Carolina. Then I met the other and... Well, everything sort of went downhill from there. The gods knew that I wasn't supposed to be the Apollyon, and they knew one of their own was seeking to betray them. Turns out that Ares, who made sure I came into existence, wanted to take over the world, bring it back to the glory days where gods ruled not just Olympus but also over the mortal realm."

Surprise shuttled through me. Ares was real? Goodness.

"The gods took precautions when I was born. They knew they needed a backup plan in case one of the Apollyons became the God Killer, so they created twelve demigods, bound their powers, and left them alone. You're one of them."

My head was spinning again. "So, I'm virtually Plan B?"

"Actually, you're virtually Plan C."

Well, damn. My birth was Plan C?

"We fought Ares a year ago. One of the ways we battled him was by releasing one of the Titans from Tartarus," he explained, and all I could think was *holy crap, Tartarus is real?* What about the guy who ferried the boat? "It was a crap plan from the get-go. Perses ended up freeing more Titans after we defeated Ares, because all the gods were weakened when we took Ares out. Due to some kind of cosmic bullshit, only the demigods can put them back in their place. So Plan C is being put into play."

"Um, I'm...I'm supposed to do what? Send a Titan back to hell?"

"Tartarus isn't hell. It's a mixture of good, bad, and something in-between. And yes. Once the six remaining demigods are together, your powers will unbind."

"Wait. Remaining *six*? I thought there were twelve?"

"There were twelve. Ares took out some of them." He placed his hand over mine, causing me to jump. A slight, knowing grin appeared on his lips as he easily pried one of my hands free from the blanket. His hand slid off mine, leaving a shiver in its wake as

67

he moved onto my other hand. "There are six, but it appears the Titans got to two of them. They aren't dead. Not yet."

I wasn't sure I wanted to know, but I asked the question. "What do the Titans want from them?"

His lashes lowered, shielding his gaze. "The Titans are weak, and they can feed off of gods and demigods to regain their strength."

"*Feed?* Oh my God."

He cocked his head to the side and lifted his lashes. "They can drain the demigods of their *aether*, which is what makes our blood different from mortals'. Gods have the most *aether*, followed by demigods, the Apollyon, pures, and then halfs."

Now that my hands weren't clenching anything and he was still holding onto one of them, I didn't know what to do with them. "That's a lot to deal with."

"Yeah, well, you've *got* to deal with this."

"I am," I replied. "I'm trying."

His hand slid up to my wrist and the simple caress sent a ripple of warmth along my arm. "I'm not sure if you are, or if you still think you're hallucinating pink elephants. Well, in your case, it would be a pink Pegasus. And yes, Pegasus is real. I've never seen it personally, but it's around."

"I shouldn't have told you that," I retorted. His thumb smoothed over the inside of my wrist. "And can you stop touching me?"

His grin spread as he slowly slipped his hand away from my wrist. A heartbeat passed, and then he leaned in. I inhaled sharply. His scent...there was something intoxicating about it. He was close, so close that if I shifted an inch forward, our noses would be touching. That wouldn't be the only thing touching, either.

"I need to make sure you understand everything I said to you," he said, his bright gaze locking onto mine. "Because they know you're here. That's why the shades are here—why one of them was in your room."

"He was another student. I think he...he lived on the seventh floor."

"He's nothing now."

I flinched, my stomach unsettled.

A muscle thrummed along his jaw. "That was a bit insensitive of me." There was a brief pause, the next words sounding almost forced out of him. "Was he your friend?"

"I didn't know him well, but that doesn't matter. He was a living, breathing person and now..." And like he'd said, now he was nothing. "This can't be good. None of this."

He shook his head and his hair slipped over his cheeks. The movement brought him even closer. "No, Josie, none of it is good, and there's more I need to tell you."

"There's more? How could there possibly be more? Or are Transformers real, too? Or aliens? What about fairies and vampires and—"

"Josie," he murmured.

"What?" I wanted to throw my hands up, but I'd end up hitting him if I did. "I didn't believe gods existed and they do, so why not the other stuff?"

He cocked a brow. "Your father fears that Hyperion is going to come directly for you. He's a Titan your father entombed."

My stomach twisted. "Isn't that why the...the shade was here?"

Shaking his head, he met my gaze. "The shade could've been scouting for any Titan. After all, they're going to be looking for any demigod to snack on." When I winced, his expression remained impassive. "But Hyperion has a revenge hard-on for Apollo and there's a chance he's going to take that out on you. You don't want that."

"No," I agreed, and my head was starting to spin again. The walls of the room were getting closer. "What does this mean?"

"It means that your life changes right now. You have to leave here, and that's where I come in. My job is to get you to the

Covenant, which is a stronghold in South Dakota, where Apollo believes you will be safe."

The twisting motion stopped, because my stomach bottomed out. "South Dakota? I'm not even sure I can point out where South Dakota is on a map."

The slight curve of his lips appeared again. "It's between nothing-there-interests-me and land-of-the-great-nothing."

A surprised giggle escaped me. Seth...he could be funny, but I clamped my mouth shut, because I was afraid that if I started laughing, it would become that crazy kind, and then I wouldn't be able to stop.

Squeezing my eyes shut, I tried to let everything soak in, but my brain felt like an overflowing bathtub. A bit of fear trickled into my blood like a small, icy stream. I cut it off before I slipped into the kind of panic that left people rocking in the corner. I had to be smart about this, because the last thing I wanted was to end up dead. "So, I can't stay here and my life as I know it is virtually over."

"Or your life is finally starting," he suggested. "You could look at it that way."

I wanted to lean back, but I was already pressed against the headboard. There was nowhere to go. "I need a shower," I blurted out.

His brows knitted. "You need to shower?"

"Yeah. Yes. I need to shower. It helps clear my head," I went on, the words coming out in an anxious rush. "And I really need to get my head clear, because this is a lot. So I need to shower. Lots of steam. It helps me think."

For a moment I thought he was going to tell me no, but then he pulled back and pushed off the bed. Suddenly feeling chilled, I watched him back away from the bed, but I could finally breathe with the space. "There's a Jacuzzi tub in there."

I hesitated for a moment, and then I tossed off the covers. Springing from the bed, I headed straight for the bathroom door, my head full of so much I thought it would explode.

"Joe."

Clenching my hands, I faced him. "Don't call me Joe, *Sethie*."

"Sethie?" A laugh burst from him.

I folded my arms across my chest, ignoring the fact that he really did have a nice laugh even if he wasn't human. Well, if I believed him, I wasn't completely human, either. "What?"

His bare chest rose, and I forced my gaze back to his face. "I..." He shook his head. "Nothing. I'll be waiting. Don't take forever."

I stared as he turned to a bag resting on a large chair, and I hoped he had a damn shirt to pull out of it. Turning back to the bathroom bigger than my dorm room, I pulled the door shut behind me and all but collapsed against it.

Closing my eyes, I listened to the absolute silence of the hotel room. If he was moving around out there, he was part ghost. So much information rolled around in my thoughts. Part of me wanted to deny everything, but he...he had to be telling me the truth, and that caused little darts of panic to shoot through me. My body trembled. Demigods. Gods. Apollyon. Titans. Even Pegasus. All of it was real, and I was one of them? And all of this... It felt too real to not be.

I opened my eyes and stared at the huge tub.

I seriously hoped Seth found a shirt.

CHAPTER

8

WHEN I heard the water come on in the bathroom, I exhaled loudly and then tugged the shirt on over my head. There were no windows in the bathroom for her to make a crazy escape, and while she could be using the quality one-on-one time to convince herself none of this was real, at least she was still in there and not running screaming back to campus.

This conversation had gone better than the last, which was a positive.

Sighing, I zipped up the bag and then moved to the wet bar. Opening the mini-fridge, I grabbed a beer and then walked over to the chair. Popping off the cap, I didn't even bother trying to summon Apollo. I knew he wouldn't show.

I took a long drink before I dropped down in the thick cushioned chair I'd parked my ass in when I'd brought Josie to the hotel. I'd sat there for a few hours, watching her sleep like some kind of creep before I'd hopped in the shower to wash away the faint, lingering scent of the Underworld. But I did have a valid reason for keeping an eye on her. She had cracked her head pretty good. It had to have been the blood she carried in her veins, even though her abilities were bound, that kept her from needing a trip to the ER.

Tipping the bottle to my lips, I wondered if there'd been situations in the past where she'd walked away from serious accidents or injuries virtually unscathed. Had she ignored them, chalked them up to luck?

Did she also know she slept like the dead?

From the moment I'd laid her down in that bed and tugged the blankets up, she hadn't moved from where I'd put her. Not once. Didn't flip onto her side. Roll onto her stomach. Didn't even twitch.

The constant drum of water ceased in the bathroom. Finally. There had to be enough water in that tub for her to drown herself.

I lowered the bottle to the arm of the chair as I turned my narrowed gaze on the bathroom door. She wouldn't...

I didn't know her at all, so I had no idea what she was capable of. The girl had been worried that she was sick like her mother, and maybe she was.

Dammit.

Pushing up from the chair, I set the bottle on the wooden stand and went to the bathroom door. Unease gathered in the pit of my gut, the sensation traveling upward. I reached down, turned the knob, and found it locked. Not a problem. The energy of the fire element rolled down my arm, and heat wrapped around my palm, searing the knob and melting the insides of the lock.

Lock be gone.

Ha.

Mentally preparing myself for anything, I pushed open the door. What I saw I was definitely not prepared for.

Josie was in the bathtub, not drowning herself, which was a good thing. Bad thing was being in the bathtub meant she was completely naked. Maybe that wasn't a bad thing. Okay. *Definitely* not a bad thing.

She froze in the jetted tub for a few seconds—seconds that felt like the longest of my life but still not enough time.

She was tucked into one of the rounded corners of the tub, her knees breaking the whirling water. Her hair was pulled up, but light-brown and blonde tendrils snaked around her neck, sticking to her damp skin. My gaze followed the longer strands that traveled well beyond the slope of her shoulders. As I tall as I was, I had a clear view into the tub. At that point, I should've looked away. Maybe apologized. That's what a decent person would have done.

But I was not a decent person.

So I looked my fill.

I'd been right. She'd been hiding some major assets under the baggy sweaters. Gods, the top half of her was perfect. They were more than a handful, but not overly large, with creamy swells and rosy pink tips.

Sweet. That's what came to mind. Everything about what I saw was *sweet*.

Then she moved.

Josie shrieked as her arms shot out and over her chest. Water flew like a little rocket had hit the tub. She curled up, pressing her knees against her arms, covering all that glorious skin. "Oh my God! What are you doing?"

Good question. For a moment I'd forgotten why I'd come in here. "I was making sure you didn't drown yourself." My voice was deeper, rougher.

Her wide eyes narrowed on me. "Well, obviously I didn't drown myself."

No. No, she had not.

"Have you ever heard of knocking?" she demanded, her gaze doing a quick scan of the room. "And I locked that door."

"Knocking is...cumbersome. And locks are annoying."

Her brows rose quickly, and I was fascinated by the way a pink flush spread across her cheeks and down her throat. I bet it flowed over her breasts too, but unfortunately, she had them covered. A moment passed. "You're still in here," she said.

"I am."

Her lower lip thinned. "You shouldn't be. It's rude."

"Is it?" I leaned against the doorframe, getting comfortable.

"Yes! I'm in a bathtub. And naked!"

My lips curved up. "You are most definitely naked."

"That's the point!" she shouted, and my grin spread. "What? Do rolly-pollys not have basic manners or any personal boundaries?"

"Apollyon," I corrected absently. "And like I said, I'm not good with boundaries."

"Whatever." Her voice pitched high.

A chuckle rolled out of my throat, surprising me. I needed to get out of here before...before I did what? Stripped off my clothes and joined her? Parts of me really liked that idea, but that wouldn't be smart.

Josie wasn't some girl I had picked up for a few hours.

Forcing myself to move, I turned, but her voice stopped me. "Seth?" she called, and I looked over my shoulder at her. Her tongue darted out, wetting her bottom lip, and I swallowed a groan. She had no idea. "Your eyes...they're kind of glowing."

"They do that sometimes."

She looked like she wanted to ask another question, but seemed to remember that she was naked in a bathtub. I really needed to get out of the room. Grabbing the virtually useless doorknob, I stepped out and shut the door behind me.

"Damn," I groaned.

I was as hard as I was the first time I saw breasts, and that was a long time ago. I thought I might even be harder this time.

What was I doing here?

Adjusting myself sure as hell didn't ease anything. I walked over to where I'd left the beer and grabbed the bottle. Taking a long drink, I wondered how I'd ended up in this place, at this very moment, with a naked chick a few feet from me, and I *wasn't* in there with her.

My life was completely out of my hands.

Laughing out loud, I dropped back in the chair and kicked my feet up on the bed as I rested the bottle in my lap. That shit was funny. Since the day I'd been born, I hadn't had an ounce of control over my own life. I'd been groomed to be an Apollyon, which meant I was trained like any other Sentinel.

Truth was, if Apollo released me tomorrow from the deal I'd made and told me I had control of my life, I wouldn't know what to do with it. Hell. I didn't know who I really was anymore.

The Elixir, a special brew that had been used to sedate halfs who went into servitude, was gone now. So were a lot of the rules, but I hadn't been around the Covenants or in the communities to see how much things had changed. I doubted they'd changed very much at all. I guessed I'd be finding out soon enough.

I glanced over at the bathroom door, exhaling softly. She'd been in that bath long enough to be a prune by the time she climbed out. What a shame to wrinkle all that pretty skin.

Now I was thinking about all that pretty skin.

And I'd seen a decent amount of it.

Had I thought she was plain before? Plain and pretty? I was reevaluating that observation when the bathroom door finally opened and Josie emerged.

Oh for the love of the gods hiding in Olympus, she was wearing a robe. Not even one of those awful terrycloth, unisex robes a lot of hotels had. That wasn't how this hotel rolled. She'd found a thin, silk one that had been hanging on the bathroom door. It was cinched tight in a way that drew attention to her small waist and rounded hips.

The robe was beige and damp in interesting areas, like right below her navel, above the belt, and in the valley between her breasts. She sucked at toweling off. Not that I was complaining. My gaze moved to her breasts. Her nipples were clearly visible, pressing against the thin material.

Gods.

I spread my legs, hoping she didn't look at my lap. Nylon pants don't do much when it comes to hiding an erection.

She walked over and sat on the edge of the bed. "I didn't want to put the other clothes back on," she said, peeking at me through thick lashes. "You're...you're the one staring now."

My eyes were glued to her. "I am."

Her stare met mine for a moment, and then flickered away. "Rude," she muttered, glancing back at me.

I grinned. "Your friend is supposed to bring your clothes over. It will probably take her a while. Some of the mortals were too close to your dorm room when we were there. She needs to make sure anyone who thought they might have heard or seen something doesn't repeat it...or remember it."

Sucking her lower lip between her teeth, she looked away. "How will she do that?"

Dropping my feet to the floor, I set the empty bottle aside. "She'll use a compulsion to make them either forget what they heard or saw, or she'll make them think something else happened."

That got her attention. Those deep blue eyes were on mine again. Her brows knitted in confusion, pinching her face in a way that was almost...cute. I drew back. *Cute?* "So a compulsion is kind of like mind control?"

"Yeah." I brushed my hair back off my face. "Pures can do it. Any of the gods can. Halfs can't. They are vulnerable to compulsions like a mortal would be."

She seemed to consider that. "Can you do it?"

I nodded.

Her fingers nervously fluttered over the knot in her belt. "Does compulsion work on me?"

"It shouldn't. You're a demigod." I paused. "But your powers have been bound, so who knows? I can give it a try." The look on her face said she'd rather I didn't, but that didn't stop me. My gaze met hers and held it. "Take off your robe."

Her lips parted, and then her mouth gaped open. "What the hell?"

Disappointment rippled through me. "Guess it doesn't work."

"You're a pervert."

I shrugged. "Been called worse."

"I bet," she muttered crossly.

"You have no idea." I stood, raising my arms above my head and stretching. Her next question surprised me.

"You said you can use the elements? Can you...show me one?"

Lowering my arms, I watched her. "So you want a show and tell?"

She hesitated and nodded.

My first instinct was to tell her no, because I'd had enough of that in my life, but that's not what I did. Lifting my arm toward her, I opened my hand, palm up. While pures usually only excelled at using one element, usually the ability that ran in their families, summoning any of the elements was second nature to me. I guessed it would be the same for her once she was able to tap into her abilities.

I didn't even have to really think about it.

Heat rolled across my skin, licking into the air around me. A spark appeared above my palm, followed by the faint scent of burnt ozone. A second later, a small ball of amber-tinged flames appeared, the outer layers of the fire encasing my hand.

"Holy wow." Josie pushed off the bed. "Your hand is legitimately on fire!"

My lips twitched. "It doesn't hurt." I moved my hand, flipping my palm down and then up. "It goes where I want it to."

"Wow..." she repeated, walking around the bed, inching closer to me. She stopped a few feet shy and the glow of the fire reflected off her dewy cheeks. "That's...just, wow."

I closed my fingers, extinguishing the flames as I met her awed gaze. "You'll probably be able to do it, too."

She shook her head as her fingers went back to fiddling with the knot on her robe. "I can't even wrap my head around that."

The edges of the robe had started to gape under her throat, teasing me with a flash of pale skin. "You will. You'll have to."

There was a pause. "I've been thinking."

"So that's what you were doing in the bathtub for twenty hours?"

"I wasn't in there for twenty hours." Her arms lowered to the side, and the material gaped further, revealing the gently curving swell. Back to sweet again. "You said I have to go to South Dakota."

I dragged my gaze to hers. "Yes."

"And then you're just going to leave me there?"

I didn't have an answer for that. Apollo's orders were to get her to the Covenant. That was all. I sure as hell wasn't hanging around there.

Her eyes closed and her chest rose sharply, straining the robe. Fuck me. Seriously. This girl was off-limits for a multitude of reasons, especially considering who her father was, and while I would have loved to piss him off, I didn't want a lightning bolt in the ass. But my fingers itched to touch the skin peeking out from the robe, to slip my hands under the material.

"My life here is important. Everything I've been working toward means nothing now—my education, what I wanted to do with my life."

I really needed to stop staring at her chest. "You are a demigod. You will eventually help save the world and blah blah. That's more important than...What were you studying?"

"Psychology," she answered. She laughed, the sound soft and sad. "I know that probably isn't important to you, but it is to me. It means a lot to me, and now that's been stripped away and I..." She stopped talking, her expression taking on a distant quality.

She had no choices now. She had a destiny she'd never known about, probably didn't want, and might end up getting her killed. I got how much that sucked. My heart pounded in my chest for no reason. "I'm sorry."

She blinked as if surprised, and then she turned to the side. That expanse of exposed skin was killing me. "I just realized something."

79

I wasn't really listening. Moving toward her before she could speak another word, I caught the edges of the robe. The backs of my fingers brushed her skin, revving me up. Her breath caught as her body stiffened. Her neck craned as her eyes widened, met mine. There was so much depth in them, more than what I'd realized before. There was so much emotion. Confusion. Unease. Innocence. Oh, but there was more. Fear existed in their depths, but so did curiosity. There was a crater-sized part of me that wanted to slip the robe off her shoulders, to see how she'd respond, how deep that innocence ran, and if the curiosity I was tracking in her gaze, in the way her lips parted, was stronger than the fear.

I tugged the edges together. "Distracting," I murmured.

She exhaled softly as pink infused her cheeks. Reaching up, she grasped the edges just below my hands. Our hands didn't touch, but my knuckles pressed against her skin, scalding me. For a moment, neither of us moved. We seemed to be stuck in a moment in time.

"Your eyes are kind of glowing again," she whispered.

They tended to do that when I was feeling anything strongly, and I had lot of feels right then—all of them inappropriate. I let go and forced a step back from her. "What did you realize?"

Several moments passed before she spoke, and when she did, I noted the change in her voice. The sound was huskier, softer. Interesting. "I don't know if my mom is crazy anymore," she said, and talk of her mom effectively slaughtered my hard-on. "She said my father was an angel who visited her. It wasn't an angel. It was... God, I can't even believe I'm going to say this, because it does sound really crazy, but it was Apollo."

"Yeah, it was him, creeping into the bed of a young lady," I muttered, eyeing the wet bar. I wanted another beer.

Josie forged on. "And she said that everything that happened last year with the natural disasters, the whole world on the brink of war, was the world on the verge of ending. She was right, wasn't she?"

I nodded. "Kind of like the gods bowling with Earth."

"There...there must've been so many times when I thought she was hallucinating—it might all have been true, and we—my grandparents—they put her on meds. Antipsychotic meds. And those meds, if you aren't schizophrenic, it can... You shouldn't be on them. Oh my God..." She plopped down on the bed, her expression starting to crumble. "We probably made it worse for her."

My gut twisted with helplessness as I stared at her. The glassy sheen to her eyes told me she was seconds from crying, and I wasn't good with that shit. Emotions—they were bad. But I stepped toward her.

Her chin rose as she drew in a deep breath, squaring her shoulders. The shininess in her eyes was still there, but no tears fell. I stopped halfway to her, wondering what I was doing. She exhaled roughly. "I want to go home. I *need* to go home. Now."

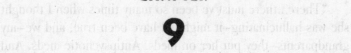

CHAPTER

9

"**Y**OU WANT to go home?" Seth repeated. He stared at me like what I'd just said was the craziest thing spoken that night. And there had been a lot of crazy.

I'd used every moment soaking in that tub—that *awesome* tub—focusing on keeping my head on straight, and I'd barely pulled that off. Having him bust into the bathroom hadn't helped. I still couldn't believe he'd thought I was in there drowning myself. And I really couldn't believe I'd been totally naked in the same room as him. I was kind of naked now, since this robe left so little to the imagination, but I wasn't going to think about that. I was pretty sure he'd gotten an eyeful of my breasts in the bathroom anyway.

At least now he was a couple of feet from me, staring at me like I was insane. That was better than him *right* in front of me, his fingers curled around the edges of my robe, his knuckles against my skin, and staring at me like... My breath hitched as a strange flutter danced low in my stomach. He'd been staring at me with eyes that were slightly luminous, and he'd looked *hungry*.

I couldn't recall any guy ever looking at me like that unless I was holding a basket of chicken wings or something. But in that moment, with the back of his hands searing my skin, if he had

82

lowered his mouth to mine, there was a good chance I would've stood there and let him.

I wasn't sure what that said about me.

Pushing those thoughts aside, I rose as I reached for my belt, making sure it was still tight. "I need to go home to see my mom. I need to talk to her." Guilt churned through me even though I knew it was ridiculous. Who would've thought that any of what she had been saying for years was true?

Seth folded his arms as he eyed me. "And you can't just, I don't know, pick up the phone and call her?"

"I can, but I want to see her." Frustrated and feeling about a thousand other emotions, I reached to tug my hair loose, but stopped when the stupid top of the robe gaped open again. Clutching the edges, the flutter was back when I noticed the way he seemed to breathe deeper. I needed to focus—and not on the flutter. "I don't expect you to understand or even care, so I'm not going to go into the million reasons why what I need to say to my mom—the huge apology I need to deliver with probably a garden of flowers—is not phone-call appropriate. I want to be with her. I want to hug her. Okay? So I need to see her. Not call her."

Those elegantly arched brows climbed slowly. "Do you realize you ramble? A lot."

Heat swept over my cheeks. "No. I've never been told that."

"I find that hard to believe," he responded dryly.

My eyes narrowed, and when he grinned, I was torn between wanting to knock it off his face and...and grin back at him. That was an infuriating response. "You're supposed to take me to South Dakota. Why can't I stop in Missouri and see my mom on the way?"

"I never said you couldn't."

My eyes met his. "Then I'm going to see my mom before you cart me off to the middle of nowhere."

He tilted his head to the side, and his hair, now dried in soft waves, brushed his face. "I don't think it's smart."

"And I didn't ask your opinion."

One eyebrow rose.

I squared off against him, drawing in a deep breath as my grip on the robe tightened. "You can't stop me."

He stared at me a moment and then tipped his head back, laughing deeply. A shiver curled around my spine. Such a nice laugh. "I can't stop you? You can't stop *me*, Joe."

"Don't call me Joe!"

His chin dipped as amusement curled his lips. "Sorry, *Joe-sie*."

"Oh my God, you're so annoying," I muttered as I started pacing along the length of the bed. "What is your job? Like, why are you here with me? You're my babysitter, right?"

His amber gaze tracked my movement with unnerving intensity. Did he always stare at people like he could see right into their innermost private thoughts? "I prefer the term 'guard' over 'babysitter.' I'm supposed to keep you alive, not fed and watered and entertained with Disney cartoons."

"Whatever. You're a hot, ninja-esque babysitter who has to *protect* me," I amended, distracted for a moment by the sudden glimmer in his tawny gaze. Drawing in a shallow breath, I raised my chin. "Because my...my father ordered you to do so. And he's like Apollo—the real deal—and I'm guessing he's super-powerful and not someone you want to tick off. And I'm also guessing, since he had other...people watching over me, he doesn't want me dead, so he'd be pretty ticked off at you if I end up not breathing, right?"

His lips pursed as the glimmer faded in his eyes. "Something like that."

"So, to make your job easier, you should just let me go see my mother. If not, you're going to have to spend half the time worrying about killer mythical creatures gunning after me, because the moment I can make a run for it, I'll do it. I can promise you that, *Sethie*. And then, if I'm there running amok with no protection..."

His mouth opened slightly as he cocked his head to the side, and then he shocked me. He laughed again as he unfolded his arms. "That was clever."

I tried and failed to hide my triumphant grin. "I thought so myself."

"It's not smart," he added with a shrug. "But, hey, what's the worst that could happen? You end up dead and I end up wishing I was dead. Or the Titans or shades follow you home and put your entire family in danger. It's a risk, but no biggie."

My grin slipped off my face. Well, that didn't sound good.

Walking over to the other side of the bed, he picked up a pillow, fluffed it, and dropped it back against the headboard. Then he pulled the heavy blanket and sheet back.

"When are we leaving? Now? If so, I need clothes." I needed clothes like five minutes ago. "And probably my purse and cellphone. I guess I need my identification stuff. You never know when–"

"Your friend will be bringing that stuff over, probably in a couple of hours. Not only is she doing clean-up, she's out there scouting and making sure nothing gets close to this hotel."

I had to wear this robe for a few more hours? I could put my old clothes on, but they smelled weird–musty and dank.

Seth looked over at me. "So we're not going anywhere until the morning."

"The morning?"

"Yep." He threw himself on the bed, causing the mattress to bounce, but he did so with a level of grace that was sort of astonishing. Sprawled on his back, he folded his arms behind his head. Nice biceps–that position really showed them off.

"What are you doing?"

He wiggled his hips. "What does it look like?"

Whatever it was, it looked good.

Those lips formed another grin, and I prayed that he couldn't read minds. I might need to ask about that later. "Unlike someone, no names mentioned." He looked pointedly at me. "I didn't just take a four-hour nap. So I'm going to use these next couple of hours to sleep."

My mouth opened, but I clamped it shut. I couldn't complain about him wanting to sleep. That was just rude. But what the heck was I supposed to do while he was getting some shuteye? Holding onto the robe for dear life, I shuffled my weight from one foot to the next as I looked around the spacious hotel room.

"Josie."

I turned to him, my breath catching. How in the world did anyone look that...that good simply lying in bed? "What?"

His eyes were at half-mast, drawing attention to the thick, spiky lashes. "Come here."

Another shiver slipped over my skin. "Are you trying that mind-control thing again? Because it's not working."

He chuckled. "No, I'm not. Just come here."

My heart tripped up in my chest. "I don't think that's a good idea."

"Really?" he murmured, grinning lazily. "Why?"

I didn't have a good answer, because what I was thinking was really presumptuous of me. When I didn't answer, he rolled onto his side and extended his arm over the empty space between us.

"Come here," he said again.

Digging in, I shook my head. "Why?"

"Because it'll make me feel better."

"That's definitely not a good enough reason."

He chuckled again. "That wasn't very nice, Joe."

"I don't like you," I whispered.

His grin spread until it transformed his face, taking some of the raw edge off his beauty. "Look. I'm not going to molest you or anything." He wiggled his fingers while I dealt with a really weird and really disturbing sense of disappointment, which made me feel like I needed therapy. "I need to get some sleep, so I can be alert later on, but it's hard to do that when you look like you're seconds away from darting toward the door. All I want you to do is sit here. You can even watch TV. I'll sleep through it, but I need you here, beside me."

I need you.

I nibbled on my lower lip. Of course, he hadn't meant that he *needed* needed me, but there was still a dangerous coiling low in my belly. Mentally slapping myself, I needed to get control of my hormones. I didn't know this guy. I didn't even know *myself* anymore. Sex and all things naughty needed to be the furthest things from my mind.

The bed was huge. I could easily sit on one side while he slept on the other. His reasoning sounded logical, and I wasn't going to be stupid and make a run for it as long as he played nice. I knew I wouldn't be able to defend myself. I didn't have any cool powers like setting my hand on fire.

I *needed* him, and God, that sucked.

Gathering up my courage, I didn't take his hand as I put one knee on the bed while still holding the edges of my robe. I teetered there for a moment.

Seth was on me before I even realized he'd moved. One second he was lying there, all lazy-like, and the next I was flat on my back, my eyes wide, and his leg thrown over mine, all but trapping me in place.

With shallow, uneven breaths, I turned my head toward him. Those eyes were half-open, the grin full of mischief. He moved his hand, wiggling something black and slender in my face. The remote! How in the world did he get the remote between lying there and doing nothing and practically tackling me?

The fucker *was* a ninja!

"Want to watch TV?" he asked.

I started to count to ten. I made it to three. "That was completely unnecessary."

"I don't think so."

My indignation rose swiftly. "I'm not going anywhere."

"I know you're not." He winked and then placed the remote below my white-knuckled hands, right on top of my breasts.

87

I gaped at him. "You arrogant, annoying son—"

"Naptime," he interrupted. "Watch TV. Or not. Stare at me or not, but I'm going to take a nap."

So much aggravation built up inside me I thought my head would spin off my shoulders. I tried to wiggle his leg off, but the jerk weighed a ton. "Move," I ordered with as much as dignity I could muster. "Move your fu—"

"I can't nap when you're talking. And I need my naptime. If not, I'll end up driving off the road on the way to the airport tomorrow."

Every muscle in my body tensed up. I forgot about the fact that his leg was on mine. "Airport?"

"Mmm-hmm." Both eyes were closed. "How else do you expect us to get from here to Misery?"

"Missouri," I corrected.

"Same difference."

I ignored that. "It's a town called Osborn. Well, it's more like a village, but we can drive. I have a car."

He sighed. "I have a car, too."

"Good," I rushed on quickly, knowing my poor car needed a lot of work before I made that hike again. "It's only a thirteen-hour drive from here and—"

"Thirteen-hour drive? Are you high?" One amber eye opened. "I'm not driving thirteen hours."

Panic curled around me. "Then I'll drive! I can drive. I've done it a billion times."

"Really," he said blandly. "It would be like an hour or two flight. We're flying."

"No. No way. I'm not flying. I'm not getting in a tin can that could fall out of the sky at any moment. Screw that. Have you ever thought about how they get planes in the sky and how they stay in the sky? No? I have. It's a lot of science I don't understand."

Both eyes were open now. "You're afraid of flying."

I briefly considered lying, but that would've been stupid. "Yeah, it's never interested me."

Seth stared at me for a moment, and then he muttered something under his breath that sounded like a different language. "Fine. We'll drive."

The next breath I took relaxed my muscles as my gaze flickered over his face. "Thank you."

That appeared to be the wrong thing to say, because the earlier teasing tilt of his lips was completely gone, as was the glimmer of annoyance in his eyes. His face was absolutely stoic, showing nothing as he stared at me.

"What...what did I say?" I asked.

His eyes held mine for a moment, and then they drifted shut. "Nothing," he murmured.

And he didn't say anything after that. Neither did I. Remaining quiet, I kept still as I watched him until I knew he was asleep, because his face relaxed and his lips parted. And I kept watching him. In his sleep, he looked...he looked *young*. Vulnerable. Not normal, because even at rest, there was an unreal quality in the angles and planes of his face, but... I didn't know. He looked different. Still insanely good-looking, but there was a quality of humanity there, and that was a relief to see, especially because I knew my life was literally in his hands.

MIRACULOUSLY, I actually dozed off during what was probably the epitome of creepy behavior—a.k.a. staring at Seth while he slept. If being a creeper was an Olympic sport, watching someone while they slept was gold-medal worthy.

I only realized I'd fallen asleep when I blinked—or at least that was how it felt—and the soft glow of morning was filtering in through the partially opened curtains.

Huh. Hadn't they been closed when I was all but catapulted into the bed? And my pillow really sucked. It was as hard as a bag of rocks, but incredibly smooth. The pillow had a weird beat, too.

Pillows didn't beat.

My pulse accelerated as I really became aware of my surroundings and who, and not what, I was lying on. Seth. And I wasn't really lying on him. I was completely tangled up in him. My head was on his chest and my right arm was curled against his trim side, and my other hand was resting on the hard slab of his lower stomach. One of my legs was under his, the other curled around the top and somehow shoved between his. My thigh was really close to a part of him that it had no business being that close to.

Oh wow.

One of his hands was tangled in my hair, that must've come undone at some point, and somehow I'd ended up under the covers, which was not how I'd fallen asleep. So at some point, he'd tugged the covers up. How embarrassing. Because it was so obvious I'd rolled onto him and turned into a clinging parasite during my sleep.

Crap.

His chest rose and fell under my cheek in deep, steady waves. He was still asleep, so I needed to somehow disentangle myself before he woke up and discovered that I was using him as my personal Pillow Pet.

Man, I missed the Pillow Pet I'd had growing up. I'd had a ladybug that I'd taken everywhere with me, even to the lake. I'd had it with me once when Bob had showed up, and he'd stared at that thing like it was some sort of mystical creature. I wondered if my grandparents still had it stowed away—okay, who cared about the stupid Pillow Pet? Rolling my eyes, I told myself to focus. But how in the world was I going to move his hand? Or get my leg out from under his? Or not accidentally knee him in the—

A throat cleared softly.

My heart skipped a beat as my gaze darted around the room, landing on the tall, dark-skinned girl sitting in the chair in front of the desk.

Oh gosh.

Erin sat there, arms folded over her chest. She looked normal, like the girl I'd met two years ago when I shuffled into my dorm for the first time, wishing I'd had my Pillow Pet with me. There were no leathery wings or all-white eyeballs. Her skin was smooth and flawless, not charcoal gray, and her fingers weren't sharpened into deadly claws. She looked human. Our eyes met, and my stomach hollowed as I stared at her. Everything she had told me was a lie.

"Weeell," Erin drew the word out as she hooked one slender leg over the other. "I'd heard about his reputation, but I have to admit, I didn't think he was *this* good."

For a moment, I didn't get what she was suggesting, then I remembered where I was and who I was lying on. Ah, awkward.

"This isn't what it looks like." I started to sit up, but the hand that had been in my hair slipped down the curve of my back in a slow slide that caused my breath to hitch and my toes to curl.

"It's totally what it looks like," came the deep voice.

Erin arched a brow.

My head whipped around. Seth gave me a lazy grin from where his head was propped up on the pillows. "You're awake!"

"I have been."

"For a while," Erin added, and I twisted back to her. "We were debating on waking you up or not. Especially when you were making those noises."

"Noises?"

Seth's hand was a heavy weight on the side of my stomach. "Yeah, it was kind of like little whimpers."

Heat blasted my cheeks. "I d-don't make noises when I sleep."

"Yes, you do." Erin tapped her fingers on the arm of the chair. "Kind of like what a baby kitten sounds like."

My mouth dropped open.

She shrugged. "It's cute."

It was *mortifying*.

Planting my hand on Seth's stomach, I pushed up. His stomach didn't give an inch. It was like pushing on a wall. Gathering up the edges of the robe, I scooted to the far side of the bed.

Seth sat up, stretching his arms above his head. Joints cracked as he twisted at the waist. As he lowered his arms, his lazy gaze swept over me, lingering where my hands clutched the robe, and then moved to where Erin sat. Then he said, "I'm hungry." He looked at me, sleep clinging to the relaxed line of his jaw. "You hungry?"

I was always hungry, so I nodded.

"Perfect." He swung his legs off the bed and stretched again. This time, when he raised his arms, his shirt rode up. Not that I hadn't seen it all when he'd paraded around shirtless before, but the glimpse of hard abs still caught my attention.

And Erin's.

He sauntered past her on his way to the bathroom. "I would ask if you were hungry," he said to her. "But I assume you ate your fill of babies last night."

My eyes widened. "You...eat babies?"

Her eyes rolled. "No, I don't." She shot him a nasty look as he chuckled. "Asshole."

Seth disappeared into the bathroom. I didn't know what to say to Erin in the silence that followed, and he returned in a few seconds, the hair around his face damp. He tugged the ends back, securing them at the nape of his neck as he toed on a pair of sneakers I hadn't noticed before. "I'll be back," he said as he walked to the door. "With bacon. Pancakes. Eggs. Sausage. Maybe some fruit," he continued, opening the door. "And waffles. Oh. Omelets sound good, too. With lots of cheese and peppers..." The door shut behind him as I wondered how he'd get all that food back here.

Silence.

Smoothing a hand over my hair, I looked over at Erin. She was staring at the closed door. "I've heard a lot of stuff about him," she said, her voice soft. "Rumors. Some of it probably true. Some of it not. He *did* kill one of my sisters." She turned to me. "Granted, they were trying to kill him."

I wasn't sure if that made it any better.

Uncrossing her legs, she dropped both feet to the floor and leaned forward. "He's just not... He's not what I thought."

"What do you mean?"

Erin shrugged. "It doesn't matter. I brought you all the clothes I could grab, and some of your other stuff, too."

On the floor under the desk were several gym bags and backpacks that looked full to bursting. My tongue felt woolly as I spoke. "Thank you."

Her features pinched. "We need to talk before he gets back and pisses me off. I know you're probably confused."

"Confused?" My laugh was as dry as dust. "Twenty-four hours ago, I thought Greek gods were nothing but myths, and now..."

"And now you know you're *one* of the myths," she finished. "A demigod—a very important one. Besides the fact that there hasn't been a demigod since, well, a very long time, you're *Apollo's* daughter. The freaking sun god is your father."

My father. I still couldn't wrap my head around that, but I did know I wasn't comfortable with the way it sounded. "Please stop saying he's my father. He might've donated some sperm, but that's all he did. He's not my dad. My grandpa is the closest to a dad I have, because he raised me. He loves me."

She cocked her head to the side as her brows knit together. "Apollo loves you, too. I know that may be hard to believe, but he does. He made sure you were always safe. Protected."

The thing was, I hadn't needed that when I was growing up. Or if I had, I'd been completely oblivious. What I had needed was a dad. Grandpa was great and did everything he could, but it wasn't the same.

I swept those thoughts aside. "He sent you to watch over me."

She opened her mouth and then closed it. As she nodded, a twisty motion enveloped my stomach. "He did."

"So you're not really from DC, are you? And you didn't run track in high school." When she shook her head, my chest squeezed like it had been dropped in a juice grinder.

"I grew up on Olympus, but I've visited DC many times. I like the museums," she said sheepishly. "I know that's not what I told you."

Did they even have high schools in Olympus? "You're right. Everything about you—about *us*—has been a lie."

She stood, flipping her curly ponytail over her shoulder. "I couldn't tell you the truth. You wouldn't have believed me."

She was also right about that, but she didn't get it. "You know that I didn't have friends growing up, right?"

Casting her gaze to the window, she nodded. "I know."

"Other kids weren't nice to me, because their parents weren't nice to my family," I said, swallowing against the sudden tightening in my throat. "When I came here, I was expecting the same. I didn't really know any better, but I met you and you were so nice and so open, and..." Pressing my lips together, I shook my head. "You *had* to be friends with me."

Her eyes widened as her head snapped back to me. "I had to be close to you, yes, but that doesn't change that I sincerely like you." She took a step toward me. "I wasn't faking that."

Part of me got that, but I couldn't help wonder how our relationship would've been if she was...normal.

"I'm sorry," she said quietly, and my gaze drifted to her. Sincerity was etched into her beautiful face and soulful eyes. Seeing her like this made it hard to believe that she could turn into a giant bat-like creature with snakes for hair. "I know *you*, so I know this has hurt you. And I wish I could've sat you down and talked to you about what I am and why I was here, but we were ordered to keep the truth hidden. And for your sake, I'd hoped you would never find out. No. Don't take that the wrong way," she said when I opened my mouth. "Not because I wanted to continue to lie to you, but if you lived the rest of your life not knowing about any of this, that meant you were safe. None of us knew this would happen with the Titans. We were preparing for..."

"What?" I asked when she didn't finish.

Erin glanced at the closed door. "We were preparing to fight the God Killer. He told you about what he could've turned into, right?"

I nodded. "He mentioned something about that."

Tension crept in her movements as she folded her arms across her chest. "We prepared for a different kind of battle. None of us planned for the Titans or for..." Her forehead wrinkled as her shoulders hunched. "Apollo trusts the Apollyon—Seth. He trusts him with you."

Tiny hairs all over my body rose. That didn't sound good. "Should I be worried about more than just the Titans?"

She was still for a moment and then shook her head. "There are things about us, about our world, that you don't understand and will hold to mortal social norms and judge by mortal standards. And anyway, you're leaving in a few hours, right? Where are you going? I'm leaving, too. I've been called back, now that Seth is here."

"Called back? What about school?" I asked stupidly.

She picked up one of my bags and placed it on the foot of the bed. "I don't need to be here any longer."

"But how can you just disappear?"

Another bag joined the one on the bed. "The same as you have. People will think you went home. Family emergency. And well, people leave college all the time." She shrugged as if it was no big deal. "So where are you going?"

"We're going to see my mom first," I answered, distracted by how she was organizing my bags and what she had said. "Then I guess we're going to someplace in South Dakota."

"Ah, the University. It's kind of like Radford, but cooler. Full of pures and halfs and maybe a god or two." Opening one bag, she grabbed a pair of jeans and tossed them on the bed. She laughed, the sound like wind chimes. "Sorry. I'm trying to picture Seth in Osborn, Missouri. I do think it's cool you're going to see your mom. Maybe knowing what you know now will help you understand her better. And also will stop you from worrying that you'll have some kind of illness later. You won't."

"Yeah, I guess that clears up that worry." I caught the bra and undies she threw at me. "So you're not going with us?"

She shook her head. "If I did, I'd probably end up maiming Seth at some point, and that kind of defeats the purpose of him watching over you. But it's not like you're never going to see me again. You will. But I need to help locate the other demigods. They also need protection."

I'd forgotten about the others already. Standing up and holding my undergarments close to my chest, I watched Erin pull out a lightweight pink sweater, and it hit me again that, at some point, I was going to be required to fight the Titans, to help entomb them in Tartar Sauce Land.

"Holy shit," I whispered.

Erin looked at me sharply. "What?"

"I can't even walk a straight line sober, but I'm basically a weapon, aren't I? So are the other demigods. I'm going to have to fight a Titan."

Her eyes met mine before flickering away. "You'll be okay, Josie."

I'll be okay? That's like telling someone who was about to jump into shark-infested waters they'll be okay.

She came around the bed and shoved the jeans and sweater into my arms. "You should shower and get ready before Seth comes back. Unless you want him to see you in that robe again, which by the way, does nothing to hide your goods."

Oh Jesus.

I let her push me toward the bathroom, but I stopped just inside and faced her. Our eyes met, and somehow I knew—I just knew—that after I closed this door, she was going to be gone, and I wasn't sure, no matter what she said, if I would see her again.

Our friendship had been built on lies. There was no ignoring that, but the last two years... She had been there for me when I was the scared and naïve freshman, away from home for the first time. She was there the first time I drank tequila, and she held my hair while I vomited it all back up later that night. She'd been there when I went out on my first date with the boy from my Soc 101 class, and then rescued me when he started talking about inviting me to meet his mom five minutes into our awkward dinner. She'd also been there when my mom had a terrible relapse and had gone missing for days, ending up in Tennessee. She had become my best friend, and that wasn't something I could forget. No matter how much it sucked and hurt to know that the foundation of our friendship had been precariously built on a house of lies, it didn't change everything she had done for me.

I couldn't hold a grudge.

Dropping my clothes on the floor, I sprang forward. Her eyes widened as my arms circled her shoulders. I pulled her in for a tight, fierce hug. And I didn't say anything. Neither of us did as she hugged me back. We stood there for a few minutes, and when we pulled apart, her deep eyes glimmered with tears.

"You better get ready," she said, her voice thick as she smiled faintly.

The lump in my throat was hard to talk around, so I nodded as I drew back. I needed a deep breath before I spoke. "You're my best friend, no matter what."

Her eyes squeezed shut briefly as she whispered, "You're my best friend, too. No matter what." Then she stepped back, her smile spreading as she flashed me the peace sign.

For some reason, knowing what she was, that made me laugh as I gripped the door. But it wasn't until the bathroom door was closed that it really set in she was leaving and I...I wanted another hug.

Throwing the door open, my shoulders slumped. Like I'd suspected moments earlier, the hotel room was empty. Erin was gone.

JENNIFER L. ARMENTROUT

CHAPTER

11

TIME WAS ticking and we had a thirteen-hour-and-then-some drive ahead of us, and here I was, standing at the back of the silver Porsche Cayenne that I had *borrowed*, staring at Josie's ass.

In my defense, I was a guy, so when I had the choice between staring at a bunch of trees or a female's ass, it was probably going to be the ass. And it was also a nice ass, too. Plump. Not too hard to imagine peeling down those jeans that hugged her ass and shapely thighs. The pink sweater she was wearing rode up, exposing a ribbon of skin along her lower back. Huh, it was a very tempting area of the body I'd never paid attention to.

I reached out before I knew what I was doing. My fingers hovered just above the hem of her sweater, preparing to tug it down, when I jerked my hand back. A series of tingles rippled across my fingers, almost as if my skin was protesting not touching her.

What the fuck?

Searching for a distraction, I scanned the parking lot of the hotel again. No vengeful shades lurking around—unfortunately. My gaze moved back to Josie, and to her ass as she wiggled it, stretching even further.

I sighed. Maybe groaned a little, because her ass stopped wiggling, and I wasn't sure if I should be relieved or disappointed by that.

"Why don't you go ahead and climb in the back?" I suggested.

Her body stilled. "I'll just be another second."

"What are you looking for in there? The answers to life?"

"Ha. Ha," she responded, her voice muffled. "Erin packed everything, so I don't know where anything is at. A-ha!" Triumph rang out in her voice. "Found it."

"What? Did she accidentally store some cow hearts in there?"

Josie flew out from the back of the Porsche, clasping a slender black rectangle electronic thing in her hand. She took a step toward me, and that black thing smacked into my arm.

"Hey!" I stepped back, folding my hand over my stinging upper arm. She'd actually hit me. She'd seriously *swatted* me with something. I was freaking stunned. "What the hell was that for?"

"She does not eat babies or cow hearts!"

"How do you know?" I challenged, damn well knowing furies tended to not eat babies or hearts, but whatever. Her sweater was a V-neck. Of course. The swells of her breasts all but defied the limitations of her sweater. I shifted, spreading my legs. This was just ridiculous. "Did you Google a furie's diet while you were hanging out in the back of this car? Was that what you were doing this whole time?"

"Erin's a vegan, smartass." Her lips pursed and her nose scrunched in that cute way again. *Cute?* Dammit. "Or at least veggies and crap is all I've ever seen her eat. And I wasn't Googling crap. I was looking for my Nook, which I've now found. It's a requirement for any road trip."

"Nerd."

Her arm flew back as she prepared to swat me upside what appeared to be my head this time. I caught her arm before she delivered the blow. "Do not hit me with that again."

Deep blue eyes flashed. "I'll hit you with it again if I want to."

"If you hit me with that again, I'm going to bend you over the back of this car, right in front of everyone and all the gods, and smack your ass like your momma should've done."

Her mouth dropped open. "You wouldn't dare."

Not even using any amount of strength, I tugged her forward, and before she could pull away, I circled my other arm around her waist, keeping her in place. My body immediately warmed in every place we were connected. She was a good head shorter than I was, but we lined up well enough in all the important areas. As focused as I was on all of her softness pressing against me, I forgot what the hell I was doing. Something about spanking her ass?

That was a damn good plan.

"I would *so* dare," I told her, my voice dropping low. "And I would also really, thoroughly enjoy it."

She tipped her head back, lips parting as our gazes locked. "I would so *not* enjoy that."

I dipped my head, coming so close to kissing her that my groin tightened with need. The sudden rush was all-encompassing. "I think the blush traveling across your cheeks tells me you'd enjoy it just as much as I would. Maybe more."

Her soft exhale sent another jolt through me as her breath danced over my lips. "I'm not blushing," she said. "The breeze is chilly. And I have sensitive skin. I burn really easily, which is funny considering I have some sun-god blood in me. Go figure—"

I placed the tips of my fingers on her cheek, stopping her chatter. Her eyes widened then, the blue going so deep if I wasn't careful I could tumble right into them and do something really idiotic.

And there were a lot of idiotic ideas that were coming to mind right now.

I trailed my fingers to her mouth, my touch feather-light. When I reached her parted lips, the softness of them against the tips of my fingers spiked the need into something damn near primal. The feeling was raw, and as I pressed her lips together,

101

the whole fucking thing backfired on me, because parts of me were aching now.

"Liar," I said to her.

Josie jerked back, but her chest rose and fell quickly. "I don't like you."

I bit down on my lower lip, but it didn't stop my grin. "I don't like you, either."

She shot me a dirty look over her shoulder as she rounded the side of the SUV, heading toward the passenger side.

This was going to be one long-ass trip.

❦

Three hours in and it was already feeling like a long-ass trip. We'd spent too much time this morning dicking around and now there was no way we'd reach Osborn by nightfall. We'd have to stop somewhere along Interstate 64 for the night, because driving straight through was stupid when the potential for facing anything was high.

Josie had been playing the quiet game, glued to her Nook from the moment I'd climbed behind the wheel and started the SUV, which had been fine with me, but I did wonder what she was reading. Probably romance. Or Harry Potter. She seemed like the kind of chick that would dig boy wizards. But it was around the time we crossed out of West Virginia and hit Kentucky that she powered the thing off and started staring out the window.

My fingers tapped on the steering wheel. A lot of stuff had been dumped on her in such a short period of time, but she was holding it together like a champ, like...

Like Alex.

Fuck.

If I could carve out all those memories and every shitty thing I'd caused and everything attached to Alex, I could look at this objectively. I could see that Josie had some of Alex's strength. Obviously not the physical kind, but strength... It went beyond muscles and the ability to fight. Josie had the important kind—mental strength. The girl had...*grit*. Most mortals, after finding out they weren't exactly mortal, that spirits and Titans were after them, and that their father was a legendary god of dickdom, would've flipped their shit by this point.

But she was just staring out the window, her profile thoughtful, a little distant. Maybe I should have said something, like point out how well she was doing—positive reinforcement and all that good stuff. But the words weren't there, and every time I glanced over at her, her expression hadn't changed.

As the tires smoothly ate away the miles, my mind wandered to those moments outside of the SUV, to how her body had felt pressed against mine. There was no denying that I was physically attracted to her, and while she was a different type of girl than I normally went for, I wasn't surprised by wanting to get in her pants and between her legs.

It just wasn't something I *should* act on. But not acting on it wasn't looking too good. It had only been a handful of days since I'd first seen her and not nearly as many hours that we'd been together, and I was already feeling my tenuous grip on restraint slip. I wasn't known for my self-control, especially when it came to something I wanted.

And yeah, I wanted her. Wanted her in a way that was purely physical and inherent to who I was. And it was official. Apollo was a bigger idiot than I realized for putting *his daughter* under my guardianship, knowing everything he knew about me.

I laughed out loud at that.

"What?" Josie asked, looking at me.

Grinning, I shook my head. "Nothing."

She was quiet for a moment, then she blurted out. "I forgave Erin."

The statement caught me off-guard and I glanced at her again. She was staring at me, the hollows of her cheeks pink. "Okay."

"Do you think that makes me, like, too forgiving?"

As I coasted around a slow-moving van in the passing lane, I smirked. "I'm probably not the best person to ask, Joe."

"Why, *Sethie*?"

My smirked turn into a grin. "I hold onto grudges. I feed and water them, growing them into happy little pools of bitterness."

"Well, that sounds fun and lovely." She shifted in the seat, stretching out her legs. "I don't see the point in holding onto grudges, because that happy pool of bitterness will turn on you and start eating away at you."

Already was.

"It sucked that she lied to me, but she's still my friend. She was still there for me," she said. "And that's what matters. Anyway, I guess some of this is kind of cool," she went on, "I mean, there's this whole world existing right alongside ours, interacting with ours, and we've had no idea. It's like something in a movie or a book. Like Hogwarts coming alive."

Yep. I called it. Totally into boy wizards.

"You've read Harry Potter, right?"

I snorted. "No."

"Seen the movies?"

"Nope."

"Been to the Wizarding World of Harry Potter?"

I laughed. "That would also be a no."

"I've never been there either, but still." She twisted toward me so fast, it was a surprise she didn't choke herself on the seatbelt. "Have you been living in a cave?"

"I've been busy," I replied as I checked the rearview mirror. "You know, fighting automatons and saving the world."

"What's an automaton?"

"Something you do not want to see," I said, and when she huffed, I sighed. "They are one of Hephaestus's creations. He's like the ultimate blacksmith. He can create just about anything. Automatons were basically half-robot and half-bull. They breathed fireballs."

She turned back to the windshield. "That doesn't sound like any fun. How do you even pronounce his name? Can I just call him Hippo?"

I laughed under my breath. "We call him Hep. He hates it, as much as he hated Ares for sleeping with Aphrodite while they were married. Ever hear of unbreakable chain and net? It's real. He used it to catch the two of them getting it on."

"Oh. I...I thought Aphrodite was with Adonis or something?"

"Aphrodite has pretty much been with everyone. She even hooked up with one of the Sentinels I know, and he ended up with a nice scar as a reminder of the no-touchie-touch policy."

"The Sentinels... You've mentioned them before." She tapped the Nook on her knee. "You said they were mostly the halfs, right?"

"Yeah. Now the Sentinels are more of a mix of pures and halfs."

The Nook continued to bounce. "And the Sentinels are like the godly version of the army?"

"Something like that. All halfs go before the Council—well, used to. A lot of this has been abolished for about a year, but back in the day, at the age of eight, we went before the Council—twelve pures who oversaw each of the Covenants, which are schools near the largest communities, and it was determined if we were to train to become Sentinels or to go into servitude. I obviously went into training. We got basic education, but it was more focused on different styles of fighting and defense, ranging from hand-to-hand combat like grappling and krav maga, to basic martial arts, to gun and dagger play. There's thousands of Sentinels. Used to be more..." *Before I helped kill a whole truckload of them.*

"So you're a Sentinel, too?"

"Yes. And no. First and foremost, I'm the Apollyon, but I was trained just like any other Sentinel. Probably pushed harder, and I was never really *with* them. Even when I was in classes with the others, I was always separate somehow."

"Why?" she asked. Obviously the quiet game was officially over.

A huge part of me had no idea why I was telling her so much. "The halfs and pures knew what I was. They knew I was different, and since I could easily knock one of them into next year, it didn't make them real comfortable around me. Neither were a lot of pures. Everyone liked to stare when I was around, but people didn't get too close." Unless the pures and halfs were female, most steered clear of me. All except the few connections I'd made with those who'd been at the Deity Island Covenant, and I hadn't seen any of them for over a year.

The Nook stopped moving. "You really didn't have friends growing up?"

"I had no one," I admitted, surprising myself.

"No one?" she whispered.

I glanced at her, and she was staring at me, not with curiosity but with a visible need to understand, to relate. It was written all over her face. Maybe that's why I kept talking, telling her things only one other person knew. Maybe it was because I thought, out of everyone I'd ever known, this girl...she'd understand. "The very second I opened my mouth and took my first breath, my pure-blooded mother—and using the term 'mother' is a fucking joke—handed me over to a caregiver who was as warm and fuzzy as Medusa. She hadn't wanted me. You see, relationships between halfs and pures were forbidden. We knew it was because of the potential for an Apollyon, but it's also because halfs have always been looked down on, but my mother... There was no great love affair between her and whoever my father was. She liked getting it on with the help, until she got pregnant by one of them. Then not so much. She probably would've drowned me in the Mediterranean Sea."

She gasped. "No, she wouldn't have done that."

"Pures did that all the time, Josie, and that would've been my fate if it hadn't been for the god who came to her before I was born and told her what I was."

"God, that's just terrible."

My hand tightened on the steering wheel. "Then I became her party favor. For years, I only saw her when she wanted to see me—twice a week for dinner and whenever she wanted to tote me around society parties as her *special* son, the Apollyon. No one called me that then, but everyone who saw me knew what I was. It was my eyes—the color gave me away. I'd been a prop then, the equivalent of a fucking expensive and rare handbag. Stared at. Whispered about. Touched. Stroked. Then stored away until she wanted to impress more of her pure friends, who had lost respect for her the moment she'd gotten pregnant by a half-blood, but probably wanted to gawk at my ass. Needless to say, I grew to hate pures." I cut myself off, dragging in a deep breath. "Anyway, I wasn't allowed to address her as 'mom,' but by her given name, 'Callista.' Mommy Dearest would shit a brick if she knew the truth—that I wasn't supposed to be the Apollyon. Maybe she *had* known. Either way, there'd been no friends. The only toys I'd found were ancient things that no kid wanted to play with, and then I went before the Covenant. They'd taken one look at me, knew what I was, and I was taken away from the Cyclades Islands and sent to the Covenant in England where I began my education. From there, I was shipped to the Covenant in Nashville."

I paused, caught up in memories. That had never been a good place for me. "I haven't been back to the Islands since that day, and I was eighteen when a Minister at the Covenant in Nashville informed me that my mother had been found dead."

That had sucked.

Even though she hadn't been much of a mom, she had been my flesh and blood. She mattered, even if I hadn't mattered to her.

In the silence, I could feel Josie watching me, and I couldn't look at her, because I knew there'd be pity in her gaze. I probably should've kept my damn mouth shut.

"So...so that's why you have a little bit of an accent?" she asked.

Relief eased the tension in my shoulders. That...that was cool of her. "Yeah, that's why."

She shifted in the seat again. "So there are that many Sentinels? Is it really that dangerous?"

"Yeah, Josie, it's really that dangerous." I sighed as the Porsche picked up speed. "There are daimons—pures and halfs that had become addicted to the *aether* that's in our veins. *Aether* is what fuels our abilities—gods have the most, second would be demigods and Apollyons, the gods' various little creature-features and lesser deities, then the pures and finally the halfs. The pures who get addicted to it, it changes their entire chemistry—the way they appear and everything. To mortals, they look normal, but halfs have this weird ability for seeing them for how they really look. Pures don't. I'm not sure about you, with your abilities being bound."

"What do they really look like?"

"Pale faces with no eyes and a mouth that would make Jaws envious."

"Ugh." She drew back, visibly shuddering. "So, let me guess, they use their teeth to feed?"

"Yep. It's not the only way one can drain the *aether* from someone, but the *daimons* like to bite because they also like to cause pain." I frowned as I squinted into the already fading sunlight. Kentucky was a boring-ass state to drive through. "They'll also go after mortals for the fun of it. Probably where the whole legend of vampires came from. But then there're also pures who get power hungry without the *aether*. People break laws in our society, just like they do in the mortal world."

She fiddled with the Nook, turning it over and over in her hands for a few moments. "I'm sorry, Seth."

My gaze swung to her. "You're sorry for what?"

"All of that sounds lonely and just... It sucks, growing up that way. I didn't have friends, but I had a childhood, you know? I got to be a kid." Her wide gaze moved to the road, which reminded me that I was driving. "My mom...she told me once when I was little that there had to be a reason why her life ended when mine began."

Jesus.

"But she still loved me," she added quietly, and when I glanced at her again, she was staring straight ahead, the Nook pressed to her chest. "I know she did. That didn't make things...easy all the time, but I can say that about her and it doesn't sound like you can say that about your mom. So, I'm sorry."

A weird constriction seized my chest, peeling the scabs off old wounds I'd either forgotten about or had managed to ignore all of these years. Yeah, my childhood sucked ass, but I didn't deserve sympathy. Not after all the terrible shit I'd done.

WE DIDN'T talk after I told Seth I was sorry for what he'd experienced as a child, or in a way, what he hadn't experienced. I had difficulty with my mom, but I still had my grandparents, and it sounded like Seth had no one. A huge chunk of me felt bad for Seth. I knew what it felt like to *know* you weren't wanted—the sting and burn that existed inside of you every day knowing you were just an accident. You came into this world with your parent wishing they could undo the act that brought you there. That kind of knowledge festered, and it rotten and ruined parts of me even though I knew my mom, underneath it all, loved me.

The sky outside the Porsche faded from dusk to night. We hadn't spoken more than a few words to each other when we finally stopped for food. The burger didn't settle well and another hour went by before he spoke again.

It was close to nine when his deep, slightly accented voice rolled through the dark interior. "I think we should stop for the evening. Get some rest and hit the road early so we reach your house by the afternoon."

My stomach tumbled as I sat up straighter. "I think we can keep going. I still have a key to the house. We can let ourselves in, and we have an extra bedroom you can sleep in. I mean, we're not too far from St. Louis, and it's just another four hours or so from there."

"I've been driving for about nine hours. I'm done."

"I can drive."

He snorted. "Not going to happen."

My eyes narrowed. "Why not? You think I can't drive? I can so drive. I could drive in NASCAR if I wanted to."

His lips twitched as he shook his head. "It's not that. I'm tired. I need to be alert, and that isn't going to come from sleeping in the passenger seat while you're playing NASCAR with a Porsche." He slid me a long look, and in the dim light, his features were shadowed. "Are you nervous about staying another night with me, Josie?"

Whoa. He didn't just hit that nail right on the head. He slammed that nail through the wood.

His gaze flickered back to the road as he eased the Porsche into the right lane. "Because tonight isn't going to be the only night. You're stuck with me, babe, at least until I get you to South Dakota."

My mouth opened and then I snapped it shut. Irritation prickled across my scalp like a hundred fire ants had just done a dance through my hair. "I really do not like you."

He chuckled darkly. "You don't need to like me."

I rolled my eyes.

"I saw that."

"Oh, there is no way you saw that!" I smacked my hands on my legs. "Unless you have, like, cat eyes or something."

"I see better in the dark than a mortal does," he replied. He was grinning that smart-aleck grin when I sent a death glare in his direction. "I think this is a good enough place."

Folding my arms as he took the exit, I sat back and resisted the urge to throw a major hissy fit that would make a two-year-old proud. He picked the first lodging we came across.

"This isn't even a hotel," I pointed out as he turned into the gravel parking lot. "It's a motel, as in the doors are on the outside. The kind of doors that serial killers kick in while you're sleeping."

"It'll work." He double-parked the SUV. "It's not a high traffic area. Looks like only two other people are here, and if a serial killer kicks in our door, it'll be the last door they'll be kicking in."

"It looks like the Bates Motel," I muttered.

Seth laughed.

I hated his laugh. Okay, I didn't *hate* his laugh. It was a nice, deep sound. He was already out of the Porsche by the time I unlocked my seatbelt. He tapped my window, a look of impatience settling into his features. I rolled my eyes again, and he responded by opening the door for me.

"Need help?" he offered. "I can pick you up, toss you over my shoulder, and carry you in." He leaned in, placing one hand on the seat beside my leg. A strand of his hair fell loose, curving toward the corner of his lips. "We could pretend we're newlyweds."

I gaped at him. "No way."

"Maybe they have a honeymoon suite. Oh, this sounds like a plan." He stepped back. "I hope they have a heart-shaped bed."

Sliding out of the seat, I *gently* slammed the door shut behind me and then shouldered past him. Did places really have heart-shaped beds? That was kind of gaudy.

He caught right up with me with his long-legged strides. "Stick close."

I didn't respond as he opened the door below the neon-pink OPEN sign. It was a small lobby, surprisingly clean and kind of cozy, full of country décor. Lots of baskets and red berries, green vines, and small, wooden ladders covered every square inch. The smell of vanilla and some kind of fruit was pleasant.

Seth strolled up to the desk and smacked his hand on the bell. A white door opened and an older lady bustled out, folding a magazine. She took one look at him and her mouth dropped open. He propped his hip against the counter, his lips forming into a slow grin that probably even had Granny fanning herself.

"I need a room for me and my girl," he said in that voice of his.

Turning away, I rolled my eyes yet again and started inspecting the nearest basket. There were little toiletries inside. Cute. I moved along the shelf, coming to a set of baskets that appeared empty.

"Well, Sugah, we do have quite a few rooms tonight, so you're in luck," the lady said, and then Seth spoke, his voice low.

My fingers slipped over something smooth. I picked it up, and my mouth dropped open.

The baskets were full of condoms.

Oh my God. What kind of motel had baskets full of condoms in their lobby, in cute little woven baskets? I stared at the wrapper marked extra-large, ribbed-for-her-pleasure. Where were we and what kind of people typically stayed here?

"Josie."

I turned to Seth. His gaze moved from me to my hand as his brows rose and his grin transformed into a heart-stopping smile that reached his eyes, lightening them and warming them up. Seth not smiling or smirking was beautiful, but him smiling? It was...wow. Breath-stealing.

And I was still holding the condoms.

Heat blasted my face.

"They're on the house, honey," the lady said behind the counter. "Take as many as you want." She winked. "I would if I was you."

Oh my God.

As if it was a tiny pit viper, I dropped the condom back in the basket, folded my arms, and refused to touch anything else in this place.

Seth turned back to the lady and he got a room key. Oddly, I didn't see him pull out any identification or money before he came to where I waited. "Did you get enough condoms, *honey*?"

"Shut up," I hissed, storming out the door he so gallantly opened for me. "Did you pay her?" I asked once we were both outside.

He laughed. "No. That's the cool thing about compulsions. Get a lot of free stuff. Like that sweet Porsche."

I tripped over my feet. "That's so...so wrong."

"You're just jealous you can't do it yet."

Okay. Maybe I was a little jealous. I followed him past several doors, and we ended up at the very last one that was next to a field and a thick grove of trees. I bet he'd made sure he'd gotten this room for some ninja reason. When the door opened, I was relieved to see this wasn't a honeymoon suite.

Carrying the same theme from the lobby, it was all kinds of country up in the room. Baskets. Wooden ladders covered in vine and berries. A pumpkin-spice scent greeted us.

There was one bed.

Not even a big one.

Or even a couch.

I whirled around. "There's only one bed."

"Yeah," he replied, turning to the door. "There was only one last night and we made it work. Well, you turned me into a full-length body pillow, but it worked."

Oh geez. I closed my eyes and took a deep breath before I reopened them. "This isn't acceptable. We need two beds."

"It'll be fine. Stay in here. I'm going to get our bags."

Then he was gone, and I stomped my foot. Once. And then twice, like a five-year-old, but I didn't care how stupid it was. I couldn't sleep in the same bed with him again, because apparently I was a cuddler, and I was so not going to do that a second time.

My gaze drifted over the cozy room. There was a narrow door to a bathroom that looked nothing like the one from Seth's hotel room. And there was another with a small window beside a dresser. I walked over to it, peeled back the burgundy curtain, and spied a small deck with privacy walls.

Hearing the front door open, I twisted back around. Seth came in, dropping his stuffed bag on the floor and the three bags Erin had packed for me on the bed. I waited for him to make some kind of snarky comment, but he didn't. All he did was turn to his bag and root around until he pulled out a pair of nylon pants. Then he disappeared into the bathroom.

I resisted the urge to bang my head against the wall and figured finding something to wear would be more productive. I opened the first bag and found a bunch of clothes. Then I moved onto the second bag that was packed full of tank tops, undies, and bras. The third bag was full of more clothes and some shoes, but nothing I could sleep in.

My heart turned over heavily. I went back to the first bag and double-checked it as my stomach started to sink.

"You're looking a little panicked."

I jumped at the sound of Seth's voice. He was standing behind me, and I hadn't even heard the door open or him come out of the bathroom. "God, how do you move so quietly?"

His lips tipped up at one corner as he tossed the clothes he'd been wearing onto the carpeted floor. "It's an acquired skill."

I wanted that acquired skill since I felt like I was trotting around like a three-legged mule. My gaze dipped below the neck. He was shirtless. Again. The nylon pants he wore seemed to be held to his narrow hips by some kind of act of God. I couldn't help but wonder if he was born with awesome genes, or if he had to work for his abs like the rest of mankind.

"I like your hair down," I blurted out, and then mentally smacked myself. I like your hair down? Who said that to a guy? But it was true. Not a lot of guys could pull off longer hair, but he did. It added a wildness to him.

Seth looked at me, head tilted to the side. He didn't say anything, but seriously, what did one say to that? Feeling like an idiot, I turned back to the bags. My search for nightclothes was hopeless.

"I'm going to kill Erin," I said.

He stepped closer, reaching out and running a finger over the strap of one bag. "I can get behind that, but I gotta ask why you want to kill her when you said you'd forgiven her."

My gaze tracked his hand. "She didn't pack anything for me to sleep in."

"You can sleep naked," he suggested. "I'm not going to complain. And I'll sleep naked if it makes you feel better."

Shoulders slumping, I sent him a dry look. "Thanks for being so accommodating and supportive."

He chuckled as he moved to his bag. Reaching down, he pulled out a shirt. "You can sleep in this." He tossed it to me, and I caught it before it smacked me in the face. "Or naked. Option's yours."

Holding up the shirt, I had to admit that it worked better than anything I had with me. I muttered a "thank you" as I dug around until I found the tiny make-up bag that had all the essential items in it. I headed into the bathroom, concentrating on getting ready for bed, tugging my hair up in a ponytail, washing my face, and brushing my teeth. I didn't let my mind wander to anything else.

When I left the bathroom, Seth had already moved the bags to the floor and one side of the somewhat narrow bed had the covers turned over. I hesitated at the foot of the bed, nibbling nervously on my lower lip.

Seth straightened, seeming to forget what he was doing as he stared. The shirt was super-long on me, ending a few inches above my knees, virtually shapeless, but his eyes suddenly glowed a tawny color, and I felt like the shirt was skintight.

"Thanks for, um, the shirt," I said again. My fingers twisted around the hem as I glanced around the room before settling back on him. He was still staring. "There should be stuff at my house I can get, so I won't need to keep borrowing your clothes."

His throat worked on a slow swallow, but he didn't say anything as he nodded curtly. He dropped the pillow and started to turn toward the bed but stopped, eyeing me again in that wholly intense way of his. "I don't really see females wearing my clothes often."

For some reason that made me happy, which was stupid, because I didn't care if an entire dorm floor wore his clothes. "Well, I don't usually, um, wear male clothing, so..."

His lips twitched. "That's good to know."

I shuffled my weight from one foot to the other as a series of shivers coursed over my skin.

And he kept his eyes on me. "I never got it before."

"Got what?"

A strange tension crept into his expression, sharpening his features. "Why it's such a turn-on to see a girl wearing your clothes."

My eyes widened until they felt like they were going to pop out of my head.

He dipped his chin and strands of his hair fell forward, brushing his jaw. "It's *really* a turn-on."

Warmth zipped through my veins in a heady rush. Unable to hold his gaze a moment longer, I looked away as I drew in a deep breath that didn't seem to do anything for my sudden shortness of breath. I thought about standing in front of him in the robe, when he'd dragged the edges together. Like I was compelled, my gaze moved right back to him.

Without any warning, he was right in front of me, so close that his bare feet brushed mine. I sucked in a breath that seriously didn't go anywhere as he placed the tips of his fingers against my throat, right on my wildly beating pulse. It was such a light touch, but I felt it in every part of my body.

"Does knowing that make you uncomfortable?" he asked, his voice soft and low.

Yes. No. "I don't know," I admitted.

His fingers moved down my neck, to where the collar hung loose. My heart kicked against my ribs as two of his fingers slipped under the collar, following the line of my collarbone to where it dipped at the base of my throat. I had no idea what he was doing or if I wanted him to stop touching me or to keep touching me. Common sense said I should want him to stop.

He tapped a finger there and then his hand moved up and to the side, curling around the base of my neck. His thumb was against my pulse, and it went crazy as he tilted my head back. He lowered his head until his mouth was above mine, so close I could taste his minty breath.

Time seemed to stop and then he tilted his head. "It makes me uncomfortable," he spoke just above a whisper, and as he did, his lips brushed the corner of mine, sending a riot of sensations through me. Panic. Confusion. Want. Desire. He shifted closer, his legs touching mine. When he spoke again, his lips were near my ear. "Only because I'm going against my nature right now."

I shuddered from the combination of our closeness, the feel of his soft hair on my cheek, and the way his thumb pressed against my pulse. An almost painful heaviness moved into my chest and then lower, much lower. My fingers trembled as the crazy notion of lifting my hands and placing them on his chest smacked into me.

"When I want something, I go for it," he continued in the same low, seductive voice. "I don't even think twice about it, but with you...I've got to think." His lips hit a surprisingly sensitive spot right under my ear. I jerked as a tiny, raspy sound crept out of my throat. "And that probably makes you very, very lucky."

Seth stepped back, his gaze lingering for a moment before he turned away and left me standing there, at a complete loss as to what had just happened and wanting, oddly, to not be so lucky.

I let go of the breath I didn't realize I was holding. My throat felt insanely tight and my heart was doing an unsteady little dance in my chest. Even though he wasn't near me now, there was still an edginess in the room that made the shirt I wore feel too heavy. I'd never had such a...visceral reaction to a guy before, especially one that I'd known for two days.

Two days, and I'd already slept in the same bed as him, would be doing so again, when I'd never shared a bed with a guy before.

Two days since my life had started to unravel upon meeting him in the stairwell, and only one day since I learned the truth about the world and myself, but the time felt longer than that. Maybe that was why everything was heightened. I'd been thrust into this, into Seth's world, spending hour after hour with him, and with all these crazy things happening, even my body was reacting differently.

But none of it mattered. Once we reached South Dakota, it sounded like he'd be gone, and only strangers would surround me. Even though we had just met, I really didn't consider Seth a stranger anymore. My knees were shaky.

Seth sat on the bed and he lifted his hand, scrubbing his hand through his hair as he looked over at me. "Would it make you feel more comfortable if I took one of those chairs for the night?"

Surprise flickered through me. I hadn't even thought he'd offer that, especially after last night, but the mere fact that he offered that drew some of the rigidity out of me. I softened a little bit more.

"No," I said, forcing my feet to move to the other side of the bed. "That's not necessary. You're a big boy and I'm a big girl."

He cocked an eyebrow, but remained silent as I climbed into bed, quickly shoving my bare legs under the comforter. As I settled onto my back, getting my legs pressed together and my hands fitted across my chest, he stood and made his way to the light switch. The moment the room plunged into darkness, I started retracting the "big girl" part immediately. When the bed dipped under Seth's weight, I might have stopped breathing a little. And when the mattress shifted again as he rolled onto his side, facing me, I might have had a minor heart attack.

"Josie?" His voice was soft in the darkness.

"Yeah?" I croaked.

There was a beat of silence. "If you want to use me as a body pillow again, I won't mind."

I opened my mouth and a startled laugh erupted out of me. Moderately embarrassed and partly amused, I turned my head

119

toward him. As my vision adapted to the darkness, I could make out the planes and angles of his face. "Thanks."

"Just thought I'd let you know. I actually like cuddling. And I like what typically comes before and after cuddling," he went on, and I couldn't fight the stupid grin tugging at my lips. "I bet there's condoms in those baskets on the dresser."

"Oh my God," I said, and another laugh escaped me as looked away, smacking my hands down on my face. "What kind of motel has condoms in baskets in the lobby?"

Seth chuckled as he reached out, tugging the closest hand away from my face. He didn't respond, but he also didn't let go of my hand. Both of our hands lay in the miniscule space between us, his fingers wrapped loosely around mine. I don't know why he did it or why his hand stayed like that, but when the quietness stretched and his breathing deepened, his fingers remained entwined with mine. The very last thought I remember before slipping away was there was no way I'd get any sleep that night.

I HAD used Seth as a giant body pillow. Again.

When I woke before dawn, I wasn't lying on my back any longer. Nope. At some point during the night, Seth had shifted and I had shifted *on top* of him. Our legs and arms were tangled together and my head was tucked into a surprisingly comfy spot in the crook of his arm.

And he had been awake when I woke up, because his hand... The hand that belonged to the arm that I'd been lying on had been on my shoulder, but it hadn't been still. His fingers had been moving, tracing odd symbols that went beyond circles and squares—symbols I didn't recognize. But I had no idea how long he'd been awake doing that, or why he hadn't shoved me off and gone about his business instead of lying there, somewhat peacefully waiting for me to wake up.

When I'd finally scrounged up the courage to pull myself off him, he hadn't said something snarky or annoying. All he'd done was look at me in a very quiet way, and then we got ready to hit the road again.

I got the shower first. Not wanting to suck up time blow drying my hair, I towel-dried it off the best I could, and then pulled it up in a loose knot. Seth said nothing as he disappeared into the bathroom.

I puttered around the room aimlessly. It was too quiet and I was restless, full of unspent energy. My gaze landed on the bathroom door when I heard the shower come on.

He was totally naked in there.

I rolled my eyes. Of course, he was naked and now...now I was picturing him naked, and that didn't seem right. I was attracted to him. Duh. That was also probably stupid, considering I barely knew him, he planned on leaving me, and for a buttload of other reasons.

In the short period of time I'd been around him, I'd seen so many different sides of him. It was like the Faces of Seth. He could go from sullen and serious, to teasing and downright annoying, to mischievous and playful, to seductive and dangerously deceptive in a matter of minutes. I'd never known anyone in my life like him, and I doubted many people, mortal or not-so-mortal, could claim to know how his head worked.

And I really wasn't in the frame of mind to start that monumental chore.

So many thoughts swirled and crashed together as I stood in the middle of the quiet room. Whatever calm and control I'd had since my life imploded was beginning to slip. It wasn't like I hadn't realized how much trouble I was in before. I just hadn't let it get to me.

Now it was getting to me.

It had started when it crossed my mind that I'd totally missed my psych exam, and the tight knot in my stomach fisted when it hit me again that missing the exam was the least of my problems. I wasn't going back to Radford. There would be no more exams in my future. There would be no more classes or internships.

Because I was a mythical creature.

I dropped my head into my hands and bit back the urge to scream at the top of my lungs, total crazy-chick style. My heart rate picked up, pounding in a way that made those knots in my stomach squeeze tighter and tighter. Nervous. I tried to take a breath, but it got stuck.

Remembering the tiny deck I'd spotted the night before, I padded over to the door and went outside, closing it behind me. In the pre-dawn darkness, a lamp attached to the wall cast a yellowish glow across the small deck and onto the grass.

The cold wood quickly chilled my bare feet as I walked to the edge of the tiny deck, and I took what felt like the first real deep breath in forever. Having cold toes was so worth the clean rush of air moving down my throat, expanding my lungs.

Folding my arms across my chest, I stared across the neatly trimmed patch of grass and the still trees beyond it, focusing only on breathing and letting the cool air rearrange my head into something manageable.

I'd never had a full-blown panic attack—at least not one that wasn't totally understandable, like when Erin had spread wings and displayed some wicked sharp teeth. That didn't count as a panic attack, because I like to think most people would freak in a situation like that.

But I had felt like I was on the verge of one in there. A powerless demigod that experienced anxiety attacks? I coughed out a dry laugh. Maybe Seth and Erin and everyone were wrong. Maybe I wasn't Apollo's daughter. That would make more sense.

Wishful thinking.

Wishful, wasteful thinking. Because even if this was some giant mistake, it wasn't like I could forget any of this and go back to the way things were. I could never go back. No one could—

A twig snapped in the silence, the crack as loud as thunder, causing me to jump. Another snap came, quickly followed by another. My throat dried as I shifted my weight from one foot to the other. The sun hadn't risen yet, and I doubted many people would be out at this time in the morning. It was time for me to get back inside, because other than freaks like me, I couldn't imagine who'd be roaming around out here. I started to turn, but I wasn't fast enough.

Someone stepped out in front of the opening of the small deck—a woman. Maybe in her late twenties, with dark hair and eyes, the woman had a stunning face, but even in the soft yellowish glow of the little lamp beside the door, I could tell her clothing was filthy and torn, stained dark just under the collar and on the knees of her jeans.

Even though I didn't want to, I smiled at her as I reached for the door behind me, because that's how my grandparents raised me. Always be polite.

The woman didn't smile back, but she stopped at the opening, tipping her chin up as she stretched her neck to the side. Her nostrils flared. Was she...*sniffing* the air? Uh...

Quiet as a shadow, a man appeared behind her. Probably a few years older than her, also rocking a gorgeous face and ratty clothing. The faint, fake smile that would've made my granny proud faded from my face as the man's dark eyes drifted over me. Definitely time to get inside. My fingers wrapped around the door handle.

"Wait," the woman spoke.

Something about the voice was like wire dragging over my nerves. Tiny hairs on my body rose. I didn't wait. I started to turn the knob when the deck creaked under footsteps that weren't mine.

I didn't even have a second.

A hand clamped down on mine, yanking it back from the door as another hand smacked down on my mouth, smothering my startled yelp of pain. Immediately, a metallic taste flooded my mouth, my senses. My lips burned as they were forced back against my teeth, but the scent of blood...it wasn't from me.

It was the man holding me.

My feet were lifted off the floor as he turned away from the door. Real fear, such I'd never felt before, exploded like a buckshot, pinging around inside me. Instinct kicked in, and I went wild, clawing at the hand around my mouth and swinging my legs back, digging my heels into his legs.

"Get her legs," he grunted.

The woman moved up the two steps and reached out to grasp my ankle. Her grip was startlingly strong, but I still kicked out, catching her in the chest with my other foot.

Dropping my ankle, she stumbled back as she hissed. She actually *hissed*. Like a pissed-off cat, lips pulled back and teeth bared. Terror punched through my stomach. Not normal. Not normal at all. I dug my fingers into the cold, clammy man's hand, trying to pry it away from my mouth as he neared the steps of the deck.

"Gods," snapped the man, and my heart dropped. *Gods*. Oh crap. "She's just a stupid mortal and you can't even grab hold of her legs. You're fucking helpless."

Horror swamped me as I grabbed for anything to slow him down. My fingers slipped over the plastic privacy wall, digging into the raised edge. With all my strength, I held on as he moved down the steps. Muscles in my arms stretched, screaming out as he tugged harder with his arm around my waist and the hand at my mouth, wrenching my neck back until I thought for sure he was going to snap my neck.

"He's inside," I heard the woman say, her voice dipping in a whine. "I can sense him. Why are we messing with her? I can *feel* him. I need—"

"Because," he said, yanking again. "She smells of the Apollyon. We'll use her to get him out here. Unless you plan on going in there after him. Be my guest."

The man dropped me, cutting off whatever the woman was saying. Losing my grip, I fell into empty space, swallowing a scream as the deck steps rose up to meet me. Pain exploded as my knees cracked off the ground and the side of my head smacked into the corner of the steps. Light burst behind my eyes. Stunned and jarred to my very bones, I couldn't move as I was roughly flipped onto my back and yanked the rest of the way down. I was sprawled in the damp grass before I could get my lungs to work again.

He was over me and on me in a second, and there was nothing I could do as he wrapped a hand under my chin, pushing my cheek into the grass. His nails scraped along my neck as his fingers caught the collar of my sweater and ripped it to the side.

"She'll bring him out," he said, lowering his head. His cool lips brushed the same area Seth's had only a few hours earlier. Nausea twisted my insides as his mouth moved to the space between my neck and shoulder. "Won't you, darling?"

My heart jumped and then faltered as *something* ripped through my skin. Had to be a knife, because it couldn't be what I thought it was—it couldn't be his *teeth*. Red-hot pain blasted through me like a cannonball as I opened my mouth and screamed—*really* screamed.

I was on fire. Someone had dropped a match inside me and my veins were full of gasoline. I was burning up—I had to be. Sharp pinpoints of pain shot out from every cell and there was this tugging deep inside me, this wrenching that came from my very core and burned a mixture of fire and ice. The woman was saying something, but I didn't understand her words. They sounded like they were a different language.

The thing jerked off me, his legs slipping over mine as he planted his hands in the grass beside my head. I blinked his face into focus. Blood—my blood—smeared his lips. Then my vision blurred back out, and...

"What...what are you?" he asked, voice slurred, sluggish.

Icy fingers wrapped around my arm and then there was that tearing feeling again, above my wrist, and I wasn't screaming. I couldn't make a sound.

⇐

No more than a minute after I stepped out of the shower and dried off, glyphs raced across my skin. I exhaled as I snatched the briefs and jeans off the sink. The feeling curling down my spine was a signal, just like the appearance of the wards on my skin.

Tugging the briefs and then the jeans on, I threw open the door. The room was empty, and as I took a step forward, I felt the wicked sixth sense kicking in. The glyphs moved quicker.

Daimons were near and Josie....

"You've got to be fucking kidding me." I whirled, grabbing a titanium dagger off the nightstand. The handle warmed to my touch.

Her stuff was still where I'd placed it, near the front door. The chain-lock was also set. My gaze swung to the back door. In less than a second, I was throwing it open and stepping out into the night, and into a nightmare.

Two daimons had Josie pinned on the ground. A female was at her wrist and a male was on her, his face buried in her neck. Both were tagging her, feeding from her in a way meant to cause pain. And the male daimon, his body covered hers completely. All I could see was a still leg. Not moving. Nothing.

Rage like I'd never known before detonated like a nuclear bomb, becoming a metallic, bitter taste in the back of my mouth. The world tinted amber as I flew forward off the deck. Landing beside the female, I grabbed a chunk of her hair and ripped her head back, seeing right through the glamour that hid them in the mortal world.

Dark holes where eyes should've been met mine. Black veins twisted like snakes under ghastly pale skin. Her mouth was hanging open, revealing a row of jagged teeth covered in blood—Josie's blood.

I slammed the titanium dagger into one of the holes, cutting off the damn wail daimons were known for before she could let it loose. They were highly allergic to anything titanium. Allergic as in a single slice-and-dice from a titanium blade took them out. As I yanked out the dagger, her face crumbled into itself and then she imploded in a shower of shimmery dust.

The male daimon reared to his feet and stumbled back a step. Josie didn't move. Her neck was covered in blood and her sweater was torn, revealing more than that bastard ever should've seen.

"She tastes like a god." He staggered, tripping over her still leg. His lips curved into a gruesome, bloody smile. The son of a bitch was high. "Bliss..."

"You're so fucking dead," I growled.

He dipped his chin and opened his mouth, letting out an eerie howl that was a cross between a bobcat getting run over and a screaming infant. Then the stupid fuck charged me. All hocked up on the hidden *aether* that must be in Josie's blood, the daimon moved like a freight train. I dipped under his extended arm, popping up behind him. The need to make the bastard hurt, to make him pay overrode the years of training that taught Sentinels not to play with their prey. The daimon whirled on me. I was going to break his fucking neck. Then his arms. Then his legs. Then I was going to find something rusty and dull to cut his balls off. Then I would kill him. Slowly. As painfully as possible. I started to toss the dagger aside as it barreled toward me again.

A soft whimper came from behind me, echoing through my head a thousand times, louder than a gunshot or crack of thunder. For a second, a tiny moment in time, I was torn between the lure of losing myself, losing everything in the revenge, in the art of fucking payback, and the girl on the ground—the girl who needed me. With no time to spare, I snapped out of the haze of violence.

I launched forward, meeting the daimon halfway. Catching him around the neck with a hand, I held him off as my eyes locked with the soulless, black depths. "You are so very lucky."

Then I shoved the dagger deep into its chest, yanking the blade out. I spun around before the bastard imploded into nothing.

Dropping down to the ground beside Josie, I placed the dagger within reach. I brushed her hair back from her cheek. Her face was too pale. The skin above her temple was bruising, turning red and swelling.

"What's going on out here?"

I looked over my shoulder. An older man in slippers and a dark robe stood a few feet away, his watery eyes moving from me to Josie and coming up with gods knew what. I didn't have time for this shit. "You didn't see or hear any of this," I gritted out, packing a powerful compulsion. "Just a dream. Go inside. Go back to sleep."

The man didn't blink. He was frozen for a second, and then he wheeled around and walked stiffly across the grass.

Heart pounding, I turned my attention back to her. Carefully moving more strands of hair out of the way, I got a good look at her neck. The tag wasn't deep and blood had already stopped oozing out of the crescent-shaped bite mark. I checked her wrist. Same.

"Fuck," I grunted, shifting so I could slide an arm under her. I lifted her up into a sitting position. Her head lolled back and I quickly adjusted her, cradling her against my chest. "Fucking mother *fucker*."

She didn't make another sound. Didn't move.

"Come on. Open your eyes, Josie. Come on, baby, open your eyes." I got an arm under her knees and lifted her as I stood, swiping up the dagger. My heart was still pounding. There was a weird dropping sensation in my gut. I carried her inside, my jaw aching from how hard I was grinding my teeth together. What had she been thinking going outside like that? If she were awake, I would've shaken some godsdamn sense into her.

But that wasn't entirely fair.

Josie had been thrust into this world and she still had a lot of mortal traits in her. She probably hadn't even thought once that going outside wouldn't be safe.

I kicked the door shut as she finally stirred, moaning softly. I stopped. "Josie?"

Her features tightened, pinching as her lashes fluttered. Potent relief rushed through me as she slowly blinked her eyes open. Her gaze was a little unfocused, but her eyes were open.

"You with me?" I asked.

Her lips parted, and I saw the angry red cut on them then. Anger replaced that relief, tearing through me as an unsteady breath expelled from her. "I think...I think they bit me," she croaked out.

"Yeah, you most definitely were chewed on," I told her.

Her eyes shut, staying close long enough that I felt the punch of panic again, but they swept open again. "They...they were daimons, weren't they?"

Nodding, I moved to the bathroom. "You think you can sit up?"

She cleared her throat, wincing. "Yeah. I can." Her words were mushy.

"Good." Carefully I set her down on the closed toilet, then placed the dagger on the edge of the sink. Her eyes were closed again and that worried me. The sweater was torn, slipping off her shoulder and revealing a lavender strap and the dainty lace covering one swell. My gaze flicked up to the bite mark as I inhaled deeply. There was something in the air, more than a metallic scent—something potent and alluring. *Aether*? Shit. I was loosing my mind. I couldn't smell *aether* like daimons could. I could sense it, so maybe that was what I was picking up, and that made me cagey, because a yearning took root in my stomach, striking deep, making my mouth water.

Moving quickly, I tugged the sweater up. "How are you feeling?"

Her lashes lifted. "Like someone...bit me."

"The tags aren't deep," I said, standing. "But you need water—fluids. Sit still." I wasn't sure if fluids would really help her, but I went into the room, drawing in several deep breaths as I opened up the small fridge under the TV. There was a bottle of Gatorade. Grabbing it, I went back to the bathroom, placing the bottle next to the sink.

Kneeling down, I grabbed for her arm. She flinched, recoiling, and I felt something acidic burning deep in my chest, replacing the empty craving. "Hey," I murmured, dipping my head close to hers. "You're okay. You're safe, Josie. You're all right."

Holding my gaze, she exhaled softly. "Okay..."

I gently pushed the sleeve of her sweater up. "I'm guessing with your powers bound, it made you susceptible to their glamour—old magic that disguises them." I reached up, grabbing a towel. I ran it under the tap. "Or maybe you're wired like the pures. They can't see through the glamour, either."

She didn't say anything as I handed over the bottle. "Drink this. It should help."

Josie took the bottle. My attention was drawn to her fingers. The nails were dirty, broken. "I'll be okay," she said, taking a drink as I looked up at her from where I was crouched. Her hand shook the bottle but she didn't drop it as she raised it to her lips again. "You know, I...I've never been seriously ill or injured before, even when I should've been." Her gaze tracked over the room while I mopped up the blood on her arm. "Once...when I was younger, I climbed up this tree, all the way to the top."

As I cleaned her arm, an image of a younger, smaller Josie took form. Probably all legs and arms with a headful of multicolored hair and probably loads of trouble.

"I fell out and I remembered being...in a lot of pain," she continued as I tossed the towel and reached for a new one. "I thought I broke my leg. I was sure I broke my leg, but...by the time my grandparents got me to the hospital, I was just bruised. The doctors said I was lucky."

It wasn't luck. It was what she was. Dampening the other cloth, I stood, my eyes meeting hers. I opened my mouth to say something, but I didn't have any words.

"I've bled all over you," she whispered.

I looked down. She was right. Streaks of crimson slashed across my bare chest. A lead ball settled in my gut. "It's okay."

Her eyes closed. Dark shadows had bloomed under them. The attack had taken its toll. I leaned in, lowering my voice so only she could hear me, and the question came out rough, strained. "Are you hurt anywhere else...that I can't see?"

The lashes flickered up. Confusion skittered across her expression, and then understanding crept in. Muscles in my back and neck tensed. All daimons cared about was *aether*—was getting their next fix—and they could be dumb in that relentless pursuit. Halfs who'd been turned into daimons were far more dangerous, but all of them could be cruel and sick.

"No," she said quietly.

Another dose of relief hit me, and I nodded. Carefully peeling the torn material aside, the lead ball in my gut expanded, feeling like I'd taken a punch in the chest.

Josie had been tagged—tagged in the same place as *her*—as Alex. The coincidence was more than unnerving. It blasted through me as I wiped around the bite mark. No matter who or what you were, a daimon tag scarred. Just like *she*...just like Alex had carried scars all over her.

My hand shook. Rawness flowed through me. I didn't like what I was feeling, so I latched onto the anger boiling inside me like a lit furnace. "Are you too stupid to fucking live?" She drew in a sharp breath, and I felt like a fucking ass for saying it, but it needed to be said. "What were you thinking? Going outside while I was in the shower? Am I going to need to chain you to the chair from here on out?" I tossed the bloodied towel in the bathtub. Giving her palms a cursory glance, I opened the cabinet under the sink and hit jackpot—a first aid kit. It was unlikely that she'd die from some kind of infection, but with my luck, I wasn't willing to risk it. I yanked out a packet of disinfecting wipes.

"You're right," she said, surprising the hell out of me. I even stopped what I was doing, standing there holding a wadded disinfecting wipe. She glanced over at the door before her tired, bruised gaze drifted back to me, and if I thought I'd been punched in the chest before, I'd been wrong. I felt it now. "I wasn't thinking. I couldn't stay in the room. It was too quiet. I went...outside without thinking it through. It was a 'too stupid to live'...kind of move."

That shocked the shit right out of me. Kneeling down in front of Josie, I looked up at her. "This might sting a little."

She nodded.

I pressed the alcohol wipe against her palm. She jerked but didn't make a sound. I gently cleaning up the scratched skin. When I was finished, I rose so that we were at eye level. "I shouldn't have said it like that earlier." My voice was gruff, strange to my own ears. "You're still operating like nothing has changed. That's normal. It's just...it's a lesson you didn't need to learn." Straightening, I ignored the curious look she sent me. "I'll get you another sweater."

She stopped me by grabbing my arm. I looked back at her. "Thank you," she said, letting go of my arm. "I...need a few minutes. I should clean up."

I hesitated for a moment. Something uncanny and weird opened up in me—a need to comfort her. Obviously what she'd experienced had to have been traumatic as shit. Before I knew what I was doing, I'd taken a step toward her. An urge to gather her close and tell her everything was going to be okay rode me hard, which was bullshit. Everything would *not* be okay in the end. Not for me. And not for her. She was just a tool, a last resort against the Titans, just like *she*...like Alex had been a last resort.

And look what that had gotten Alex. Look at what that had gotten me.

I stopped before I reached her. I didn't need to go down this road with her. As soon as she saw her mom, I was getting her ass to South Dakota, and then I was done. Turning away, I headed out and went to her bag, grabbing the first sweater I saw and handing it over. "Come out when you're ready," I said gruffly.

Then I closed the door behind me. Leaning against it, I swore as I shut my eyes. If I hadn't sensed the daimons and gone out there, they would've kept tagging her. They would've kept on her until there was no aether left, just like the Titans would do if they got hold of her.

"Shit."

Opening my eyes, I stared blindly at the room as I heard the water come on in the bathroom. What in the hell were daimons doing out here anyway? We were close to St. Louis, and there was a community of pures near the city, but still. It was strange they would be here. They wouldn't have sensed me until they were damn near on top of the motel. Coincidence? I didn't believe in that shit.

We needed to hit the road.

Reaching up, I stopped short of running my hand over my chest. The red streaks had begun to dry—her blood. That churning was back in my gut, twisting and whirling as I moved away from the door, stopping in front of a small, dusty mirror over a dresser.

I was still standing there when Josie came out, dressed in a new sweater, her hair in waves of blonde and brown around her face. Neither of us spoke for a long moment.

"Stay in here," I said. "I need to...I need to clean up."

Her gaze bounced around the room, not settling on me as she sat on the edge of the bed, chin ducked. "I'm staying."

I stood there in the door to the bathroom for a moment, wanting to tell her...to tell her that I wished she'd never experienced what being tagged felt like, that she wouldn't have to live with those scars, but those words wouldn't form.

And those words would be pointless, because I was sure this wouldn't be the last time she'd experience something I wished she hadn't. It was only the beginning.

CHAPTER

14

WE WERE quiet as we got into the Porsche. We still had that remaining four-hour drive ahead of us. There was nothing that needed to be said. I'd screwed up and I could've died. I could've gotten Seth hurt. As we pulled away from the parking lot, I was glad to lose sight of the motel. I wished I could scrub the whole thing out of my head.

I quickly zoned out, beyond exhausted and still feeling the pings of residual fear darting around me like little aftershocks... and I was *disappointed*. Utterly disappointed in myself. Seth had warned me that this world was dangerous. I believed him, but I hadn't acted with any thought. My mind was still stuck in the world where things like daimons, gods, and Titans didn't exist. In a world where I could walk outside and not worry about being nom-nom'd on like Toaster Strudel. That was too stupid to fucking live.

And that was a hell of a lesson to learn.

When I'd seen my neck and wrist, I hadn't known what to think. The skin was ugly and pink, forming perfect crescent-shaped bite marks. The areas were still tender, and there was a dull ache in my head and knees. But it wasn't the pain or the bitter

135

taste of terror that lingered from those moments outside, but the fact I hadn't been able to do a single thing to defend myself.

Nothing.

They were on me in seconds and I hadn't been able to fight or anything. I doubted that I'd turn into a ninja when my abilities were unbound. And I also knew that the Titans had to be way more powerful than shades and daimons.

I was *so* dead.

The exhaustion got to me, and I drifted off to sleep...and I dreamt. A warm, soft touch slipped over my cheek, tucking hair back behind my ear, careful to not touch the tender skin along the side of my neck. I was dreaming a phantom touch. I had to be, because such a gentle, careful touch didn't make sense in real life. My body unconsciously sought the caress. I leaned into it as I thought I heard my name called. The touch moved across my lower lip, stopping short of the raw spot at the corner of my lip. I liked that—a lot. Warmth traveled though me, stirring up a pleasant haze. This was a sweet dream. I could stay here forever.

The voice came again, louder this time, and then I heard, "Joe. Wake up."

Fog lifted from my thoughts as I forced my lids to come unstuck and open, and when they did, honey-colored eyes met mine. Oh crap, I wasn't dreaming.

And his hand was still curved around my chin, his thumb resting just below my lower lip. My breath hitched as I stared at him. Surprise flitted through me and my sluggish mind couldn't catch up.

"You're awake now?" he asked, tracing my lower lip with his thumb, creating a stir of hyperactive butterflies in the pit of my belly. "I can drive up and down the street again if you want to continue to nap."

"Huh?"

A small grin appeared and those butterflies decided to invade my chest in an army of flurries. "We got to your house, but you were still sleeping, so I drove back through town," he said, and my eyes widened. We were in Osborn? I'd slept the entire way? "We're about a mile out now. I figured you'd want some time to get yourself together."

That was incredibly considerate, surprisingly so, and actually kind of sweet. My lips curved into a smile. "No, I'm awake."

"How are you feeling?"

"Okay." I swallowed hard. "Do I look...like I've just gone toe-to-toe with Jaws? I don't want my mom or my grandparents to worry."

He looked me over. "No. Keep your hair down. It covers the tag and the sweater takes care of the rest. Your lip...it's not that noticeable." His gaze dropped to my mouth, and oh boy, those butterflies were turning into pterodactyls. It was silly. All of this was. But I could easily recall the way he'd stared at me when I'd walked out of the bathroom wearing his shirt, the things he'd said, and yeah, how I'd fallen asleep with him holding my hand... all the stuff before I'd almost gotten myself killed.

"You were making noises again," he said. "Little murmurings."

Oh my God, seriously? "I *so* do not like you."

That didn't even sound believable to me, and he grinned. "You," he said, tapping the tip of my nose, "are a terrible liar."

I blinked.

He slid back, shifting the car out of park and into drive. Pulling off the shoulder, he coasted back onto the road. I stared at him another moment, realizing his hair was down again, the soft-looking ends brushing his broad shoulders, softening the cut lines of his face.

God, he really was something to look at it, and I needed to focus on what was important. I was minutes from seeing my mom, from *really* seeing her after knowing the truth, and I needed to get my head together.

A bundle of nerves formed in my belly as we drove down the familiar country road. Sunlight filtered through the heavy branches, casting shadows across the hood of the Porsche and the windshield. What was I going to say to Mom? What *could* I say?

"Nervous?" Seth asked.

I glanced at him. "How can you tell?"

"You're bouncing around in the seat like there are springs under your ass."

Oh. Well then. I made an effort to sit still. "I don't know what to say to her. I don't even know if she'll understand."

His long fingers closed around the steering wheel as he squinted. A moment passed. "Do you need to say anything?"

At first that didn't make sense, and then I got what he was saying. Turning my gaze to the side window as the SUV slowed, I knew I didn't have to go into detail with her. I could just tell her that *I knew*, or I could just hug her and let her know that way that I understood.

"You're a smart girl," he said, turning down the narrow road that led to the house. I think I stopped breathing as I clenched the seatbelt. "You'll roll with it and figure it out."

My heart was pounding like a steel drum as the house came into view. The two-story home was well over a hundred years old and had to have been a beauty back in its glory days. Not that it was decrepit or anything, but the white paint was peeling off the exterior wooden slabs and the roof needed to be replaced, especially over the porch. But for me, it was home—beautiful in a sad, aging kind of way.

Aging? It struck me then as gravel crunched under the tires of the Porsche. Would I stop aging once my super-special powers were unleashed upon an unsuspecting world? I looked at Seth. "Do demigods age?"

His brows knit as he stopped the SUV near my granddaddy's old Ford pickup truck. "Wow. Random. But no, they don't. Back in the day, there was always some trial they went through, and then they were at full demigod status. Some are...they are made and they stop aging at that point."

Whoa. I slumped back against the seat, staring at the swing on the porch that probably couldn't hold my weight anymore. I would stop aging. Holy crap. I could be stuck between twenty and twenty-one forever. Like *forever*. "Do you age?"

There was a pause. "Yes, I age, but that's not really going to be a problem."

I looked at him sharply, not liking the way he said that. "Why?"

Seth hit the engine button, turning it off. His jaw was set as he tugged a leather band off his wrist and pulled his hair back into a short ponytail. "That is not something you need to be worried about right now, Joe. You've got to get inside. I hate to say this, but we don't have a lot of time. We need to get back on the road, because we're really pushing it stopping here. I need to get you to South Dakota."

"So you can drop me off and leave?" The question came out before I could stop myself, and he looked at me sharply. I sucked in a breath, wondering why I had even asked that. "And stop calling me Joe." I unbuckled my seatbelt. He had a point, but I was stalling. "When's your birthday? You're twenty-one, right?"

He looked at me, mouth curled at the corners, as if he didn't know if he should smile or frown at me. "My birthday is May second. I'll be twenty-two."

"My birthday is October thirteenth. Sometimes it falls on Friday the thirteenth, and that's kind of creepy, right? Like I'm a walking black cat or a living ladder no one wants to walk under."

He sighed as he shook his head. "You want me to stay here and wait for you?"

Guess no more procrastinating. Reaching for the door, I started to tell him yes, but that wasn't what came out of my dumb mouth. "No. I mean, can you come inside, too? My grandparents might think you're my boyfriend or something, but I'll introduce you as my friend, and they'll be pretty cool. I think they were hippies back in the day."

139

His lips were doing that curling thing again. "Why not your boyfriend?"

I stared at him. "Because you're not my boyfriend." That seemed obvious.

"I'm your friend?"

He'd sounded genuinely curious, and that made him more socially awkward than me, and I kind of liked him for that. "Yes, you're my friend," I decided, and he cocked a perfect, golden eyebrow. "I don't know why. You're moody, but you can be funny when you want. Kind of dirty-minded, though. Sometimes even nice, and I know we've only known each for a couple of days, but you saved my life earlier and I think...I think I know you just about as well as I knew Erin. So, yeah, friends."

Seth stared at me for a moment, and then he chuckled deeply, shoulders shaking. "Get out of the car, Joe."

I got out of the car. "Thanks, *Sethie*."

He shot me a look that was full of amusement as he rounded the front of the Porsche. Gazing up at the front door, my heart leapt into my throat. I took a deep breath. "You sure I look okay?"

"Yes," he said.

Then I dashed up the stairs, ignoring the aches and pains from taking a hard landing earlier, as the wooden boards creaking under my feet. Opening the screen door, I wasn't surprised when I found the interior door unlocked. The only kind of crime around these parts was stolen cows. Walking into the narrow foyer, I called out. "Mom? Granny?"

Seth slipped in behind me, quiet as a freaking ninja, somehow closing the door behind him without causing it to make the annoying shriek it had when I'd opened it.

I started down the hall as my grandmother walked out from the kitchen. What had happened this morning with the daimons ceased to exist the moment I saw her. Granny wasn't that old, only in her late fifties, more round than narrow, and even though her face was weathered, her brown eyes were always so bright and full of life.

"Honey, what are you doing here?" Wiping her hands on the front of her jeans, she charged forward and barreled into me before I could respond. Her hugs were always fierce and squishy. It hurt a little this time, but I didn't care. I'd missed these hugs. She drew back, smiling broadly. "This is such a surprise!" Craning her neck, she yelled, "Jimmy! Josie's here!"

I winced at the pain in my eardrums.

Granny stepped back, holding onto my hands as she looked over my shoulder. Her eyes widened. "Honey, who is this?"

Feeling my face heat, I turned to Seth. "This is, um, this is Seth..." And I realized I had no idea what his last name was. "He's a friend."

"A friend?" Granny sent me a look that clearly said I was doing something wrong, and I wanted to throw myself under the small table butted up against the wall. She winked, and not at me, and I swallowed a groan. "Well, come in. Both of you. I'll get you two some sweet tea. It's fresh, just like you like, honey. Jimmy's in the kitchen, eating pie, even though the doctor told him he needed to start eating more vegetables and less sweets and meat because of his diabetes, but you know how he is. I swear he's eaten half of the apple pie since I took it out of the oven last night, so if you two want a slice, I suggest finding a shotgun and threatening his life with it. Oh, and if you want, the coffee's still warm."

My lips pursed as Granny spun and disappeared through the doorway. Seth stopped beside me, knocking my shoulder with his. He was grinning as he lowered his chin, whispering in my ear. "I'm going to hazard a guess and say you take after your grandmother."

"We're not friends anymore," I grumbled.

He chuckled as I walked through the large dining room. A vase of tulips, Mom's favorite, sat in the middle of the oak table. Seth stayed slightly behind me as we made our way into the eat-in kitchen, and like Granny had said, my grandfather was at the table, a slice of pie the size of my head in front of him and a newspaper in the other hand. My grandfather had the most awesome head full

141

of hair—great genes or something, because there wasn't even a streak of gray among the brown strands. Or he was rocking some Clairol for Men.

Peering up over his dark-rimmed glasses, he lowered the paper as his hazel eyes shifted from me to Seth. "Who's this?"

"Seth. No last name apparently, because I wasn't given one," Granny answered, grabbing two mugs and placing them next to two glasses. "He's a *friend*."

I opened my mouth, but my grandfather opened his first. "Do you like pie, boy?"

Oh God, did he seriously just call Seth "boy" and ask him if he liked pie? This conversation wasn't going as planned.

There was something like a choked laugh from behind me. "I love pie, sir."

His eyes narrowed on us as he sat back, folding his arms across the flannel shirt he'd had since I was a little girl. "Good. I don't trust anyone in my house that don't like pie."

Before this conversation could continue, I jumped in. "I can't stay really long, but I need to see Mom. Is she in her bedroom?"

Granny finished scooping at least the tenth spoonful of sugar into my grandfather's cup, which made me frown, considering that wasn't going to help with his diabetes. She placed the mug in front of him. "Hilary's not here, honey."

"Not here?" That was different. Mom didn't leave the house without one of my grandparents. "Where is she?"

She smiled as she whirled toward the fridge, opening the door and yanking out a giant jug of tea. "She's with a friend."

The nervous knots from before were back, multiplying like mogwais fed after midnight. I shook my head. Mom didn't have friends. "What friend?"

"A really nice one. They're on a mini-vacation." She glanced at my grandfather as she poured the tea. "Or something like that."

Seth moved closer, a suddenly tense presence in the cozy kitchen. I took a breath, but it got stuck. "Okay. You guys are just being funny. Is she upstairs?"

"She's gone," my grandfather answered, picking up the newspaper. "When did she say they'd be back? Her and that nice young man who also liked pie?" His brows knitted. "I can't... remember."

Granny shrugged as she sat at the table, placing the glasses down. "It's no concern of ours. Now, do you two want to drink this tea or not?"

I stared at them, sort of dumbstruck for a moment. There was no way in hell my grandparents would let my mom leave with anyone—especially a "him"—and think it was no concern of theirs. I watched them go about their business for a moment. Grandpa eating his pie. Granny arranging the glasses. Something was wrong here, very wrong. Taking a step back, I bumped into Seth.

"Josie," he said quietly.

Spinning around, I tore out of the kitchen and ran back into the main hall. Hanging a left, I took the steps two at a time. "Mom?" I called, hitting the hallway that smelled vaguely of mothballs and apple-cinnamon. I flew past the framed photos, past my old bedroom and my grandparents', to the last bedroom at the end of the hall.

The door was open.

I skidded into the room, breathing deeply as my frantic gaze ranged over the bedroom. The bed was empty and made. No pill bottles sat on the nightstand. Mom's slippers weren't on the floor beside the bed.

Hands shaking, I went to the dresser and yanked open a drawer. Empty. I moved to the next one and the next one. All of them were empty. Whipping around, I ran my hands through my hair, tugging the heavy strands back.

Mom wasn't there.

This wasn't right. Not right at all.

I darted to the nightstand, opened the little drawer there. It got stuck, but I pulled it open. Her favorite book—a Joanna Lindsey historical romance novel she'd read over and over again,

143

until the pages were falling out—was still in there, tucked away next to a packet of tissues. The pills she took made her eyes water.

Stumbling back, I stared at the little paperback in the drawer. What was happening?

"Josie?"

I whirled at the sound of Seth's voice. He stood just inside the doorway. "Where is she?" When he didn't answer immediately, panic eroded my fragile grasp on rational thought. "Where is she, Seth?"

"I don't know, but—"

Wheeling away from him, I stormed toward the closet and ripped the doors open. Mom didn't have a lot of clothes, mostly comfortable things like lounge pants and worn jeans, but she did have a few dresses.

They were gone.

Seth said my name again, and this time he was closer than before. "She has to be here somewhere. Maybe she's at the lake." That didn't explain the missing clothes or pills, but I jumped on it like a lifeline. "Sometimes she goes down there. And the weather isn't bad today."

He shook his head. "I don't think she's there."

"No." I sidestepped him as he reached for me, hurrying toward the door, but he was right behind me, wrapping an arm around my waist, pulling me back against his chest.

"Stop for a sec, Josie. She's not at any—"

A burst of strength I didn't even know I had in me allowed me to break out of Seth's embrace. He shouted my name, but I took off into the hallway, spinning out of control as fear for my mother took hold, sinking its razor-sharp claws into me, digging deep. I gave into it and I ran.

"Shit."

This was about fifty levels of suck. Things were definitely off, and it wasn't just the conversation about pie.

I took off after Josie. Damn, that girl was fast when she wanted be, and strong, too—abnormally strong in that moment she broke free, especially considering what had happened this morning. She was already downstairs, flying out the front door. Cursing under my breath, I leapt from the stairs and landed in the hall.

"Jesus H. Christ on a crutch." Josie's grandfather stumbled into the wall beside the doorway, his hand against his chest.

Shit on a brick.

"Forget you saw that." I headed for the still-open door, turning back for a second, tossing out another compulsion. "And...I don't know...go eat some more pie."

Then I was outside, crossing the porch with one jump. Hitting the gravel, I spotted her breaking off at the treeline. I took off after her, chasing her through the tall oaks, and then she disappeared around a bend. Picking up speed, I burst out from the trees and skidded on sand-colored pebbles, kicking the tiny rocks into the air.

Josie was a few feet in front of me, standing near a pile of driftwood, staring across the still waters of a huge-ass lake. I brushed a strand of hair that had come loose behind my ear as I stared at her stiff back.

Gods, the last thing I needed was for her to run off like this, but dammit, her emotions were heavy, tangible in the cooled breeze, practically a third entity between us.

"She's gone," she said, turning around. Her blue eyes shone as she stared at me, her expression pleading, and there was a tug in my chest, an unsettled feeling, because I couldn't answer that unspoken plea. Squeezing her eyes shut, she reopened them and walked past me, back toward the stand of trees. I turned, relieved when she stopped, her back to the trees. "Something's wrong with my grandparents. They would never be okay with her leaving...or with someone taking her."

Stepping forward, I stopped when a look that said she was ready to bolt again flickered across her face. "I think your grandparents are under a compulsion."

"A compulsion?" she whispered, and a sudden gust of wind picked up her words, tossing them around. "Someone like you has been here? Took my mom and messed with my grandparents' heads?"

I could already tell this wasn't going to go over smoothly, but there was no point in lying. "It could be a pure, or a god or..."

"Or what?" She took a step back, her hands balling into fists. "Or what?" she shouted.

It could've been a Titan. But taking her mom and placing her grandparents under a compulsion didn't make sense. If they knew where Josie lived, knew about her mom, I doubted anyone would've been alive in that house. But then again, the only Titan I'd ever met was Perses, and he was whacked enough to show me that Titans were capable of anything.

"God. This isn't right. My mom hasn't done anything wrong."

"I know," I said as carefully as possible. "I understand."

"You understand?" She laughed as she raised her hands, pulling her hair back. "How in the hell do you understand, Seth? Have you ever had your entire world turned upside down? Told things you never thought possible were true? Had your mother possibly kidnapped by a mythical creature?"

"No." And then I surprised the hell out of myself. "But I know someone who has. I *knew* someone who had their entire world turned upside down, who lost their mother and a lot of other people." I couldn't believe I was actually talking about her—about Alex—but I forged on. "So I've seen this before. I know it's hard, but you've got to keep it together. Your grandparents are okay, so that leads me to believe that whoever took your mom didn't want to upset or harm them. That's a good sign."

Her throat worked as she swallowed hard. Some of the panic receded from her expression, but her muscles tensed, and I knew she was going to run again. I really couldn't blame her. The girl had been through a lot and she probably needed space and time, probably someone who could comfort her, but I couldn't chase her around Bumfuck, Egypt, and I sucked at the whole comfort thing.

And we were running out of time.

Josie let out a sound that tore into me just as intensely as claws from a furie would, and she twisted at the waist, about to take flight. I took a step forward, ready to tackle her ass if need be, but before she could run, the ground under my feet began to tremble. Before I could take my next breath, a great and terrible sound—like a thousand shouts booming along a mountain—erupted.

Awareness curled its way down my spine as the glyphs bled onto my skin, swirling in warning, and gods, that was a really, really bad sign.

147

CHAPTER

15

ALL AROUND us, the trees rattled and shook as a wave of birds suddenly took flight, streaming into the air in a flurry of snapping wings and frantic shrieks, blocking out the sun as they blanketed the sky.

Seth shot to my side. "Damn, this...yeah, this is not good."

The ground quaked as the sound of hoofs pounded from the direction of the shaking trees. I stumbled, plastering myself against the tree as deer broke out from the trees. Not one. Not a few. *Hundreds* of them. They ran, hopping over the slight dip where the grass turned to pebbles, their white tails twitching.

But among the deer were smaller critters—rabbits, squirrels, skunks. Stunned, I watched as an entire cast of cute Disney-type creatures veered sharply at the water's edge, following the lake until they disappeared out of sight.

Seth twisted toward me, brows raised, and I swallowed hard around the knot of fear in the base of my throat. "That's not normal," I said. "At all."

"What? You don't have a mass exodus of animals every weekend?"

Before I could respond to his smartass comment, a loud sound clapped again, causing me to jump. Louder than thunder, it rolled through the blue, cloudless skies, an endless roar that raised the tiny hairs all over my body. It sounded like trumpets, like the apocalypse kind of trumpets.

Or Godzilla.

And the sound was coming from where all the animals had run from, the direction of my grandparents' home. My stomach dropped to my toes. "My grandparents..."

I pushed away from the tree at the same moment Seth grabbed my hand. He didn't try to stop me. We ran together toward the noise. From above, branches broke away from the trees, streaking down and snagging my clothes and hair. Seth was sure-footed, avoiding every exposed root and boulder. We burst out from the trees, and there was my grandparents' home, the Porsche next to the Ford, and everything looked normal except for the trampled bushes my grandfather had planted around the driveway a few years ago. I rounded the side of the house and the porch came into view. The front door gaped open, the screen door hanging off its hinges.

Oh no, *no*.

Seth's grip tightened and he drew me to a halt. "Something's not right."

Fear crowded my thoughts. "I need to make sure my grandparents are okay. Let go."

With his free hand, he pulled out one of those wicked-looking daggers he had stowed God knows where. "You are *not* going into that house."

I whirled on him, but the look in his eyes stopped me dead. I shook my head. "No. Not—"

Seth hauled me to him and twisted, going down on his knees as another loud crack reverberated and the windshield on the Ford exploded in a shower of glass. "Gods," he grunted, pushing me the ground and back against the Porsche. "Stay down."

He sprung up and around, scooting down the narrow space as another shot rang out, smacking into the hood of the truck. I pushed onto my hands and knees.

My grandfather stood in the doorway, a sawed-off shotgun in his hands. He whipped it around, aiming straight for Seth. I scrambled to my feet. "Granddad! No!"

He didn't hear me as he came down the porch steps, firing another round. I screamed as Seth darted to the right as the buckshot whizzed past him.

Seth moved as fast as I imagined a panther did in the jungle, rushing the steps. He gripped the barrel of the gun, twisting it out of my grandfather's hands and tossing it to the ground in front of the Porsche. The sun glinted off the dagger as Seth raised it high.

"No!" I screamed, shooting out from between the two vehicles. "Seth! Don't!"

Seth hesitated a fraction of a second as he looked in my direction. My grandfather stepped to the side, lifting his leg and landing a vicious kick in Seth's midsection, knocking him back. With a grunt, Seth crashed through the wooden railing on the steps.

"What the...?" I skidded to a stop at the bottom of the steps, staring up at my grandfather. I hadn't seen *that* coming.

My grandfather faced me.

"Josie, get back!" Seth shouted.

I saw my granddad's eyes...or the lack of them. They were pitch black. No pupils. Just pure black. I took a step back. I took a sharp breath, and the scent of dirt and decay surrounded me.

He smiled. "We've been looking for you, daughter of Apollo." Oh shit.

"That's not your grandfather." Seth was suddenly in front of me, edging me back. "Not anymore."

My head couldn't process that. I got what he was saying, I saw what he meant with my own eyes, but I just didn't want to understand. I *couldn't*.

Granddad kept coming, and Seth tensed in front of me. "Don't look, Josie," Seth said softly. "Don't watch."

Breath strangled in my chest, and I couldn't look away. He'd been right—Seth had been right. He tried to tell me that it would be too dangerous to come home, but I hadn't listened.

I'd led these...these things straight to my family.

"It's too late." My grandfather laughed, and it was nothing like his normal laugh. It was cold as death, dank as underground tunnels. "He's here."

An icy shiver coursed down my spine.

Seth took a step toward my grandfather, and I knew what was about to happen. A scream built in my throat, but before it could escape, my grandfather threw his head back, and black smoke poured out of his mouth, thick and murky like dirty oil. I didn't even see where it went.

My grandfather crumpled, folding into himself like there were no bones or muscles in his body. I shot around Seth, but he snagged my waist with one arm, lifting me clear off the ground. Through a haze of tears, I stared at the lifeless body. He lay in a messy pile of skin and clothes. My heart cracked, fissuring straight down the center.

"Pappy?" I whispered, reaching for him.

"He's not there," Seth said into my ear. "He's gone, Josie, and we need to go. We need to get out here before—"

Dust plumed above the roof as it cracked down the center. The windows in the house exploded, one after another. Glass flew through the air like tiny missiles, heading right for us. My throat closed up as Seth started to turn, to use his own body as a shield, but the glass shards stopped. They just froze in midair and stayed there. Light reflected on the slivers, turning them into diamonds. And then they dropped to the ground.

The house shuddered and the porch trembled as something—*someone*—stepped out from the warped doorframe. Planks of wood snapped under booted feet. Legs the size of tree trunks were encased in leather, and the wide torso was covered with a half-buttoned white shirt.

151

It was a guy—a massive guy who had to be seven feet tall, or damn near close to that. He was huge, steroid-size *huge*. Head completely shaven, eyes exotically slanted at the corners, wide mouth and broad cheekbones, his skin tone was the strangest mix of ethnicities. He wasn't white or black or Hispanic; he appeared to be several different shades all at once. As he strode forward, the roof over the porch peeled up like a can opener had been set across the middle. The man was beautiful until I saw his eyes. They were pitch black—soulless.

Yeah, I didn't need to be up on my mythology to safely assume that this—*this* was a god. *Please be a friendly. Please be a friendly*.

Seth continued to edge me back, his body coiled with tension. "Hyperion."

Totally not a friendly.

Hyperion stopped at the top step as he tilted his head to the side. "Step aside, Apollyon," he said, his voice echoing *through* me. "Or I'll burn everything you cherish."

"That sounds fun and all," Seth said, blocking me. "But I think I'll pass."

The Titan was on the porch one second and then in a heartbeat he was right in front of us. Seth swore violently as he twisted, but even he—as fast as he was—wasn't fast enough.

Seth was seized by the shoulders and tossed to the side like he weighed nothing more than a bag of potato chips—a *half-eaten* bag of potato chips. Full of rising horror, I watched him slam into the side of the house, cracking the exterior. He hit the ground, and I didn't see him move.

Hyperion cocked his head to the side. "You are rather... boring for a demigod, but your father's scent is all over you."

Instinct propelled me into action. I spun around and took off between the vehicles. Where was I going? I couldn't leave Seth. I could circle back, and then what? Scream for help? It didn't matter. As I reached the opening, Hyperion was in front of me. Crying out, I skidded across the gravel and began backpedaling.

One side of his lips curled up. "Don't run. It's rude."

Forget that.

Whirling around, I ran back to where I came from, breaking out between the cars, but then he was *right* there. Shrieking, I couldn't stop in time and bounced right off his rock-solid chest. I fell back, landing on my ass.

He looked down at me, the shit-eating grin on his face. "It's also pointless to run, little one. I am a Titan."

I scrambled back across the gravel, heart racing as he casually strode forward. His arm snapped out, digging his hand into my hair. Fiery pain erupted over my scalp as he hauled me to my feet. I grasped at his thick wrist and dug my nails in.

He didn't even blink as he lowered his head. "Do you know how long I've waited for this?" he asked, and a silver color flashed across his black eyes. "Thousands of years I've been trapped with nothing but the thirst of vengeance to keep me sane." He jerked his arm, and my back bowed as he leaned over me. "Well, the sanity part is up for discussion." A warm hand circled my neck, cutting off my strangled gasp. "You don't even know why, do you?"

I opened my mouth, but there was no air. No words. I smacked at his hand, trying to pry the fingers off of my windpipe. Stretched up on the tips of my toes, I was beyond the point of panic and knee-deep in terror. Like with the daimons, there was nothing I could do to fight him, no way to defend myself.

"Oh. Can't breathe? Sorry about that." Hyperion's grip loosened enough to allow a ragged breath to scorch down my throat, but he curled his fingers, digging his nails into my skin like talons. His head came closer and when he spoke, I felt his breath on my cheek. "You think I want to kill you?" He laughed and the cars trembled around us. "No. I don't want something quick for you. Oh no, I'm going to drag this out for *years*. Soon, you will call me Master, and when—*only* when—your father is broken and Olympus is ours, will I release you into the abyss. But until then, you're going to be my personal PowerBar. Looks like someone already got to you."

I kicked out, but my feet bounced off his legs with no effect.

"You fight like a girl," he said, laughing coldly. "So weak. So helpless. There's almost no sport in this." He let go of my hair and shoved his hand against my chest. "As I can see you know, there is one painful way to feed off of *aether*. The other is less painful. *Less*," he stressed.

"You're going to scream," he said. "And you're going to lure your father out." He let go of my hair as he lined up his mouth with mine, and I swung on him as my fear squeezed my chest in an iron vise. He caught my hand before it connected and turned, slamming me into the side of the truck with enough force to rattle my bones. Moving his hand from my throat, he pressed his palm between my breasts. For a horrifying second I thought he was about to seriously grope me, but he inhaled and his palm—it seared straight through to my breastbone.

Something inside me woke up like a slumbering giant, uncoiling in the pit of my stomach. Warmth swirled like a mini tornado, whirling to where his palm was. Thin slivers of silver in his eyes crackled as the Titan smiled. My body jerked and the warmth turned to scalding hot water. Something was happening inside me—leaving me—and it *hurt*, like when the daimon had bitten me, but more intense. I cried out.

"Hey, Hyperion."

The Titan drew back, lifting his head. The tugging sensation eased off as I slumped back as far as I could go, dragging in deep breaths. Wet warmth ran down the front of my throat. He'd scratched me.

"Yeah, you. Asshole." Seth stood there, one hand curled around the handle of the dagger. A trickle of blood ran from the corner of his lips. "So you're Hyperion? Disappointing. I'd expected someone bigger."

"Seriously?" he asked, releasing me. "You have a death wish, something I am more than happy to fulfill."

I fell forward, hitting the ground on my knees. Rocking back, I pressed my hand against my stomach. The burn receded to a pulsing ache as I lifted my head.

Seth and Hyperion were going toe to toe.

It was insane—a death match. Punches were thrown. Powerful, brutal kicks delivered. Seth was landing more, but the Titan was virtually unaffected. Pushing to my feet, I staggered out from between the vehicles, spying the shotgun. I wasn't sure if it would help, but it was better than nothing.

Seth dipped down and kicked his leg out, but Hyperion reared back, avoiding the kick, and as he turned, he swung out, catching me in the back and knocking me forward. I hit the ground, coughing as my ears rang.

For a moment I couldn't move. I was frozen. My palms pushed into the dirt, my back aching from the blow and my entire body burning. I could hear them grunting, could hear the sound of flesh hitting flesh. The sky lit up a bright amber color, like tawny lightning.

Hyperion laughed.

We were going to die. The panic dug in deep. I lifted my chin, saw the shotgun, and saw my grandfather's body. Tears blurred my vision. I didn't want to die. Not like this. I didn't want Seth to die.

Calling on every bit of strength I had, I rolled and grabbed the shotgun. Hands shaking, I shifted onto my back, rolled up, and leveled the weapon at the Titan. He had Seth by the throat. I threw up a prayer and pulled the trigger. The kickback flattened me back down, but I saw the buckshot hit Hyperion in the back. He dropped Seth and stumbled to the side. Smoke wafted out from the decent-sized hole in his back. Turning around, he smiled as he spit out a mouthful of blood that coagulated the moment it hit the dirt.

Holy crap.

"That wasn't very nice of you." He took a step toward me, and he actually smiled. I shot him in the back and he smiled!

My fingers trembled as I tried to squeeze off another round, but in that same moment, Seth shot up behind him, spinning with lethal grace.

Something whizzed over me, making a high-pitched whistle. Hyperion staggered back and then went down on one knee. I hadn't pulled the trigger. Seth hadn't delivered a blow.

An arrow was sticking out of the Titan's shoulder—a wooden arrow that caught fire then disappeared into a poof of ashes. Another slammed into his chest.

A hand curled around my shoulder, pulling a startled shriek out of me. I twisted, ready to unload the weapon, but I came face to face with what could only be described as an ethereal, beautiful woman.

She looked like an elf.

A *Lord of the Rings* kind of elf.

Pointy ears and chin. High cheekbones. Long brown hair. And her skin had a faint sheen, a dewy glow. She wore a skintight, forest-green jumpsuit, and her eyes were all-white as they focused on me. I inhaled sharply, and all I could smell was rich soil and sun.

"Your father sent us," she said, her voice as light as spring showers as she propped a crossbow on her shoulder.

Us?

Then I saw them—dozens of them coming out from the woods. All the females were just like the one kneeling next to me. There were men, too. They wore some kind of animal-skin pants. Their skin shimmered in the sunlight. All of them carried bows.

She helped me onto my feet. "You must go. The poison will only hold him for a few minutes."

Breath catching in my throat, I looked down at Hyperion. He was frozen on one knee, staring straight ahead. "Poison?"

"Blood of Pegasus," she answered, smiling slightly. "It freezes anyone and anything for a limited period of time."

Seth was on my other side, staring at the woman with a mixture of awe and trepidation. "You're a nymph, but..." He trailed off as he glanced at the male striding up behind Hyperion, pointing an arrow at the back of Hyperion's head.

"We're all nymphs," she answered. "Contrary to the stories they tell, there are both males and females. Now you two must go. His body will adapt quickly."

"Thanks. Have fun with this douche." Seth sheathed his dagger and then started to pull me toward the Porsche.

I dug my heels in. "Wait. My grandmother—"

"Gone." The nymph was suddenly in my face, at eye level. Seth stiffened next to me as sympathy crossed her face. "She is gone. There is nothing alive in that house."

Her words thundered through me, and I cracked open. My heart hurt in a way that felt so very real, that shattered me straight through. My grandparents had raised me. They had loved me, and I had loved them with everything I had in me, and now they were gone. There just a few minutes ago and now gone, and for what? I couldn't say anything, couldn't process as Seth gently pulled me away from the nymph, leading me to the passenger side of the car. My eyes were dry, but I could barely see. I was quiet, but it felt like I was screaming myself raw.

When he opened the door, a male nymph was suddenly there. Up close, I realized, numbly, that he was as unearthly pretty as the female. "Your mother is safe," he said. "Your father made sure of that."

I stared at the elfin creature, unable to speak. Seth loaded me up and I sat in that front seat, staring straight ahead but not seeing anything, not hearing a single word Seth spoke to me as he got behind the wheel and spun the Porsche around.

It wasn't until we hit the rural road that I realized I still clutched the shotgun to my chest.

GODS, THAT couldn't have gone any worse.

Fucking Hyperion. Apollo had been right. The Titan had gone straight for Josie, and he'd tried to tag her—maybe he had. He'd had his hands on her, positioned in the way to feed. I knew how it was done that way.

My hand tightened on the steering wheel and a flare of pain danced over my aching knuckles. The fucker had a hard head. My knuckles weren't the only things hurting, but I wasn't concerned about the ass-kicking I'd just gotten handed or even the fact that the Titan had been the only thing in a very long time that *could* kick my ass.

For the hundredth time since we got into the SUV, I glanced over at Josie. She was still, her eyes on the road ahead. At some point, she had let go of the shotgun and it now rested across her knees. The only words she'd spoken to me since we'd left the house were when I asked if she was okay, which was a lame-ass question. Her lip was bleeding again. Blood had dried along the front of her throat, but the bruise around her neck was painfully visible, forming a handprint, and wasn't that a punch in the gut to know that Hyperion could have choked the life out of her or snapped her neck, while I'd been right there.

Fuck.

Before, when Apollo had told me about the Titans and I'd thought he'd wanted me to go after them, I hadn't cared if I fell in a fight against them. Hell, there'd even been a little part of me looking forward to it, but now it was different. If I went down in a fight against Hyperion, so would Josie.

But I shouldn't care about that. I couldn't. Caring about anything or anyone was futile at this point in my life.

I had to get her to South Dakota and then she would be safe. Sort of. And I would be...I needed to get away, but right now I was focused on her.

"I think we can stop for a few," I said, breaking the silence as I glanced at her again. We'd been on the road for about five hours, with about four more to go. "Enough time to get a look at you and—"

"I'm fine," she cut in, still staring straight forward. "I don't want to stop. I just want to get to where we're going."

A wisp of unease curled in my gut. "Josie, you were tagged this morning—twice—and you faced off with a Titan. Your throat was bleeding and I..." I also wanted to make sure she was okay, and not just in the physical sense. What she had seen happen to her family, on top of everything else, it was a lot. Too much for anyone to really handle.

"I'm...I'm okay. Like I said, I...I don't want to stop. I want to go. I want to keep going and get as far away from there as I can."

The muscle in my jaw spasmed in response to her words. Aw, damn, this...this wasn't good. "Josie, I'm...I'm sorry about your grandparents. I wouldn't wish that on anyone."

"You were right. You said it was dangerous, but I didn't listen. I shouldn't have gone back home." She drew in a sharp breath that hitched. "It's my fault."

"It is *not* your fault. You didn't hurt your grandparents, Josie. Hyperion did. Don't put that kind of shit on yourself."

She didn't respond, and when I looked over at her, I could tell that those words hadn't changed a damn thing. My gaze focused back on the road. Traffic was getting congested the closer we got to Sioux Falls. There'd be tons of hotels, but there was also a rather large pure community nearby, which meant there'd be more daimons.

After a few minutes, she spoke again. "The guy...the nymph, he said my mom was safe. That Apollo took her. Would he do that?"

If so, he failed to mention that fact, but then again, Apollo rarely told anyone what he was doing. I decided to be Positive Paul with this. "He probably knew that Hyperion would eventually learn where your family was and knew he could use your mom to lure you out."

"So, she's safe?"

I didn't say anything, because I hoped for her sake that she was.

Josie drew in another ragged breath. "I couldn't fight him. I couldn't do anything to stop him or to help you."

Wasn't what I expected her to talk about right now, but at least she was talking. Shifting into the next lane, I passed a slow-ass sedan. "You're not trained, Josie. You're not—"

"Can you train me?" she said, and I could finally feel her gaze on me, and I was sure she saw my mouth hanging open. "Can you train me to fight like you?"

I had no idea how to respond to that. Slowly shaking my head, I pushed away the rising memories of training another person— another girl. Then again, training Alex had been completely different. Alex had already known how to fight, and I hadn't been the only one working with her. "I am the best fighter that is breathing, and I'm not even trying to be arrogant about that. But I barely held my own against Hyperion. Besides that, training you won't change what happened to your grandparents."

"I know that, but at least I'd be able to do something other than stand there and scream. Or watch other people get their asses kicked, or watch them die!" Her lips trembled when I glanced at her. "If he comes after me again, I won't be able to defend myself or anything."

"You'll be safe at the University," I told her, and acid churned in my stomach, because I wasn't sure how safe she would be. It wouldn't take Hyperion long to find out where she was stashed away, and I had no idea how they planned to keep the Titan out. There were probably wards—protective spells—but no ward was a hundred percent foolproof.

"I can't stay there forever," she replied, raising a hand to her neck. She started to touch the spot where the daimon had tagged her earlier, but jerked her hand away. There was a tense pause. "Will you do it? Train me?"

Muscles in my shoulders tensed. Training Josie, like I'd trained Alex? I almost laughed at the fucked-up irony of it all, but nothing about any of this was funny. "Josie, I'm...I'm not sure what I'm doing after I get you to the University. Your father might have other plans for me and..."

And I couldn't stay there.

"That's right. You're leaving," she said quietly, and looked away, casting her bleak gaze out the passenger window. "Do you think someone there would train me?"

It was possible. Sentinels were still trained at the University, and there'd be plenty around. All she needed was for the Dean of the Covenant to agree, and I was assuming that was still Marcus Andros, the former Dean of the North Carolina Covenant and Alex's uncle. He'd go for it, especially once he learned what she was and *who* she was to him. Someone would help her.

But it couldn't be me.

I wasn't going down that road again.

Dusk had turned into a starry, cloudless night. I'd forgotten how dark it got up here, when there was nothing between us and the sky. The University was nestled in the Black Hills, not near

Mount Rushmore, but in a part of the protected Northern Hills. People had to know what to be looking for to find the entrance road. Five bumpy miles later, we reached the repaired outer walls of the University. The last time I'd been here, burnt-out cars had lined the roadway and huge chunks of the outer marble walls had been blasted through. The walls were all shiny and new now, looking as if nothing evil had ever crossed their path.

My hands tightened on the steering wheel.

Josie stared up at the twenty-foot walls that circled the acres and acres of land, and then her gaze landed on the titanium-encased gates, speaking for the first time in hours. "Holy crap."

She was staring at the Sentinels. Kind of hard not to when they had semi-automatic weapons pointed at our SUV. Dressed all in black, they were nothing more than shadows as they drifted forward.

Josie shifted. "Seth...?"

"It's okay." I hit the window, rolling it down. "They're just very cautious." I rested an arm on the open window, hoping none of the Sentinels approaching were ones I'd tried to kill at some point. That would be awkward.

A male Sentinel leaned down, his shrewd gaze sweeping over me and getting stuck on Josie. His jaw tightened as he lowered his weapon. "What is your purpose, Apollyon?"

I arched a brow. "It's none of your business." The Sentinel cocked his head and I gave him my best smile, the kind that pissed off everyone in a ten-mile radius. "I need to see the Dean."

The Sentinel's lips curved into a smirk. "You have a mortal with you."

"And that is also none of your business." I held his gaze even though I heard Josie inhale sharply. Like I was going to tell some random Sentinel who she was. More than anybody, I knew it was never a great idea to trust anyone. "I need to see the Dean. Now. And if I have to repeat myself, you better hope you not only have great aim, but that you can pull that trigger fast."

"Oh dear," Josie murmured.

Holding my stare for a moment that tested my patience, the Sentinel finally straightened. Pressing his free hand to his earpiece, he spoke quickly into it.

Josie was still staring at the Sentinels in front of us. "Do you think you could've been...um, nicer to that guy?"

I chortled. "No."

Slowly, she turned her head toward me and raised her brows. "They could shoot us. They *look* like they want to shoot us."

A smile appeared on my lips. "They won't shoot us."

She didn't appear convinced, but the Sentinel raised his arm and motioned toward those at the gate. A second later, the heavy thing swung open. "See? They aren't going to shoot us."

"That's good to know," she mumbled, staring wide-eyed as we passed a bunch of mean-looking Sentinels.

We traveled on, and she ended up pushing the shotgun aside and leaning forward, placing her hands on the dashboard. "What...what happened to those trees?"

The trees surrounding the inner walls of the University had taken a huge hit. Hundreds of them were still tipped over, their limbs stretching to the ground. Exposed roots were the color of ash.

"Ares," I said. "When it all started to go down, he went after the University. He couldn't get in—not at first. But he did eventually." A dry laugh rattled my chest as I slowed the Porsche. "He'd been around us since the beginning, pretending to be an Instructor at the Deity Island Covenant. That's how he got into the University here."

"What happened?"

A big part of me was glad she was talking now, but I wasn't particularly fond of where this conversation was heading. "He got in, killed a bunch of people, and hurt quite a few more."

She pressed her lips together as we were guided toward a large parking area that was within walking distance of the second gate. I ended up parking beside a dozen Covenant-owned Hummers, and after killing the engine, I turned to her.

"We're going to walk from here," I told her, and I watched her throat work. "What you're going to see will probably be a bit overwhelming, but you're safe. I'm not going to let anyone hurt you."

"But you're leaving," she replied immediately, and only then did I realize what I'd said. My chest hollowed out as she looked away, closing her eyes briefly, and then she nodded curtly. "Okay. Let's do this."

I sat there as she opened the door and climbed out, wincing when she put her feet on the ground. *I'm not going to let anyone hurt you.* What kind of fucked-up statement was that? It had been my job to get her here in one piece and I had. Sort of. Definitely not unscathed. My job of keeping her safe was over.

Almost over.

Getting out of the Porsche, I slammed the door shut, headed to the back, and loaded up with our things. She was waiting for me by the passenger side, her chin dipped and arms folded across her chest. My gaze flickered over the Sentinels *casually* lounging near the wall. Over a dozen of them. I ignored them as I dropped my bag on the ground. Using the tips of my fingers, I urged her chin up. Tired blue eyes met mine. Gods, exhaustion was carved into her features. I had no idea how she was still standing, because her weariness went beyond the physical.

I wanted to gather her in my arms. Comfort her. Hold her tight and lend her whatever strength I had to give. But that wasn't me. Or was it? There had been a time when I'd had the luxury of comforting someone, holding her through the raw pain of losing someone she loved, but that felt like forever ago, and I had been a different person then.

I didn't know who I was today.

Feeling about seven kinds of awkward and knowing several eyes were on us, I dropped my hand. "Are you okay, Josie? You ready for this?"

She nodded again, and after a few seconds, she spoke. "I can carry some of the bags."

"I got them." Picking up my bag, I turned toward the gaping gate. "Stick close to me."

Josie listened as we made our way across the marble walkway near the wall. In the dim light, I wondered if she could see the etchings in the stone—the glyphs and drawings of the ancient gods, or see the very same things carved into the inner walls.

As we passed under the archway, under the scrutiny of Sentinels who seemed to be repopulating faster than we could walk, I heard her ragged exhale. "Holy good Lord," she whispered as she looked around, getting her first good look at one of our Covenants.

It had to be something pretty amazing to see for the first time.

The campus was a sprawling monstrosity of everything Greek, spreading between two mountain peaks. From the marble and sandstone walkways and benches, to the elegant, hand-chiseled statues, to the columned buildings, it was like ancient Greece had thrown up all over the valley.

Courtyards filled with every flower known to the mortal world surrounded us—flowers that shouldn't grow in South Dakota, but did inside the Covenant walls due to some crazy godly reason—casting a balmy scent that clung to my skin.

Her mouth was open as we rounded a bend and the high walls of the Courtyards tapered off. She was staring at the statues.

"There used to be twelve of them there," I told her, gazing up at the marble likenesses of the core Olympians. "Looks like they tore down Ares's statue. Can't really blame them."

They were big, well over ten feet, and each probably weighed a ton. They lined the walkway. And then there were the stone Muses, guarding the entrance to each academic building we passed. Dorms rose in the background like skyscrapers, lights glittering from windows, and I knew from memory that below them were the training facilities and community buildings that were full of every modern convenience one could come up with.

"How in the world do people not know this is here?" she asked, looking everywhere all at once.

165

"Planes don't fly over the area. Never have. And those who have seen it think it's some rich private college with really exclusive admission criteria." I shifted the strap on my shoulder. "Mortals see what they want to see. Never what's really there."

She looked at me sharply, but didn't say anything.

In the circular structure up ahead, busts of the Olympian Twelve, including Ares, were carved into the sandstone pillars. When I glanced at Josie, her expression was floored, the surprise of someone unexpectedly transported to Greece. A small smile pulled at my lips. The building where the Council met did look like a Grecian amphitheater.

As we climbed the wide steps of the main building, she glanced around, spying the Sentinels who were not so covertly following us. A frown appeared as she looked at me. "You said this is a college, right? Where are all the students?"

"Good question. When we showed up, they probably had them all confined to their dorms."

Her steps faltered. "Why?"

"They've been through a lot, Josie. They don't trust anyone."

She seemed to mull that over as we passed the statue of Themis. The scales she held were balanced. Before we reached the titanium double doors, they opened for us, spilling bright light out onto the veranda, and Josie drew up short, gasping.

Out of instinct, I moved closer to her, attaching myself to her hip since I couldn't put her behind me when we had a shit ton of Sentinels breathing down our necks, and a shit ton standing in front of us, forming a loose line that prevented our entrance.

Every muscle in my body tensed as energy coiled tight inside me, ready to be unleashed if they made one wrong step toward us. "All of you are here to welcome us?" I drawled slowly. "I'm honored."

None of the Sentinels replied. Nope. They were too restrained for that shit, and as my gaze flickered over them, I noted all of them were halfs and none of them looked like they were about to roll out the red carpet.

Josie shivered.

That pissed me off.

Anyone could take one look at the girl and know she was a hairsbreadth away from falling on her face. This shit wasn't necessary.

But the wall of Sentinels parted as a tall pure strode between them, and it was the guy I was looking for. Looks could be deceiving when it came to this pure. He was Rambo in pressed khakis and could kick ass with the best of them. His dark-brown hair was styled back from his face, and while there were more lines around his startling green eyes and his mouth than I remembered, he looked as cool and calm as I recalled.

The only time I'd ever seen Marcus Andros lose his shit was when Apollo had told him that his niece had...that she had suffered a mortal death.

I'd been there. Chaos had reigned supreme. The Covenant in the Catskills had been burning to the ground, and in the glow of the unnatural fire, Marcus had punched me.

It had been the last time I'd seen him.

Behind him, I saw a familiar face. A Sentinel stood just off from the rest, his thick brown hair pulled back from a face only his mother could love, with a jagged scar cutting from one eye to the corner of his lips.

Solos Manolis.

I wasn't surprised to see him here. From what I'd gathered, the main Council had been moved to the University since the Catskills had to be rebuilt. He wasn't a bad dude—actually pretty legit. But he was part of a group that I wanted nothing to do with—the group that I knew was here. His father was also a pure, a well-respected one who had lobbied on behalf of the half-bloods for years. Solos had taken a seat on the Council—the very first half-blood to ever do so, taking the place of *saint* Aiden St. Delphi, who'd given up the prestigious spot.

Marcus's cool gaze flickered from me to Josie, stayed there a moment, and then settled back on me. "Seth, this is... unexpected."

"I know," I replied, meeting his gaze. "We need to talk."

The Dean of the Covenant stared at me for a moment and then he glanced at Josie. A long moment passed. "Yes. We do."

CHAPTER
17

WITH WIDE unblinking eyes, I watched the elegant-looking man who was almost as tall as Seth pivot around on the heel of a polished loafer. "Follow me," he ordered.

And he didn't wait for us. Nodding to the man with a scar on his face, he kept walking, thankfully bypassing a huge spiral staircase I knew I would never be able to climb, since right now I felt like lying down in a fetal position and not moving for a month.

Every muscle ached and burned, and my body throbbed as I trudged along beside Seth, grateful when the very unhappy-looking people in all black kept their distance as they followed us through the absolutely awe-inspiring lobby.

I focused on the intricate designs etched into every square inch of the building, instead of letting my mind wander back to Missouri. If I did, I *would* be in that fetal position and I wouldn't get out of it. Part of my heart had been shattered in Osborn, and I gathered every cord of strength I had in me to hold it together. So I focused on the drawings of tall men and women wearing togas, on the beautiful writing that had to be an ancient language, and on all the glossy white statues.

I'd never seen anything in my life like this, not even in museums.

The man crossed under another archway, down a narrow hallway, and then we entered a brightly lit common room with a large sofa and several armchairs. The scarred man followed, closing the door behind us before leaning against a wall that looked like sandstone.

Seth dropped our bags on the floor by the door, and I stopped. Dead on my feet, I swayed a little as the stranger moved to the center of the room, crossing his arms over his chest as he watched us.

Reaching down, Seth took my hand and led me to the couch, never taking his eyes off the men, but there was no missing the surprise that flickered across the older man's face when his gaze dropped to our joined hands.

"Sit," Seth said in a soft voice.

I was not going to argue with that. The moment my butt hit the thick cushions, it thanked me. Seth didn't sit. He stood beside me, arms also folded. For a moment, the three of them engaged in some kind of weird stare-off, and it didn't take a genius to figure out there was some history there. Not a good history, but I was too tired, too whipped, and just...too numb to even care.

Then the older man looked at me, and I knew he stared at my neck. The neckline of the sweater had been stretched in my pitiful fight with Hyperion, revealing the tag. I must've looked a mess, but I also didn't care about that. He softened his hard expression with a slight curve of his lips. "We haven't been introduced." His voice was deep, cultured. "I'm Marcus Andros, the Dean of this University, and you are...?"

I resisted the urge to glance at Seth, because I couldn't rely on him at this point. He'd made it clear earlier that he was leaving as soon as we got here, and we were here now.

Clasping my hands together to keep them from shaking, I shoved them between my knees. "My name is Josie Bethel, and I'm..." My brows knitted. "I'm not quite sure what I am."

His brows inched up his forehead as he glanced at Seth. The man with the scar chuckled softly and said, "Honey, I don't think any of us quite know who we are, but that's probably the strangest introduction I've heard in a while."

Seth stiffened. "I do believe she said her name was 'Josie,' and not 'honey,' the last time I checked, Solos."

The man with the scar, who I assumed was Solos, laughed again, but it was Marcus who almost looked thunderstruck as he stared at Seth, who appeared as if he was on the verge of throwing someone through a wall.

I shifted and winced when a dart of pain shot down my leg. My patience with—*with everything*—started to slip. "He brought me here because he was ordered to do so. It's his job."

Seth's head swung toward me and his golden brows knitted as his eyes narrowed. What had I said to earn that look? Only the truth, so whatever. I bounced my knee, ignoring the licks of dull pain that shot up my leg.

"May I ask why?" Marcus sat in a leather chair across from us. "I'm assuming you know what we are, based on your...condition." There was a pause. "No offense, Josie, but I cannot fathom why he would bring you here."

"Because she's not mortal," Seth replied, and boy, the room got so quiet I could've heard a cricket hiccup.

Marcus blinked as he shook his head. "Seth, she isn't one of us."

"I didn't say that she was, but thanks for pointing out the obvious," he replied, and white lines formed around Marcus's mouth. "She isn't one of us. She's completely different."

Solos arched a brow. "You gonna give us details or drag this out as long as possible?"

I thought for a second that Seth was going to wing something at Solos's head, maybe one of those sharp blades, but he sat beside me, so close that his entire leg pressed against mine. "Are you all aware of what happened with the Titans?"

Across from us, Marcus straightened. "Of course. And we've taken the necessary steps to ensure that our students and those here are safe, and not only from them."

Seth smirked. "Message received," he replied, and I had no idea what that meant. "So you're warded against the Titans."

He nodded. "We are, but what does this have to do with her?"

I wondered how you could ward against something as powerful and scary as Hyperion. Probably involved the blood of a dozen virgins or something equally archaic and creepy.

Seth leaned forward, meeting the brightest green eyes I've ever seen, and then he dropped the bomb. "Josie is Apollo's daughter. She's a demigod."

Marcus and Solos swung their gazes on me. Both men's eyes were wide, and they stared at me like I had suddenly morphed into a three-headed dragon. "No," Marcus said. "There aren't any demigods on Earth, and anyway, we would sense her if she was one. What kind of–?"

"Her powers are bound, Marcus. That's why you don't sense her. And she's not the only one," Seth explained as he reached over, clamping his hand on my knee, stilling it.

"Sorry," I muttered, casting my gaze to his hand. As Seth started talking again, explaining to our rapt audience what I was, how many of us there were, and all of that good stuff, he kept his hand on my knee. I stared at the long, elegant fingers. Graceful, but deadly.

The weight of his hand made me feel funny, and I didn't like it at the same time I acknowledged there was something comforting about the pressure, almost grounding.

"Gods," Marcus murmured, drawing my attention to him. He was still staring at me. "A demigod–a born demigod. Never thought I'd be around to see that."

I squirmed uncomfortably, and Seth removed his hand. "Apollo told me to bring her here. She needs to be kept safe, Marcus, until the rest of the demigods can be located."

The next breath I took hitched. Why did I care if I was just a job to Seth? It wasn't like he was Erin, but for some reason, knowing that he'd also been ordered to be a part of my life, no matter how brief, also stung like I'd walked into a nest of hornets.

"Yes." He blinked, looking away for a moment before his gaze moved right back to me. "She's very important."

This was getting really awkward, but at least he wasn't kicking me out on my butt. I needed to use this to my advantage. "I want to be trained," I announced, and yep, everyone was really staring at me again, including Seth. "Like the...the Sentinels. Can you do that while I'm here?"

Marcus sat back as he rubbed two fingers over his brow. "Trained?" He glanced at Seth and then shook his head. "Josie, our Sentinels are trained from—"

"From the age of eight. I know, but I got my butt handed to me twice—when we ran into daimons, and then Hyperion. I couldn't do anything as those...those things bit into me like I was a cheeseburger. Then Hyperion handled me like I was a ragdoll. And he used these things...these shades to kill my—" My voice cracked, and I swallowed hard. "To kill my grandparents, and I couldn't do anything. I'm absolutely helpless if he gets in here."

"Josie—" Seth started.

"You're planning on leaving, but that doesn't mean there isn't someone here that can help me." I turned my gaze to the Dean. "Please. What can it hurt? If not, I'm just going to be sitting around, right? I can't do that. I can't just sit here. I have to do something. *Please*." And then I laid the only cards I had on the table. It was a crappy thing to do, but I had no choice. "If you can't do it, then I can't stay here."

Seth whipped toward me, eyes narrowing into angry amber slits. "You *are* staying here."

"No one can watch me twenty-four hours a day. I'm smart. I'll find my way out." I met his glare with my own. "If no one can do this, then I'm out. And wouldn't that suck, being how *important* I am?"

His mouth opened as he stared at me. "I didn't just bring you halfway across the United States, get you to a place that is safe, for you to do something as incredibly stupid as threaten to leave. Do you have a death wish?"

"Do you?" I shot back.

He cocked his head to the side. "That response doesn't even make sense."

"Whatever," I snapped, crossing my arms. "I don't even like you and I didn't ask for your opinion."

"You're going to get my opinion, like it or not, Joe." His eyes flashed a bright tawny color. "You're not going to risk your life because you're not getting your way."

"Why do you even care?" I shouted, throwing my hands up. "Seriously? So shut up, *Sethie*."

Seth drew back as the cut line of his jaw hardened. "You test my patience."

"Children," Marcus murmured tiredly.

I tested *his*? "You make me want to nunchuck you in the throat! But I can't. Because I don't know how to use nunchucks!"

His lips twitched, and I swore, if he laughed, I was going to physically hurt him with my bare hands. "Sentinels don't use nunchucks, Josie."

"I've used nunchucks before," Solos commented.

Seth cast him a long look. "Seriously? Not helping."

The Sentinel shrugged, but he was grinning, and not even trying to hide it.

"Then can you help me?" I asked the man. I wasn't picky.

Seth turned on me. "He is *not* training you."

"Stop interjecting yourself where you don't belong!" I all but shrieked.

Solos made a deep, gruff sound. "Gods..."

A strange looked crossed Marcus's handsome face. "You two remind me of..." He trailed off, shaking his head, and Seth cursed under his breath. "Well, it doesn't matter." Standing, he looked at me. "We'll talk more about this tomorrow, Josie. Right now, it looks like you could use some rest."

I pushed myself to my feet and bit down on my lip as my muscles protested the movement. "We talk about the training now."

"For gods' sake," Seth muttered, shoving to his feet. "You have no idea how hard training is, Josie. I don't even think you can do it."

Something ugly and hot twisted in my chest. "Again, I didn't ask for your opinion."

Rolling his eyes, he shook his head. "This is getting repetitive."

"No shit." Then I flushed as I glanced at Marcus.

He stared at me, and I felt my resolve start to crack a little. I wasn't a ballsy person. More like go with the flow, so it took a lot for me to stand there under his sharp, emerald gaze. But then he smiled, and it wasn't a big smile, never reaching his eyes. "You remind me of my niece," he said, and a burst of tension exploded off Seth. "I hope you two get to meet one day. I think you'll like her."

"Uh, okay." And just like that, whatever energy I had left in me seeped out. My shoulders slumped. I was so tired, absolutely spent.

"We'll find someone to train you," Marcus continued, and I almost ran up and hugged the man, but he didn't look like a hugger and it felt like that would get real awkward real quick, so I held myself back.

"Thank you," I said, feeling a measure of relief. "Really. Thank you."

He nodded as he looked at Seth. "We'll talk more tomorrow. With that being said…" His gaze shifted from Seth and he eyed me with a mixture of awe and a measure of distrust. "Welcome to the Covenant."

Anger reverberated through every inch of my being, and I wasn't sure if it was directed at the now-quiet Josie, at Solos who was leading us to the dorms, or at myself.

Irritated on so many different levels, I ignored every attempt Solos made to make conversation, and he finally gave up by the time we crossed another courtyard. And I ignored the outright curious looks from the students when we entered the lobby of the first dorm.

Pures and halfs were actually huddled *together* around the couches and under the big-screen TV hanging from the ceiling. Josie must've been out of it, because she wasn't paying attention to them or to the few Sentinels stationed in the lobby. I kept her close to my side whether she liked it or not. The students stared openly. They knew what I was, but they had no idea what Josie was. Josie would be a mystery to them, and they would be nosy, and she really didn't need that right now.

Solos walked down one of the wide hallways on the lower level, passing several closed doors. "These are the suites we use for guests." At the end of the hall, he stopped. "These two rooms, across from each other, are empty. Have your pick." He smiled at Josie, and my hand tightened around the strap of the bag I carried. When he looked at me, the fucker laughed under his breath. "You can have whatever room for however long you plan on staying."

I said nothing.

He laughed again as he turned to Josie. "I'll come for you in the late morning, give you enough time to rest up, and then I'll take you to see Marcus."

She nodded. "Okay."

"If you need anything, find any of the people in black and they'll get me, okay? Like you heard, my name is Solos."

When she nodded again, I was this close to knocking him upside the head with the bag. She turned to the door to her right and Solos handed her one of the keys. Murmuring her thanks, she opened the door and disappeared inside. I caught it before it slammed shut, cracking it open.

I looked at Solos, meeting his dark gaze. "She won't need anything."

176

Solos cocked a brow. "Because you're here? Sounded like you're leaving." Before I could reply to that, he clapped his hand on my shoulder. "Seth, she's a little too young for me. Chill."

What the fuck? I didn't get a chance to respond to that either, because he continued on, "But, man, if what you said is true about her being Apollo's daughter, you've got the biggest balls known to man. Have fun with that."

With that, he turned and made his way down the hall. I stood there for a moment, wanting to pretend like I had no idea what he was talking about. Gods, I hadn't pissed a circle around Josie, marking my territory, but I couldn't have been more obvious.

So, yeah, what the fuck?

Pushing open the door, I entered the room and left it open behind me. The room was bigger and nicer than the one she'd had back in Virginia. My kind spared no expense when it came to furnishings and living arrangements. A small living area, complete with a loveseat, coffee table, and kitchen nook, led into a bedroom large enough to fit a full-sized bed and a dresser. There was even a bathroom and a walk-in closet.

I dropped the bags in the living area as I stopped just outside the bedroom. She stood in front of the neatly made bed, staring at a painting on the wall. I looked, and any other time I would've laughed.

It was of her father.

Apollo.

And it was a rendering of him in his true form—wearing white pants, head full of hair so blond it was almost white. In one hand was a golden harp. There was no way anyone seeing her standing there near that painting couldn't see some of the shared characteristics.

I had no idea what was going through her head right then.

Her wide eyes met mine for a moment, and then she turned her cheek. The side of her neck was exposed again.

That fucking daimon had tagged her, leaving behind a crescent-shaped wound that would eventually fade to a scar a shade paler than her normal skin tone.

Tagged her in the same spot Alex had been tagged—Alexandria Andros, Marcus's niece. The other Apollyon—the one who *was* supposed to exist. The girl I had helped train once it was discovered what she was. And the girl I'd given up the rest of my life for so she could spend hers with the man she loved.

It had been a long time since I'd let myself really think about her, really allowed any thought concerning her follow through. It wasn't because she'd broken my heart or picked someone else over me. I'd cared for her—as much as I'd been able to care for anyone back then. No. Not being able to think about her had nothing to do with the brief relationship we'd had.

It had everything to do with how badly I had screwed her over.

I had no idea why I was thinking about this now or allowing myself to do so. Maybe it served as a reminder to get the hell out of here, because when I looked at Josie, I couldn't help but think history was on repeat.

Here was yet another girl who had a fate laid out before her that she never chose, and I knew, when gods were concerned, she could fight that fate all she wanted, but it wouldn't change a damn thing. Her life was on autopilot. And with me involved, that autopilot was set to crash and burn. She didn't *need* me in her life, and if she knew everything about me, she wouldn't want me there.

I needed to leave. Right now. Go ahead and get back on the road before Apollo appeared and I ended up stuck here. But it was more than that. I needed to leave before it got to the point that I *didn't want* to leave.

So I should have been turning away and walking right out that fucking door. Saying goodbye. Wishing her good luck. She was going to need it, and then some.

Turning away, my hand curled on the frame of the door. My heart pounded in my chest as I closed my eyes and pushed it shut. A moment passed and then I pivoted around and crossed the few feet between us. Without saying a word, I took her hand and led her into the bathroom.

She needed to be cleaned up.

And I wasn't leaving.

MY HEART was somewhere in the vicinity of my throat as Seth led me into the bathroom. I had no idea what he was doing, but his hand was making me feel warm and weird again. He sat me down on the closed toilet, and I felt like we'd been here before.

Oh yeah, we had been.

"What...what are you doing?" I asked.

Kneeling down, he was staring at our joined hands, his brows furrowed together, and even though fifteen minutes ago we were arguing and I was threatening to nunchuck him in the throat, he was holding my hand like it was the most fragile thing in the world. "What is the real reason why you want to learn how to fight, Josie?"

The question caught me off-guard, and then he looked up, and he was staring right into my eyes, like he could see inside me. There were a lot of reasons why I wanted to train. I'd been helpless back there. It was something to focus on when *everything* had either been pulled out from underneath me or destroyed right in front of me.

I took a deep breath and I gave him the main reason, the one that sucked to say out loud. "I don't want to be afraid, and I'm scared to death. If I can fight, I won't be so afraid."

His amber eyes flared brightly for a moment, and then he placed my hand on my knee. Letting go, he rose fluidly. "You'll still be afraid, Josie."

Well, that was helpful. "I thought you were leaving."

He reached over my head, grabbing a hand towel. "You sound eager to get rid of me now."

Pressing my lips together, I said nothing at first, because that was far from the truth. I didn't want him to leave, but I couldn't stop him from going. I shook my head. "You don't need to do this..." I waved my hand, indicating the bathroom. "I'm fine. I can clean myself up."

"Are you wearing anything under that sweater?" he asked, ignoring me.

"Um..." I swallowed. "Yeah, a tank top. Why?"

He shifted, turning on the faucet. "Take it off."

"What?" My voice pitched high.

With the damp towel in hand, he was kneeling in front of me again. "I need to look at your neck again. It was bleeding earlier. You wouldn't let me do it on the road, so let me do it now," he said, and I opened my mouth to tell him hell to the no, but he spoke again. "Please."

I don't know why that single word held so much power over me, but it did, and besides, I wasn't naked underneath. Grabbing the hem, I tugged the ruined sweater over my head, flinching at the movements. I dropped it on the floor.

Seth's gaze stayed on my face before dipping to my neck. His lips parted in a rough exhale. I clasped my hands again as he slipped a finger under the thin strap of my cami. I jerked when he grazed my skin. The soft caress rippled over my body in a way that was kind of embarrassing.

He halted, his gaze flicking to mine. "Did I hurt you?"

My cheeks heated. There was something wrong with me. The last thing I should have been feeling was any kind of arousal. "No," I whispered.

He held my gaze a moment longer, and then gently placed the towel against my neck, where Hyperion's nails had sliced into my skin. It didn't hurt, but I had to hold myself still. "My last name is Diodoros."

I blinked. "Dio-what?"

A soft laugh came from him as he tossed the dirtied towel into the tub and wet a fresh one. "Diodoros."

I had no idea how to even begin to spell it, but somehow I knew not many people in this world, if any, knew this about him. It was in the way he said it, his voice gruff and raw. He was sharing something personal, and he'd chosen me to share that with. I didn't know why, but I wanted to cherish that fact, hold it close.

"You know what it means in Greek? 'Gift of Zeus,'" he continued, sliding the towel to the top of my cami, wiping up dried blood and dirt. "That's the height of irony."

My breath caught as the cloth dipped lower than my shoulder, the edges brushing over the swell of my breast, and thank God I had a bra on under the cami, because I could feel my nipples hardening, and that was just beyond embarrassing. It had to be the trauma of today. Okay. That was an excuse.

"Why?" I finally asked.

"Because I'm more like a pain in the ass to Zeus than a gift." He sighed, rocking back on his heels as he lifted his gaze. "The cuts aren't deep and he didn't tag you like the daimons did, but I saw him. He was going for your *aether* too. Did you feel anything?"

"It hurt." The reminder of how that felt grounded my butt back in reality. "Like he was pulling something out from deep inside me, just as bad as when the daimons got me."

He said nothing as he moved the towel along my face, wiping up what felt like a week's worth of dirt. Then he tossed the second towel and took my hand again. Hauling me up, he placed his other hand on my hip when I stumbled. A heartbeat passed as our gazes locked.

We were standing toe to toe in the bathroom, barely any space between us. His chin was tipped down and mine stretched up. It felt like we were about to dance, which was silly to imagine. I don't know why I did what I did next, but it seemed natural to do so, and I was so tired, so emotionally spent, that I didn't really think about it.

Closing my eyes, I leaned in and rested my cheek against his chest, right above his heart. Seth stiffened like he'd turned into one of those marble statues I'd seen earlier. His chest rose sharply, and I held my breath, waiting for him to shove me away.

But he didn't.

Seth's hand slipped off my hip and made its way to the center of my back. He also dropped my hand, loosely circling his arm around my shoulders. My breath hitched as I placed my hands on his waist. A long moment passed and he dropped his chin to the top of my head, and while that seemed like it wasn't a big deal, my chest squeezed.

His arms tightened just a fraction as he cleared his throat. "One of the first things they teach you when you're training is to never let your opponent get a good grip on you or get you on your back."

A shiver rolled down my spine. "The daimons got me on my back. Hyperion...well, he didn't get me on my back. He sort of just lifted me up with one hand."

"And there's that." His hand slid up, tangling in my hair as his fingers curled around the nape of my neck. "I'm going to train you."

At first I didn't think I heard him correctly. I started to pull back, but he held onto me. "What?"

"I don't know if your father will show up and send me off somewhere else," he continued as if I hadn't spoken. "If he does, I won't be able to deny him."

My mind was racing. "Why?"

"Doesn't matter. These are my rules if you want me to train you. You have to agree to listen to me and not to whine when it

183

gets hard, because it *will* get hard, Josie. You think your body hurts now? You haven't seen anything yet. You're going to hurt. You're going to want to stop, but you're not going to be able to." He pulled my head back, and our eyes met. "I'm going to own you through this process."

Own me? Um, well, that didn't sound right, and I shivered again, which also wasn't right.

He continued. "But, most importantly, you have to trust me. Can you agree to all of that?"

"Yes," I said immediately. "I can agree to that."

His gaze held me in those amber depths a moment longer, and then he stepped back, slipping his hands off me in a slow slide that got yet another shiver out of me. "We'll start tomorrow, then."

"Tomorrow," I whispered, nodding. "You're staying then."

"I'm staying."

I had no idea what made him change his mind, but I didn't push it, because I wanted him to be the one to train me. Even though he was a puzzle I probably had no hope of figuring out, I *did* trust him.

Seth started to turn, but I reached out, grabbing his arm. His skin was so warm and tight under mine. His gaze flicked to where I held him. "Will you stay?" I asked.

One eyebrow rose as he raised his gaze to mine. "You want to use me as a body pillow again."

He got what I wanted without me really having to say it. I nodded once more, even though it was more than the fact that he made an awesome pillow. As needy as it sounded, I just didn't want to be alone right then. I didn't want him to leave. I wanted him there.

A half-grin appeared on Seth's face. "Come on then. I'm tired. Tomorrow is going to be a long day."

Seth left the bathroom, and I hesitated for a moment, squeezing my eyes shut against the raw rush of emotions that swirled inside me like a tornado. Tears pricked my eyes, but I willed them back down. Once I had it all in check, I opened up my eyes and I saw myself in the oval mirror above the vanity.

With skin pale and dark smudges under tired eyes, I looked haggard. I looked messed-up with my hair in knots and my neck shredded. The crescent-shaped bite mark was red. My stomach dipped as residual adrenaline pulsed through me before quickly evaporating. I swallowed hard, my gaze tracing over my own familiar features.

Looking in the mirror, I saw...I saw *me*. Other than looking like I'd gotten run over by a truck and trapped in a wind tunnel, I looked like me, but I wasn't *me* anymore. Like I had said to Marcus, I wasn't quite sure what I was, and that showed in my eyes.

You'll be whoever you want to be, baby.

My throat constricted. That was something my granny had said to me when I had brought home college applications. Back then, it had been all about choosing a career, not something that sounded like destiny or fate, which was what it felt like now.

Thinking of my granny hurt, and I couldn't deal, because all of that was too fresh and it was something training couldn't fix, something I couldn't go back in time and change, and that...that I *wasn't* ready to face.

I stared at my reflection for a moment longer, and then I pushed away from the sink, shutting it all down. Tuning it out and turning it off.

Seth was standing where I'd stood earlier. His gaze drifted over me. "You okay?"

Taking a deep breath, I nodded. "Yeah."

He tilted his head to the side, a small smile gracing his lips, and it was kind of sad. "You're still a terrible liar."

I was.

Seth had left to clean up in the room across from mine, and I had done the same thing while he was gone, scrubbing the rest of the funk off me. Leaving the door unlocked, I'd climbed into the surprisingly comfortable bed, rolled onto my side, and turned off the light. If I hadn't, I would've stared at the painting of what had to be Apollo, and that would've wigged me out more than it already did.

So it was dark when I heard the door open, and like a doofus, I'd held my breath as Seth strolled into the bedroom. He'd gone to the other side of the bed first, and then had stopped. Pivoting around, he'd walked over to the painting of Apollo and had muttered something under his breath before he'd taken it down and placed it against the wall.

"Sorry," he'd said as he'd turned toward the bed. "Really don't want to fall asleep with his freaky-ass eyes on me."

I'd laughed, and it had been a light and strange sound after everything. Nothing was said after that point. Seth had gotten into the bed, shifted onto his side, and I'd felt his warm breath on the back of my neck. I didn't think that I could fall asleep with everything crashing around in my head, but I did.

And when I woke up, I was sprawled across Seth. It was ridiculous. Really. My head was on his chest, my arm on his abs, and my leg was thrust between his, pressing on a very interesting part of him. It was like I was trying to become one with him or something, but he also had one arm around me, his hand resting on my hip, *under the covers*, and the other was curved around my forearm.

I didn't dare move, since he was still asleep, his chest rising and falling steadily, and his heart beating under my cheek. There was something surreal about lying in his arms like this. I'd always thought it was something people did when they were in a relationship, the whole cuddling thing, but it made me feel that strange warmness again. It also made me feel a lot of other things, like his defined chest under my cheek. And those hard abs under my arm. I couldn't help it. Every part of me was hyperaware of how my body was plastered to his. He was just so long and lean, and as I lay there, I didn't think about all the dark and terrible things that were waiting at the edges of my consciousness, ready to pounce and push sorrow through me like dirty, messy slush.

The hand on my waist suddenly flexed, and my eyes widened. Was he awake? The answer came when his hand slowly slid to my hip and his fingers splayed. A ripple of tingles spread across my body, centering between my thighs. I squeezed my eyes shut, but it did nothing to stop the sudden pounding of my pulse in all the interesting areas. I should move and definitely get off him before...well, before my hormones started to climb out of my body and do a little jig on top of us. I shifted, straightening my leg, and the hand on my hip tightened, as did the one on my arm.

"*Josie*," Seth said, his voice gruff with sleep and something else, something more raw and rough.

For a moment I didn't understand, but then I felt *him* against the inside of my leg, the one between his. Holy crappers, I really did *feel* him. My eyes popped open, and I started to move, but the hand on my hip stopped me. It didn't just still me, but pressed me against his hip, and the contact sent a jolt through me. I squirmed, and that only made the feeling stronger. No. It wasn't just a *feeling*. I knew what it was. Arousal. Want. Desire. Lust. Whatever. I'd felt it before, many times before, and it made my breath reedy, and my body acted out of instinct, not common sense. I moved my hips forward and was rewarded—or maybe punished—by the acute rolling of sensations that started at my core and undulated through me.

"If you keep moving around, this is going to get super-awkward," he rasped, voice husky and shivery.

My mouth dried because I felt him swell and thicken against my thigh. Heat burned my cheeks, partly due to embarrassment, but also due to the slow fire that had started building in my veins. I was stunned by the intensity of what I was feeling. I'd liked guys before, even wanted them, but I'd never felt *this* strongly.

"Or maybe not awkward," he drawled as he moved that hand on my hip, sliding it up to my waist, creating tiny coils in the pit of my belly. His hand halted, as if he was testing me, his thumb barely brushing the underswell of my breast. "Maybe something totally different."

I didn't know what to say, nor did I get the chance. A startled gasp parted my lips as Seth rolled. I was on my back in a heartbeat, and Seth was above me, his powerful arms on either side of my head.

The next breath I took lodged in my throat. His hair was loose, curving around his cheeks as he stared down at me. "What are we doing, Josie?"

Heart pounding, I forced my breathing to slow. "I don't know."

"You don't? I think you do."

Nervous energy rushed me, mixing with that burn in my veins. The tip of my tongue darted out, wetting my lips, and his eyes drifted shut, as a large shudder seemed to roll through him. When his lashes lifted, his gaze was as scorching as the summer sun.

"We shouldn't do this." Even as he spoke those words, his lower body settled on mine. "We shouldn't be doing anything like this."

Every muscle in my body tensed at the weight and feel of him. My hands settled on his shoulders as his forehead dipped to mine. Air around us thickened as my heart threatened to tear itself out of my chest. I recalled when he'd said in the hotel room outside of St. Louis that I should feel lucky he wasn't caving in to what he wanted, but I didn't feel lucky then, and I sure as hell didn't feel it now.

I gathered whatever courage I had inside of me. "Why not?"

"Several reasons," he said, shifting his body, and suddenly the hardest part of him was pressing against the softest part of me.

I wasn't prepared for that or how my body would react. I dampened. I *ached*. The long shirt—*his* shirt—that I wore, my undies, and the thin material of his sleep pants were a frail barrier between us, but, at the same time, it was too much. My fingers gathered the material of his shirt as I clutched his broad shoulders.

"Your father would have my balls if I got between those pretty legs." His voice was deep and rough as he spoke, his breath warm against my parted lips. "But, you know what? Losing my balls would be worth it."

"I can't believe we're talking about balls."

"Seems relevant, don't you think?"

My lips curved into a smile. "Yeah...yeah, it kind of does."

"Mmm..." His head tilted and the ends of his hair dragged over my cheek. "Gods, I can't even believe I'm going to say this, but you've been through a lot. Dealing with that can make you think you want things you really don't." A look of surprise flickered across his striking face as he lifted his head, like he'd actually shocked himself.

For some dumb reason, that made my chest all squishy, because he was *thinking* of me, and well, that had to mean something, right? "You're a...you're a good guy, Seth, when you want to be."

He stared at me for a moment, and then laughed outright.

"But I know what I want and what I don't want," I continued, feeling a flush travel down my throat.

There was an electricity-filled moment before he spoke. "Do you?"

I did. Right or wrong, I really did, and I didn't care about what the driving force behind it was. I didn't want to investigate that too closely, to poke and prod at it. I couldn't find the words, because my bravery had disappeared as my inexperience took center stage. I'd kissed boys before, but I'd never been in a bed with an unbelievably gorgeous guy who was a complete mystery to me, and I felt clumsy, naïve even, but I wanted him to kiss me. I *needed* him to.

Drawing my leg up the side of his, the movement settled him closer, deeper, and there was a burst of fiery sensation. A low, sultry groan rose from the depths of Seth, and there was an answering rush of warmth in response. This was crazy, but it was going to happen. I saw it in the way his golden eyes burned bright with need.

"You're going to regret this," Seth said, and before I could process what those words meant, he dipped his head. Those well-formed lips of his swept over mine, as light as a feather, once and then twice. My grip tightened. His head slanted, and I—

A *thump* thudded off the dorm door, jarring us out of the heady daze. I jerked back, pressing my head against the pillow as Seth lifted his and swore as he cast a damn near deadly look in that general direction.

The knock came again, louder and more insistent this time, sounding like cops were about to burst through the door. I cleared my throat. "Maybe it's Marcus? He said we needed to talk today."

"It's early." Seth shifted off me, and I lowered my hands to my sides, feeling hot and cold as he rose from the bed and looked at me. The fire still smoldered in his gaze, but his jaw was tight. His gaze dipped to my chest. A muscle popped along his jaw. "Stay in here."

Pressing my lips together, I sat up and tugged on my shirt. He rounded the bed easily, heading into the little living area, and I scooted forward, wondering if I had time to find an oven and go shove my head inside. Nope. I heard the door open.

And then I heard Seth say, "Dammit."

Lips pursing, I started to strain forward, but an unfamiliar voice froze me. "So it's true," a guy said. "Everyone was all like 'the Apollyon is here,' and there was a lot of excitement. I didn't believe that Seth the awesome Apollyon would dare grace our steps again."

"It's true," came another unknown male voice, and my eyes widened as I started to yank the blanket up to my throat. "Everyone is talking about it. We had to see for ourselves."

"Yeah, I'm here. You've seen me," Seth replied. "Now you can go—"

"But the thing is," the second guy spoke again. "Solos told us you were in the room across the hall. We knocked. You didn't answer. So Luke got the key."

"You got the key?" Seth asked. "Yeah, can I have that key?" There was a pause. "Thanks."

"*Anyway*," the guy I assumed wasn't Luke said. "We knocked on this door and you answered."

"Thanks for the blow-by-blow description of what just happened," Seth replied dryly.

"And we also heard you didn't show up here alone," the guy named Luke chimed in. "All the peeps are talking, Seth, saying you brought a *mortal* here."

"So, of course, we're here," the other guy added. "Because we need to see this."

What the...?

I started to ninja-jump off the bed and dive into the bathroom, but I heard Seth's very loud and very exasperated sigh right before he said, "Whatever. This was going to happen sooner or later, so come in."

Come in?

My eyes nearly popped out of my head, but I had no time to do anything. A second later, two very tall and very good-looking guys steamrolled into the bedroom.

They stared at me.

I stared at them.

One of them had bronze-colored hair that was artfully messy, and he was dressed in a long-sleeved black shirt and dark blue jeans. He was built—huge arms, an obviously toned stomach—and he looked like he knew a thousand ways to kill someone.

The other was more slender, had a head full of blond curls and the most startling gray eyes I'd ever seen. He was wearing plaid pajama bottoms and a deep-blue V-neck sweater. He was already grinning, but it spread into a wide smile. "Hey there."

I glanced over to where Seth looked like he wanted to bang his head against the wall. "Hey."

The blond continued to smile, while his friend continued to stare at me.

Seth sighed again. "The one grinning like he's crazy is Deacon, and the other one is Luke."

"We're *friends* of his–of Seth's," Deacon threw in, and Seth did not look like they were friends.

"This is Josie," Seth continued. "Please don't be weird and scare her."

"Be weird?" Deacon rolled those gray eyes. "Ha. Whatever, dude. All you need to know about me is that I'm like a dolphin in a sea of less-smart fish," he announced, spreading his arms with a flourish.

Luke turned to him slowly as his eyebrows inched up his forehead. "What?"

He shrugged. "Just saying I have a lot in common with dolphins. They're smart. I'm smart."

Seth rubbed his hand down his face.

There was a beat of silence, and then Luke sighed and shook his head, lips twitching. "It's a good thing I think you're fine as hell."

As unbelievable as it sounded, Deacon's smile stretched even further as he turned to look at me. "We're together."

"Oh," I said, glancing between the two. "You two make a great couple."

"We know," he replied.

Luke folded his arms. A moment passed. "You have awesome hair."

"Um..." I raised one hand, smoothing it down. This was *so* weird. "Thanks."

Deacon's smile started to slip a little as he eyed me. Then it was like chess pieces moving on a board. He took a step toward the bed, and I locked up, and Seth shifted closer. Luke got between Seth and Deacon, who seemed oblivious to all of them. Then, Deacon's eyes narrowed as he stared at me. "Your eyes are *really* familiar."

192

Tension eased out of Seth as he sat on the edge of the bed. A slight smile pulled at his lips as he looked up at the two guys. "Oh, this is going to be great once you put it together." He leaned back, his elbows pressing into my legs, and he chuckled. "I cannot wait."

I had no idea what was going on, and Luke looked just as confused, but Deacon... His lips were moving, but no words were coming out, and then he drew back, straightening as if someone had dropped a steel rod down his spine.

"Holy shit," he said, paling.

Seth tipped his head back, laughing deeply—laughing so hard I wanted to knee him in the back.

"What?" demanded Luke.

Deacon shook his head slowly. "It's not possible."

"Oh, yes, it is," replied Seth.

"What?" I repeated.

Luke unfolded his arms, turning a pointed stare on Deacon. "Yeah, you want to let us in on whatever is going on here?"

"Her eyes... I know those eyes. Like, I *really* know those eyes." Deacon thrust a hand through those wild curls. "They're the same as..."

"As Apollo's," Seth filled in for him. "When the son of a bitch actually has eyes."

Luke's brows flew up again. "Wait. You're not saying..." He laughed, but it sounded strangled. "She can't be..."

Since I figured that Seth must trust these two dudes, I decided to get to the point. "Apollo's supposedly my... He's like my dad or something. My demigod...whatever is bound, so everyone thinks I'm...mortal. And Seth's...he's going to train me." All of this was so incredibly awkward.

"Yes," agreed Seth. "To all of that."

"Holy. Shit." Blood rushed to Deacon's cheeks.

Seth chuckled again, and I still didn't get what was so funny. "Needless to say, Josie here is very important, and not everyone

193

on this campus needs to know who or what she is. So, you two keep your mouths shut."

"Doable," Luke murmured, and then he knelt down, shaking his head. "A fucking demigod? Wow. That's...well, that was unexpected, Seth. Leave it to you to surprise the hell out of me."

Seth grunted.

Deacon was a statue. "Holy. Shit. Balls."

I glanced at him, starting to get worried.

"Wait," Luke said, frowning. "If she's Apollo's daughter, wouldn't that mean in some weird way, she's related to—"

"I think Deacon's going to pass out," Seth cut in smoothly while I was wondering who else I could be related to. I wasn't sure if I wanted to know.

Luke looked over his shoulder and rolled his eyes. "Dude, chill. It's not like you slept with *her*."

"Wait. What?" I said, distracted.

Deacon bobbed his head. "Yeah, that's a good point."

A chuckle rumbled from Seth, and he tipped his head back so he was looking at me. "When I said your daddy got around, I wasn't exaggerating."

I stared at Seth for a moment, then looked at Deacon, and then put two and two together. Whoa. "My *father* slept with you?"

Deacon winced as he shrugged. "I wouldn't say we slept together. I seriously had no idea who he was, and he was all about free love, and so was I, and the next thing I know, the dude I'd fooled around with turned out to be Apollo, and well... Shit gets kind of awkward sometimes."

"I can imagine," I murmured.

Seth snorted. "You have no idea."

"How old is Apollo?" I asked.

Luke chuckled as he rose. "Depends on how he wants to look, but even in his true form," he said, shrugging, "he looks like he's in his late twenties. He's hot. But that's probably gross to you."

"Of course he's hot." Deacon rolled his eyes. "It's not like I'm going to get with someone who isn't, but anyway." He turned to Seth and took a deep breath. "I'm glad you're here, because I never got to thank you."

And just like that, the amusement disappeared and Seth tensed up. "That's not necessary, man."

"No, it is. It's really necessary. I know what you did for my brother. I know what it *means* for *you*," Deacon rushed on, and now I was even more confused than before. "So, thank you."

Seth said nothing as he focused his gaze on the wall, and silence poured into the room. The tension was thick, and while I was as curious as a bored cat, I didn't like the sudden stiffness to his shoulders. I liked it when he was laughing.

"So," I said, drawing out the word. "My father can change the way he looks?"

"Oh, yeah. He can pretty much do anything," Luke said, and the corners of his lips tipped up, and I smiled back, mostly out of relief. "Also has this horrible habit of popping in at the most inopportune times."

"I second that." Seth sat up.

Deacon plopped down on the end of the bed, tilting his head to the side as he grinned at me. "The whole hooking up with your dad thing aside, I can't believe I'm sitting on a bed with an Apollyon and a bound demigod."

"It's like the start of a bad joke," Luke said. He grinned as he reached out, patting my blanket-covered leg. "My life just got so much more interesting."

CHAPTER

19

A **TINY** bit of guilt pricked at me for leaving Josie alone with Luke and Deacon. One of them alone could be a lot to deal with, but two of them were something else, something overwhelming.

I cracked a grin, imagining Josie at the moment. Those eyes— eyes I'd never thought were beautiful before, but I sure as fuck thought so now—were probably wide, and that pretty mouth was also probably hanging open.

But I trusted these guys, the four of them—Solos, Marcus, and those two. And before I had ducked out, knowing I needed to chat with Marcus alone, I had pulled Luke outside and reminded him of two things: that Josie *was* important and she needed to be kept safe, and that he needed to keep his mouth shut about me. He hadn't looked happy about it, but I also knew he didn't want to piss me off either.

What Luke and Deacon knew, Josie didn't need to know. Or maybe she did, and I just didn't want her to know. It didn't matter. What'd almost happened back there... Well, nothing uncomplicated could come from it. If she had been any other girl, I wouldn't have thought twice. I'd have been in and out of her, thoroughly enjoyed myself, and then forgotten about the whole thing. But I did rub some brain cells together when it came to her.

Strange thing was, knowing she should have a big "No Touching" stamped all over her soft, curvy body, didn't change the fact I wanted to touch, kiss, link, slam into, and take it slow with that body.

Great. The hard-on had let up when Deacon and Luke showed, but now was back to the point it made thinking or walking—hell, breathing—difficult.

I didn't even know what it was about her. She wasn't a classic beauty, and gods knew, in the past, that was about all that it took to get me off. She wasn't strong, and that was something I admired in anyone. But her beauty was different and she sure as hell wasn't weak.

In just a handful of days, she hadn't just gotten under my skin. She had crawled in there, set up camp, and wasn't leaving for a while. I couldn't remember a time when I'd ever been that affected.

Stripping off my clothes, I turned on the shower, let the heat fog the bathroom mirror, and then got my ass under the steady stream. There was no thinking about right and wrong now. I slid my hand down my abs, gripping the base of my heavy erection. An image of Josie formed in my thoughts, of her underneath me, staring up at me with heavy eyes and rosy, parted lips. A groan broke free and my back bowed. It didn't take much. A couple of tight strokes later, and I was like a fifteen-year-old boy jacking off for the first time. Release tingled down to the tip of my dick, and the orgasm crashed into me, stronger and fiercer than any time I'd actually been with a chick, and it had been *my* hand that had brought that on.

Hell, it had been more than my hand. It had been the thought of Josie, and wasn't that messed up? Gods, I needed to get my head on straight and my hand off my cock. With that in mind, I actually used the shower for what it was meant to be used for, toweled off, yanked my hair back, and once the clothes were on, I was out the door.

In the hall, across from Josie's room, I stopped and considered checking in, but then I assumed I'd probably end up getting hard again, and the last thing I wanted to do was talk to Marcus with an erection.

Which begged the question, how in the fuck was I supposed to train her when I was a walking boner? And that thought immediately led to, how in the hell had Aiden pulled it off when he'd trained Alex?

I laughed drily as I headed down the empty hall.

Aiden *hadn't* pulled it off. He'd been a pure and Alex was an Apollyon, but ultimately a half, so a relationship between the two should've never happened, but it had. And when I'd helped train Alex, I'd been able to separate whatever I wanted from what we needed to do, but oh, I didn't think this time around was going to work out that way.

And why in the hell was I thinking about those two? They had their happily ever after—well-deserved, but fuck. Probably had to do with Aiden's slightly crazier, albeit cooler, younger brother currently cozying up to Josie.

I was outside in the brisk March wind, ignoring the open gawking from nearby students who'd never had the pleasure of seeing the Apollyon in real life, and boy, didn't that change up their Monday morning routine? I'd just passed the training facilities and was rounding the marble-columned library, when it hit me with the impact of a cement truck.

Holy shit, I was turning into Aiden St. Delphi.

Being all saintly and shit, tampering down urges because it was the *right* and *decent* thing to do, and instead, masturbating in the shower like a loser. Holy fuck, I was probably starting to *care*. Before I knew it, I'd be holding hands with her.

Oh shit, I'd *already* held her hand.

This was why I didn't want to be back here to stay, but it was a little too late for that, because I wasn't leaving.

A chill got inside my chest though, burrowing itself deep, because there was that feeling again, of the button being reset, of history chugging along, bound to repeat itself. And once that iciness got in there, it was hard to shake.

It was like coming face to face with an oracle who communed with the gods, and she was about to drop some messed-up shit in your lap.

My steps picked up and, as I entered the main academic building, I held the door open for the two Sentinels who had been trailing my ass since I'd left the first dorm.

"Try to be a little more inconspicuous next time," I suggested, turning just as the female Sentinel flushed.

"No offense," said the male, stepping inside. "Orders are orders."

Strolling past the elaborate statue of three gods joined at the hip or something equally fucked up like that, I flipped him off.

"He's waiting for you in his office," the female called out.

Of course he was. Pushing open the doors, I hit the stairwell and climbed about a thousand steps. One would think, at some point, someone at one of these damn Covenants would invest in an elevator.

The Dean of the Covenant's office was down a wide hall, past a bunch of pointless offices. The last time I'd been up here...it hadn't been good. Dark and bitter memories clogged my thoughts as I forged forward, but no matter how badly I didn't want them there, images appeared.

Images of all of us in the Dean's office, of Apollo showing up and yanking the gods Phobos and Deimos out of Alex, and her losing her shit afterward, because she...she had sensed something different about her. She had thought she'd been pregnant. So had Aiden, and the whole time, it had been that bastard Ares's children invading her body, enhancing her fears and doubts.

My stomach churned as I ignored the stoic guards outside of the office and welcomed myself in.

Marcus was behind the desk, and a brow rose as I came in. He sat back in his chair, his chest expanding with a deep breath. The setup was different. There was some kind of terrarium behind him, taking up the length of the wall. Upon another look, I realized there was a huge yellow-and-white snake in there.

Did not picture Marcus as a snake guy.

I was right behind the set of chairs in front of his desk when I realized we weren't alone. I spun around and my eyes narrowed on the silent, older man lounging against the wall, arms folded across his black thermal.

My eyes widened with recognition.

Oh, fuck me with a rusted fork. Seriously?

The older Sentinel's weathered face crinkled with a tight smile that did not reach his whiskey-colored eyes. Yeah, I doubted he was happy to see me, being that he was Alex's father.

I had a feeling I was going to get punched again.

"Alexander has been overseeing the Sentinels here," Marcus explained, and the man didn't chime in, because he couldn't, since his tongue had been cut out years ago. "Have a seat. I figured there was something you wanted to talk to me about without Josie being present?"

Not really wanting my back to Alex's dad, but having no choice, I turned. I just didn't sit. "I'm going to train her as long as I can."

He didn't look particularly surprised by the news. "What do you mean by, 'as long as you can?'"

The back of my skull tingled from the holes Alexander was drilling into my head. "You know I made a deal with Apollo. He tells me to head to Switzerland, I've got to go. I don't know what he plans for me next. He's got people out there looking for the other demigods, so he could put me on that. Until then, I'll work with Josie."

"Then you should get Luke to help you in case you are... reassigned. I'd suggest using Solos, but his responsibilities to the Council take up a lot of his time." Marcus closed a folder on his desk, and then folded his hands on top of it. "I assume that, when more demigods are found, they will be brought here?"

I shrugged. "He didn't tell me that, but you know how Apollo is. I haven't seen him since I found Josie."

He shook his head. "Apollo's daughter... Amazing, but this could become problematic."

Tension drew my shoulders back. "She's very important, Marcus. And yeah, it'll be problematic, but what's the point once the Titans are fully charged and decide to go psycho on the world? You know they'll go after the pures and halfs first, and then mankind."

His eyes flashed emerald fire. "I know she's important, Seth, and I'm also well aware of the threat. It's not like this is the first time I've been on the front line of a massive disaster, but I cannot allow what happened at the Deity Covenant to happen here."

A muscle started throbbing along my temple.

"You remember, don't you?" He leaned forward, and he met my stare. "After the stunt you pulled with the Council, you recall what happened?"

Stunt? On Lucian's orders, I had...I had done unforgivable things. "Personally, I wouldn't label that as a *stunt*."

His chin dipped as his hands curled into fists. "I could do nothing as Poseidon destroyed the Covenant. Do you know how many people died that day? Three-hundred and five, Seth. I will not have that happen again."

Hearing that number was like swallowing a lead bullet. It made my skin raw, uncomfortable. "I'm not planning to pull a *stunt* like that again."

He pushed off the desk and rose, and out of the corner of my eye I saw Alexander ghost forward. "I'd hope not, but I have a responsibility to these students and those who have sought refuge here."

"I get that, but this is sounding like a lot of bullshit to me."

A brow cocked. "Is that so?"

"Yeah, it is." The glyphs bled onto my skin. He couldn't see them, but I knew he was picking up on the rush of energy whirling around inside me. "Because what it sounds like is that you're willing to dump Josie outside those gates."

"I never said that, Seth. What I am saying is that, if her presence here, or anyone's presence here, threatens the safety of the Covenant, I will have to take steps to rectify that," he said. "Hopefully, that will never mean turning her or anyone else away."

That told me nothing, and as I stared at Marcus, I had to give him credit for not pissing his pants and for protecting what was his. But I would have to do the same thing.

Marcus sighed as he glanced over to where Alexander stood. "I'm going to say something I know you're not going to want to hear."

"Great," I muttered.

He ignored that as he pressed his palms onto the desk. "A lot of things have changed. Some are the same. You haven't been around to see any of that, but I know—*I know*—you've changed, and that's the only reason why you're standing in this office."

Part of me wanted to ask him exactly how he thought he could've stopped me, but then he must've read my mind. "If I thought you were going to screw us over, I would've walked out to that first gate myself and put a bullet between your eyes. I know it wouldn't have killed you, but it would've put you down long enough for me to dismember your body, and then discover how an Apollyon puts itself back together."

My lips tipped up at the corners. "Well, that's a brutal imagination you got going there."

He smirked. "Like I said, you still have the attitude, and I know you could end my existence in a heartbeat, but you've... you've changed."

I held his gaze then looked away, working my jaw. "Is there a point to this part of the conversation?"

"Not really. I just like to hear myself talk." Marcus sat down, hooking one knee over the other as he eyed me. "As we mentioned yesterday, there are wards up against the Titans, but I'm sure you realize they won't last forever."

Back on more comfortable ground, I shifted my weight. "There are also shades. One got hold of Josie's grandfather." I paused. "She saw him die."

His lips thinned. "That is truly unfortunate. How is she handling it?"

"She's not." And that was the truth.

He inclined his head. "She's with Deacon and Luke?"

"How did you guess?"

A real smile formed. "I figured it would take them no time to find you and her. Deacon will be good for her, considering he lost his parents." A thoughtful look encroached upon his features. "If you had arrived a few months earlier, she could've talked to Alex. Of all our people, she would understand."

Inhaling through my nose, it took everything not to look at her father. Alex *would* understand. After all, she had seen her mother turned by daimons and, subsequently, had had to end her own mother's life.

Happy times.

"Do you care for her?" Marcus abruptly asked.

I blinked.

"Josie," he clarified, like that was fucking necessary at that point. "Solos said you did not sleep in your room last night." He held up his hand. "Yes, Solos kept an eye on you two, and, no, I do not care to know the details."

"Then I don't know what kind of answer you're looking for," I replied.

Marcus studied me for a moment, and then I heard the door open. I turned in time to see Alexander slipping out of the room. Very few people could be quieter than me. He was apparently one of them. When I turned back to Marcus, he was staring at the closed door. "He does not trust you."

"I don't expect him to."

Marcus's gaze shifted to mine. "He will one day."

I smiled, but everything was brittle and wrong about it. "Why would he? It was his daughter—"

"She *is* also my niece—not was, Seth, and you've paid a heavy restitution."

Something knocked around in my chest, a cold and hollow thing—a very real reminder. "No. No, I haven't."

204

CHAPTER

20

My head was spinning on sensory overload.

From the moment Deacon and Luke had walked into the room, they hadn't stopped talking. Well, one of them had disappeared–Deacon–long enough for me to shower and change, and he was back by the time I walked out of the bathroom. He was wearing jeans and a sweater instead of the pajama pants, and his hair was a damp, curly mess of adorableness.

They had a way about them of coaxing information out of me. They could've been spies for a Greek Secret Society or something, and I was just forking over details on my life in Missouri and at college. Erin had been welcoming, but these boys were something else. The only thing they didn't get out of me was anything about my grandparents or my mother. I wasn't...I just couldn't talk about them right then.

I didn't know if Seth would be happy with me leaving the room, but the boys didn't seem to care. They took me out and in the morning sunlight, which seemed harsher and stronger in South Dakota, then guided me to a one-story square building that housed community rooms and a cafeteria nicer than the one at Radford. Nicer, as in there were granite countertops in the prep

205

areas, the people serving the food were extraordinarily gorgeous, and the place smelled great—like peaches and not like greasy food.

Deacon, chatting on about something, loaded me up with bacon, and Luke plopped a bottle of OJ in my other hand before they ushered me toward an empty, sparkling clean, round table.

My eyes were wide and I barely heard anything they were saying to me. I couldn't stop staring at the people at the other tables.

And they were staring at us.

Not for the same reason I was staring—my eyes were glued to them due to their crazy insanely good looks. Everyone looked like they had stepped off a film screen or runway. Almost everyone had startling eye colors—bright sky-blue, emerald-green, whiskey-brown, and even purple.

Who in the hell had amethyst-colored eyes?

Some of the students—I guessed they were students—weren't paying attention to us. They were huddled in little groups at the tables, textbooks spread out between them. It was so painfully familiar that it forged a lump in my throat, but others were looking, and I couldn't say their looks were all that friendly.

A nearby icy blonde with deep, forest-green eyes stared in our direction, her full lips pressed together. Beside her, a tall and lanky guy with reddish-brown hair had his baby-blue eyes narrowed in our direction. Maybe I was paranoid.

I twisted around and glanced over my shoulder in the other direction. A brunette with a perfect nose curled her lip up.

Okay. Not so paranoid.

Popping back around, I met Deacon's gray gaze. "Is it just me or...?"

"Is everyone staring over here? Yep." He leaned forward, holding another strip of crispy bacon. "Some of them are staring because they think you're mortal and they don't understand why you're here."

Sitting beside him, Luke nodded. "We've never really been close to mortals. Having to hide what we are makes any kind of relationship with them difficult, so seeing a mortal here is like spotting a unicorn or chimera."

I arched a brow.

"Plus...well, I'm a pure," Deacon explained as he munched away.

"And I'm a half," Luke explained. "They don't give a crap about the fact we're both guys and together, but a half and a pure? Gasp!" He widened his eyes as he dramatically clutched at his chest. "Oh, the horror."

"Seth said something about that changing?" I pushed my bacon around on my plate, not really hungry when I could feel a hundred beautiful people staring at me. Everyone knowing about my family's business reminded me of high school; the only difference was that everyone here was hot. "A Breed Order?"

"Yeah, the whole law saying we can't be together has been abolished, but you can't erase thousands of years of assholery in a year." Luke shrugged a shoulder, but his jaw strained. "Some pures think we're below them and have looked down on us since the dawn of man. It's going to take a while for that to change."

"That's terrible," I whispered, fiddling with my bottle.

"It was just this last year that I finally had some control over my life," he said, brows knitting together. Deacon reached over, placing his hand atop Luke's, and my chest got all gushy. "I was always going to be a Sentinel. Trained since I was eight for it, because I didn't have a choice."

"And now you do." Curiosity got the best of me. "So what are you doing now?"

He glanced at Deacon and grinned as their gazes met. A moment passed, and it was like they forgot about me for a second. "I still train. It's stupid not to, since there's obviously a lot of crazy things going on, but..."

"But he's not an active Sentinel." Deacon leaned back, folding his long arms across his blue sweater. "He's taking classes."

Luke's grin spread. "A lot of halfs are now doing that. Some decided to keep on the path they were on, but it's good...it's good to have options."

I couldn't even fathom a life without those options. Then again, it seemed like Luke and I had reversed roles. The moment I found out what I was, I'd been stripped of those choices. And that thought messed with my already fragile grasp on everything, so I swatted it away for the time being. "So what are you studying?"

"Horticulture," he answered.

My brows shot up. Was *so* not expecting that.

Luke chuckled. "Sounded different and interesting, so why not? He's studying—or pretending to study—ancient history."

Deacon snorted. "What about you?"

That knot swelled. "Psychology, but I guess...that doesn't matter now."

"Why not?" Deacon frowned, which seemed like it might be a rare sight on his handsome face.

I raised my hands. "Well, with this. It's not like they're letting me enroll in college. I'm here to...to basically be hidden. Not to continue my education."

Luke studied me closely for a moment. "I'm sure, if you wanted to, Marcus would let you."

Maybe he would, but what was the point? If I survived this, could I go back to my old life and be a psychologist? Could I go back and be anything knowing what really existed out there? Hell, all of that was banking on the very unlikely *if* I survived.

"Anyway." Deacon said as he snatched a strip of bacon off my plate. "So, you and Seth? Have you hooked up yet?"

I nearly choked on my OJ. "What?"

"Hooked up? You know, got naked and had wild, animalistic sex," Deacon clarified like I had no knowledge of slang. "It has to be animalistic sex, because I can't picture Seth doing anything gentle and soft, like holding hands and gazing into each others' eyes kind of stuff."

Oh. My. God.

Luke rolled his eyes.

Warmth poured into my face as both guys waited for an answer, but I was kind of picturing that rough and raw in the flesh. Feeling like I needed to fan myself, I squirmed. "We haven't... um, we haven't hooked up."

Both of their mouths dropped open, and that made me wiggle under their scrutiny more. To hide my embarrassment, I shoved bacon into my mouth, and almost moaned.

Holy shit! My taste buds orgasmed all over my mouth. It was the best bacon I'd ever tasted—salty and yet sweet, like it had been battered in maple syrup. What had I been missing sitting here and not eating?

"Wait a second," Luke said, leaning forward. Over his shoulder, three students walked by, whispering as they stared at us. Neither guy appeared to care. "He *did* sleep with you last night, right?"

I nodded.

"And you two didn't have sex?"

Shaking my head, I smashed another piece of bacon in to my mouth. God, it was the *best*.

Deacon stared at me like I was a mythical creature. Wait—I kind of was. "You two haven't had sex *at all*?"

And yet another piece of pig made its way into my mouth as I shook my head again.

"Holy shit." Luke rocked back in his seat. "I think that is more shocking than you being, well, what you are."

Sadly, there was no more bacon on the plate. "Why is that so shocking?"

Deacon cocked a brow. "Seth's a bit of a...*playa*. I mean, he kind of is a man-whore." He chuckled. "And I'd know what it takes to be a man-whore."

"True," quipped Luke. "Deacon's what I'd like to call 'equal opportunity' when it comes to sex. Well, not since me. We're monogamous, but before...?" He shook his head.

Um.

"When he first showed up at the Deity Island Covenant—that's where we're from, originally—he went through half the dorm in record time," Deacon continued.

I slowly lowered the OJ to the table as I felt my stomach drop to my toes, and that was an uncomfortable feeling when it was full of bacon. Went through half of the dorm?

"And then when he was at the Catskills, he was hooking up with this one chick." Luke looked at his boyfriend. "What was her name?"

He shrugged. "I don't know. Alex always called her Boobs, but I think it was something like Thea or Tori. Something with a T. She's around here somewhere. Can't miss her."

Sitting back, I forced my lungs to work slowly. "We haven't had sex. I mean, we just met each other."

Luke wrinkled his nose. "That doesn't matter when it comes to Seth."

"Wow," Deacon murmured.

I bit down on my lip as I tried to sort out the awful twisting motion in my belly. I shouldn't have cared that he'd had sex with an entire college worth of girls before we met, because that was dumb. I shouldn't have cared, because we weren't together.

The twisty motion increased.

But there was something there between us, wasn't there? This morning…I had seen my feelings reflected in his gaze, hadn't I? He'd looked at me like…like he'd wanted nothing more than to kiss me.

Yet just because he wanted to get in my pants didn't mean there was something starting between us. But he did stay—he agreed to train me, and he didn't have to, and that had to mean something.

"You know, I think this is a good thing," Deacon announced, jerking my gaze to him. "The fact that he hasn't hooked up with you has to mean that he's into you."

210

And just like that, because I was stupid, the twisty motion turned into this balloon thing that was full of hope and was lifting me up right out the chair, and God, that was probably a bad sign.

"And I think it would be really good for him, you know, to be into someone, because—"

"Why don't we take you on a tour?" Luke cut in, and Deacon looked at him sharply. "You've got to see this place."

And just like that, we were up and out of the cafeteria, the guys on either side of me, and there was no more talk about Seth hooking up with me or anyone else, and within minutes, I was distracted by everything going on around me.

The place...it was something entirely foreign to me. The academic buildings were huge and ridiculously clean. The courtyards were out of this world, filled with everything from garden-variety roses to tropical flowers that smelled sweet. Marble and sandstone statues of the Greek gods were everywhere, a constant reminder that this place, no matter how nice and spectacular it was, wasn't entirely normal.

As we followed the walkway with the strange symbols on it, I started to feel edgy—like a rush of nervous energy. I asked what the symbols were. "They're glyphs forming wards," Deacon explained. "Basically, spells that keep things out we don't want in here. Like Titans. It doesn't always work. Daimons could still get in if they got past the guards, but that's what they are. Seth even has them on his skin."

I frowned. "What? I didn't see any tattoos. And he walks around shirtless a lot. Are they on his ass or something?"

Luke chuckled. "That would be interesting, but the tats on his skin can only be seen by gods or another Apollyon. Maybe even you, once you become the special sauce."

Special sauce? Interesting, I thought, as I turned my gaze back to the large building in front of us, another one that looked like it was straight out of ancient Greece. A wave of goosebumps broke out under my sweater.

"And this is the library," Luke announced, gesturing at the building. "We don't go in there."

Folding my arms against the brisk chill, I squinted my eyes up at him. "You don't?"

He shook his head. "Libraries always weird out halfs."

I glanced at Deacon. Shrugging, he said, "I have no idea. A lot of halfs are like that. It's weird. They can sense daimons when we can't. Maybe they sense something under the library."

Another shiver curled around my stomach, a weird yearning sensation. "Under?"

"Yeah, there are always catacombs under the libraries," Luke explained. "I have no idea what's kept in them. Don't plan on finding out. Come on, there's more to see."

Then Deacon reached down and took my hand, causing me to trip. When I glanced up at him questioningly, he just winked and kept walking, swinging our arms between us like we were small children, and I couldn't help but grin.

And I also couldn't help but look over my shoulder as we passed the library, and I couldn't help but to keep looking back, wanting to go in there. Yeah, that was weird. But I was living in weird now, rolling around in it.

Lunch came and went. So did dinner with the boys, who I was guessing had decided not to go to class that day. They spent the entire day escorting me around and putting so much food in my stomach I was sure they were going to have to roll me back to my room.

Although I had thought I'd start training today, and the raw loss of my family lingered on the fringes of my thoughts, I enjoyed hanging with them. They were funny and lively and just great. Even Luke, who hadn't seemed too keen on me this morning, spent half of his time with his arm around Deacon's and the other around mine.

The sun had started to go bye-bye when we made our way back to the dorm, and as we entered the lobby, I saw Seth immediately. It was like my eyes were drawn past all the pretty faces right to the ultimate pretty face.

Wearing a black thermal, like Luke, and faded jeans, he stood between two bright red couches, muscular arms folded over his chest, hair pulled back.

My belly did a little jig upon seeing him, and then dropped when I realized every butt in those seats was female, all stunningly perfect and in every flavor, it seemed.

Seth turned, his amber gaze flickering over to us. He said something to a brunette, who glanced over her shoulder, and then laughed. It wasn't a mean laugh. More like a response to whatever he said, but I sort of wanted to stab something.

He walked over to us. "Have a moment?"

"I've had several moments *all day*."

Seth arched a brow.

Deacon whistled under his breath.

I'd said that out loud.

Flushing, I looked away and found myself staring at the back of the brunette's head. Great.

We walked over to an empty nook, and I got busy staring at my sneakers, feeling like an idiot. There was a slight touch on my arm, and I looked up at Seth.

"Sorry about today," he said, dropping his hand. "I got tied up doing some things."

Words like "okay" and "all right" rolled to the tip of my tongue, but I didn't respond, because was it okay and all right? Was I just being a bitch?

He stared at me a moment, and then turned to Luke. "I was hoping you could help us with the training, if you got the time."

Surprise filled his expression, but he quickly masked it. "Yeah. I can do it in the afternoon. Got classes in the morning."

"Classes? What the hell are you studying?" he asked.

Deacon beamed. "Horticulture."

213

Seth frowned, opened his mouth, and then snapped it shut. "Never mind." Glancing back down at me, I felt my breath catch. "I'm going to get you some training clothes. Okay?"

I nodded.

And that was it. Seth was out the door before I knew it, and I was in my room alone for the first time since…holy hedgehogs, since this all began. What was today? I scrubbed my fingers across my face as I sat in the middle of the bed. Monday? Tuesday? Less than a week had passed since I'd met Seth.

Less than a week.

It felt like *months*.

Wow. I lowered my hands and stared down at them. Everything in the whole entire world had shifted in less than a week.

That screwed with my head in a way that made it hard to breathe evenly. My trembling fingers blurred. Twisting at the waist, I stretched and snatched the remote off the nightstand, flipping on the TV and settling on the first channel I saw, because I really wasn't seeing anything.

An hour passed and there was a knock. My heart doubled its beat as I all but dive-bombed off the bed and ran to the door, throwing it open.

It was Luke. He smiled. "I brought you some workout clothes. Seth put the order in and guessed the size."

Trying not to let any disappointment show, I took the clothes and saw that they really were my size. Um. Okay. I didn't know if I should be awed by that or kind of wigged out that Seth was that good at guessing women's sizes.

And that he *knew* my size.

Well, no point sucking in my belly around him now.

"Thanks," I said, glancing up at him, and then over his shoulder to the closed door that belonged to the guy who should've brought the clothes to me.

"I gotta run."

I kept that stupid smile plastered on my face. "Okay. Goodnight."

Luke started to turn, and then swiveled back to me. "Are you okay?"

I guessed the smile looked bad, so I wiped it from my face. "Yeah. Just tired." I took a step back. "Oh. Thank you for today. It was nice. I had fun."

"No problem." He tilted his head to the side as he scratched at the scruff that had appeared on his jaw. "You sure you're doing all right? If you want, I can hang out—"

"Yeah, I'm fine. Really, but thank you." Holding the clothing close, I nodded at him. "I'll see you tomorrow. I guess."

"Yeah. In the afternoon." He paused again. "Have a good night."

Kneeing the door closed, I took my clothes into the bedroom and spilled them across the bed. Black pants that reminded me of yoga bottoms. Gray T-shirts, long and short-sleeved. Sighing, I glanced at my bags, and then the empty closet.

I made the next hour or so productive. Hanging up my clothes and putting them away since I figured I was going to be here...for a while. Then I got ready for bed, donning Seth's shirt again. I really needed to find some sleep clothes and a washer and dryer.

Another hour was wasted staring at the TV screen, and by then, it was close to ten. No sign of Seth. Fidgeting until I couldn't take it any longer, I sprang from the bed and went to the door, opening it. I stepped out, digging my toes into the carpet as I froze, my eyes fastened to the door across from me.

What was I doing?

Seth wasn't coming over. I'd slept every night by myself since forever. I didn't need him or anyone to go to sleep.

I hesitated, and then I turned, quietly pushing my door shut. Closing my eyes, I leaned forward and pressed my forehead against the door. The knot from earlier was back, lodging at the base of my throat, and my arms felt tired, so did my legs, even though I hadn't done anything all day but walk around and eat. But I missed—

I cut the thought off as I pushed from the door. A weight settled over me as I tugged the covers back and slipped into bed, pulling the blankets up to my chin, and as I lay there, the image of my grandparents formed in my thoughts—them at the kitchen table, sweet tea in hand and pie on plates between them. A sharp pain whipped through me, and I squeezed my eyes shut, forcing thoughts of them away and focusing on taking deep and even breaths until my eyelids became heavy.

And Seth never showed.

SETH DID show up the next morning, about fifteen minutes after I dragged my butt out of bed. I opened the door to him, still half-asleep but aware enough to note that he looked damn good in dark nylon pants paired with a black henley.

God, he always looked damn good.

He handed over a coffee that I took without thinking. "Get moving, Joe. We're training today."

Scowling, I took a sip of the coffee. "Don't call me Joe."

"But I want to." Placing his hands on my shoulders, he turned me around, toward the bedroom. "By the way, you still look great in my shirt."

Heart skipping, I looked over my shoulder at him. I wanted to ask why he hadn't come over last night, but the question seemed wrong and needy, incredibly needy. So I said nothing as I sipped my steaming coffee.

He cocked a brow. "Anytime now."

"I don't like you," I murmured.

A quick smile appeared and disappeared. "Yeah, you do."

"I really don't like you." I turned, using the rim of the Styrofoam cup to hide my grin.

Seth was sitting on the bed, chin in his hand and elbow propped on his knee when I was finished getting ready. His gaze tracked from the tips of my sneakers, over the black pants and gray shirt, to where I'd pulled my hair into a ponytail.

"The training uniform also looks good on you," he murmured.

A pleasant rush invaded me, and I wanted to ignore it, because I shouldn't be so easily flattered.

"The tag has already starting to fade," he commented, and he was right. It was a faint pink when I peeked at it in the mirror. "How's you're head?"

"Okay." That bruise was also nothing too serious.

He stood fluidly. "You sure you want to do this?"

"Yes, I'm sure." I nodded, just in case he didn't get it. "I–I need to do this."

Holding my gaze for a moment, a look that was akin to pain flickered across his face, but then it was gone as he extended an arm toward the door. "Then let's do this."

I followed him out into the hall, but he stopped and said, "Hold on a sec," and then disappeared into his room. Yawning, I waited the few seconds it took for him to come back out, holding a zipper hoodie and a gray scarf.

"For me?" I asked.

"Yep." Not meeting my gaze, he handed the items over. "I picked them up yesterday and forgot to give them to you. It's cold here at the beginning and the end of the day. Will be until sometime in May."

"Thanks." I slipped the hoodie on.

His lips curved up on one side as he stepped in front of me and reached out, catching the sides of the hoodie. He slipped the zipper together and dragged it up, and I stood there, holding the scarf like an idiot.

He winked and then turned on his heel. "Time's ticking, Josie." God, I really disliked him.

Wrapping the scarf around my neck, I hurried after him. We didn't talk as we made the trek outside, and I immediately huddled down in my hoodie. The wind whipped across the courtyard, catching thin wisps of hair and tossing them around my face.

The boys hadn't taken me to the training facilities that were situated just beyond the library, so I was eager to see what they looked like inside. As we passed the library, the tiny bumps on my skin returned, and I couldn't fight the urge to keep my gaze on it once again. Something stirred inside me restlessly, and I figured maybe it was a sign of needing to gobble up an armful of books to pass my extra time. Or maybe it had to do with the fact I had spent many weekends inside the tiny library back home.

"You're going to trip and break your neck before we even get started," Seth commented.

I forced my gaze toward him. "Whatever. I'm not a complete klutz."

His shoulders shook with silent laughter, and my eyes narrowed. "Soon I'll be able to kick your ass," I warned.

The laughter was loud and clear now. "Yeah, keep dreaming, Sweet Cheeks."

"Sweet Cheeks?" I caught up with him. "That's the worst nickname ever."

"Then Joe."

"How about just 'Josie?'"

He cast a glance at me as he veered off onto a walkway leading up to double doors at the back of the large, square training building. "That's boring."

"Then I'm going to call you 'Sethie.'"

Opening the door, he tipped his chin down. "I like that."

I rolled my eyes. "Well, there's no fun in that, then."

He chuckled. "Figured."

The hallway was wide and traveled the length of the building, ending in a burst of sunlight that came through large windows. On each side of the hall there were doors every thirty or so feet. No windows on any of them.

"It's early. Most training classes start in the afternoon, since the students do academic classes in the morning," he explained,

219

walking toward the fourth door on the left. "This room is going to be ours. Get used to it, because you're going to be in here a lot."

That didn't sound good, but as he pushed open the door, I got my first look at the inside of a Covenant training room.

With wide eyes, I stepped further inside as Seth closed the door. Tile covered the floor at the entrance, but thick blue mats took up over half of the room. Three fleshy-looking dummies sat to our right, and as I walked up to one of them, I ran my finger along the deep slashes across the thing's chest. There were cut marks everywhere—neck, arms, shoulders, legs.

"Sentinels use these for target practice." Seth's voice was so close that I nearly jumped. "They train mostly to fight daimons. As long as you have a titanium blade, if you get them anywhere on their body, it does the trick."

"Stabbing people," I murmured, shaking my head. The very idea of shoving a sharp, pointy object into someone wasn't something I could comprehend.

One second I was staring at the dummy, and then the next I was staring up at Seth. He'd whipped me around that quickly. "Daimons are not people, Josie. That is your first lesson. There is nothing humane about them. They thrive on *aether*, and they are cruel, dangerous creatures." His eyes flashed a fiery amber as he stared down at me. "You need to understand that."

"Bad choice of words," I said.

A muscle flexed in his jaw. "Do you understand, Josie?"

My heart turned over heavily. "I get it."

I didn't wait for him to respond. Turning around, I headed toward the mats as I unwound my scarf. When I got a good look at the opposite wall, I almost did trip over my own feet.

The entire wall was covered with stabby things.

Knives. Blades. Daggers. Swords.

Honest-to-God swords—like Samurai swords and something King Arthur might've pulled out of a rock.

I'd seen Seth with daggers and I totally got that they were the things that had inflicted the damage on the dummies, but seeing all of them up there was like reality had kicked me in the face.

"I'm not just learning how to defend myself," I said, my gaze traveling over all the sharp objects. "I'm learning how to *kill* things."

There was a beat of silence and then, "Yes. Are you still sure you want this?"

I drew in a shaky breath as my throat thickened. This was my life now. That was my reality, and it felt like the floor moved under my feet for a moment as I stared at the silvery dagger in the center, the one with the five-inch blade and thick, cross-style handle. Could I kill something?

The answer weakened my knees.

I had already tried to kill someone—or something. Hyperion. When I'd pulled that trigger and shot him in the back, it hadn't been a love tap. God, what would my grandparents think of this? They were live-and-let-live kind of people. And they were dead.

A sharp pain sliced through my chest. "Yeah, I'm sure."

A moment passed and then I felt his hand on my shoulder, turning me away from the wall of death. "Good news is, you aren't anywhere near close to touching a single thing on that wall."

I shot him a look.

"What?" His tone was light. "You'd end up cutting off five fingers and a foot if you started messing with those things right now."

"Your faith in me is staggering." I tugged off the hoodie, dropping it on the corner of the mat with my scarf.

He smiled as he stood in the middle of a thick blue mat. "The first thing you have to learn, before we can move onto anything, is how to correctly take a fall when you're knocked down."

"There's a correct way to fall?"

His golden brows rose as his lips twitched. "Yes, there's a correct way. And that way allows you to absorb the hit with minimal impact and also allows you to get right back on your feet.

221

And that's the most important thing, Josie. If your enemy gets you on your back and keeps you down there, it's over."

"Okay." I reached up, tightening my ponytail. "So that's what I'm going to learn?"

"That's what you're going to start with, then we'll end practice with running."

My lips curled. Running? Ugh.

"You need to build up your endurance. That's the easiest way to do it." Seth stretched his arms above his head, back bowing. Joints cracked. "To take a landing correctly, you roll your hips in and keep your chin tucked down. This will cause you to take the fall on your upper back."

I ran that through my head. Hips rolled in. Chin tucked. "I got this."

A dubious look marked his expression. "All right."

Shaking my arms out, I started to tell him that I was ready, but the next thing I knew I slammed into the mat. Pain exploded along my spine and across the base of my skull, knocking the air right out of my lungs. The overhead lights turned into a hundred dazzling stars before the corners of my vision darkened.

Uh oh.

Holy shit.

The moment Josie went into the air was the exact moment I knew I'd fucked up. So used to training with other halfs and Sentinels, I hadn't checked myself. Even though she was a demigod and her body had to be resilient, her powers were bound and she obviously had never done any real fighting, so knocking her down like she was any other person I was training with was a fucking huge miscalculation on my part.

Holy shit, I fucked up.

Unease exploded in my gut as I dropped onto my knees beside her. A wave of muggy loathing wrapped itself around me. Thick,

222

dusky brown lashes fanned her pale skin. I reached for her, my fingers hovering above her cheek. "Josie?"

My heart literally skipped a damn beat as those lashes fluttered and then swept up. Clear blue eyes met mine. "Ow."

A strangled laugh escaped me as I picked up her limp hand, rubbing it between my palms. "Shit, Josie, I'm sorry. I should've held back. Are you okay?"

She wet her lips, and that sent a jolt straight to my cock, which officially made me an ass. "Where were you last night?"

The question almost knocked me on my butt. Out of everything I expected her to say, that wasn't it. I placed her hand on the mat as I rocked back on my heels. "The day got away from me."

That was absolute bullshit. The day hadn't really gotten away from me. It had dragged on after I'd met with Marcus. I'd spent a good part of my day trailing Josie and the guys like a grade-A stalker, and then, when I'd headed back to the dorm, I'd run into Thea, and that was about three shit levels of awkward. I shouldn't have been surprised that she was here, since the Covenant in the Catskills was still out of commission. If Josie and the guys hadn't shown up, I probably would have chewed my arm off to get away.

I'd thought Josie and I needed space.

Well, *I* had needed space, because what had almost happened between us yesterday morning was something I didn't...I hadn't deserved. It was that simple. Affection wasn't in my cards. So I spent most of last night unable to sleep, out by the damn cemetery, sitting on the bench, staring at the repaired statues I'd destroyed the last time I'd been here, and wanting nothing more than to somehow forget the last two years of my life.

Josie stared at me a moment, and then swallowed. "Oh. Okay," she said hoarsely, and I did my best to also forget that. She started to sit up and I got an arm around her shoulders, helping her. "I...I suck."

223

Way inappropriate visions danced in my head like a streaming porn flick. Nice. I got her up on her feet. "You don't suck, Josie. That was my fault. I needed to pull back and—"

"Will Hyperion hold back the next time he finds me?" She stepped away, and I let my arm fall. "No? Will a daimon, if it gets its hands on me? I'm guessing that's a no, too. So let's do this again."

Tucking a loose strand of hair behind my ear, I was mentally halfway to the door, because I didn't want to do this. With Alex, I hadn't thought twice about the possibility of accidentally injuring her, but it was a real concern with Josie, and that sucked ass. My stomach churned as I forced myself to stand behind her.

But it was more than that.

My gaze traveled to the wall, to where all the weapons were displayed. No matter what she'd said, she hadn't fully accepted the knowledge that she'd have to kill to survive. All of this training was pointless if she couldn't do that. It was such...such a mortal moral to cling to, one I'd never had any problem tossing aside. For a moment, I thought of all those I'd hunted down in the past year. If Josie couldn't kill to protect herself, what would she think if she knew how many I'd killed?

"When you fall, cross your arms over your chest." Shaking those thoughts out of my head, I grabbed hold of her arms from behind her and crossed them over her chest. Then I got a damn good handful of her hips, and I heard her soft inhale. Ignoring that was impossible. "Tilt your hips like this and tuck your chin down. Okay?"

"Okay," she said, her voice thicker, huskier.

My jaw worked overtime. "Let me see you do it a couple of times. The mechanics of it."

Josie did what I asked. Under my hands, her hips tilted forward as she dipped her chin, getting her arms across her chest. And every time I felt those muscles tense, it took everything in me not to grab those hips and haul them back to mine.

Her hips moved again, and I almost groaned.

I needed to get my head into the game. Refocusing on her for the right reasons, I had her keep doing the motions until they were smooth, but my hands lingered as I stepped back, having a mind of their own as they slid off.

She turned, facing me. Her bottom lip was stuck between her teeth.

"Ready?"

There was a nod.

Cursing this and about a dozen other things, I swung out, catching her on the shoulder. Down she went, smacking into the mat. Not the correct way.

"Dammit," she moaned, unfolding her arms as she stared up at the ceiling. "That...that stings."

Walking over to where she lay, her legs at awkward angles, I extended a hand, and hated myself for what I said next. "Get up. Do it again."

Josie groaned as she folded her hand in mine.

I hauled her up.

We squared off.

I knocked her down again.

And she didn't land right.

This was going to be a long day.

CHAPTER
22

THE LONG-ASS day turned into a nightmare of sorts once Luke arrived after lunch and also tried to get her to land right. Frustration was like a heat rash on every square inch of my skin—made worse by the fact that Luke had also gotten all hands-on with her, trying to help her out with the hip motion.

I wanted to rip his hands off at the wrists and shove them into his mouth, which was stupid, all things considered.

Then there was the group that had formed at the door. Halfs. Pures. Deacon had also shown up, but he was sitting on the edge of the mat, arms resting on his knees, looking like all he needed was a bowl of popcorn. But those by the door, they were all curious to why a half and an Apollyon were training what appeared to be a mortal. Thea was among them, the shirt she was wearing so low-cut and tight that her generous breasts were defying gravity and practically training along with the three of us.

Josie had also noticed.

Every time she picked herself up off the mat, she checked out the group huddled at the door, and her eyes always strayed to Thea. It was hard not to, since the girl was basically fucking me with her eyes.

I was going to have to do something about that.

"You got this," Luke said, standing in front of Josie. "You almost had it right last time. We'll do this again, and then you've got to run."

Josie shifted her gaze to mine. "Running sucks."

"I'll run with you," I told her.

Luke patted her shoulder. "So will I."

"Yay. Can we all hold hands while we run?" she asked.

I snorted. "Let's pass on that."

"I think that's a great idea," Deacon chimed in. "*I'd* even run with you guys if we all hold hands."

Luke shot him a look before he stepped back from Josie, and I moved a few feet behind her, mentally bracing myself to watch Josie turn herself into a living, breathing bruise.

She shook out her shoulders. "Ready."

The half shot forward, hitting her in the shoulders, and she took the jarring knock like a champ. Her hips were in the right position, but her neck and shoulders weren't, and I knew, when she hit the floor, it was going to sting like a bitch.

I didn't stop to think.

Springing forward, I caught her at the waist before she slammed into the unforgiving mat for literally what had to be the hundredth time that day.

A slight grunt came out of her and her eyes popped wide. "Seth," she gasped, gripping my arms as I righted her.

My gaze met Luke's questioning stare, and I quickly looked away. "She wasn't going to land right. No point in letting her break her back."

"Good point." Luke folded his arms as one eyebrow climbed up. "I guess we call it a day and run."

"Sounds good to me."

A half-smile appeared on his face. "I think you need to let her go first, though."

Frowning, I looked down. Josie was staring up at me, the hollows of her cheeks pink. My arms were around her like I was a

227

rubber band. I let go of her so fast that she stumbled and I had to catch her again. This time I didn't hold on.

Deacon chuckled.

I sent him a look that said I was more than willing to light his ass up, and all he did was grin at me.

I was losing my touch.

We started toward the door to take our run outside. The group scattered like cockroaches. All except a few—one of them being Thea.

She sauntered right between Luke and me, causing me to draw up short. A body—Josie—bounced into my back and there was a muffled curse from her.

I sighed.

Thea was beautiful. There was no way around that. Stunning face and a body that could grace a *Sports Illustrated* swimsuit edition. And she was a nice girl. She liked to have fun, especially my kind of fun, but the perfect face and body weren't doing anything for me.

She smiled, flashing straight ultra-white teeth. "Hey."

Josie bumped into me as she stepped around, eyeing Thea. I fought the urge to smile or outright laugh. "Hi, Thea."

Catching the end of her braid with long fingers, she tilted her hips to the side. "I was wondering if you were doing anything tonight."

If doing something meant sitting out in the cold like a jackass, then yes. "Yeah, I'm kind of busy tonight."

She pouted, but the light in her jewel-green eyes didn't dim. "Maybe another time."

I forced a smile, but didn't respond as I edged around her. Josie was staring at the floor, the skin white around her lush lips. I started toward her, to do what, I didn't know, but I stopped myself before I looked like a complete fucker.

Deacon arched a brow, murmured something about getting food, and bounced away.

The running didn't suck as bad as the training did, but by the time we had circled the campus once, which was pushing two and a half miles, I was sure Josie was going to keel over and die, and I let Luke drag her off to fuel up. The chicken-salad sandwich she'd eaten for lunch must have completely burned off by this point.

I headed over to the med building, grabbed what I needed, and came back out just as the sky was darkening to dusk. I'd taken maybe two steps when I felt a nerve-grating intensity aimed my direction.

Turning around, my eyes searched the thickening shadows. I immediately found the source.

Alexander was several feet back, eyes on me. Nothing about his expression was friendly. My fingers curled around the jar I'd picked up in the med building. I waited for him to approach me, to do whatever it was that he wanted to do, which probably was a lot.

A full minute passed, and then Alexander pivoted on his heel and disappeared into the shadows. I stood there for a moment, feeling oddly hollow. It wasn't like I wanted a confrontation with the man, but in a weird, twisted kind of way, I wanted him to do whatever it was that he felt he had to do. Hit me? Try to kick my ass? I wouldn't stop him.

The jar suddenly felt heavy in my hand, and I lifted it, thinking of its purpose. Standing here all emo-like wasn't going to get anything accomplished.

Back in my dorm, I took a quick shower, changed into whatever was nearby, and then grabbed the jar. Maybe a half-hour had passed by the time I exited the room, took a step, and was in front of another door.

I rapped my knuckles on the door, and then waited.

A few moments passed before the door swung open and there she was, freshly showered. Damp hair stuck to her cheeks and shoulders. She still sucked at drying off, and I still wasn't complaining, because the shirt she wore clung in the best possible

229

places, like across her belly and between the swell of her breasts. And what lovely breasts they were.

Seriously.

Man, my mouth literally watered as her nipples hardened against the thin, damp shirt. I bet they were perfect, pink and small. My pants suddenly felt a couple sizes too small. Great.

"Hey," she said, and when I dragged my gaze back to her face, her cheeks were flushed prettily.

"Can I come in?"

Her delicate brows knitted. "Yeah, you...you don't have to ask." She stepped back, sucking her lip between her teeth.

I smiled tightly in return. "How are you feeling? How's your back?"

She winced as she shuffled into the bedroom. With the bed. The very same bed she'd been under me in. Perfect. She sat on the edge. "It's definitely a little sore."

"I brought you something that will probably help you with that." Yeah, because I had a reason to be here that didn't involve staring at her tits. "It'll help with the swelling and soreness, get the bruises to fade quickly. It was created for halfs when they're training, even though we have a higher than normal pain tolerance..." And now I was rambling.

"Oh, that would be great." She eyed the jar. "What's in it?"

Moving to sit next to her, I unscrewed the lid. The sharp menthol scent was strong. "It's a mix of plant extracts—arnica and mint extracts, mostly. It'll help. And you'll probably need to use this every night until your skin and body toughen up."

Her eyes met mine. "You knew this would happen?"

I nodded.

"Thank you," she murmured.

At that point, I needed to hand the jar over and get the hell out of there. She could figure out how to get the salve on her back, even though it would be kind of tough to do so. But she was smart. She'd figure it out.

"Did you get something to eat?" I asked instead of leaving.

"Yeah, Luke took me to the cafeteria. I ate, like, a pound of fries." She smiled quickly and then cast her gaze to the muted TV. "Everyone stares. It's awkward." With a shrug, she winced. "Did you eat?"

No. Are you offering? Gods, my mind was wallowing in triple-X territory. "I'm good." That would've been the perfect moment to leave, but I twisted toward her. "You want me to put this on your back?"

What the hell was I doing? Part of me prayed she'd say no.

She worried her lower lip and that flush ran deeper as her lashes flicked up and her eyes locked with mine. "Can you?"

Air leaked slowly out of my lungs. This was a bad idea. Actually, it was a great idea. Awesome. Best I'd had.

Fuck me.

"Lie on your stomach." My voice sounded rough to my own ears, and if Josie noticed it, I had no idea what she was thinking. But she got up and did just that, got down on her belly, folding her arms under her cheek.

Her eyes were closed and that lip was still between her teeth, and I had no idea why I found that so sexy. Getting up, I walked around the side of the bed and set the jar on the nightstand.

Swearing to about every god I knew, I carefully scooped the heavy, wet strands of hair out of the way, tossing them over one shoulder. Then, before I got down to business, I looked over my shoulder and made sure the damn painting of Apollo was still where I'd moved it, the face turned to the wall.

I slipped my fingers under the hem of her shirt, dragging it up the length of her back. She rose up a little, and the shirt gathered under her breasts, but I had it so far up that it bared her shoulders.

"Gods," I grunted, staring at her back.

"Is it that bad?"

I shook my head as I stared at the already red and purple marks along the top of her shoulders. A giant collage of contusions from hitting the mat over and over—it was normal to see during training.

231

Even more so when a Sentinel was out in the world, fighting. But seeing the violent splotches on *her* skin rocked me. I didn't like it.

"Seth?"

My gaze drifted to her face. Those eyes were open and she was looking over her shoulder. I exhaled softly as I picked up the jar. "You didn't complain."

A lopsided grin appeared as she settled her cheek back on her arm. "I think I complained."

No, not like most people who'd believed they were mortal up until a week ago would have. I scooped some of the thick gunk up, and then sat beside her, starting with her right shoulder.

The moment my fingers touched her, she jumped and let out a hoarse giggle. "Sorry. It's cold."

Nothing about this felt cold as I rubbed the salve gently over the bruise that traveled the width of her shoulders. Nothing about this should've been a turn-on, but the simple act of *touching* her got me going. There was something else under, a slight humming in my blood that had my gut hollowing in response, causing a tingling in the back of my throat. I didn't want to look too closely at it.

More goo ended up on my fingers and made it onto her skin. Before I knew what I was doing, both hands were on her back, and even with the cooling menthol, her skin was warming under my fingers as I worked out the tense muscles.

Ten minutes had to have passed before either of us spoke. "By the way, your hair looks great down," she said, sighing like a kitten that was dozing out in the warm sun. "Even wet. You have awesome hair. I'm jealous."

My lips split into a grin as I glanced up from where I was working the slight dip in her back, where there were absolutely no bruises. "Thanks, Joe."

"You're welcome, Sethie." There was a pause. "I really sucked at training."

"It was just one day. You'll get the hang of it."

"You really think so? Or are you just trying to make me feel better?"

"Maybe a little of both."

She laughed, and I could *feel* it.

"I guess it worked, huh?" My voice was low.

"Yeah," she whispered.

I liked the soft smile on her face—a contented smile. The kind of smile I imagined would grace her lips after having an orgasm. That flush would be there, too, just like it was then. But I bet it would be deeper, richer.

I grabbed more of the salve, and my hands moved to her lower back, following the slight, sexy curve. There were faint bruises here. Nothing major, but that didn't stop me. Even though I was well past the amount of time it would take to do this, my body was on autopilot. My fingers reached the soft sides of her waist, and I heard her inhale. The sound ricocheted through me like a boomerang. I was so hard, I ached. This was pure, senseless torture, but again, I couldn't stop myself.

Rubbing the salve up her sides, to where her shirt was bunched up, my gaze flicked to her profile. Her eyes were open in thin slits and her lips were parted. Chest rising and falling unsteadily, I dragged my hands back down her sides as I kept my gaze glued to what I could see of her face. The pink *was* deepening, spreading. My fingers trailed to the center of her lower back, and there wasn't even a speck of salve left on my fingers, the scent of menthol faded, as I worked my thumbs along her skin, dipping them under the hem of the loose sweatpants.

Her hips jerked up toward me and her eyes widened as my thumbs worked in short, pressured circles. Then they jerked again and her legs pressed together, like she was unconsciously seeking something—something that I could give her, that I wanted to give her.

I shuddered as I closed my eyes. The feeling of her skin under my hands, her body so close to mine, and knowing that if I took this further, she wouldn't stop me, nearly blew the head right off my cock. Being that stiff *hurt*, but that throbbing pulsed deeper. Yeah, I wanted to strip her out of these clothes, part those thighs and ease into her from behind, blissfully losing myself in her and forgetting everything else, but I wanted more. I wanted to get so close to her that there was not an inch of space between our skin, and I wanted to stay with her. The nights I had slept next to her, were the nights I had gotten the best sleep of my life.

I didn't deserve that.

Sure as hell didn't deserve something as fresh and fucking pure as Josie, because that's what she was. Totally untouchable.

It took everything in me to move my hands up and off her, and she stayed still, her breath coming in quick, short pants. I forced my hands to the mattress on either side of her as I stood and leaned over her.

"You want to know something?" I asked, my lips so close to her cheek I could almost taste her skin. "Sucked today or not, nothing in the sky is shining brighter than you."

And then I pushed up off the bed, and I left with her calling out my name like a church bell leading a sinner to the promise—to the illusion—of salvation.

CHAPTER
23

IN A blur, days turned into weeks faster than I could ever imagine they would, taking me further away from the life I had known and turning it into something foreign. Hours during the day were spent getting to know all the different areas in my body that could hurt, places I'd never even thought about before.

My legs felt like they had permanent shin splints from running in the evenings. It didn't matter if it was indoors or outdoors. My thighs ached from the uneven terrain when we were outside, *and* from when we were inside, and Seth jacked up the treadmill incline to run-or-die levels. The cheeks of my butt hurt from both the running and falling on them. I didn't even want to think about my back, because the word b-a-c-k made it ache.

About a week into training, I'd finally taken a fall correctly. Once in an entire day, and it wasn't until two days later that I was able to consistently land the correct way, but in the big scheme of things, that was a minor triumph, even though Luke and Seth insisted it was a big deal. But after learning how to take a fall without knocking the air out of my lungs or giving myself a concussion, I had to learn how to get back up.

Quickly.

And like a ninja.

Seth and Luke had taught me that I didn't want to roll up or get up by turning my back on the attacker, which was a big duh, but they expected me to get up just by pulling my legs in and propelling myself onto my feet.

What?

So this new phase of training had my stomach muscles feeling like someone had karate-chopped my nonexistent abs and my b-a-c-k was hurting even worse because I'd finally been able to get myself off the ground, kind of horizontally, only to fall right back down. It took almost another week for me to learn that I needed to roll onto my shoulders and to gain enough force when swinging my legs back down to propel myself up.

Then I spent another two days doing this repeatedly until the guys figured it was time to move onto defensive techniques, which resulted in lovely shades of purple, blue and red up and down my arms.

After the training sessions, I usually ate dinner in the cafeteria with Deacon and Luke, and there I saw more aspects of this strange world. I got to see pures using the elements to do things, like moving their plates or chairs without touching them, or causing it to rain over the unsuspecting heads of other students.

Other than Deacon and Luke, no one else really warmed up to me, even though a lot of them ended up watching the three of us train. The chick named Thea, with the huge boobs, was there every other day visually molesting Seth, and I didn't want to think about what it could mean.

Seth hadn't spent an entire night with me since our first night at the University. And while I knew I shouldn't be affected by his absence and I understood there was no reason for us to keep sharing a bed, I missed it, especially after he left in the evenings.

Another torturous ritual had begun after the first night of training, when Seth had given me that downright frustrating backrub. Every night since then, barring the random days off, after I ate dinner and then showered, Seth would show up with the jar that seemed to be bottomless.

We would chat for a little while, sometimes talking about nothing important, like what character we thought would be the last man standing on *The Walking Dead* or who was the better Winchester brother. Other times, the conversations ran deeper. He'd talk a little more about his mother and how beautiful she was, and what it was like to be shipped off to a school in a remote land. And I would tell him what was like to spend my summers on the lake and how lonely it was during the school year. Then I would lie on my belly with my shirt tucked under my breasts and Seth would apply the ointment, and when that ointment was gone from the slightly rough fingertips, he didn't stop. Not right away, at least.

His fingers and hands had mapped out every dip and curve of my back and sides. He was intimately familiar with each small ridge in my spine and the line of my shoulders. His touch... I don't know if it was because of *what* he was or because of *who* he was, it was like lightning in a bottle for my senses. From the moment he'd touch me, my body warmed—liquid heat pooled deep in my core and simmered in my veins. My breathing became more shallow with each passing moment and a different kind of ache invaded my body.

I was totally aware of how my body responded, how my hips would twitch and how I'd press my legs together to try to elevate the tension building. And he had to have known what he was doing to me, the state he was leaving me in.

And he did leave every night, and I had no idea where he went. Back to his room? Out somewhere on the campus? Because I knew there were parties. I heard Deacon talking about them. I couldn't imagine that he was spending every night by himself, especially since I also knew he was just as affected by the nightly rub-down as I was. When he'd stand to leave, I could *see* how affected he was. He wanted me, but he didn't act on it, and I couldn't help but wonder if that meant he was acting on it elsewhere.

Sometimes he brushed my hair back from my face before he left. Other times his hands just lingered on my hips when he stood. Last night he had kissed my cheek, but he'd still left.

"You look like you're about to fall asleep," Deacon commented, drawing my attention to where he sat across from me. We'd broken for lunch, and Seth had gone off wherever he went. I grabbed a quick sandwich with the boys in the cafeteria. "Do I need to get you a pillow?"

I smiled tiredly. I hadn't been sleeping well, partly due to thinking about things I didn't want to think about. Like my grandparents. Like my missing mom. Like how much I missed Erin. And like how much I sucked at training.

And the fact Seth had my body wrung so tight I felt like I was going to snap didn't help.

"I'm good." I picked a huge slice of tomato off my sandwich.

Luke finished off his mammoth bottle of water. "How was this morning?"

"Still working on defensive blocks—punches and kicks." I sat back, sighing. "I still suck."

He frowned. "Josie, you don't suck. You're doing great, and I don't think you understand how long we've been training. We make it seem easy, only because we've been doing this stuff since we were eight, but we know it's not. We know—"

Someone shouted behind us, and Luke twisted in his seat. I saw Deacon's eyes widen, so I cautiously turned around.

A tall guy with black hair and olive skin was facing off with another dude, who wasn't as tall, but definitely broader.

"What did you say to me?" Black-Haired Guy demanded, bright green eyes flashing.

Shorter Dude cocked his chin up. "I said, fuck you. And I'll say it one more time and I'll add onto it. Fuck you, you fucking *Hematoi*. You think you're better than me, but you're not, so fuck off."

"Hematoi?" I searched my memory for that word, finding nothing.

"Means pure-blood," Deacon answered quietly. "This isn't good."

Luke pushed back from the table. "Nope."

A loose group was starting to form around the two guys, and the Sentinels at the other end of the cafeteria started toward them.

"I'll say it again for you, too. Your kind doesn't belong here." Black-Haired Guy raised a hand. "Yeah, so fuck *this.*"

Shorter Dude lifted off his feet as if an invisible wrecking ball had slammed into his stomach. He was knocked back several feet, into a few of the guys crowding around him. The pure had to have been using the air element. Shorter Dude gained his balance easily, and then lurched forward, a large arm cocking back to land a powerful strike.

"Shit," Luke muttered, standing.

"Stop," Black-Haired Guy commanded, his voice moving like a ripple over the cafeteria, and holy crap, the Shorter Dude drew up short and stopped, arm frozen in midair. A sneer formed on the pure's lip. "Go to the top of the tallest building you can find, and then jump out the window."

My brows flew up, because that had to be the lamest comeback in history and I expected better from a descendant of a mythological creature, but then Shorter Dude spun around and started walking off. Unease churned in my stomach as I watched him cross the cafeteria.

"Oh my gods," Deacon said, coming to his feet as he raised his voice. "Someone stop him! That was a compulsion!"

My stomach dropped. The guys had filled me on a lot of things during the last couple of weeks, and I remembered clearly that, even before the Breed Order was abolished, using compulsions on halfs was forbidden. I'd found it ironic that they could use it on mortals as long as it did not place them in danger, but I knew that what the Dark-Haired Guy had just done had been a major no-no, a huge violation.

Luke shot forward, getting in front of Shorter Dude and slamming his hands into the guy's shoulders, but the guy kept trying to move forward.

"What the hell?" someone shouted—a girl. She came out of nowhere, all lean muscle and beautifully smooth dark skin. She shoved the pure back into the table and then snapped forward, curling a hand around the guy's throat like a pro. "If you even try to pull that shit with me, I'll break your neck. Undo the compulsion, asshole."

"Screw you," the pure grunted out.

Chaos broke out. Plates crashed to the floor. Bottles of water and soda toppled over. Tables were overturned as fists flew and bodies smacked into the floor. The double doors at the center of the room exploded as Sentinels rushed into the room, diving into the melee, and they were completely swallowed by the fighting group.

At the door, Luke was still wrestling with the half who was under a compulsion, and Deacon was with him. He had his arms around the half from the back, his sandaled feet digging in, trying to hold him back.

And then it turned horrific.

A flash of bright red went up in the corner, and someone screamed. The smell of burnt ozone and…and charred skin quickly filled the room. I jumped to my feet, my mouth dropping open as a human-shaped ball of flames ran out between two overturned tables, whirling and twisting. Shrieks erupted from the poor soul.

Oh my God.

Horror seized me in its grip and a part of my brain couldn't process what I was seeing—witnessing a person being burned alive. I started forward, not sure how to help, but someone—a girl—rushed toward the person, holding a glass of water. She threw it into the air as she raised her other hand. The stream of water rapidly expanded, pulsing as it spread out like a web of water.

A hand landed on my shoulder, whipping me around. I tensed, prepared to go all ninja on someone's ass. I didn't recognize the guy, but he was tall and had stunning, jewel-like eyes, as all pures did.

His hand tightened on my shoulder, fingers digging in. "A freaking mortal. You belong here even less than those halfs do."

Before I could say a word, his grip lessened, and then he pushed me back with enough force that I hit the chair and knocked it over. I didn't stop to think. A month ago I would have, but not now.

I reached behind me and grabbed the heavy, ceramic plate. The Covenant didn't do plastic or paper, and that turned out to be a huge benefit to me. I swung that plate right at the guy's head. The impact jarred my arm, and the guy dropped like a sack of apples.

"You really shouldn't have done that."

The cold voice sent a chill down my spine, and before I could turn or grab anything else that could be used as a weapon, a hand fisted in my ponytail and jerked my neck back sharply, causing me to cry out.

"And you really shouldn't have done *that*, asshole."

Then the hand was gone, and I spun at the sound of Seth's voice and my eyes met his narrowed gaze. His lips were thin, his cheeks sharp as he grabbed my hand. He was furious. "Let's go."

Whoever had grabbed me was in a crumpled heap on the floor, and he didn't look like he'd be getting up for a while. "But—"

"This is not our problem, Josie. And it's going to get worse before they stop. You're getting out of here before someone sets your sweet ass on fire."

I scanned the packed cafeteria, spotting Luke and Deacon still struggling with the half, and I started to dig my feet in, because it didn't seem right to leave them, but Seth was having none of it.

Cursing, he spun around toward me and dipped low. I was tossed over his shoulder in a nanosecond, and then he was moving forward, easily dodging the flying chairs and bodies rolling across the floor.

Out in the hall, he didn't put me down, and when I started to wiggle, his hand smacked down on my butt, causing me to yelp. "Hey! Seth, put me down!" When he didn't answer and kept walking, I knocked my fists off his back.

"Knock it off, Joe."

"Seth—"

"I don't trust you if I put you down. You'll probably run back in there and get yourself turned into a toasted marshmallow." He kicked open the door, and I winced as cold rain washed over my back. "Shit back there isn't going to calm down for a while."

My fingers dug into his thermal as rain ran up my back and across my neck, causing me to gasp. "Oh my God, I don't like you."

There was an extra bounce in his step that had me cursing. Chuckling, he tightened his hold on me. "Hold on."

I squealed as he took off, running across the rain-slick walkway with the grace and speed of a damn gazelle, but we were still soaked by the time he burst into the lobby of the dorm, and the bastard still didn't put me down, not until we were inside my room.

The second he deposited me on my feet, I knocked the loose strands of hair out of my face and then shot forward, smacking his arm. "That wasn't necessary!"

He arched his brows. "Apparently it was."

Scowling at him, I backed off before I hit him again. I had to take several deep breaths as I plucked the wet clothing off my skin. "Does that stuff happen regularly?"

"I have no idea, but I'm not surprised. Some of those pures are real bastards."

Giving up on my shirt, I exhaled roughly. "The pure used a compulsion on a half. Told him to go jump out a window."

"That sucks." Seth started to turn. "Stay in here until either Luke or I tell you it's okay to come out."

I don't know what did it. Maybe it was the fading adrenaline from what had gone down in the cafeteria. Maybe it was the rough and tough training. Maybe it was the frustration that was pent up inside me. Maybe it was everything.

Either way, I lost my shit a little.

"You're going to leave again? How typical."

He turned back to me, both brows raised. "What?"

"You! You're going to leave again. Because that's all you do. So I'm supposed to just sit in here on my hands until someone tells me it's okay to come out again. That's bullshit."

His brows slammed down. "It's for your safety."

"It's bullshit!" I repeated. "We could be training right now! And I need to be doing that because I can't just sit here and do *nothing*."

Seth moved a step forward. "You have been training nonstop, Josie. A day or two here and there isn't going to change anything."

My hands closed into fists. "You don't get it," I said, heading into the bedroom. "Whatever. Go do whatever you do in your free time."

"What the hell, Josie? What is your deal?"

What was my deal? Kicking off my sneakers, I plopped down and yanked off my socks, tossing them into the corner of the room.

Seth was in the doorway. "Josie."

I yanked my hair down and slingshot the rubber band across the room, and when I looked at him, I *really* lost my shit.

Shooting onto my feet, my hands balled into fists. "You don't get it, Seth! I don't want to sit around in my room alone, because I don't want to sit here and think about how fucked up everything is!"

He straightened. "I know—"

"No, you don't!" I shouted. "I just saw someone get lit on fire, and you're acting like it's really not that big of a deal. People just get burned alive all the time around here, apparently. And I

243

saw someone get told to jump out of a window and that person was seriously going to do it! That's crazy. That's legit insane!"

"Josie," he said softly, carefully.

"And it took me almost three weeks to learn how to take a fall and to get up correctly. Three weeks! Hibernating bears learn faster than that."

His lips twitched and his voice dropped, "Josie."

"Don't you dare laugh, you asshole!"

"*Josie*," he drawled, amber eyes twinkling.

"And I can't think about my grandparents without it hurting, or my mom without wondering if she's even alive!" Squeezing my eyes shut, I drew in a shaky breath. Tears burned my eyes as I plopped down on the edge of the bed. Except, of course, I misjudged it and ended up landing on my butt on the floor by the foot of the bed. The pain didn't even register as I pulled my knees up and pressed my palms against my eyes.

"Hey." His voice was closer, and I felt his hand wrap around my knee.

The next breath I took got stuck. "They're dead, Seth." My voice cracked, because it was the first time I'd said it since it'd happened. "They're dead, and because of what? They were good people—great people. They didn't deserve what happened to them."

His hand moved up to my arms. He pulled one down, and I lowered the other as his steady gaze locked with my teary-eyed one. "You're right. They didn't deserve that, Josie. But you can't bottle that stuff up in you. No amount of training or anything will help you if you keep the lid on it. It's not healthy."

"No shit," I retorted, pulling my arm away. I wiped under my eyes with the backs of my hands. More tears were building. The knot in my throat was getting thicker. I could feel myself starting to crumble, and I forced my thoughts away from them and my mom, and latched onto the next thing. I blurted it out without really thinking. "And then there's you..."

"Me?"

I looked at him. "You come in here every night and you touch me and you...you make me feel these things—"

Seth rocked back, putting distance between us. "Josie—"

Warmth infused my cheeks, but I continued on, because why not? It was either embarrass myself or cry all over him. I was going to go with the former. "You touch me, and then you leave me, and I want you to stay. I want you to keep touching me, but you...you *leave*."

He turned his head, dipping his chin down as his chest rose. "You don't want that. Trust me, you—"

"Don't tell me what I want!" I shifted onto my knees and slammed my hands into his broad shoulders.

Unprepared for what I'd done, he fell back on his ass. His eyes widened on me, like he couldn't believe I'd just done that, and yeah, it was wrong.

But I didn't care. "Don't tell me what I want. You don't live in my head or in my body. Don't you dare make that call for me."

His jaw clamped down as he stared at me with narrowed eyes. "I make the call for you, because I know better."

"Oh, that's lame, *Sethie*. Lame and stupid, and you can take that and shove it up your ass! I know what I want!" Too caught up in anger and frustration and grief and so many other things, I couldn't stop myself. "I want you to kiss me. I want you to—"

A second passed, and then he was in my face, hands on my shoulders, causing me to gasp. "Don't push this, Josie. Seriously. You have no idea what you're asking for."

Maybe I didn't. Probably didn't, because I had no experience, but what he did every night by coming in here and then leaving was wrong. I met his stare. "Then you don't come in here and touch me and then leave, going off to do God knows what while I'm in here wondering what the hell is going on."

A muscle throbbed along his jaw, and then he dropped his hands. "Fine. If that's what you want."

My mouth dropped open, because that was exactly what I didn't want and it hurt—it *burned* inside my chest and my throat—

how easily he could just be okay with that. And it *hurt* more than I thought it would. "Fuck you."

His head tilted to the side as he stared at me, his eyes glowing a tawny amber. "Godsdammit, Josie."

I glared at him.

He glared at me. "Fuck."

A heartbeat passed, then Seth's large hands were on my cheeks and his mouth on mine.

CHAPTER
24

I **HAD** absolutely no self-control.

Kissing Josie was the last thing I should be doing, but I was so done with fighting what I wanted, fighting what *she* wanted. Had it all been leading to this? Was I fooling myself every night I came to her, touched her, and then left, thinking I wasn't building something between us?

Yeah, I was a fool.

But my mouth was on hers, and the action seemed to have caught her off-guard, her body stiff, but I was insistent. As my lips moved over hers, something rose up in me, something wild and electric, and I needed more than this...chaste gesture. I needed to go deeper. I needed to taste her.

Tilting my head, I caught her lower lip between my teeth, putting the slightest pressure there, and her hands landed on my chest and her fingers dug into the shirt I was wearing.

I flicked my tongue over her lower lip, and then across the seam of her mouth, coaxing a tentative gasp out of her. In the back of my head, I could sense that she was inexperienced, that I needed to hold back, but when her lips parted, I delved right in, stroking my tongue over hers, tasting her for the first time. And holy fuck, that taste went straight to all my nerve endings. I

247

dropped a hand to her back, balling the thin, damp barrier of her shirt. She sucked in a breath, and I wanted it for my own. I took it, deepening the kiss, until one of her arms came up, looping around my neck. Second by second, her body relaxed into mine, and a deep, possessive sound rose from within me.

This was fucking insane.

But I couldn't stop.

Savoring her mouth, the feel of her lips against mine—it had been forever since I wanted something this badly, and I *wanted* her. I pulled her body against mine, sliding her knees across the carpet, fitting her hips where I wanted them. The breathy sound she made into my mouth went straight to my cock, and I knew she felt that. There was no hiding it, and I wanted her to feel it.

Her hand caught in my hair, tugging my neck, and I nipped at her lips as I lifted my head, staring down at her. Those silky lashes fluttered open. Our gazes locked. Those blue eyes were deep, the color of the sky before it turned to night.

Something moved in my throat. I ran my tongue along my lower lip, tasting her.

"Seth," she whispered.

I could hear her shaky breaths in the silence between us. Knowing I didn't deserve this, I dropped my hands to my thighs, trying to gain some thread of control, but it was like grasping at raindrops. Our gazes met again, and the hunger and need pooling in those bright blue eyes undid me, snapping the restraint like a band pulled too tight.

Shooting forward, I clasped her cheeks again as I took the next kiss to a whole different level—none of that soft and coaxing bullshit. And she was ready. With a breathy moan, her mouth opened under mine. This kiss went deeper, was rougher, and the force propelled us. Josie went down, and I followed, my mouth never leaving hers, and the sudden change in positions was like hitting payday. Our bodies were flush, chest to chest and hip to hip. She was soft and wonderful under me.

Shifting my weight onto the arm planted on the carpet next to her head, I cupped her chin and tilted it back, deepening the kiss, wanting to somehow claim her very soul. Funny thing was, it was my soul that was being claimed, my breath that was being stolen, and my heart that was pounding crazy fast in my chest.

Josie was kissing me back, and there was a hint of hesitation, as if she didn't know what to do, but it didn't matter, because she was doing everything right, and that made me want to abandon any pretense of being tame. I could take her now—lose myself in the wonder that was Josie. I was rock hard, ready, but damn, if it didn't go deeper than a physical need.

I wanted what I'd never had. Real companionship. Loyalty. Friendship. Her. Me. No third parties. Just us. A future. A *tomorrow*. Salvation. And that made my fucking chest compress, because I didn't even know what to do with all of *that*.

But I knew what to do with all of *this*.

Her thighs spread, seating me against her, and a rough groan rumbled up from my chest as she flicked the tip of her tongue against mine. Fuck—so sweet. She made a soft, heady moan into my mouth and that catapulted a bolt of raw sensation through me, and all I could taste was her on my tongue, and it was wild, all-consuming.

I slid my hand down over her delicate throat, stopping for a moment to feel her racing pulse under my thumb, and then I went lower, my hand coasting to the side, barely sweeping over the swell of her breast, and yet her back arched up as she gasped into the kiss.

Gods, she was going to kill me.

I pressed my hips into hers, letting her really know just how badly I wanted this with her, that there was absolutely no question about it, and I gripped her with a trembling hand, rocking my hips again, sending a rush down to the base of my spine. And she tilted hers. A perfect dance I was so caught up in that I didn't even feel the presence until I heard the voice.

"When I asked you to watch over my daughter, I didn't have *this* in mind."

Oh shit.

I froze as tiny hairs all over my body stood, and under me, Josie stiffened. Nothing killed an erection faster than Apollo popping in while I was dry-humping his *daughter*.

Gods, his timing was always epic.

Lifting myself up, I opened my eyes and stared into Josie's wide, startled ones. I knew I was so dead, like deader than dead with my balls not intact, but right now, it was only me between her and seeing her father for the first time.

This...this was going to get messy.

Apollo sighed loudly. "Any time now, Seth."

Confusion had already begun to fill her expression, and I tried to smile for her as I touched the tips of my fingers to her cheek. "It'll be okay," I whispered to her.

Her eyes remained latched to mine as I rolled off Josie, positioning myself so that I was in front of her, giving her time to get it together. When I saw Apollo standing in the doorway, all I could think was *what the hell?*

Apollo didn't look like himself—not like his true self. His hair was dark brown, cropped close to the skull, his features slightly different, and his eyes the same as Josie's. He looked like Leon had—the way he'd made himself look when he'd been at Deity Island, pretending to be nothing more than a Sentinel.

"What is up with this?" I asked, standing.

He was staring at me like he wanted to castrate me old-school style, but his gaze shifted beyond me as Josie sat up. Putting a hand on the edge of the bed, she stood, her face pale and eyes so incredibly wide as she stared at him.

Apollo, disguised as Leon, smiled at her. "Hello, Josie."

She took an unsteady step forward, her shoulder brushing mine. "Bob?"

"Bob?" Seth repeated.

The man I was staring at—the man Seth had called Apollo, my father—was familiar to me. I knew him. I'd known him as a little girl.

"Wait a minute," Seth said, stepping forward. "You're calling yourself Bob now? Really?"

He glanced at Seth. "Why are you still here?"

Seth folded his arms. "I'm not going anywhere." Pausing, he glanced at me. "Unless you want me to go."

"No." I shuffled closer to him as I stared up at the tall man. "I want you to stay."

"Great," muttered the man I knew as Bob.

I shook my head slowly, trying to get my brain cells to function. The dizzy, pleasant rush of sensations from Seth's kisses and from the weight of his body on mine, pressing into the best possible places, had quickly faded, but I felt like I was in a dream.

"You...you used to visit me when I was little," I said, and it sounded crazy. "By the lake. You brought me candy and dolls."

"That doesn't sound creepy at all," Seth muttered under his breath.

I ignored him. "I don't understand." Maybe I did and just didn't want to comprehend it. "You're my..."

"I am your father." He glanced at Seth and smirked. "That's the second *Star Wars* nod. Keeping track?"

Seth rolled his eyes.

"What the hell?" I whispered.

The air shimmered around the man I knew as Bob, and then he...he wasn't Bob at all. In his place was a man who shared some of the same features, but was taller and broader, with a head full of blond waves and eyes that still matched mine.

"Holy crap." Heart pounding, I stumbled back, and then looked at the painting that was facing the wall. "Holy crappers."

Seth reached out, but I shook my head. "I'm okay. I've just never seen someone do a live Photoshop on himself."

The man—who was so *obviously* Apollo—smiled again, and it made my stomach tumble. "I was never supposed to know you. Not unless we needed you. That was the deal we made when we created the twelve demigods," he explained. "But...you were my child. I *wanted* to know you."

I had no idea what to say, so I just stared at him as my heart raced.

"We didn't get to spend a lot of time together, and I understand if you feel like I abandoned you, but I've always kept an eye on you, one way or another."

I still had no idea what to say.

Apollo tipped his chin up, and a long and awkward moment passed. "I am sorry about your grandparents. They're at peace now, in paradise. I hope that's a comfort to you."

Air caught in my throat as I took a step to the side and sat down on the edge of the bed without falling off it this time. Was that a comfort to me? Yes. No. "My mom?"

"She's safe. I cannot tell you where she is, but she will remain safe until the threat is over," he replied as his gaze moved over my face. "I am proud of you."

My mouth opened, but no words formed. My breath hitched again, and I felt that damn knot in my throat expand.

"You've shown remarkable strength, and you have held it together in an incredible situation," he continued, doing something akin to putting my heart in a juice squeezer. "Instead of doing nothing, you've opted to train, to defend yourself. I'm proud." There was a beat of silence as he glanced at Seth. "However, your choice in males concerns me."

"I think my choice in *males* is quite good, thank you," I snapped back before I could stop myself.

Seth's head swung toward me, as if he was surprised that I would defend him, which would make him an idiot, considering I'd just had my mouth on his.

Apollo's smile reappeared and spread, softening the cold, eerie beauty of his face. "Well, then..." His gaze shifted to Seth. "I guess she told me."

For once, Seth had nothing to say, and when I looked at him, he was still staring at me, his golden eyes wide and his face a shade paler.

"I cannot stay long. Being in your presence... Well, it drains me, but I..." His brows furrowed and he shifted from one foot to the next. "But I felt your pain earlier. I had to see you."

There. That juice squeezer was working overtime in my chest. "I don't know what to say."

"You do not need to say anything."

"No...I do. This...this is a lot. All of this is a lot. You don't even look old enough to be my dad." I laughed, and it sounded a little crazy. "And I knew you at one point. Your were my friend—my only friend, and you...you just walked in on me making out with a guy, so I feel like we just covered the teen years I never had with you."

Seth choked on what sounded like a laugh.

"Let me put on record, that was not an enjoyable experience," Apollo commented dryly.

"But you're here and you've...you've been here in one way or another," I said, smoothing a shaky hand through my hair. "And that has to mean something," I whispered, my voice raspy.

His smile faded a little. "But right now, I know it's not enough."

I squeezed my eyes shut against the sudden, uncontrollable burn, and in a heartbeat, I felt that he was closer the second before he touched the side of my face. My eyes flew open, and he—a god, *the sun god*—was kneeling in front of me. A surge of energy shot through me, like being shocked by electricity.

"You must continue to be brave, *to paidí mou, i zoḯmou*. You must continue to be strong. Nothing you face will be easy, but I will always be watching over you." He lowered his hand as he stood, addressing Seth. "And you...you are so very lucky."

And then he was gone.

Just like that, there one second, and then gone the next.

"Well, that wasn't as awkward...or as violent as I thought it would be," Seth announced, obviously accustomed to Apollo popping in and out.

"What...what did he say?" My gaze shifted from the spot Apollo had stood to where Seth was. "In the other language? Do you know?"

He nodded as his face softened. "He said, 'my child, my life.'"

My heart squeezed.

"I never thought he had it in him."

"What?"

Seth scrubbed his fingers through his hair and then dropped his hand. "I never thought Apollo really cared about anyone other than himself. Not like I think—like I know he cares about you. He has compassion. I've just never seen him that way before."

I don't know what it was about that, but the tenuous hold I had on my emotions shattered. I broke wide open. My face crumpled as a sob ripped out of me, shaking my body. I smacked my hands on my face, but it did nothing to stop the tears. They wet my palms, streaked down my cheeks and shook my shoulders.

The bed dipped, and strong, warm arms circled my waist, and knowing that Seth had stayed here, that he hadn't left, made it all that much harder to pull it back together, to stitch the rawness closed.

Seth made a deep sound in the back of his throat as he pulled me onto his lap, folding one arm around me. His hand curved around the back of my head, and without saying a word, he guided me closer, and I went. Having no experience with these kinds of tears, I burrowed in as close as I could, wrapping my arms around him, and I held on.

And he held onto me.

OPENING MY eyes, I stared up at the bluish glow flashing across the ceiling from the TV. The volume was turned down to nothing but hushed whispers. I must've fallen asleep.

You're so very lucky.

I dipped my chin, my gaze traveling over the still form of Josie. Emotionally spent, she had fallen asleep in my arms. Hadn't even woken up when I'd repositioned us at the head of the bed. She stayed in my arms, her body curled on her side, hips between mine, head on my chest.

I tucked a strand of hair back behind her ear. She stirred, but whatever she murmured was completely unintelligible. The arm I had draped over her waist tightened of its own accord.

Had I ever held a girl like this? Maybe once or twice with Alex, but with her it had never been a case of her really wanting to be there, with me. More so a case of her *needing* to be close to me, and that was a big difference. Honestly, Alex and I...we had needed each other.

We'd never *wanted* each other. Not in the way she'd wanted Aiden St. Delphi and not in the way I wanted—I cut myself off, even though it was pointless. But sometimes it felt like, if I didn't allow myself to finish a thought, it wasn't true. Dumb-as-shit logic right there.

Josie shifted again, curling her small hand into a fist against my chest. I wondered what she dreamt and hoped it was something peaceful as I stared at the faint bruises shadowing the insides of her forearms. Eventually her skin would toughen against the training, but would she? So far she had accepted everything tossed her way, but I knew she would still hesitate when it came to killing something. That last shred of morality would be near-impossible for her to leave behind and accept.

There weren't a lot of things in this world that scared me, but knowing there was a good chance she wouldn't be able to kill... Yeah, it terrified me.

I closed my eyes, sucking in an unsteady breath. If she knew everything about me, everything that I had done, she wouldn't be lying in my arms like this. She wouldn't be anywhere near me, let alone wanting me to kiss her. So, yeah, I was lucky right now.

I needed to get my ass out of there before...before what? Before this went any further. Before she got herself so deep inside me I wouldn't be able to get her out. And before she found out what I really was.

"Seth?"

My lids lifted at the sound of her sleepy voice. Her head was tilted back, her blue gaze on my face. "Hey."

She blinked slowly. "I fell asleep on you."

"It's okay," I told her. "I didn't mind."

A soft smile curved up her lips, and my gut dropped a little. A smile...I'd never known a smile could have that kind of effect. Could feel like a kick to the chest. "Thanks for...well, for also letting me cry on you." A pink stain spread across her cheeks. Fascinating. "And for staying with me."

"It's not a big deal." I tried to shift inconspicuously. Now that she was awake and moving, so was my cock. "You hanging in there?"

She settled her cheek against my chest again, apparently going nowhere, and that...that was okay with me. "I think I'm better," she said quietly as she wiggled her hips, causing my hand against her stomach to flex. "I needed to let it out, I guess. I was holding it in. But I...I really don't know what to think about Apollo. I just can't really think about him being...being my father."

"Who *would* want to think about Apollo being their father?"

She giggled, and I felt my lips respond in a grin. "Yeah, good point."

"Out of everything you're dealing with, I think it's okay to put that on the back burner for a little while. Just don't be surprised if he pops up again."

"Hopefully when we're not making out," she muttered wryly.

I started to laugh, because that made two of us, but the humor faded quicker than morning frost. "I should probably get next door."

Josie jumped off my chest so quickly I thought there were springs under her ass. Planting her hands on my thighs, she twisted around so that she faced me. "You're going to leave now?"

I opened my mouth.

"Think before you answer that question, Sethie."

Caught between wanting to laugh and kiss her and getting the hell out of there, I stared at her for what felt like a full minute. "Josie, I..." I trailed off as her eyes narrowed. "I'm not trying to be a dick—"

"Really? You kissed me earlier. Like *really* kissed me, and it sounds like you're about to write that off, and yeah, that makes you a dick."

"Damn, you're feisty when you want to be," I murmured, kind of turned on by her display of attitude. But as her lips thinned, for a second, I thought she might hit me.

"Sometimes I really don't like you," she said.

"The thing is, Josie, if you *really* knew me, you wouldn't like me." Pulling my right leg up, I shifted so there was some space between us. "You wouldn't be in the same room as me."

Josie sat back on her calves, and I wanted to get hit with another dose of anger—rightful anger. "Why?" she said softly, surprising me. "I really would like to know, because I think I know you. I know you better than I've known anyone else. So tell me why."

Shoving my fingers through my hair, I resisted the urge to pull on it.

"Come on, Seth. You saw me at my worst and didn't run. Do you think I will?"

I lifted my gaze, meeting her steady one. "Do you know what I was doing for the last year? Before I was sent to get you? I was hunting down those who sided with Ares. And by hunting down, I don't mean rounding them up to have brunch and crumpets, Josie."

"I figured you weren't having lunch with them," she said, plopping back on her ass. Her eyes never left mine.

"Did you?" I rose, shifting my weight onto my arms as I planted my hands on either side of her legs and leaned in so that we were face to face. "Those I hunted down—they were living, breathing people. Some of them pures. Some of them halfs. And some were mortals."

She still held my stare, and I wanted her to look away, to turn away and prove what I thought. "None of them were arrested or tried in a court. All of them were deemed guilty before I even laid eyes on them. My orders were to kill them. And I did."

Her chest rose sharply, but still, she did not look away.

"I cannot even begin to count how many lives I've ended with these hands. *These* hands, Josie." Lifting them, I curved them over her knees. "The ones you want touching you."

Her lips parted. "It was your job, Seth, it—"

"It was who I was. An executioner," I cut in, my voice pitching low. "I killed people. Sometimes I didn't make it quick. Do you know what that makes me?"

She didn't answer.

I gave her one. "A monster. It makes me a monster."

"No." Her hands landed atop mine, and when I started to pull them away, she held on. "You are not a monster, Seth. You did what you had to do. What you were ordered to do."

"Josie—"

"There are people—mortals—who kill other people every day because they are ordered to do so. Does that make men and women in the military monsters? What about police?" Her slim fingers gripped mine. "And would you have done those things if you hadn't been ordered?"

Of course I wouldn't have. I'd learned my lesson well before I got my marching orders, but did that change the last year of my life? No. And it didn't change everything I had done before then.

"Would you, Seth? Would you have done it if you weren't made to?"

I closed my eyes and my response was barely above a whisper. "No."

She squeezed my hands. "It's terrible. I'm not going to lie and say that it isn't a big deal, but I *know* you. You did what you had to do, not because you wanted to. There's a difference there." She paused as her hands slid up to my wrists. "I ran over a squirrel once."

Blinking open my eyes, I drew back as far as she'd let me. "What?"

"I ran over a squirrel the second time I ever drove a car," she repeated. "I also hit a deer. And when I was seventeen, I clipped a cat. Before I left for college, I backed into a dog."

"Gods," I muttered.

She nodded, lips drooping at the corners. "His name was Buddy and it was a golden retriever. Like, the most friendly of all dogs."

Oh my gods.

"And the owner's five-year-old kid saw it. Buddy survived, but I'm kind of like a mass murderer when it comes to animals and me behind the wheel."

My lips twitched. It wasn't funny. I had to keep telling myself that. "Babe, that's not the same thing."

"I know." She shrugged. "But still. I'm not happy about it, but it seriously made me feel like an animal serial killer. Like somehow that was my destiny. To kill all the furry, four-legged friends."

I stared at her. No matter what, she was so...so mortal.

Josie bit down on her lower lip as she worked her hands up to my elbows, her thumbs pressing on the insides. "I have deeper, darker secrets."

"You do?" My voice was low, rough. The constriction in my chest was lessening. "Did you cut off the heads of your Barbies or something?"

She laughed softly. "No, but I did cut their hair and tried to dye it with markers."

"Of course," I murmured.

Rising onto her knees in front of me, she tightened her grip on my elbows, and I was absolutely helpless to move. Made powerless by a girl who thought she had darker secrets than me. "I wished, more than once when I was younger, that I had a different mom. That's pretty bad."

I found myself leaning toward her. Our faces separated by scant inches. "I think most people would sympathize with that."

"Maybe. I'm just pointing out that no one is perfect, especially me."

Josie was the closest thing to perfect I'd ever met, and she had no idea. The realization was a shot to the chest. When had this happened? When had I gone from being a one-man show, always alone with nothing meaningful, to having *this* right in front of me, in me? I closed my eyes as I dragged in a deep breath. I don't even know why I said what I did. Then again, I didn't know why I'd told Josie all the things I had before. "I don't feel that way."

"What?"

When I opened my eyes, she was staring at me with those big, blue ones. "When I'm with you, I don't feel like a monster. I forget." And that was the damn truth—a scary truth. "I forget all the things I've done that make me not deserve this."

Josie didn't respond, and for a long moment, she didn't move, but then I felt her soft lips brush my forehead. The gentle, chaste touch shocked me, and I jerked back, staring at her. My heart pounded like a jackhammer.

Her smile was hesitant, but her grip on my arms was strong. "You're staying with me," she said, flushing pink as she ducked her chin. "It's settled, like it or not."

Then she sort of climbed up, forcing me back against the headboard and onto my ass, her movements awkward and shy as she looped her arms around my shoulders. I stiffened as she wiggled down, getting herself comfortable in my lap. Once situated, she grabbed my arms and folded them around her.

All I could do was stare at her, but as seconds turned into minutes, and as my muscles began to relax, I stayed with her.

" **Y OU RUN** like a girl."

I scowled at Seth's back and huffed out, "I *am* a girl."

"Doesn't mean you need to run like one," he called out, hitting the main pathway that led around the academic buildings.

This time I made a face that didn't last long, because I felt like I might pass out. Luke had bowed out on the afternoon run. Not that I blamed him. A cold snap had dropped the temps into what felt like lung-freezing territory and I couldn't feel my face.

I hated running.

However, I did not hate the view in front of me.

Long, lean muscles flexed under his deep-gray thermal. My gaze dropped to his butt, and I almost tripped. I could seriously stare at his body all day. It was a work of art.

But my attraction to Seth ran deeper than the physical. He was still that puzzle I'd only barely begun to arrange. Like I'd gotten all the outer pieces with the straight sides lined up, but the meat of the puzzle still needed to be pieced together. Those moments when he was unbelievably kind, or when he was patient during training, or when he stayed with me when I'd turned into a hysterical mess, or when his guard completely slipped, and I saw the teasing, easy-going nature that I knew was at the heart of him—all of them had lured me in.

I wanted to get inside his head. Maybe that was some of wanting to study psychology left in me. Maybe it was just Seth. I didn't know.

It had been two days since I'd seen Apollo and had a minor mental breakdown, and two days since we kissed. There hadn't been any more of that, but Seth hadn't left the last two nights. He stayed, and I guessed that was progress—*frustrating* progress.

I had gotten somewhere with him that night. I knew that, but I also knew there was so much more than what he'd shared with me. And I couldn't help but think back to what Erin had said, to how Deacon and Luke behaved around Seth.

There was more.

The strange—but becoming more and more familiar—feeling unfurled deep inside me as we passed the library. Without meaning to, I slowed down, and then I just stopped in the middle of the pathway, unmindful of the brutal wind whipping through the statues and olive trees.

My gaze crawled up the long, wide set of marble steps beyond the veranda, and to the heavy, unmoving doors.

"Hey." Seth had circled back to me, his body blocking the wind. "You okay?"

I nodded. "Yeah, it's..." Shaking my head, I smiled up at him. "Never mind."

Rays of sunlight caressed his high cheekbones as his brows knitted. "What?"

Glancing back up at the library, I shrugged. "It's just... Every time I see the library, I don't know, I want to go inside."

"That's weird."

I laughed as I pressed my chilled hands together. "I know."

"You haven't checked it out with the guys?" Seth grabbed my hands, capturing them between his. "Gods, your fingers are like ice cubes."

My gaze drifted from the library to him. His head was bowed, and shorter strands of his hair had slipped free, brushing his cheeks, as he rubbed his hands over mine. It was such an intimate thing to do that I didn't want to respond at first. "No," I said quietly. "Neither of the guys is keen on the whole library thing."

"Neither am I." He shifted closer, still concentrating on my hands.

"Why doesn't that surprise me?"

He peeked up through long, thick lashes. "I'll have you know I'm practically a genius."

I snorted.

"You'll pay for that," he warned lightly. My fingers were all kinds of toasty now. "So, you want to check it out?"

"What? The library? Don't we have to run eight more miles or something?"

Seth chuckled. "Joe, you can't run eight miles."

Yanking my hands free, I smacked his arm. "You just wait until I'm a demigod. Then I'll run hundreds of miles around you. And don't call me Joe."

He grinned as he reached up, catching a few wind-swept strands and tucking them back behind my ear. His touch lingered.

"What are you doing?" I asked.

His lashes swept down, shielding those unique eyes. "I don't know. Staring at you."

I laughed even as I felt my cheeks flush. "Okay."

His grin spread, and my tummy flopped. I thought for a moment that he might kiss me, but his gaze moved from me to over my head. The curve of his lips straightened out, and I twisted around.

Three students stood beneath a statue of some robed lady that I assumed was a goddess. They were staring openly at us, not in a bad way, but definitely in a weird way. That happened a lot, especially whenever I was out and about with Seth. Wherever we went, people stared at him. Just like they had when his mother put him on display.

My skin pricked with anger. "Let's go in. Now."

He blinked and centered his focus on me. I forced a grin. "Race you to the door?"

A brow arched mockingly. "You'd fall on the steps and break a leg."

"Dick." I shoved him in the chest, and he didn't budge. "You're going to eat your words later."

I spun to get a head start, but by the time I reached the middle of the steps, he was already standing by the large marble columns. I strutted past him, flipping him off in the process.

Seth's deep laugh floated like music on the wind. He sidestepped me and opened the door. The first look at the inside of the library almost knocked me flat on my butt.

"Good *gods*," I whispered, because seriously, "gods" was the only word fitting for what I was seeing.

Giant statues of the gods were positioned through the main floor, between deep aisles full of shelves, holding up a second floor with their marble hands. The library was deep and endless, chilly, and smelled like mothballs were hidden behind every book.

But the weird, almost nervous, energy in the pit of my stomach ramped up. I placed a hand over my tummy, feeling slightly nauseous. Confused, I broke away from Seth and walked between the dark wooden tables. No one sat in the heavy-looking chairs. It was as quiet as I imagined a tomb would be.

I headed down the first aisle, running my fingers over the thick spines of books that were free from dust. The stacks were at least eighteen feet tall, and I wondered if some of the people here could fly, because I didn't see a ladder. Then again, many of the pures could just summon the air element. So could Seth.

And I would be able to, once my powers were unbound.

Freaky.

"Live up to your expectations?" Seth murmured as he touched the small of my back.

I shivered as I shook my head. "It's pretty amazing."

"Yeah, it is."

Something in his voice coaxed me into looking up at him, and when I did, I was snared. He was staring down at me in a way... well, in a way I had little experience with. That nervous energy dropped lower, and another shiver coursed down my spine.

His gaze drifted from mine, to my mouth, and my muscles tensed as my lips parted. Immediately, I forgot the purpose of coming into the library. A pleasant hum invaded my veins as I swayed toward him, feeling hot and dizzy, like I'd been out in the summer sun all day.

Seth's chin dipped as he lifted his hands to my hips. He barely touched me there, but his fingertips seared through the thin material of my pants. I started thinking about the tips of his fingers being elsewhere, and that made me even more dizzy. I inhaled deeply and caught his scent, a mix of the outdoors and something citrusy.

He drew his hands up to my waist, and then lifted one to my temple. Slowly, he traced the curve of my cheekbone. My pulse thrummed as his intense stare followed his fingertips. He trailed them down my face and then over my parted lips.

"Seth."

He jerked back, dropping his hand as he turned at the sound of his name. I squeezed my eyes shut as I gripped the edge of a shelf. When I reopened them, I peered up over his shoulder and saw Marcus, the Dean of the University. He wasn't alone. The man with the scar was with him—Solos—and so was another older man, dressed in all black, that I saw around the campus a lot.

"What's going on?" Seth asked, shifting his legs so that his stance was wide, a movement I now recognized as a fighting stance.

Unease blossomed in the pit of my stomach.

Marcus nodded in my general direction, and then those bright eyes centered on Seth. "We need to talk."

The "in private" part wasn't spoken, but I got what they were saying. Seth glanced over his shoulder at me, and I shrugged.

"I'll be right back," he said.

"Not going anywhere." After the horrific chaos in the cafeteria, I wasn't keen on roaming around the campus by myself. I actually hadn't even eaten in there since then. The boys usually brought me something to eat in the training room or to my dorm.

Seth joined the group of very stern-looking men, and they immediately started talking, their voices too low for me to hear, but it didn't stop me from trying. I learned fairly quickly that I sucked at reading lips. Everything looked like they were saying "tomatoes" or "I love you" and I doubted that was what was being said.

I sighed as I leaned against the stack, grateful when the whole thing didn't come down on my head. That would've been embarrassing and just my luck. I could almost see it now, thousands of books raining down.

A sudden cold draft curled through the aisle, stirring the hair around my temples and fluffing my ponytail. Frowning, I turned around.

A woman stood several feet behind me. She must've been part ghost, because I hadn't heard her walk up.

She was incredibly tall, as tall as Seth, and very slender. Elegant, long-fingered hands were folded in front of her. Her blonde hair was pulled up, the mass of tight curls intricately pinned along the top of her head. Most of her features were hidden behind oversized, movie-star-quality sunglasses, but from what I could see, her cheekbones were sharp, lips full and rosy.

"Hello, Josephine," she said in a distinct, cultured accent. The corners of her lips tilted up in a slight, almost shy, smile.

Another shudder worked its way across my flesh. "How...how did you know my name?"

She drifted closer, and although she wore heeled shoes—super-pointy heeled shoes—there was no sound. There was a strong scent of patchouli and orange blossoms. "I've been waiting for you."

Okay. That wasn't creepy or anything. Part of me wanted to take a step back, but I held my ground. "Who are you?"

267

Her head tilted to the side. "I am the Librarian."

Um. Yeah. Since when did librarians wear sunglasses indoors? I glanced over my shoulder. Seth was still with the Dean, and as Solos spoke, Seth looked over. Our gazes collided, and sucking in a breath, I turned back to the librarian.

The space in front of me was vacant.

"What the...?" I strode forward, all the way down to the end of the aisle and looked both ways. Nothing—even the scent was gone.

"Josie?"

Turning back to Seth's voice, I met him halfway down the aisle. "What were you doing?" he asked.

"I...I don't know." Seemed silly to mention the lady. "Is everything all right?"

His eyes searched mine. "Let's talk as we head back to the dorm, okay?"

That didn't sound good, but I started walking with him. Once outside, he scrubbed a hand over his forehead. "Marcus limited the coming and going of the students when he learned of the Titans escaping Tartarus. However, groups of Sentinels come in and out of those gates all the time. Some are hunting. Others are doing patrols. There's no way to completely keep those gates closed for a long period of time."

I folded my arms across my chest to keep the chill out—from the air and from what I had a feeling his words would bring.

"All of the Sentinels check in hourly. No one screws around with that." His voice dropped as he placed a hand on my shoulder, steering us around a group of students who'd simply just stopped in the middle of the pathway. He waited until we were several feet beyond them. "A rather large scouting group has gone missing."

Oh no.

"That's not entirely uncommon," he continued, voice clipped. "It doesn't mean it has anything to do with Hyperion or the Titans. They could've run into problems with daimons. Or, gods know, it could be something else entirely."

"There's a 'but' coming, isn't there?"

A slight smile formed on his lips. "We need to make sure that there *is* no connection to the Titans."

A cold burst of fear clawed at the inside of my stomach. "You're going out to see if you can find them, aren't you?"

Seth nodded. "I'm the Apollyon. This is the kind of stuff I do."

But he also was just...just a guy. Yeah, he was some kind of superhero or something, but he was more than that and it didn't sit well with me, because it felt like I was seriously the only person who saw him as anything else.

Silence followed us back to our dorm, and he opened the door to my room. He didn't come in, not that I expected him to. I looked up at him, and our gazes met and held.

The muscles in my neck tensed. "You're going to be careful?"

That ghost of a smile formed. "I'm always careful." He placed a fingertip on my chin, and my heart squeezed in my chest. "I'll see you later. Okay?"

None of this felt okay, but I nodded and forced myself to step back, further into the room. When the door closed, I exhaled roughly. What if it *was* Hyperion? If he got into the University, it was going to be bad. Not just for me, but for everyone.

Needing something to do to pass the time, I took a shower, and then changed into a pair of jeans and a chunky sweater. I was just about to brave the wilds of the Covenant against orders when Deacon showed up, bearing cheeseburger subs.

"Where's Luke?" I asked, grabbing the bottles of soda out of his hand and placing them on the small coffee table.

"He's with some Sentinels right now."

My brows rose. "I thought he wasn't doing anything like that anymore."

"He's not." Deacon dropped onto the loveseat. "But he's good at it and they...they need him right now."

I sat down next to him much more slowly than how he'd thrown himself down. "You know about the missing group?"

269

He nodded as he smashed a hand down on top of the sub, flattening it. "Yeah."

Not having much of an appetite, I nibbled at the sub, my thoughts caught up in what could be going on outside the walls.

"He'll be okay," Deacon said, and when I looked up, I was amazed to find that he'd already eaten his sandwich. Damn. His gray eyes locked onto mine. "Just like Luke will be okay. That's something you've just got to believe in. If not, you'll drive yourself crazy." His gaze shifted from me to the framed photo on the coffee table.

Erin had packed it for me, but I hadn't pulled it out and placed it anywhere I could see it until yesterday evening, after the guys left and before Seth had shown up.

"That's your family?" Deacon asked, reaching for it. "Well, not including daddy?"

"Yeah," I breathed, watching him lift the frame. I pressed my lips together, wondering if I had been ready to put that picture out. "That's my...um, my grandparents and my mom. It was taken about two years ago."

He studied the picture for a moment and then placed it back on the table carefully. "I'm sorry. Luke told me. I'm guessing Seth had told him." He peered at me through a mass of curls. "It gets easier. I know that sounds lame, but I didn't think that when my parents died. I had my brother, though, and even though I was a little shit for a long time, I know it gets easier."

"How...how did your parents die?"

"A daimon attack. Only Aiden and I survived it," he said, sighing. "Sentinels ended up saving our asses. It was why my brother became a Sentinel. Back then, it was rare for a pure to make that choice."

"I'm sorry about your parents." When he smiled slightly, curiosity got the best of me. "Where is your brother now?"

He tilted his head. "That's a long story."

"We've got time."

Deacon laughed softly. "But it's not just my brother's story."

270

That didn't make much sense to me.

"Okay," he said, smacking his hands off his thighs. "Luke is going to kill me, but whatever. Time to get real."

My brows rose. "Um. Okay. I guess."

"You like Seth. Don't even try to pretend. I've seen the way you look at him."

Heat blasted my cheeks. Oh dear.

"And I've seen the way he looks at you."

Oh double dear.

Deacon leaned over, knocking his shoulder against mine. "I've seen it before, you know, the whole 'I want someone I shouldn't or can't have.' But you look at him like you want him. He looks at you like he can't or shouldn't. It's all very ironic, come to think of it. It's really like watching history repeat itself."

I faced him, unable to stop myself from saying, "He can have me if he wants me." I felt like a dork when his grin went up tenfold. "I mean, I get that he thinks he...he doesn't deserve me."

His brows rose. "Did he tell you about everything?"

"He told me about what he was doing this past year." When Deacon's face fell, I sighed. "There's more, isn't there?"

"Uh, yeah." He stared at me for a long moment, and then he leaned against the arm of the loveseat. "Seth will definitely murder me for this, but there's a lot you don't know—that I think you need to know."

A sudden shiver wrapped its way down my spine.

Scrunching fingers through his hair, he sighed. "I'm only telling you this because I think it will help you understand where Seth is coming from, but you've got to be ready to hear this, Josie. The Seth you know now is not the Seth we all knew back then."

My stomach tumbled. "I'm ready to hear."

Deacon pursed his lips as he lowered his hand. "I'm going to tell you a story—it's practically a legend among us now. It's the story of Seth and Alex."

271

CHAPTER

27

MY CHEST felt like it had a minor seizure. "Alex... That's a girl, right?"

He nodded. "Alex is short for Alexandria. She's named after her dad. He's a Sentinel here. Runs around. Doesn't speak. Kind of scares the shit out of me because he's a badass, like his daughter, but anyway, she was also another Apollyon. Awesome chick. We're good friends. But I'm going to get one part of the story out of the way first."

"Okay," I whispered. Out of everything I thought about Seth's past, I never thought it involved another girl.

"Alex is in love with my brother. He's in love with her. They have this epic kind of love. Always-have, always-will kind of shit. They shouldn't have been together, because he's a pure and she was a half, but they made it work. They did it."

That made me feel better. A little.

"But Alex was never meant to be with my brother. She was an Apollyon, born in the same generation as another—as Seth. *They* were meant to be together. It was how they were built, to be each other's other half."

I opened my mouth, but nothing came out. Okay. That did not make me feel better.

"They met when Seth was brought to Deity Island to guard Lucian. He was Alex's stepfather, also ran the Council, and a very big douchebag. Seth didn't know that Alex existed. She didn't know about him. You see, when they first met, Alex was seventeen, and the Apollyon doesn't come into their powers until they turn eighteen. Seth was already the Apollyon, and as far as we knew, he was the only one, but he wasn't. Alex swears that Seth didn't know, that he was just as shocked as she was. The two of them didn't hit it off at first." He paused. "Well, most people didn't hit it off with Seth."

I remembered what it was like when I first met him. Totally understandable.

"He could be a dick. Either you loved him or you hated him, but almost *everyone* feared him," he explained. "Anyway, turns out that Lucian knew the whole time that Alex was the Apollyon. That bastard was working with Ares, and Lucian made every attempt to keep Seth and Alex together, because when there are two Apollyons, something crazy can happen. One of them can tap into the other and become the God Killer. And if you happen to control the God Killer, you control everything. Because the God Killer can, obviously, kill gods. That's a big deal."

All of this was fascinating, but a bubble of dread began to form in my belly. I tucked my legs to my chest, wrapping my arms around my knees. "When you say 'together,' do you mean *together* together?"

There was a pause and he nodded. "Alex always loved my brother, but like I said, it wasn't easy for them at times. Aiden pushed her away to keep her safe, and with Seth and Alex both being Apollyons, they were connected in a way that is hard to explain. They knew when the other was in trouble. They could feel things about each other. I know they...they, uh, messed around, but, Josie, what they felt for one another...wasn't something deep and everlasting. Yeah, they cared for each other. Maybe even loved one another, in a way, but not in the way you've got to worry about, okay? What was between them was always a fabrication of fate. Nothing more."

That...that was hard to fully accept. That another girl out there was *connected* to Seth, could, like, feel him?

"Seth was never supposed to be the Apollyon," he continued. "Throughout history, except for one instance, Apollo has always created the Apollyon, but Seth was born a few years before Alex. The gods knew that one of them had done it, and they feared that someone was hoping to create the God Killer. One of them was, and that was Ares. Now remember, Ares was working with Lucian, right? Lucian got to Seth. No one knows how, but it became painfully clear that Lucian had some kind of weird parental control over Seth. He doted on Seth, made him feel like he was a part of a family. He got Seth good."

Oh no. Maybe that sounded weird to Deacon, to everyone else, but I got how it could happen. Seth had a crap mother. Had a crap childhood. It took no leap of logic to think that Seth secretly, maybe even desperately, wanted to belong–wanted someone who was like a parent to love and care for him. I could understand that. If I hadn't had my grandparents, I would've been lost.

And Seth...he had been lost.

"Lucian got Seth on his side, meaning he got Seth on Ares's side. No one knew this. There was a lot of other shit going on, but when it got closer to Alex's birthday, to when she would awaken as the Apollyon, the shit hit the fan."

"What...what happened?"

He stared into my eyes. "This is the part I hope you're ready to hear."

I waited a moment and then nodded.

"Seth was in deep with Lucian and Ares, and he did what they ordered. The first phase of Ares's take-over-the-world plan was to take out the Council at Deity Island, and that was done." A pinched, pained look clouded his face, like the memories were too raw. "They used Seth to do it."

I sucked in a sharp breath. Oh God.

"He took out the Council. It was...it was bad, and it sparked a chain reaction among the other gods. Poseidon showed up. Yep. *That* Poseidon. He destroyed Deity Island trying to stop Seth and Lucian, but it didn't work. A bunch of innocent people died."

Closing my eyes, I swallowed my next breath. I remembered watching the news when that'd happened. Of course, they had reported it as a natural disaster. Horror poured into me, knowing that Seth had been a part of such...such destruction.

I wasn't even sure I could kill a daimon and Seth had killed... He had killed so many people, either by his hand or as a result of his actions.

"And Seth, it turned out that he'd been trying to awaken Alex before all of that. He was tapping into her *aether*...and from what I gathered, he was getting addicted to it—to the power. That just made the whole thing worse. Then Alex awakened, and she connected with Seth because of what he was doing. It was pretty bad. The gods were pissed. Volcanoes were erupting. Earthquakes. Shit got real. Ares was on Earth, his influence sparking war and conflict, and we had to cage up psycho Alex to keep her from running off and joining psycho Seth."

My mouth dropped open. Seth was a killer...and an addict. There were no words.

"Yeah, I'm pretty sure Alex threatened to make a crown out of my ribs or something. She was such a bitch during that time." He flashed a quick grin. "But as cheesy as this sounds, love conquers everything, even fate and destiny. She managed to escape and Aiden went after her. She could've killed him, but her love for him snapped her out of it. She unplugged from Seth and wasn't so crazy anymore."

"That's...that's good to know," I murmured, staring at him.

"But, meanwhile in psycho-Seth land, he was doing whatever Ares told him to do. Fighting. Taking out those who were trying to flee Ares. He...he was a killing machine, addicted to power, completely manipulated. Totally psycho and—"

"Please stop saying that," I cut in. "Please stop calling him psycho."

Deacon blinked. "Okay. He was searching for Alex, thinking if he could reach her, he could get her back under his control, which would mean under Ares's control. Whatever bullshit that god was feeding him, it...it warped him, Josie. Yeah, he could be a smug dick before, but what he was like under Ares's thumb..." He trailed off, shaking his head, and I suddenly wanted to cry, because none of this was fair. "But something happened that changed everything, something reached into Seth and broke him free."

I exhaled roughly. "What do you mean? He turned against Ares?"

"Yeah, in the end, when it really mattered, he gave Ares the middle finger." Deacon cringed. "Sometimes the gods can be cruel. In ways I hope you never have to experience or see what they're capable of."

Understanding crept in. I guessed it. "Ares got hold of Alex, didn't he?"

He nodded, his expression full of sorrow. "He got into here, the University, and Alex was with her uncle—Marcus—and Aiden when he revealed himself. She got them out of the room, because she knew Ares would kill them. She squared off with Ares, but... but he was the god of war, Josie. He beat her so badly that there wasn't an inch of her skin without scars. It was so bad that Apollo had to take her to Olympus to be healed."

"Oh my God." Tears pricked at my eyes, pain for a girl I'd never met, a girl that Seth had cared deeply for.

"It was horrible." Deacon's voice cracked and I reached out, squeezing his arm. He smiled faintly. "My brother...Aiden heard the whole thing go down, but couldn't get to her, couldn't help her. That... Yeah, that killed a part of him. And the only good thing that came from it was...that Seth was connected to Alex when she was fighting Ares. He felt everything she felt."

Another dose of horror rose in me. How could this get any worse?

"Seth didn't know Ares was going to do something so awful, and that didn't mesh well with him. It broke the hold. Somehow he convinced Ares that he could sway Alex into joining him, and he left for the Covenant, bringing Lucian with him." He took a big breath and let it out slowly. "When he showed up at the gates, we thought it was about to go south, but he simply handed over Lucian to Alex and kind of... He kind of turned himself over. I think...I think he was just done, you know? He'd never meant for Alex to get hurt. I think, deep down, he'd never meant for anyone to get hurt."

I felt something wet on my cheek and I reached up, hastily knocking it away. God, all of this was so terrible and so sad.

"Even then, Seth wasn't the guy we knew in the beginning. He was quiet. Completely withdrawn. Kind of like he is now. That shit...it had to have messed with his head."

My eyes squeezed shut. It had changed him. And it *had* messed with his head.

"But, that's not the end of the story, Josie." When I opened my eyes, he was smiling a little. "Seth was on our side in the end. He worked with us. They ended up freeing one of the Titans to help fight Ares. Aiden had to make a deal with Hades to do so. Yeah, Hades is hot, but also a dick. Aiden had to promise an eternity as one of Hades's guards once he died in return for releasing Perses—Perses the Titan."

I gaped at him.

"Who was also a major dick."

I gaped at him some more.

"Yeah, that apparently was a bad idea, but that wasn't Seth's bad idea, so...any-who, in the end...Seth did something truly amazing."

"He did?" I whispered, wondering how, after hearing all of that, Deacon could even be in the same country as Seth, but then I remembered the first morning here. Deacon had *thanked* Seth.

His smile strengthened, turning his eyes dove-gray, and I wondered if his brother shared that eye color. "Yeah. You see, it was fated and prophesied that there could only ever be one of them—Seth and Alex. Like total *Highlander* shit."

"Huh?"

"Mortals." He rolled eyes. "Never mind. In the final battle, Alex tapped into Seth and became the God Killer. That was Seth's idea, because he knew, with his past issues with power, it was too much of a risk to let him do it. They fought Ares together. They won. The God of War is no more. But that damn prophecy could not be changed. The remaining gods appeared. They would not allow a God Killer to exist. Alex...she knew that, you know. She knew what she was doing—she knew the price and still did it. The girl...she had balls."

I stiffened, going so still I could mimic one of those statues.

"Seth was with her. He held her while the gods killed her."

"Oh my God!" I shouted, jumping out of my seat. "What do you mean, they killed her? She did all that and they—"

"Calm down, honeycombs. Apollo took care of her." He waited until I sat down, but my heart was still racing, and I couldn't shake the image of Seth holding this faceless girl as she died. "When Apollo had Alex in Olympus, turns out he'd given her ambrosia, the nectar of the gods. She died a mortal death, but ambrosia made her *immortal*. She became a demigod. Not like you, being all cool and born that way, but Apollo saved her nonetheless."

"Oh." That was kind of confusing as crap, but I was happy to hear she wasn't *dead* dead.

"Then Seth surprised all of us. He knew about the deal Aiden had made, and knowing that he couldn't be with Alex, because she has to stay in the Underworld for like six months out of the year—total Persephone rip-off right there—and the fact that Alex would never age, he made a deal with Apollo and Hades."

I held my breath, waiting.

"He pledged his life to the gods and his soul to Hades, virtually becoming their bitch, in return for Aiden being given ambrosia as well."

"Wow," I murmured.

"I don't think you get it. Seth sacrificed his future, his afterlife, his *everything* for Aiden and Alex, so that they could be together," Deacon explained, and, yeah, I got it. I just couldn't believe it. "For how long he has left here—and that's solely up to the gods—they control him, and once he dies, he will be a slave of Hades. He gave up everything in the end."

Rocking back, I stared at Deacon, totally mind-blown. "Oh my gosh, Deacon, I don't..."

"You don't know what to think or say? I get that. None of us really did. No one expected that from him, but what he did was huge. He gave my brother everything. He gave Alex everything, and in the end, he got nothing."

Deacon leaned forward, tugging on a strand of my hair. "Until now."

I blinked.

"He's got you, doesn't he?" He let go of my hair. "Don't answer that yet. I just told you the guy you're lusting after might have been classified as a mass murderer by human standards and practically became a saint by the end of it all. How do you reconcile those two things?" He shrugged. "I don't know. So let's watch *Supernatural*. The new season is On Demand."

I just sat there as Deacon found the remote, found the On Demand listing, and flipped on *Supernatural*, providing some awesome Winchester Brothers distraction.

"You know, that one season where they square off at Stull Cemetery, because it's one of the Hell gates?" he said, chuckling. "Stull Cemetery is actually one of the portals to the Underworld. Makes me wonder about the writers on that show, you know?"

I shifted my wide stare to him.

Deacon was focused on the TV.

279

JENNIFER L. ARMENTROUT

Letting out a breath I didn't realize I was holding, I sank into the thick cushions, trying to understand the puzzle that was now completed for me. There had been a lot Seth had not told me and now...now I understood why.

280

CHAPTER

28

IT WAS late.

Deacon had left an hour or so ago, there'd been no sign of Seth's return, and there was no way I was getting any sleep anytime soon. Thoughts crowded my head. I didn't know what to think about everything I had heard, and I was wearing a path in the carpet.

What was I supposed to think about him now? He had done horrific things, but in the end, he did the right thing. Did that undo everything else?

Passing the coffee table for the hundredth time, I easily conjured up the conflict I'd seen in his gaze many times, the sorrow that seemed to linger beneath the surface. He felt remorse for hunting down the traitors.

And he had been one of the biggest traitors of all.

Deacon had been right. How did I reconcile those two halves? And that wasn't even taking into consideration the fact that there was another girl. Yeah, it all seemed like a moot point, but still. He'd given up everything for her.

Everything.

I passed the coffee table again.

All I could think was that none of this was fair. Here I was, pitying myself and my circumstances, when others had fared much worse than me. This Alex. This Aiden. Seth.

He had gone from being under Ares's control and made to do terrible things, to doing almost the same for Apollo. That wasn't fair. It was wrong. And it was sad.

But that didn't change what he had done.

Was I holding mortal convictions too closely to my heart? I was training to defend myself, to fight. There'd be a chance that one day I would face off with people who, for whatever reason, believed they stood on the right side, and I might have to kill them to protect myself. Even humans did that.

As I neared the door, I heard another one shutting out in the hall, and my heart jumped in my chest. No one else was in the rooms near us. It had to be Seth. Without giving much of a pause to think about what I was doing, I threw open my door and rushed out into the hall, barefoot and all. I reached his door, rapping my knuckles on it.

A moment passed and it swung open. Seth stood there, his hair down, brushing his bare shoulders. He held the black thermal in one hand.

I was unprepared to see him, which meant I probably should've thought all of this out first.

"Hey," he said, stepping aside. "I was going to come to you."

Stepping into his room for the first time, I realized it looked just like mine. Living area. Bedroom through the narrow doorway, and a kitchen nook to my right. My heart pounded in my chest as I looked up at him.

So many secrets in those amber eyes.

"Did...did you all find anything out?" I asked, clasping my hands together.

"Nope." Stomach muscles tensed and flexed as he tossed his shirt on the armchair. He then raised his hand, scrubbing his fingers through his hair. "There's no sign of them. Nothing.

Marcus is upping the manpower at the gates, just in case. Hopefully, there's nothing to be concerned about."

"I hope," I murmured, lifting my gaze to his. He was...he was so beautiful, but there was such darkness that had to exist in him.

His brows knitted as he took a step toward me. "Are you okay? Did something happen while I was gone?"

"I know," I blurted out, and then I locked up. Every muscle.

He frowned. "You know...what?"

"I...I know about Alex," I said, squeezing my hands together as the frown slipped off his face and his eyes widened. "I know about Ares."

Seth took a step back as he stared at me. "You do?"

I nodded. My pulse pounded so quickly I feared I'd be sick. "I know everything."

He stared at me for a long moment, and then his chin lifted. His face went impassive, like a door being slammed shut. "If you know everything, then why are you here, Josie?"

I opened my mouth as I shook my head.

"You should be anywhere but here."

Should I? I folded my arms across my chest. "I don't know what to say, Seth."

"I know what to say for you." A muscle thrummed along his jaw. "I disgust you. I'm a killer." His voice was bland and even while I flinched. "You thought what I'd done the last year was forgivable? It's because you didn't know everything. When I told you that I was a monster, I wasn't fooling with you, Josie. I am."

"No," I said, and then I spoke up louder. "You gave up everything for Alex and Aiden. You gave up your life."

"Were you told I was an addict?" When I nodded, he laughed harshly. "And yet...you are here."

"Seth..."

He shrugged as he tugged the leather band off his wrist and lifted his heavy arms, tugging his hair back from his face. "What life was I giving up? It wasn't that big of a sacrifice. Trust me. I deserve this. And I deserve what I have coming to me."

"You didn't deserve any of this." I stepped forward, ignoring the way his head swiveled sharply toward me. And the moment the words came out, I knew it was how I felt. Right or wrong, it was just how I felt. "You didn't deserve to be born to a shitty mom or have a crappy childhood. You sure as hell didn't deserve to have someone use that against you."

His chest rose. "You don't know what you're talking about."

"I know that Alex didn't deserve everything that was thrown at her. Just like you didn't. That doesn't mean you didn't make some shitty choices in all of it."

"I'm pretty sure what I did could be summed up a little better than a shitty choice," he snapped back.

"Okay." Frustration got the better of me and I stormed forward, stopping short of pushing him. "You did terrible things, Seth. You did horrible things. Is that what you want to hear me say?"

He started to look away.

"No. Is that it? You just want me to keep telling you what you want to believe about yourself? That you don't deserve happiness? That you're a monster?"

"That's because I am one!" he shouted, facing me, and up close, his eyes burned ocher. A shimmer of amber danced down his arms, evaporating so quickly I wasn't sure I'd seen it. "Why can't you see that? Everyone else around you does. Wait. Are you just going to stand there and tell me more stories about how you ran over animals?"

My eyes narrowed. "Shut up."

He smirked.

"They don't see you as a monster," I shot back. "If they did, do you think they'd let you in here? That Deacon would've *thanked* you? That someone wouldn't have gotten their hands on you by now and at least *attempted* to beat the crap out of you?"

He opened his mouth, but I didn't want to hear it. "Or that Apollo would've put you in charge of me? That he wouldn't have skinned you alive when he found us kissing? Why can't you see that?"

A tense moment passed and then he dipped his chin, got right up in my face. His voice was low when he spoke. "So you can forget and forgive every horrible thing I've done? Is that what you're saying?"

I shook my head. "No. I'm not saying that. What I'm saying is—you are not the sum of only half of your actions. You can't disregard everything else."

He stared at me, and wow, I was kind of proud of that myself. I latched onto it. "I know that you cared for people. I know that you cared for Alex. And I know—*I know*—you wouldn't have done those things if you hadn't been manipulated into them. I'm not saying that you're devoid of responsibility, but that's not the only thing that makes you who you are. You are more than just the Apollyon. You are more than the guy who sided with Ares. You're...you're also the guy who made a major step in righting what he'd done wrong. You're the guy who regrets what he's done. You're the guy who didn't laugh at me when I said I didn't have friends in school. You're also the guy who let me turn him into a Pillow Pet, and you care about—"

He shot forward, clasping my cheeks. "Say it again."

"Say what?" I replied, gripping his wrists. "I said a lot of things. Help me out here."

"Say that I'm not just the Apollyon," he whispered, his voice harsh.

Tears built up in my throat. "You're not just the Apollyon, Seth."

His eyes drifted shut, his face tensed as his fingers splayed across my cheeks. "I don't even know who I am anymore. Or what I ever was."

Oh goodness, that ripped right through my chest. "You're just...you're just Seth."

A tremor moved through his arms. "And you...you're just my salvation."

I gasped as he let go and turned. He stumbled through the doorway, lacking his normal grace. His salvation? That was... powerful. Important. Folding my hands under my chin, I followed him into the bedroom. He'd stopped in front of the bed, hands on his hips, his head bowed and the muscles along his shoulders bunched. Every muscle in his back, down to the low-hanging pants, was tense.

"Seth?"

He lifted his head, and I heard the breath he took right before he faced me. I saw it happen. Whatever walls he had perfectly crafted around him had cracked right open. He stared at me in a way I'd never seen before.

"If you don't leave right now, I won't be responsible for what I'll do," he said, his voice deep and rough. "I am not kidding."

I froze as a series of shivers spread across my skin and my eyes widened. Part of me thought I knew what he was saying. Then again, I wasn't really sure of anything other than the fact that, as crazy as it sounded, I trusted him. Who knew what that said about me?

"Josie." His voice cracked as his arms fell to his side.

In that moment, I knew that he needed me to stay. He actually needed more than that. Leaving didn't prove anything I'd just said to him, and I didn't want to leave. My stomach fluttered nervously as I took a step toward him.

That was as far as I made it.

Seth was in front of me in a heartbeat. One arm curved around my waist and he hauled me against his bare chest. His other hand cradled the back of my head, tilting my mouth up to meet his.

The kiss...

It was the softest and sweetest thing I'd ever felt. Barely there, a whisper over my lips, but so potent, so shattering, I had to fight the rise of tears. And his powerful body shook against mine as he mapped the layout of my mouth. There was something infinitely tender in that moment.

The kiss...

It stole my soul, laid claim to me in a way I didn't know was possible. It reached down inside me, doing more than building a fire. There was hope in that kiss. There was a promise of more, of redemption.

Of salvation.

My lips parted under his, welcoming him in, and the kiss deepened, but there was nothing rushed to it. Like a slow, tentative exploration, he kissed me like he'd never kissed anyone before, and I seriously knew that wasn't the case. But there was something new, something tentative, about the way our tongues met, and I started to shake.

Seth pulled back, his eyes latched onto mine. "Do you want this?"

I found my voice. "Yes."

"You're crazy."

Then his mouth was on mine, and as my hands flattened on his shoulders, I felt my senses start to spin. His hands moved to the hem of my sweater and he didn't break contact until he needed to in order to lift the sweater over my head. He dropped it on the floor, and then swept his lips over mine.

His hands settled on my shoulders, fingers playing over the straps of my bra. I'd never gone this far before, so when he leaned back and his gaze traveled over my flushed face and parted lips, down my neck, I had to fight the urge to cover myself.

My body was not perfect, not like his. Even with all the training and running, my stomach was still soft and my hips were still wide. I doubted those things would ever change, but it was hard to stand there and let him look his fill.

He trailed his fingers down the straps and over the lacy cups, causing my breath to catch and a riot of sensations to flood me. There was no hiding my body's reaction from him. When his fingers reached the V in my cleavage, his hands moved out to the sides, smoothing over the tips of my breasts.

I swallowed, but found that I couldn't get my throat to work. He shifted closer, his hips pressing against my belly as he cupped my breasts. His thumbs moved, trailing idle circles that kept getting closer and closer to where I actually *ached*.

His thick lashes lifted, his stare searing into mine as his thumbs hit the hardened tips, and I cried out. Seth swept in, capturing the sound with his lips, but his fingers... Oh God, they didn't stop. He teased and taunted, tugged and tortured me in the sweetest way possible through the thin satin, working me until I was panting into his kisses and my fingernails were digging into his shoulders. One hand slipped to my back, and proving he had some mad skills, he unhooked the bra with one hand. The material loosened, and I dipped my head to his chest, pressing a kiss against the taut skin as he dragged the straps down my arms. He waited until I lowered my arms, and then he let the bra fall between us.

Seth pressed his lips against the top of my head and then the tip of my nose when I lifted my chin. The kisses kept coming. Over my cheeks, along my jaw, and then down the side of my neck, his tongue flicking out over my pulse, sending it pounding throughout me as his hands found their way back to my breasts. With nothing between his palms and my skin, the touch was nothing short of being hit with a live wire.

A sound I didn't even know was possible rose up my throat, and I felt his lips curve against the skin between my neck and shoulder. I held onto him as he wrapped an arm around my waist and lifted me up. Then I was on my back, in his bed, with my hair everywhere, completely topless, and he was hovering over me, his gaze doing just as many dangerous things to my heart as his touch had.

"Perfect," he murmured. "You know that? Absolutely fucking perfect."

I couldn't talk as I watched him lower his head, strands of blond hair falling forward, caressing over my chest, knocking the air out of my lungs. He trailed a hot, fiery path down the center of my chest as he shifted his weight onto one arm. His hand was heading south as his lips and tongue tasted every square inch of my chest, getting closer and closer to the hardened nipple.

His fingers unbuttoned my jeans. The zipper went down—the sound erotic, causing my toes to curl. His hand smoothed over my hip, fingers slipping under the waist of my jeans. He tugged, and instinct urged me to lift my hips. I did, and my jeans went down my legs, off my feet, falling to the floor. As his hand resettled on my belly, his mouth finally made it home, closing over the tip of my breast.

I cried out as my back arched clear off the bed. Holy crap. His hands had nothing on his mouth. Goodness. My fingers curled into the comforter and a throaty moan burst from me as he caught the tip between his teeth.

"Seth!" I tried to breathe around his name, but he chuckled, flicking his tongue where he'd nipped, soothing that slight sting. And then he gave my other breast the same treatment—kissed, suckled, nipped, and licked, and oh *gods*, I was so in over my head it wasn't even funny.

I was drowning in what he was doing, and when he slid his hand up over my ribs, closing it over my other breast, I surely thought I'd just die in that moment. I hoped not, because I could feel him pressing against my hip, thick and hard, and my heart pounded with need, want, and a thousand other things.

Seth took his time, teasing until my hips moved restlessly, my thighs pressed together, until my hands found their way to him and I slid them down his arms, feeling the bulge in his muscles, the slight tremor that coursed under his skin. Oddly, in that moment, I wondered if his tattoos were showing and what that must look like.

But then I stopped thinking, because his hand was moving as he rose up, bringing his mouth to mine. The kisses were slow, languid, almost questioning, and those kisses, they were sweet and dizzying. Seth *was* dizzying, every aspect of him. Sparks of electricity danced over my skin, ratcheting up everything I was feeling until I thought there was a good chance I might combust as his hand traveled down my stomach, over my panties.

"Open for me?" he asked against my mouth.

My thighs parted, and then he was cupping me. I tensed all over, partly because I'd never been touched that way and partly due to the tension deep inside me that had coiled up tight.

He murmured something in a language I didn't understand against my mouth as he moved his hand between my legs, his fingers dragging up and then down. "You like that?"

My hips rose in response, and he chuckled again, pressing his forehead against mine. I could feel his chest moving as he kept up that slow movement of his fingers. "I'll take that as a yes," he said.

"I..." I gripped his arm, feeling the muscles move under my hand each time he moved his fingers. "Seth..."

"I don't think I could ever grow tired of hearing you say my name like that." He kissed me before he drew back, hand and everything leaving me. I started to reach for him, but he had his hands under the band of my panties, and then he was dragging them down my legs.

"Oh God," I whispered.

One side of his lips quirked up as he glanced up at me, and then he had me completely bare to his gaze. "You are fucking beautiful, Josie."

I stuttered out a "thank you" that I wasn't even sure he heard. His hands were planted on either side of my waist, and he was staring at me like he'd never seen me before, but he was still in his pants. That didn't seem right, so I sat up, pressing my hot face into the space between his neck and shoulder. My fingers fumbled along the band of his pants, and he drew back, giving me access.

I tugged on them and he leaned over, helping me get them down his thighs. He took over at that point, which was good, because I had no idea how I was going to get them down his long legs without sticking my butt up in the air. When he was in nothing more than a pair of black boxer briefs, I felt like my tongue would loll out of my mouth. I could see the length of him straining against the material.

His hand curved under my chin, lifting my gaze. Our eyes met. There was something soft in his gaze, something I doubted many people had ever been on the receiving end of.

Biting down on my lip, I reached again for him. His hand left my chin, folding over my wrist before I could get hold of his boxers. Startled, my gaze rose to his again.

He was still looking at me in *that* way. "Unless I'm totally way off, there's something I think you should be telling me."

"What?" That I was about to come out of my skin?

Seth dipped his head, kissing my bare shoulder as he drew my hand to him, pressing my palm against his length. I gasped at the heat that seeped through the material, and he groaned. "Josie, have you ever touched a guy like this?"

My fingers closed around him, and his hips jerked forward. He slid my hand up the long length as he lifted his head, kissing the corner of my mouth. "*Josie...*"

"No," I whispered, tightening my hand around him, through the briefs. "I've never...been with anyone before."

He shuddered as he lifted his head, his gaze snaring me. "And you're going to give me that?"

"Yes." And I nodded, just in case he was confused.

Pulling my hand away, he rose, slanting his head to kiss me deeply as he pushed me onto my back, with his weight draped over me. "I've never had anything that was my own," he said against my mouth. "Nothing that was ever for just me and no one else. I've never been anyone's first." He kissed me and then lifted his head. I stared into his eyes. "I've never been anyone's only."

That made my heart ache for him as I raised my hand, pressing my palm against his cheek. "You're my first," I whispered. "You're...you're my only."

His lips parted. "You can't say that and not mean it."

I held his gaze as my chest swelled. "I mean it."

JENNIFER L. ARMENTROUT

He smoothed his thumb over my lip. "I really am a lucky son of a bitch."

Before I could process that, his mouth replaced his thumb. It was like those words had formed some kind of unbreakable bond, and that kiss sealed it. Like we were making our own prophecy, our own fate that couldn't be unwritten.

"We aren't going to do this," he said.

My eyes flew open. "What?"

He laughed softly and then groaned. "Yeah, I can't even believe I'm saying that, but there're other firsts I want from you. Other things that I want as mine before we move to that."

"But—"

"That's what I want," he told me as he shifted, sliding his hand down my stomach, between my thighs. "*This* is what I want." His hand folded over me, and my hips rose. "And there are a lot of ways I want it. A lot of ways I'm going to make it mine."

Oh geez.

He slipped a finger through the wetness and then inside me. My entire body tensed, and as he began to move his finger slowly, he watched me. "That's one of the ways."

"*Seth*."

His eyes flared bright and he did something with his hand that caused my head to kick back and my breath to come out in short, quick pants. "You're so beautiful like this," he said, twisting so that his gaze dragged down the length of me, to where his hand was. "You have no idea."

My hips were moving in rhythm to his hand, and the sounds that were coming out of my mouth would probably embarrass me later, but right then, I couldn't care less. I threaded my other hand through his hair.

"There's another first I want."

The smile that appeared on his face was nothing short of sinful. I caught a glimpse of it before he kissed me deeply and then worked his way down, lingering in some areas more than others. He kissed a path around my belly button and then slipped

292

his tongue in, and by then my hips were grinding against his hand. I was so close that, when he pulled his hand away, I cried out.

And then he kissed me where his hand had been.

"Seth," I hissed, my fingers tightening in his hair. "I...I've never done this either."

"Figured that, Josie."

"But, seriously, I haven't—"

"I know. And it's all mine," he said. "Relax."

I couldn't relax for a thousand reasons. He was between my legs, his breath warm against my thigh as he blazed a path to my center. When his mouth closed over me, heat flooded my veins and he made a sound that reminded me of a man starved.

"So fucking sweet," he said.

My heart doubled its beat as he kissed me just like he'd kissed my mouth. Slow and soft at first, and then deeper and wetter and hotter until I was squirming so much that he placed a hand on my lower stomach, holding me, guiding my hips to match the thrusts of his tongue. Sensation pounded through me, intense and beautiful. I didn't think how intimate this was, but instead I reveled in how perfect it was with *him*.

"Seth," I breathed out his name.

He went deeper and faster, and I was aware of his hips moving, as if he couldn't control himself, and something about that made me run red-hot. Somehow I innately knew he was as close as I was, and I wanted that. I took a breath, but the coil deep inside me sprung. I cried out, and I heard his husky, throaty sound against the softest part of me. The release pounded through me, stealing my breath, as I liquefied under the crushing, pulsing and throbbing whirl of sensations.

Seth stayed with me, easing me down and slowing it all until I could catch my breath. My hand slipped from his hair, falling limply to my stomach. He kissed me one more time, then each of my thighs, before he lifted up.

Through a haze, I thought his expression looked kind of startled, a little knocked off his axis. That was okay. He'd blown my axis apart.

Climbing up me, he kissed me softly, and there was a mingled taste of both of us. "You okay?" he asked.

"Perfect," I murmured. "I have no bones."

He chuckled. "I'll be right back."

"Uh-huh."

His face softened as he pushed off the bed. Reaching down, he grabbed a quilt and dragged it up to my waist. It felt long enough to cover all of me, but when his gaze fell to my breasts, I figured he'd done that on purpose.

With eyes half-open, I watched him stop at the dresser and pull out another pair of boxers. He looked over his shoulder at me and winked. "That was a first for me."

Completely unashamed.

I loved it.

I grinned a little as he disappeared into the bathroom. I heard water running, and I imagined he was cleaning himself up. He returned in a few seconds, and I hadn't moved an inch.

He climbed into the bed, sliding an arm under my back. He rolled me onto my side and then he hauled me back, nestling my butt into the cradle of his hips. His arm was tight around my waist, our bodies sealed together.

"You still with me?" he asked.

"I..." It took a moment to gather my wits. "I never knew it could be like that."

Seth pressed a kiss against my bare shoulder, and then he shattered my heart a little. "Neither did I."

MY HEART was still pounding, and I wasn't sure how much time passed as we lay there. Josie had a hold of my right hand, my dagger hand, and was dragging the tip of her finger along my palm, tracing idle designs.

She never knew it could be like this?

Hell, I hadn't either. For real. Never in my life had I found release without getting my boxers off, and even as powerful as that had been, I still wanted her now. Like a caveman, the word *mine, mine, mine* repeated over and over again, and yeah, that was a first. Kind of fucked with my head, feeling this strongly. Wasn't like it was something that had happened overnight. It had been building for a while.

She knew everything—every fucking thing about me, and she was here, in my arms, gloriously warm and soft. Lucky? That didn't even cover it. She was...she was a gift. Salvation.

It was dangerous feeling this way, because it made me want to think about things I couldn't have. A future, for one thing, and then there was the fact that she was virtually a weapon. One day she would face off with Hyperion. My arm tightened around her waist.

I didn't want to think about any of those things right then.

"When I was a little girl..." she said. Since we had settled in together, she started talking about random stuff, and I didn't want her to stop. I liked the sound of her voice. "I was really chubby. My granddad used to call me Butterball."

I grinned against her throat. "I like your butterball."

"Oh my God," she laughed. "That sounds so wrong."

"It's true."

"I bet you weren't chubby. You were probably born with an eight-pack."

Dipping my head, I pressed a kiss to the crescent-shaped scar on her neck, pushing down the anger that accompanied seeing that tag. "I was the fittest baby around. Could lift two bottles with just one fist."

Her body shook with her soft laugh. "You're ridiculous."

Unable to help myself, I nuzzled her neck, eliciting a shiver out of her. I was already ready for round two, but I held that in check, satisfied with holding her. It didn't take long for her to drift off to sleep in my arms. And even though I was tired, I found myself wide awake, centered on her, soaking in the slow and steady rise and fall of her chest, the way her lips were parted, and the long length of her lashes.

As I lay there, for what felt like seconds but could've been hours, the lead ball in my stomach resurfaced and got a little heavier. Doubt crept into my thoughts, diminishing the sated haze. It wasn't regret. Fuck no. I would never regret these moments with Josie. The dread ran deeper, rooted in everything I'd experienced. It was that icy, nagging sensation that even though I held her right now, she was going to slip through my fingers, and there was nothing I could do about it.

I was only operating on a few hours of sleep, but as corny as it sounded, I felt like I'd slept for a week when I woke up and found Josie right where I'd last seen her, in my arms.

She was awake, her face turned to me, and a small smile pulled at those lips. "Morning," she whispered.

Closing the tiny distance between our mouths, I kissed her softly, ignoring the sudden resurgence of what I'd been thinking about before I'd fallen asleep. Her lips were soft and warm under mine, and hell, I didn't want to move from this bed.

"Training," she murmured when I lifted my head. "We have..." She gasped as I trailed my tongue along her lower lip. "We have to do training today."

"I'm your instructor." I rolled, getting her right where I wanted her—under me—as I planted my elbows on either side of her head. Her legs parted, and I settled between her thighs. I'd do some crazy shit if I could get my briefs to magically disappear so there would be nothing between us, but the softness of her breasts against my chest was pretty damn awesome all on its own. "You can be late."

She grinned up at me as she placed her hands on my chest, the touch tentative. "Well, thanks for giving me permission."

"No thanks necessary. I'm just that accommodating."

"I have a feeling that if we don't get out of bed right now, we won't."

"I don't see a damn thing wrong with that." Lowering my head, I pressed a kiss to her temple and then another against her cheek. "Besides, I promise you'll get your heart rate up in here."

"Oh my God," she giggled as she slid her hands around my neck and tangled her fingers in my hair. I liked the way that felt. Hell, I liked everything about this morning.

My lips found hers again and the kiss... Yeah, it was wild how something I'd done a hundred times before could feel so different, so new. I wasn't sure what to really make of that, but she was right. The last thing we needed to do was to let...*this*...get in the way of training her.

Sometimes my maturity surprised me. This was one of those moments I wished I could fall back on the more selfish, don't-give-a-fuck Seth.

297

Sighing, I kissed her once more, taking it deep and making it count. This time, when I lifted my head, I rolled my heavy ass off her and swung my legs over the edge of the bed. "You're right. We'll be good today."

Josie lay there for a moment, her face flushed and her gaze unfocused. The sheet had slipped, revealing a rosy tip, and yeah, that whole maturity thing fucking sucked.

She went across the hall before I went back on my newly rediscovered restraint, long enough for us to shower and change into the training attire. Maybe forty minutes had passed before we met back up in the hall and the moment our gazes connected as she slipped the hoodie on over a tank top, her cheeks flushed pink.

Neither of us spoke for a moment. We just stood there in the silent hall, staring at one another. I honestly had no idea what to say. This... I didn't have any experience with this. Spending the night with a girl and not having sex. Seeing her again and not wanting to veer in the other direction.

Josie tucked a loose strand of hair behind her ear as she glanced up the hall. "You ready?"

I nodded and we started down the hall and we made it halfway before I did something totally cheesy. I reached between us, found her hand without looking, and threaded my fingers through her.

She looked up, surprise flickering over her expression, but then she smiled, and yeah, that smile was worth it.

Things were...a wee bit awkward.

Both of us were trying to pretend that a few hours ago we hadn't been lying in bed together. Well, I was trying to pretend that I hadn't been completely naked and I was doing everything in my ability not to let myself think about where those fingers and that mouth had been. I was seriously attempting to not think about any of that, leaving it to a more appropriate moment to obsess over.

I was failing.

Although doing training today had been completely my idea, it wasn't my brightest. My thoughts were scattered and hung up on everything that had happened last night.

Seth circled me. His chin was dipped down and his lips curled in a half smile that was totally at odds with what we were doing. So were those amber eyes. They were full of wicked secrets that made it hard to concentrate. I kept thinking about what would happen when we were behind closed doors.

He snapped forward, swinging out an arm. Unprepared, I darted to the side instead of blocking. "Pay attention," he murmured.

Lifting my arms into position, I narrowed my eyes. "I'm totally paying attention."

"No, you're not."

He whirled around, his arm flying. Instead of running, I stepped into the attack, using my forearm to block the hit. The impact was jarring, straight up to my shoulder, but I was getting used to it. The first time I'd successfully blocked a blow, I'd hopped around the mat like a demented bunny whimpering.

"Good." Seth dipped, and I knew he was about to kick. I hated those. Stepping back, I swung my arm down in an arc like he had taught me, blocking the kick before it connected with my stomach.

"You could be a little quicker." He straightened as I rolled my arms. Strutting past me, I jumped and let out a little squeak when his hand connected with my behind. I spun toward him, my mouth hanging open. He winked. "See. You should've anticipated that."

My eyes narrowed, but before I could do something really stupid, like try to kick him, the doors to the room opened and Luke strolled in.

"Yo," Seth called out to him, swiping a bottle of water off the mat. He took a drink. "You're early."

He nodded as he dropped a backpack by the door. "Yeah, well some shit went down in class. It ended a little ahead of schedule."

"What happened?"

Luke stripped off his sweater, revealing impressive biceps as Seth handed the water over to me. "Some shit, just not as bad as what went down in the cafeteria."

"Oh no." I took a sip, stomach unsettled.

Stopping in front of us, he ran a hand through his messy hair. "A pure and a half got into it. Chairs and desks ended up broken." He looked at Seth, expression distant. "I don't see this getting any better."

"Me neither." He turned to me, flicking his finger off the bottle. "You need to drink more." Turning back to Luke, he didn't see the face I made at him. "What do you think Marcus is going to do about it?"

He shrugged. "What can he do? Separating us isn't going to help anything. I told Deacon I didn't want him running around. I know he can take care of himself, but he...he tends to be a bit too optimistic about things."

"True," Seth murmured.

The comment about Deacon struck me as odd, but the guys were obviously ready to get back to training. I screwed the lid on the water and set it aside. With Luke here, we practiced more blocking techniques until I felt like I couldn't lift my arms. Then we moved onto breaking holds.

Something else I wasn't particularly great at.

I started with Luke, who did a front hold with his arms around my mine, capturing them against my sides. There were a couple of ways to get out of the hold. I could throw my weight back by lifting my legs, hoping to throw the attacker off balance. Or I could throw my weight forward, bringing the attacker with me, but that required getting my legs positioned right, and it wasn't like Luke was going to stand there and let me do it.

"You've got to stop treating Luke like he's Luke." Seth stood on the sidelines, arms crossed over his chest. "You're holding back."

"I am not."

Behind me, Luke chuckled. "Yeah, you are."

I shot him a look over my shoulder.

He raised his brows. "There are a lot of things you could've done at this point. Stomped on my foot. Or slammed the back of your head into mine."

Well, he had a point there, but...

Seth cocked his head to the side and waited.

"Shit," I muttered crossly. They were right. I didn't want to hurt Luke.

"You've got to let go of that, Joe." Seth moved forward, unfolding his arms. "If you can't, this is pointless."

Our eyes met, and Seth didn't have to say it. I saw it in his gaze. There was a huge part of him that didn't think I was capable of doing any of this. I looked over his shoulder at the wall of weapons and there was a mental recoil that hadn't faded from the first time I'd seen all the knives. If I was being honest with myself, there was also a part of *me* that was unsure.

Christ.

I could do this. I *had* to do this.

Luke's arms were still around me, and I... Hell with it. Squeezing my eyes shut, I kicked my head back. The top of my skull connected with Luke's chin. Pain flared, rippling across my scalp, but Luke's arms immediately dropped.

"Dammit." He staggered back at step. "You've got a hard fucking head."

Rubbing the back of said head, I turned to him, grinning. He was moving his jaw in circles. "I'll take that as a compliment I–"

Seth's arm circled my neck from behind, cutting off my words. "Now how are you going to get out of this?" His voice was a whisper in my ear.

301

For a moment, I was frozen. His body pressed against mine and that was the closest we'd been since this morning, when he'd been on me, literally on top of me, and I had been totally nude.

Oh dear.

Images flooded me. Immediately, I felt my cheeks heat. Once my brain went there, it really went there.

"Are you just going to stand here?" Seth asked, his voice sounding rougher.

I snapped out of it. Across from us, Luke stopped messing with his jaw and was watching. I shifted my hips as I gripped his arms, spreading my legs so one of them was between Seth's. The position would enable me to steady myself in preparation to flip him, but the position also put me in direct contact with Seth's... um, his lower parts.

He was *so* not unaffected by this.

I let myself acknowledge that and get all girly for a second, and then I realized I had a huge opportunity here. He was also distracted, which was rare. I hadn't yet been able to break any of his holds and this was my chance. Gripping his arms tight, I threw my weight forward, bending at the waist.

Bad move.

My rear pushed back into his hips and his soft groan in my ear threw me off. I shifted my hips to the side, knocking my weight off balance, and Seth followed as his arms loosened around my neck. He shifted, and all the weight was forced to my right leg. It caved.

And down we went.

Falling face first, I threw out my arms and caught myself before I planted my cheek into the mat. Seth came down on top of me, his arms hitting the mat next to mine. His legs were tangled in mine, and the position we were in, it made the tips of my ears burn and my belly tightened.

"Nice," Luke commented.

Seth lifted up so I could roll onto my back. Staring up at him, I felt the breath catch in my throat. His eyes were on fire—a bright, luminous tawny color. The shorter strands of his hair had slipped free, brushing his cheeks. The moment our eyes met, I couldn't move. A slow smile crept over his lips.

"You guys okay?" Luke called.

Seth ignored the comment as he tracked his gaze over my face, lingering over my mouth. The tightening in my belly dropped lower.

"Ya'll need some help?"

The look on Seth's face was easily readable. It begged a very important question. If we ignored Luke long enough, would he go away?

"Okay," Luke said, sighing. "This is getting kind of awkward. Maybe I should go...uh, do something. I'll lock the door behind me."

I got a little lost as I stared into his eyes and my heart rate kicked up as he lowered his head. I was sure he was going to kiss me, right there on the mats, in front of Luke, and I—

A piercing shrill blasted through the training room, jerking Seth back. Within a second, he was on his feet, and then I was on mine before realizing it. Luke had already turned, racing toward the doors.

"What's going on?" I winced as the sound picked up volume.

"Air siren—warning signal for when the Covenant is under attack."

30

DUTY DEMANDED that I head for the gates, but there was no way I was leaving Josie out here on her own. "We need to get you back in the dorm."

Her face was pale. "But—"

"This might not be anything, but if it is, you are not ready." Her mouth opened again, but I cut her off. "I'm not saying that to be a jerk. It's just the truth. You're not ready and I need you to be safe. Okay?"

She looked like she was going to argue for a moment, but then she nodded. Taking her hand, we hauled ass back to the dorm, passing running Sentinels and panicked students being ushered into buildings. I took her to my room, figuring for some crazy reason she would be safer there.

She followed me into the room. "If it's something, could it mean...?"

I looked over my shoulder at her, suddenly caught between two very different instincts. One was to stay with her, to ensure that she would remain safe. The other was to do what I had trained to do since I was eight, what was expected from me because of what I was.

You're not just the Apollyon.

Josie sat on the edge of the bed, holding the quilt around her, and I shook my head as I snatched a thermal off a hanger, pulling it over the shirt I wore. "It could mean the walls have been breached."

"Oh God," she whispered, and I heard her shuffling around. "You...you need to go."

Heading to the dresser, I grabbed weapons and loaded up. When I turned, she was standing there, eyes wide.

My heart hit my ribs as I crossed the distance between us. I cupped her face, tilting her chin back so our eyes met. "I do need to go. That's my—"

"I understand," she whispered.

A half-smile formed on my lips. What I wanted to do was blow out of there with her. Fucking disappear. Together. But that was stupid as shit, because there was nowhere either of us could go where we wouldn't be found.

"It's going to be okay. I just need you to stay in here." My eyes searched hers as she nodded. "Nothing should get to these dorms, but if they do, you'll have this." Reaching down, I unstrapped one of the daggers and placed it in her hand, folding her fingers around the handle. "I know you haven't learned how to use this, but it's fairly simple. Anything that you don't trust comes at you or through the door, you stab. You don't stop until they're down."

Her gaze flicked to the dagger she held, and a wisp of panic unfurled in my chest. "Do you understand, Josie? I need to know that you can do this."

She lifted her lashes and drew in a breath. "I understand."

The unease didn't leave, but the sirens were cycling again and I didn't have time to wait. This wasn't any kind of false alarm. "Wait here for me. I'll be back."

"I'll be here. Promise."

I nodded, but I wasn't moving away from her. There was no way I could waste anymore time. My ass needed to be out there, but she was...

Fuck.

Drawing her up against me, I dipped my head and I kissed her. Nothing soft or teasing about it. I got right inside her, parted her lips, and took her breath. I threw...well, everything I had said to her and everything I hadn't said, into that kiss. When I drew back, she looked a little dazed.

"Stay here," I told her again, letting go, because if I didn't in that moment, I wouldn't. "Lock the door behind me."

She nodded slowly, and I forced myself to move my feet to the door. Hell, it was one of the hardest things I'd ever had to do, and that... Yeah, that didn't bode well.

The halls outside the door were empty. Picking up my pace, I hit the lobby just as the elevator doors opened, and Luke stepped out, striding forward as he loaded a gun.

"Fancy seeing you again," I remarked.

"Wanted to make sure Deacon was where he was supposed to be." He didn't even try to hide the fact that he'd done exactly what he had been trained not to do.

Just like me.

Sentinels were already forming in the lobby as I arched a brow at Luke. "This whole retirement thing isn't going too well for you."

He snorted. "No shit." Holstering the gun, he hit the door, pushing it open. "By the way, I told Deacon to get his ass down to Josie's."

"She's not in her room."

Luke sent me a look, but wisely kept his mouth shut, and he pulled out a slim cellphone. "I'll text and let him know."

"Make sure he says who he is and that he comes in peace or some shit, because I left her with one of my daggers and instructions to stab anything that comes through that door."

His brows flew up, but his fingers flew over the screen of the phone, and then we were jogging down the path, around the academic buildings, and hey, it was like old times. Great.

Floodlights were on, lighting up the entire campus in spite of the thick clouds that raced across the sky and hid the sun. As we passed several groups of Sentinels heading toward the dorms, I felt a little bit of relief. The students would be well-guarded. That meant Josie would be too, by default.

As we neared the main council building, I spotted Solos. "What's going on?"

Eyes squinting into the chilly wind, he nodded in the direction of the walls. "Reports are a breach. No more than that."

"Real helpful stuff right there," Luke commented.

Solos glanced at him. "Thought you quit the Sentinel stuff."

"Thought you were on the Council," Luke returned.

I sighed, walking ahead of them. "I don't think you ever can quit. Being a Sentinel is like being in the damn mafia." I unhooked my dagger, feeling its slight weight against my palm. "You don't get out."

"You know, that's a great comparison," Solos replied. "Let's hope none of us are taking a cement swim today."

Smirking, we rounded the main campus building, and from that vantage point we could see beyond the courtyard, to the first wall. Wind picked up, carrying with it a scent of decay and soil.

"Shit," muttered Luke.

My chest turned to ice as I scanned the scene we were racing toward. "Shades. Dammit."

The three of us exchanged looks. This was not good, and that didn't need to be explained.

"Now we know what happened to the scouting group," Solos said with a sigh. "This is not going to be easy."

If shades were here, there was only one reason. They were here for Josie. I stopped dead in my tracks. "I need—"

A shadow darted out between the statues, slamming into Luke and knocking him to the ground. It was a female Sentinel, and the scent of death clung to her. I spun around, reaching for the back of her dirtied shirt. Yanking her up and off Luke, I tossed her to the side.

307

She skidded across the pathway, her pitch-black eyes freaky as shit. It was a shame, I thought, as she popped back on her feet and rushed me. Once possessed, there was nothing that could be done. I sidestepped her easily, moving up behind her. Two hands on either side of her head and the twist. The crack was like thunder, and when I let go, she crumpled like a paper bag, but not before black smoke poured out of her mouth, hitting the sky.

And that sucked, because as it zoomed over our heads, it didn't take a genius to figure out it was going to climb down the throat of another unsuspecting person.

"Well there," Solos drawled.

I flipped around, sighing when I saw five Sentinels that reeked of death.

"How large was this damn scouting party?" Luke grunted as he picked his ass up.

"Twenty-three," Solos answered, starting forward again.

To some that wouldn't sound like a lot, but twenty-three trained Sentinels possessed by shades was some bad shit. Not only were they rocking some ancient, pure evil, they were able to tap into all the training the Sentinels had, *and* all of their knowledge. And there was the fact that we could sit here and kill Sentinels all day. The shades would just possess more.

The Sentinels closed in.

I went at the one closest—the one who was smiling. Ducking under his outstretched arm, I sprung up behind him and slammed my foot into his back, knocking him forward several feet. As he caught himself and whirled on me, I sheathed my dagger and lifted my arm, summoning *akasha*. Amber light rolled down my arm. Nothing short of a god survived a direct hit from *akasha*.

He drew up short, laughed, and then tipped back his head. Opening his mouth, the shade crawled out, a thick and oily substance that zipped over our heads. The Sentinel hit the ground, unconscious and maybe alive. It looked like the pures and halfs could withstand the possession better than mortals. All that godly mojo came in handy.

"That's not any fun," I growled as I lowered my arm and turned just as a fist went straight for my face.

Oh hell no.

I darted to the side, grabbing the arm of the Sentinel I'd seen a few days ago, but who now showed me a face full of rage. Unhooking my dagger, I shoved the blade into his shoulder, digging in deep. The Sentinel roared, and as I hoped, the shade got the hell out of there, puffing into the air, and when I let go of the arm, the Sentinel dropped, unconscious.

"You don't have to kill them," I yelled toward Luke and Solos. "Disable them somehow."

Luke shot me a look, as if he was surprised that I cared, but what-the-fuck-ever. Solos was moving closer to the grove in front of the wall, and up there, bodies littered the ground.

The possessed Sentinels kept coming. Knock one down, two more took its place. Adrenaline coursed through my veins as the energy of the battle took hold. Using the handle of my dagger on the back of one of their heads, I then spun and delivered a powerful kick in the gut to the one creeping up behind me. He went down on his back, and I aimed for the same area, in the shoulder, hoping I could deliver enough pain to get the shade running, but hopefully...yeah, hopefully, not bloodying my hands any further.

Another came right at me.

Dipping down at the last possible second, I caught the Sentinel in the stomach with my shoulder, flipping the asshole over my back. I pivoted on my heel, thrusting the dagger into another shoulder, and then the air really began to stink. I straightened as Luke whirled, his shoulders thrown back, mouth nothing more than a slash across his face. He was thinking what I was thinking.

This shit was going to be never-ending, and there was too much space between me and where I needed to be, which was back in the dorm, standing between these fucks and Josie. Not here.

I spun at the sound of pounding feet and slammed my fist into the jaw of the approaching Sentinel, knocking him out at the same moment the glyphs on my skin went crazy.

Before the Sentinel hit the ground, his chest erupted as something shiny and sharp bulldozed through it. Leaping to the side, I watched the same projectile zoom past me and slam into another possessed Sentinel, right through the eye.

I whipped back around. As the first Sentinel toppled over face-first, I got an eyeful of...good gods, breasts and a whole lot more I wasn't expecting to see. I stumbled a step back.

Artemis stood in front of me, wearing a gauzy white tunic. I'd seen thongs cover more flesh than her outfit did. A bow was leveled on me, loaded with her extra-special silver arrows.

"Hello, Apollyon," she said, her full lips curving up at the corners. "I wonder, do you guys ever get tired of me saving your asses?"

"I can see your nipples," I told her.

Her laugh was like wind chimes. "Like these are the only nipples you've seen recently, eh?" Her arm shifted an inch and her finger squeezed off another arrow. The fleshy smack told me she had hit her target, and I just hoped it wasn't Solos or Luke.

"There went the 'not killing them' part," I sighed.

She shrugged as she waved her bow. "But do you see a shade making an escape? Nope. You don't. Not with my arrows. Sacrifice the few to save the many." Artemis's all-white eyes glowed as the air around her shimmered. The see-through gown disappeared, and in its place were fewer nipples and more bubblegum-pink camo get-up. "I am sure you understand that battle practice."

I ignored that jab, mainly because the marks of the Apollyon were speeding around my skin, forming multiple warnings. Another god was nearby.

Well, weren't they just dropping out of the freaking sky?

My gaze shifted up the walkway and I ground out, "Fuck."

The marble walkway was scorched, black marks forming as the stone cracked and the shape of big-ass bootprints formed, one after another. Foliage and shrubs shrank back, withering as two leather-clad legs formed, finishing off with a massive torso and chest, and then a head full of black waves.

Forming out of nothing but thin air beside him was a massive dog, like a mutated Rottweiler—if a Rottweiler had three heads and smelled like sulfur and rot.

Hades sneered in my direction. "Boy."

"I don't think I've been a boy in a long time," I replied, eyeing the dog.

The god cracked his neck to the side and spoke again, and for some reason, his accent was British. I could never figure that out. "You have no idea how much I'm going to enjoy you later."

"I doubt it's something *I'm* going to enjoy."

Artemis cleared her throat. "Really, can we save the snark-off for another time? We are here to handle the shades. You have..." She trailed off as one of Cerberus's offspring trotted up to me, sniffing my leg.

I swear to the gods, if it pissed on me it was losing one of its heads. "Nice puppy," I murmured.

It lifted its three heads and snarled, baring sets of shark-like teeth before it moved beyond me.

Solos rounded the corner, skidding to a halt as he saw the two gods and one of Hades's "puppies" prowling along the edge of the courtyard. "Holy balls..."

The god of the Underworld smiled. "Funny you mention balls..." He looked at me pointedly.

My eyes narrowed.

Shaking his head, Solos refocused and his stark face caused my stomach to drop. "A group of Sentinels who'd been protecting the dorms made it out of the campus. It's believed they were possessed."

I didn't even stop to think.

Pivoting around, I took off toward the dorm, running past bodies that didn't move, others that moaned in pain. My heart was in my throat and I was vaguely aware of Luke behind me, but the space between us grew larger.

I raced up the dorm steps, my stomach knotting as I saw the glass doors blown out. There were no Sentinels in the lobby. The place was a ghost town. Veering to the right, I hit the hall at a dead run.

The moment I saw the open door, I knew—I fucking knew.

Rushing inside, I struggled to catch my breath, and I'd never been out of breath before in my life. The living area was a mess. The coffee table was shattered. A stupid painting of a god was on the floor, broken.

A soft moan came from the bedroom.

Stumbling back, I pushed through the door, gripping its frame. The blanket from the bed was pooled on the floor. Red blotches were sprinkled across the sheet. Pillows were torn, the down filling lying on the carpet. And there was the dagger I'd given Josie.

Dread exploded in my chest as I made my way around the bed. Deacon was struggling to sit up, the side of his hair matted with blood.

I dipped down beside him, gripping his shoulders. Unfocused gray eyes drifted over my face as I held him up. "Where is she?" I demanded. "Deacon, where is she?"

"They were Sentinels," he said, gripping my arm. "We thought they were safe. I tried...to stop them."

A potent kind of terror gripped me. "Dammit, Deacon, where is she?"

His pained eyes met mine. "They took her."

CHAPTER
31

MY TEMPLES throbbed and my jaw ached as I came to. It wasn't the only part of me that hurt. My stomach was still recovering from a vicious kick. I started to sit up, but a hand pressed down on my center of my back, getting my face smushed into what felt like vinyl.

"Stay down, or I will put you down."

I sucked in a sharp breath at the sound of the guy's voice. They were Sentinels. They were supposed to be good. Deacon had opened the door... My sore stomach seized as concern for Deacon flooded me. It had been quick and brutal. With the minimal training I'd had, I sure as hell hadn't been prepared for it. They had taken out Deacon first, slamming his head into the wall with enough force to crack the plaster.

Oh God.

They smelled like death, like the guy back at Radford had. My mind raced. They had to be shades and that meant—

The vehicle rolled to an abrupt stop and my heart seized. I had no idea how long I'd been out, but from what I could tell, it seemed darker than before. I had no idea how in the hell they'd gotten me out of the University and into a car, but we were here.

I already knew who was waiting for me.

313

Hands landed on my shoulders as several car doors opened. I was yanked out, and my knees cracked off cold, hard ground as I fell forward onto my shaking hands.

The thin nylon pants were nothing against the icy, night air. I was lifted up onto my bare feet—what'd happened to my shoes?— and pushed forward with a rough shove in the back.

"Go," the man said.

In the dark, I could make out a set of steps that led up to a porch. Trees crowded what appeared to be a cabin. I had a feeling we were still in the Black Hills, or at least I hoped that we were.

There was no way I was going in that cabin.

I only had one chance to get away, so I didn't stop to think about it. Pushing to the side, I kicked off and started to run, my arms and legs pumping, my eyes trained on the trees. I had no idea where I was running. There were spots of the ground covered in snow. I obviously wasn't dressed for this, but anything would be better than facing off with what I knew waited for me inside.

I made it a couple of feet before an arm snagged me from behind, lifting me clear off the ground and depositing me in front of the steps again.

Someone laughed as the air froze in my lungs.

The cold burned the soles of my feet as I climbed the steps. I started to look behind me, but the push came again. Anger flared and I tried to turn again, but a sharp point suddenly pressed into the skin under my throat.

"Do not test us," the voice was a slick whisper in my ear. "Get inside." When I didn't reach for the door, the man—the thing— cursed as he grabbed the knob. The hinges groaned as it opened, and a stale scent tinged with metal rushed to greet me as I was shoved inside what appeared to be a mudroom.

The door slammed shut behind me, and I jumped, sucking in a shaky breath. Oh Christ, I was so screwed. Stepping forward, I winced as the boards creaked under my feet.

A single candle placed in the middle of the floor lighted the next room. The small flame flickered, not penetrating the thick shadows seeping out onto the floor.

I folded my arms across my chest, shivering as I inched forward. My breath puffed out in front of me, forming small, misty clouds. Through a narrow hall, I could see another room. A dim light was on in there.

Something somewhere in the room moved, a shuffling of clothing. A moan stopped my heart, halting my slow progression. I turned toward the sound, scanning the darkness. One of the shadows seemed to be thicker. Something lay against the wall in a crumpled heap.

Knowing that this could be a trap, but unable to keep walking forward, I bent down and picked up the thick pillar candle. I held it out in front of me, holding my breath as I moved toward it.

The soft glow of the candle cast a light over the wall and as I lowered the candle, I exhaled roughly.

Oh my God.

Almost dropping the candle, I rushed forward and knelt, pressing my knees into the dirty floor. I reached out with my other hand, hesitating, because... "Erin?"

The broken body on the floor stirred. No part of her that I could see was not bruised or scratched. Her face was swollen, raw-looking, and she appeared to be stuck between her mortal form and that of a furie. Her body was shades of gray and mocha. A wing was twisted over her, shielding her nude body. My chest cracked wide open as I saw the chain around her neck, attached to the wall.

Bile rose in my throat as I placed the candle down beside me. "*Erin.*"

Her head moved, but her eyes were sealed shut. Cracked lips moved restlessly, punching out two words. "I...failed."

The flame went out.

My heart stopped.

Tiny hairs all over my body rose, and I opened my mouth, but the scream was cut off as a hand curled around my neck, dragging me to my feet. I immediately went on defense. Reaching behind me, I clutched the thick wrist and tried to twist out of the hold.

A deep, dark laugh rippled through the room like an ominous cloud.

Erin whimpered.

"I think you should give your friend some time to rest. After all, I've worked her over hard."

Horror rose, but fury snapped on its heels, drenching every cell of my body with its red-hot venom. "You son of a bitch!" I shrieked. "You nasty son of—"

He wasn't holding me any longer. I wasn't even standing. The next thing I knew I was flying down the narrow hall. My arms flailed, but there was nothing to grab hold of.

My back hit the floor, pushing the air out of my lungs as pain exploded along my back. Stunned, I lay there for a moment, unable to move or to even think.

Two booted feet appeared on either side of my legs and Hyperion bent over me, his expression carved from ice and black eyes absolutely soulless. "You know what I hate more than anything?"

I opened my mouth, but his hand closed over my lips. "No. I don't want you to answer." His smile was creepier than his eyes. "I hate waiting. And I had to wait far too long to get my hands back on you."

A second later I was on my feet. He crowded toward me, forcing me to limp backwards.

"Did you also know that the gods watch over the Covenants? They would've seen my friends causing a little havoc." He kept coming, and I forced my body to move. "And we're not very far from the campus."

I darted to the side, keeping him in front of me as I tried to pull together the training Seth had given me.

"They will find us. And they will come." He turned to me slowly. "Your *father* will come."

I choked out a laugh as I searched the room for a weapon. There were dusty chairs and an old table with a lamp. I started toward it, not sure if I could really use it against him, but I had to get out of there. I had to get Erin and get out of there. "No, he won't."

Hyperion dipped his chin. "Oh, he will."

Twisting at the waist, I reached for the lamp. My fingers brushed over the metal base as I was jerked back and was pressed into the wall with one hand in the center of my chest. Before I could react, he spoke in a language that burned my ears, and then it happened. Fire ripped through me. Not a spark. Not an ember. A full wildfire erupted. My last thought, before the pain took over, was that I'd promised Seth I'd be there when he returned. I'd *promised* him.

There was no way I could shake the feeling that history was repeating itself in the worst kind of way.

Marcus stood in front of me, trying to talk me down, to wait, just like he had when Alex had gone missing all that time ago, when she'd left the Covenant to find her mother, but he had been talking *Aiden* down then.

Big difference here was that, with Alex, I had been able to feel her. I'd been able to track her down, but with Josie I felt nothing.

"Wait," Marcus said carefully, glancing over to where Artemis stood as still as one of the statues in front of the window. "You run out there, you have no idea where to even begin to look for her. Let Artemis do her thing."

Once we discovered that Josie had been taken, Artemis had popped up and summoned some giant fucking golden hawk that was out there now, scouring the mountain.

And I was in here, standing around with my dick in my hand. Night had fallen and Josie, she was....

Turning away from Marcus, I shoved my hand through my hair. Luke was in the corner, dabbing some shit on Deacon's skull. The pure hadn't really spoken much since everything had gone down.

The door to Marcus's office opened. Two Sentinels stepped aside as Solos strode in. "All of the shades have been removed from the campus. Hades and his...uh, dog took care of it, and I think...I need to go vomit now."

Marcus sighed as he paced the length of the room. I knew he wanted to talk about how screwed up everything was, about how he needed to protect the whole campus, but he got one good look at my face and apparently decided he valued his life.

At the window, Artemis suddenly turned, and holy shit, her eyes were all birdlike, bright yellow with large pupils. "I've found them."

"Where?"

Her head tilted to the side. "They are about thirty miles from here, still in the Black Hills. In a cabin. There are five Sentinels guarding it." She blinked and her eyes were all-white, which somehow, was an improvement. "It must be a trap. They did not go far."

"I don't care. Can you poof me there like Apollo does when he's bored?"

Artemis arched a brow.

"Seth," Marcus moved toward me, but drew up short. "If it's a trap, you should stop—"

"I don't care." I focused on the goddess. "Can you do it?"

Marcus tried again. "Seth—"

"I was supposed to protect her!" I snapped, whirling on the Dean. The glyphs reacted to my anger, swirling across my skin. Paintings on the wall rattled and the room tinted amber. "I was supposed to keep her safe."

He raced his hands passively. "I know it was a job, but—"

"It wasn't just a job to me," I seethed, and Marcus's eyes widened in surprise. "Going out there and defending the

Covenant *was* a job—one I should've walked away from, but because I did my duty, I failed *her*, and she is *anything* but a job to me."

"I will take you," Artemis said calmly.

I started to say "hell yeah," but she popped out from where she stood in front of the window, appeared in front of me, then placed a hand on my shoulder. A split second later we were in the woods, under a starry night, breathing in cold wind.

"Gods," I murmured, trying to gather my bearings.

Artemis stepped back. "This is as far as I can take you. A Titan awaits you and...I will fall to him."

Well, wasn't that reassuring as fuck?

"Just beyond the stand of trees, he awaits." Her form shimmered, fading out. "Good luck, Apollyon."

And with that, the goddess of the hunt and see-through clothing was gone.

I had no idea why Artemis was choosing to help me. Yeah, Josie was important to the gods, but they rarely stepped in when needed, usually only after their help would've been handy. But I wasn't looking a gift horse in the mouth. And I also knew I was walking in to face off with a Titan.

But I was going to walk back out with Josie, even if it killed me.

I raced through the cluster of trees, jumping over boulders, and clearing the last within seconds. Nothing I'd done was quiet. The cabin came into view, rising out of the gloom, and the five Sentinels were waiting.

The whole "not killing them" thing was dust in the wind.

Summoning *akasha*, I felt my cells light up as I tapped into the fifth and deadliest element. The coil ripped down my arm, arcing out from my hand. It smacked into the first Sentinel, and look at that, he went over and there was no black smoke pissing out of his mouth.

No wonder they'd run last time.

Moving forward, I took out the second, the third, and then the forth. The last one rushed me, practically ran right into my hand. I gave it to him, right up and close, sending a jolt of *akasha* right from my palm and into his chest. It lit him up from the inside, turning all the veins amber under the skin before blowing out his eyeballs.

I was already on the steps by the time he went down.

There was no way I was fooling myself into thinking that Hyperion wasn't aware that I was here, so I didn't bother ghosting into the house. Entering the enclosed space, the first scent I picked up was blood, and as my eyes adjusted to the darkness, I stepped into a large dark room.

I saw her immediately, and my stomach roiled. Going to her side, I knelt down, gritting my teeth as she drew back from me. The chain around her neck was keeping her here, and as my eyes swept over her, I couldn't even bring myself to drudge up a flicker of the animosity I normally felt for her kind.

What had been done to her was monstrous, cruel, and beyond anything I could understand. Even in my darkest moments, there had been a line. The Titan had traipsed all over that.

Sliding my fingers under the chain, I called on the element of fire, melting the links in the chain she had obviously been too weak to break herself. I freed the furie, and leaned down, whispering, "Get out of here now, Erin."

I didn't wait to see if she listened or if she responded. If she was smart, she would get out. I went down the hall, toward the dimly lit room, unable to mentally prepare myself for what I could see.

If Josie was... If she was hurt...

I stepped into the room, my gaze immediately moving to the chair in the corner. My heart stuttered, and I suddenly thought back to after the fight with Ares, to when I'd held Alex in my arms, up to the moment she'd simply turned to nothing.

Hyperion sat in an old armchair, and he faced the door. He was waiting. In his lap, draped over the arms of the chair, was

Josie, her face leached of color. I could barely see her chest move under the thermal she wore.

"I was hungry," he said, placing a large hand on her stomach. "I'm sure you know, Apollyon, that demigods have such an interesting value to us. This one in particular."

Rage I have never ever known erupted inside me, intense and violent. "Let her go."

"Or what?" Hyperion replied, glancing down at her as she began to move. Her lashes fluttered open, and then her chest heaved as her gaze focused on me. She started to sit up.

"Seth," she whispered hoarsely.

Akasha crackled over my skin, casting shadows. It took everything to not charge forward, putting her at further risk. "What do you want in return for her safety?"

Josie gasped, but Hyperion eyed me, curiosity marking his expression. "What could you possibly give me that I would want?"

"Anything," I swore.

Hyperion stared at me for a moment and then he stood, dumping Josie at his feet. I started toward her, but he faded out and reappeared in front of me. "What I want is revenge for thousands of years of being entombed. How in the world can you give me that?"

I couldn't.

Moving lightning quick, I slammed the Covenant dagger deep into his chest, where I assumed the bastard's heart was, if he had one, and then I dipped low. Spinning around, I kicked out, hitting the hilt of the dagger, shoving it in deep.

Hyperion didn't even move.

Looking down at the dagger, he looked back at me and arched a brow. "Seriously?"

Fuck.

Swinging out, Hyperion threw me through a nearby chair. It collapsed under my weight. I rolled onto my side, trying to get back up.

He was on me in under a second, picking me up by the scruff of my neck and introducing his fist to my jaw, snapping my head back. He let go and I landed on my knees. I lifted my arms to block the kick, but my movements were too slow. His boot landed in my stomach, flipping me onto my back.

I caught his boot before it came down on my neck. Muscles straining, I held him off, an inch from crushing my windpipe.

"I have a secret," Hyperion said.

Struggling to hold his foot back, I grunted out, "You envy my hair?"

He laughed coldly. "Titans can kill an Apollyon, you silly little fuck."

Ah well, *shit*...

"Apollo!" Josie screamed immediately, her voice cracking. "Apollo! Please!"

Hyperion turned from me, laughing. "Yes. Call him. Call him—"

Shoving his foot to the side, I powered onto my feet and slammed my hands down on his massive shoulders, feeding *akasha* straight into him. The big fucker jolted as the back of his skull lit up. He let out a roar that shook the walls. Using the distraction, I gripped both sides of his head and twisted.

Cracked like a dry board.

Except when I let go, Hyperion didn't go down. He wheeled around, his neck twisted at a painful and disturbing angle.

"Oh come the fuck on," I said.

Hyperion struck out, his fist catching me in the chest, knocking me back into the wall. Plaster cracked and dust plumed into the air as I fell forward, breaking my fall with my forearms.

He reached down, grabbing a handful of my hair, and Josie's screams pierced the room. "You have mettle, but I am so very tired—"

A bright light filled the room, like a burst of sun in the night. Hyperion dropped me, spinning around. As the light receded I couldn't believe what I saw.

Apollo stood in the middle of the room, as tall and powerful as the Titan. Head thrown back, white eyes glowing and spitting tiny bits of electricity into the air, he wasn't dressed for combat in his white linen pants, but he was there, and I couldn't believe it.

Hyperion dematerialized and reappeared by Josie, gripping her by the throat, cutting off her next breath.

"You wanted me," Apollo said, hands at his sides. "I'm here, but you do not have me."

The Titan eyed the god, lips pulled back in a sneer. "That's what you think now."

"Paidí apó to aíma mou kai sárka mou." Apollo's voice traveled like thunder through the room. *"I apelefthérosi dýnamí sas."*

Of my blood and of my flesh, I unbind thee.

My gaze riveted onto Josie, and...and nothing happened. Her dilated eyes bounced from me to her father.

"That's all?" Hyperion laughed darkly. "Really anticlimactic, Apollo. I am almost embarrassed for you."

He smiled coldly. "Come on, Hyperion, you know I'm flashier than that."

Then Apollo moved, brandishing a wicked-looking dagger. He moved so quickly it was hard for even me to track. His arm cocked back and he let go of the dagger.

It flew through the air, handle over deadly end.

Hyperion let go of Josie, stepping to the side, but the...the dagger was never aimed at him. I didn't realize until it was too late.

Shoving to my feet, I felt my stomach twist with raw terror. It rose through me like a monster snapping its massive jaws.

"No!" I shouted, stumbling forward, drawing on *akasha*.

But it was too late.

The blade struck true, right where Apollo had aimed.

It slammed into the center of Josie's chest, knocking her back against the wall, and my step faltered, as if I'd taken the mortal blow myself. Pain ripped through my chest, feeling so very physical. Oh Gods, I'd been here before. With a different girl, a different situation, but I'd been here before.

History *was* on repeat.

It happened so fast.

I'd seen the dagger in Apollo's hand. I saw him cock back his arm and let the dagger go, but I didn't understand as a fiery pain knocked the air out of my lungs and pushed me back against the wall. Had Hyperion hit me?

Looking down, a strangled sound parted my lips. Apollo's dagger was buried in my chest, to the hilt. A swath of red stained the front of my shirt. Blood?

This couldn't be happening.

I lifted my hands, but I didn't know what to do with them. I tried to take another breath, but it was like there was a plug in the base of my throat.

"What in the fuck?" Hyperion roared, his anger like a furnace.

My pulse pounded erratically in my ears as I lifted my chin. My gaze collided with Seth. He was staggering toward me, his face pale and amber eyes full of horror. Oh God, I thought about what had happened before. This wasn't right. This was so wrong. How could Apollo do this to him again? How could he do this to *me*?

Only seconds had passed from the point of impact to when my trembling fingers curved around the handle of the dagger. I had to get it out of me. In the back of my head, I knew that was probably a bad idea, but I couldn't breathe and I wanted it out.

My legs felt detached as I gripped the handle of the dagger. Someone—Seth?—shouted as I doubled over, my hair falling forward. I yanked—yanked hard. My body jerked as a scream tore through me. The dagger clattered off the wood floor. A buzzing, a low-level hum, filled my head like an army of a thousand pissed-off bees. Something...*something* was happening.

I inhaled past the sharp, tangy pain and breathed in fire. I was on *fire*. Worse than when I was tagged and fed on, the blaze was in my veins, infiltrating every molecule. The pain throbbed throughout me, stealing the ability to think around it, but I knew this wasn't death.

Death could not be *this* painful.

A great and terrible force started at my toes, rapidly traveling up my legs, beyond my waist and to my skull. My body straightened, bowing as my head kicked back. My mouth opened but there was no sound. Air seemed to build underneath me, and I was vaguely aware of my feet no longer touching the floor. I was in the air, my arms floating out to my sides.

I could feel it.

A coil of power that had slumbered my entire life, something that had always been there but had been at rest, built inside me. It had woken up, rushing through me, filling me, and it tasted like sunlight and strength. It was so warm, so incredibly hot. I heard a thousand voices—a thousand prayers uttered throughout the many years, in many different languages.

My eyes peeled open, and I saw Hyperion.

A stranger in my body smiled.

"Damn it," he growled, backing up.

The heat inside me exploded free, pulsing out in a giant wave from the wound in my chest. It rippled out, creating a shockwave. Furniture lifted up, toppling over. The scent of burnt ozone filled my senses. The wave streamed, like a solar flare, pulsing as it reached Hyperion. The light burst, capturing his hoarse shout and sucking it in before the wave whirled its way back, slamming into me.

I fell to the floor, landing hard on my hands and knees, jarring my bones. All the wonderful strength, the glorious warm light, was gone. It took everything to lift my head.

The room was destroyed.

Glass was blown out, the windowsills on fire. The wood floor was warped, boards completely missing in some areas. Curtains were gone. Chairs were demolished into pieces.

Hyperion was gone.

So was Apollo.

In disbelief, my eyes scanned the wreckage of the room. I cried out when I saw Seth. He was lying on his back in the center of the room. He wasn't moving. What had I done?

I forced myself across the floor with shaking, sore arms until I reached his side, my entire body trembling and my vision full of weird black spots that danced.

"Seth?" I placed a hand on his chest.

His eyes were closed, thick lashes fanning the tops of his cheeks. When there was no response, I pulled myself closer. I needed to get us out of here, but my head felt too heavy on my neck, and the next thing I knew, my cheek was on his chest, and the last thing I heard was the steady, strong beat of his heart.

CHAPTER I ARMENTROUT

CHAPTER
32

WHEN I opened my eyes, I was staring up at fluorescent lights. For a couple of moments I didn't move or think beyond those lights. I recognized that I was in some kind of hospital room, but there were no sounds of an IV dripping fluids or of a blood pressure machine or a heart monitor. My mouth was dry and my chest a little sore, but other than that I felt okay. No. I felt more than a little okay. I felt kind of awesome, like I could get out of this narrow bed, and I don't know, kick some butt or something, which was strange—

Holy crap.

My chest.

Pushing up into a sitting position, I knocked down the thin blanket and found that I had on some kind of horrible bright-pink hospital gown. I yanked the collar out and gaped.

Apollo—my father—had thrown a knife at me. The knife had hit me, square between the breasts. A kill shot if I'd ever seen one, but it hadn't killed me. It had done something else entirely, and now there were faint white marks on my chest, and those marks formed a shape.

A straight line about five inches long with two lines looping around it—at the top, the design almost looked like tiny wings.

Smacking my gown back in place, I squeezed my eyes shut. Okay. "That's not a normal scar."

"No. It's not."

A shriek erupted out of me at the sound of Apollo's voice. My head whipped to the side. He sat in a chair next to my bed, one leg hooked over the other, and there was no way he'd been sitting there a few seconds ago.

At least I hoped he'd hadn't been when I'd been checking out my boobs.

"It is my mark. One of them," he said, smiling slightly. "Kind of like a rite of passage."

I stared at him for a moment, and then I exploded. "You threw a knife at me!"

"I did," he replied calmly.

"You hit me with the knife!"

"I did." He leaned forward, dropping his foot onto the floor. "As I told Seth, unbinding you myself would not be easy. I wish I hadn't had to do it that way. The last thing I wanted was to cause you pain. I didn't enjoy any part of that—well, besides the look on Hyperion's face—but the only way for me to finish unbinding you was to pass you through a mortal death."

My head got tangled up on that, but there was something else important he'd said. "Seth. Where is Seth?"

Apollo stared at me with eyes that matched my own, and when he didn't respond, I tossed back the thin blanket. "Where is he?" I demanded, my heart rate picking up. I remembered seeing him down on the floor. I remembered crawling to him. Knots twisted up my stomach, and I tasted fear once more in the back of my mouth. "Apollo." My voice cracked.

He closed his eyes briefly. "He's in the very next room, sleeping. He is fine, my daughter." When I started to swing my legs off the bed, he raised a hand. "I know you are eager to see that for yourself, but trust in me, he is okay. He is the Apollyon. You will not be able to kill him."

Relief loosened my shoulders. "Thank God."

The look on his face said he felt differently. "I hope one day that relief never turns to dread."

Staring at him, it felt like someone had reached around my neck and squeezed, much like Hyperion had. I swallowed—swallowed hard, but I held myself back and pushed that feeling away. I knew everything about Seth. It wasn't surprising that Apollo would have some...misgivings. Several seconds passed. "What about Erin? She was hurt very badly. He..."

"Seth freed her. She's in Olympus. Healing."

I closed my eyes, but was unable to un-see the condition she'd been in, the damage Hyperion had done to her. "Will I see her again? Soon?"

"Yes."

That was a relief—kind of. I hurt for her, and I needed to see her with my own eyes to believe that she was okay.

"Daughter..."

I opened my eyes, focusing. "I'm a...a demigod now?"

"You know the answer to that."

Of course I did. People didn't levitate off the ground and have solar flares erupt from them if they were mortal.

"Your powers are not complete," he continued. "Hyperion is not entombed. You basically put him in a time-out. When he comes back, he's going to be very, very upset."

For some reason, I got stuck on what was probably the least important part of all of this. "I'm not going to age anymore, am I?"

His golden brows furrowed.

"Sorry," I sighed. "It's just that's kind of a... It's a big deal."

"It is."

"Mortal death. So I...I died?" My voice pitched on the last word.

"Yes. And no. Your mortal self passed on. You are a demigod, now immortal in most ways. You still can perish, but it will not be easy. Human illness will no longer touch you. Mortal wounds will not kill you."

I slowly shook my head. I had no idea what to say to that. I felt the same, only a little different, so it was hard to fully grasp what had happened to me. Part of me wanted to, I don't know, jump out of a window and see if I'd land on my feet.

He reached up, rubbing the palm of his hand across the center of his chest, the movement weary. "But there is more that you must do. There is an icon of mine you must find, as the rest of the demigods will need to find theirs. Once unbound and with all of the icons, you all will be able to face the Titans."

"An icon? What does that mean?"

"There's a certain librarian I think you should speak with," he said mysteriously, and then he rose, exhaling raggedly. Fine white lines appeared at the corners of his mouth, and a nugget of concern wiggled free. He looked...tired. I hadn't thought it possible that gods could get tired.

Apollo leaned forward, pressing the tips of his fingers against my cheek like he'd done in my dorm, but now his touch was cool. Unbinding me had weakened him. It took something from him. But if he hadn't made that choice to unbind me, I would've died, or worse. With Hyperion—with the Titans—there were things far worse than death.

"Thank you," I said, clearing my throat, but the words still rasped out. "Thank you for saving my life."

His eyes met mine, and he lowered his hand as he straightened. He shimmered a brilliant blue before disappearing.

I stared at the spot where he'd stood as I reached up, placing my hand against my cheek. Tears burned my eyes. I don't know why I wanted to cry. Probably because I had a lot of reasons to do so.

Drawing in a deep breath, I swallowed those tears and pushed off the bed. The tile floor was cool under my feet. I wiggled my toes, and then I took a step, and then another. I opened the door, and somehow, I just *knew* to take a right, like by some weird instinct.

The next door didn't have a window, but I turned the handle and slowly opened it. My breath caught, and my knees suddenly went weak even though I felt more energized than I had in...well, in forever.

It was like I was seeing him for the first time. As if a thin film had been removed from my eyes.

Seth lay on the bed. A blanket had fallen to his waist, as if he'd tossed and turned at some point. He wasn't in a hospital gown. He was wearing the black thermal I'd last seen him in.

The door swung shut behind me as I walked to his side. A faint blue bruise covered one side of his forehead, just above the eyebrow. His hair was down, falling perfectly around his head while I knew mine was a tangled hot mess. There was a cut on his lower lip, another reddish bruise along his right cheek.

But he still was the most beautiful man I'd ever seen.

My chest rose and fell raggedly as I stared at him. He'd come for me. He'd fought for me, and had taken a brutal, vicious beating for me. And I'd heard him scream for me when Apollo's blade had struck.

Emotion swirled in my chest, potent and consuming. I didn't know what it meant, or maybe I did, but just didn't want to give a name to it yet, and that was okay, because I was here, and so was he.

Even knowing I should probably let him rest, I still couldn't stop myself. I reached out and touched his arm.

A shock passed from him to me, jolting through my body. Before I could pull back, his eyes flew open, bright and golden, and his other hand snaked out, wrapping around my wrist. The jolt came again, stronger as it zipped through my veins.

Then I saw them.

From where his hand was wrapped around mine, shapes begin to take form on his skin, forming patterns that my eyes tracked as they swirled and shifted up his arm and then to his neck, and onto the side of his face. They were tattoos that moved and constantly shifted, forming different designs.

Amazingly, my brain started to sort those glyphs out, reading them—understanding them, and well, that was odd, because I couldn't read Greek, but I knew these symbols were definitely of Greek origin.

Strength.

Invincibility.

My gaze shifted as his chest rose and fell sharply. "I can see them," I said, awed. "The marks of the Apollyon—I can see them."

Seth moved so quickly.

He shot up as he pulled me forward, tugging me off-balance. One arm went around my waist, and muscles in his arm tensed as he lifted me up. My legs went flying as he twisted me around.

Air rushed out of my lungs as I was suddenly on my back, in the bed. He was half on his side, half on me, and my heart pounded as I rose onto my elbows. Then he shifted, one hand curling around my chin, guiding my head back against the pillow.

"Seth—"

His mouth was on mine. There was nothing questioning or tentative about the way he kissed me. It was demanding. Fierce. My lips parted with a moan, and he took the kiss to the next level, slipping his tongue in, twisting it around mine. I tasted him on my tongue and every place his skin touched mine, I was hypersensitive. My skin tingled and my body burned to feel more of him, for there to be nothing between us.

It had been crazy intense between us before, but this...*this* was something different, stronger and intensely raw. One of my hands curled into his hair as the other slipped under the sleeve that had pushed up to his elbow. I could barely breathe around the kisses, around the way he drew me into him. I yanked on his hair, and the kisses turned deeper somehow, and I never wanted to stop.

And then he lifted his mouth enough that his forehead rested against mine, and his breath broke on my swollen lips.

"Seth," I whispered his name this time.

He moved onto his side and the hand at my chin dropped to the neckline of my gown. Without saying a word, he yanked it down, and cold air rushed over my chest.

It quickly became obvious that he was checking for the knife wound, but my body had a different, more sensual idea. A flush swept over my skin, and the tips of my breasts tightened.

I bit down on my lower lip as he ran a finger along the odd scar—along Apollo's mark. My toes curled and my hips twitched. It was a difficult task to breathe as his finger moved beyond the scar and he dipped his head. The edges of his hair brushed over my breasts, creating a crazy rush of sensations.

Seth kissed the center of the mark, causing my heart to explode into a gooey mess. Then he lifted his head, pulling the top of the gown up, tucking it back in place almost reverently. "You're a demigod," he said hoarsely.

It was the first thing he said.

"Yeah," I replied, my voice breathy. "Is that...um, okay with you?"

His gaze flicked up to mine, and he arched a brow. "Do I need to kiss you again?"

My lips twitched. "Maybe."

He cupped my cheek, spreading his fingers out. "How are you feeling?"

"Okay. Better than before. What about you? I didn't mean to do...well, whatever it is that I did, but when I saw you down, I thought I—"

"No. I'm fine." He pressed a finger to my lips for a second, and then dragged it over my lower lip. A tense minute passed. "Did he hurt you in any way I can't...I can't see?"

My stomach tumbled and a shudder danced over my shoulders. I didn't want to think of the time with Hyperion, of the things he'd said. "No."

There wasn't any real measure of relief in his golden stare. "You should never have fallen into his hands. My job is to protect you, and I left you unguarded. He was hurting you. He would've—"

"Stop." It was my turn to place my finger over his lips. "We're here. Both of us. You did nothing wrong."

The look that pinched his features said he wasn't convinced, so I did the only thing I thought I could do. I moved my hand as I stretched up, replacing my fingers with my lips.

I kissed him softly.

It was nowhere near as skilled as his, or as suave, but he made that sound in the back of his throat—the sound of approval, and he shifted his hand behind my head, holding me to him.

This time, when we broke apart, Seth eased onto his side, got me on mine, and managed to get the blanket up over our hips. Somehow both of us fit on the bed, our cheeks resting on the same pillow.

We stared at each other.

And then Seth got closer, brushing his lips over the curve of my cheek. The tip of my nose was next, then each of my eyelids, and then he kissed my forehead.

We didn't talk for a long time, even though there was so much to talk about, so much to deal with and to think about. There was the fact that I was a demigod now. I didn't know where to even begin with that, and everything that would now change because of what I had become. Like, would another solar flare emit from me unexpectedly, taking out hapless pures and halfs? What about the elements? Would I now be a ninja like Seth? There *was* also the fact that Hyperion was still out there and he was going to come back. So were the other Titans. I had to find an icon. We *needed* to find the other demigods before the Titans did.

There was so much to deal with, and I could see it in Seth's eyes that he knew it too, but he remained quiet as he drew his hand up and down my arm. With each pass, that weird jolt lessened but didn't completely go away. If he felt it, he hadn't said anything about it.

I let out the breath I hadn't realized I was holding. "Guess what?"

"What?"

Meeting his amber-colored eyes, I admitted what probably wasn't a secret, but what I felt like I needed to put into words. "I like you, Seth."

He stopped his hand over mine, staying there, as he gave me a lopsided smile. "Guess what?"

"What?" I whispered.

Seth shifted so that his lips brushed mine as he spoke. "I like you too, Josie."

ACKNOWLEDGEMENTS

None of this would've been possible without Kate Kaynak and the wonderful team at Spencer Hill Press—Rachel Rothman Cohen, Kellie Sheridan, Rich Storrs, Cindy Thomas, and Damaris Cardinali. A big thank you to Kevan Lyon, the awesomely awesome agent, for keeping me stable and sane. Thank you to Stacey Morgan, Lesa Rodrigues, Dawn Ransom, Laura Kaye, Sophie Jordan, Jen Fisher, Molly McAdams, and Wendy Higgins for either supporting Seth and *The Return* by letting me talk nonsense to them or by reading an earlier version that was probably pretty crappy.

And of course, thank you—the reader. Every time you pick up one of my books, a baby Pegasus is born. Okay. That's a lie. But you are the reason I do this and I'm *able* to do this, so seriously, thank you.

In the *Covenant* series...

AVAILABLE NOW
IN EBOOK AND PAPERBACK

In the *Covenant* series

AVAILABLE NOW
IN EBOOK AND PAPERBACK

In the

LuX *series . . .*

CONTINUE YOUR LUX JOURNEY WITH *SHADOWS*, A PREQUEL NOVELLA

AVAILABLE NOW IN EBOOK
COMING SOON IN PAPERBACK

Withdrawn Stock
Dorset Libraries

**THIS BOOK IS INTENDED
FOR A NEW ADULT AUDIENCE.**

It contains a sexy, sexy hot guy with mad skillz that will
be described in swoon-inducing detail. Even the scenes
where he's just walking around with his shirt off (yeah,
that happens) may prove too intense for younger readers.
Please consider yourselves warned.

Withdrawn Stock
Dorset Libraries

DORSET COUNTY LIBRARY

400 166 096 W

Jennifer L. Armentrout lives in West Virginia. All the rumors you've heard about her state aren't true. Well, mostly. When she's not hard at work writing, she spends her time reading, working out, watching zombie movies, and pretending to write. She shares her home with her husband, his K-9 partner named Diesel, and her hyper Jack Russell Loki. Her dreams of becoming an author started in algebra class, where she spent her time writing short stories . . . therefore explaining her dismal grades in math. Jennifer writes Adult and Young Adult Urban Fantasy and Romance.

Find out more at www.jenniferarmentrout.com

Withdrawn Stock
Dorset Libraries